Phil
Cornell
2014

SHERLOCK HOLMES

AND

DOCTOR WAS NOT

Conceived of and Edited by

Christopher Sequeira

Foreword by

Leslie S. Klinger

Sherlock Holmes and Doctor Was Not

Printed in Palatino Linotype and Nightmare Pills.

IFWG Publishing International
Melbourne

www.ifwgpublishing.com

Respectfully dedicated to the memory of both

Harlan Ellison

and

Marty Shapiro.

Some years ago I was speaking to Marty Shapiro (a wonderful man who once did me a great professional kindness at no charge that avoided me getting into a very awkward contractual situation) and I asked Marty if he thought his client, Harlan Ellison, might like to consider writing a story for this anthology idea I had. Marty was an agent to greats; not just Ellison, but also to other grandmasters, like Robert Bloch. But in all of our few dealings Marty treated me—a comparable nobody who he'd only ever known via email or phone—with friendliness, candour and incredible generosity.

So, Marty again treated me with largesse, and he talked to Mr Ellison, and Mr Ellison eventually insisted on me phoning him directly.

The details of that astounding phone call (Ellison! Live, on the phone! Sounding as energetic, and brilliant, and as no-bullshit as in any video or audio presentation I'd ever heard him on!) deserve a full description by me in another forum one day, but suffice to say for now that Mr Ellison (he told me to call him 'Harlan', and I still have trouble with that) told me he loved my anthology idea (which back then I was entitling 'Sherlock Holmes and Doctor-WHAT?!').

I can also reveal Mr Ellison had an idea for writing a particular type of encounter of Holmes and a very particular Doctor. Sadly, timing and the stroke he had later made that impossible, and of course he passed away in recent months (as did Marty). But Mr Ellison's idea, I have to say, was of his typical genius-level of creativity. One day, if I'm lucky, I may find a suitable and properly respectful way to present that idea to the millions of fans he had.

Regardless, both Marty and Harlan (OK, I'll refer to him that way now), those two sterling men, are part of the reason I persevered to make this anthology become a reality when the original publication plan went by the wayside. It is therefore very important to me they both be thanked upfront of this volume.

They were titans in their respective professions, and as such giants usually are, they displayed the effortless, uncontrived, uncommon generosity-of-spirit that people who have not a single damn thing to prove to anyone possess. I was just so, so lucky to have personally experienced that.

To Marty and Harlan.

Christopher Sequeira
Burwood, NSW, Australia.
February, 2019.

Table of Contents

Foreword: Sherlock Holmes Among the Doctors
        (Leslie S Klinger)..1

The Final Prologue (Christopher Sequeira)......................7
The Forlorn Death of Sally at the Crossroads
        (Dennis O'Neil)..35
The Sign of Two: Sherlock Holmes and Dr Jekyll
        (Philip Cornell)...51
The Adventure of the Madman (Nancy Holder)............71
Sherlock Holmes and Dr Nikola:
        The Adventure of the Empty Throne.
        (Brad Mengel)...83
The Adventure of the Reckless Resurrectionist
        (Will Murray)...101
The Angel of Truth (I. A. Watson)................................127
The Locked Cell Murder (Ron Fortier)........................165
The Adventure of the Slaughter Stone
        (Rafe McGregor)...189
The Adventure Of The Walk-Out Wardrobe
        (Julie Ditrich)..207
Curtain Call (J. Scherpenhuizen)..................................261
The Investigation into The Dawning Od: A Sherlock
        Holmes and Dr Arthur Conan Doyle
        Mystery (Andrew Salmon)..............................293

Contributors..317

Foreword: Sherlock Holmes Among the Doctors

LESLIE S. KLINGER

During Sherlock Holmes's active years in the late 19th century, doctors of medicine were relatively populous in England, in a ratio of slightly more than one per one hundred persons. This is in sharp contrast to the ratio in the U.S. today, which is about two per 1,000 persons. In addition to 'doctors,' patients were served by 'surgeons' (only one hundred years after being classed with barbers) and 'apothecaries.' Despite the popularity of the profession, however, medical education was little regulated in the 19th century, though London University and Edinburgh University—training grounds for two men familiar to us—were highly regarded, and doctors still suffered from middling reputations, often regarded as primarily motivated by sales of (their own) nostrums.

It is little wonder that the Sherlock Holmes canon is similarly well-populated by doctors. Doctors appear in thirty-six of the sixty stories, as might be expected from tales largely penned by a physician, even one as inactive as John H. Watson, M.D. Arthur Conan Doyle, who had a great deal to do with the Sherlock Holmes stories, albeit in a vague role, was also a physician, and it is certain that his involvement with the stories was spurred in large part by his association with Dr Joseph Bell. Dr Bell, one of Doyle's instructors at Edinburgh University, was possessed of legendary observational skills and, although the details are vague, seemed to be employed by Queen Victoria as some sort of special investigator. Bell apparently believed that Sherlock Holmes was a creature of fiction, however, and in 1892, he wrote an essay for *The Bookman* magazine in which he claimed that he was the 'model' for Sherlock Holmes. There is no suggestion that Holmes knew or even knew of Bell, and the evidence that Holmes knew Doyle is slim. Watson may well have come into contact with Doyle, however, for there is an apocryphal suggestion ('The Field Bazaar') that Watson may also have attended Edinburgh University. Whatever the case, Bell's essay was reprinted (probably at the behest of Doyle, in an effort to bolster sales) as an introduction to the 1893 edition of *A Study in Scarlet*.

Doyle himself seems to have viewed his career in medicine as thrust upon him. "It had been determined that I should be a doctor, chiefly, I think, because Edinburgh was so famous a centre for medical learning," Doyle wrote in his autobiography *Memories and Adventures*. "It meant another long effort for my mother, but she was very brave and ambitious where her children were concerned, and I was not only to have a medical education, but to take the University degree, which was a larger matter than a mere licence to practise." Although later he expressed his joy in putting the practice of medicine behind him to pursue a literary career, he obviously took great pride in the medical profession. Doyle penned a number of stories and books about physicians, including the self-revelatory *Round the Red Lamp: Being Facts and Fancies of Medical Life*, a collection of medical stories, some undoubtedly reminiscences, published in 1894, and *The Stark Munro Letters* (1895), a thinly disguised version of Doyle's medical experiences in Southsea; and of course doctors appeared in many of his other works as well.

John Watson's medical practices appeared to have placed little demand on his time, to the good fortune of readers everywhere. Although there were spurts of professional enthusiasm—usually generated, it appears, by the urgings of a wife—his uncanny ability to drop everything to take up an adventure with Holmes, or to call in a *locum tenens* to cover for him on a moment's notice, placed him in the centre of many an adventure. Among Watson's accounts, 'The Resident Patient,' 'The Engineer's Thumb,' and *The Hound of the Baskervilles* arose out of a doctor's concern for his patient, and stories like 'The Creeping Man' and 'The Blanched Soldier,' neither of which involved a crime, essentially revolve around proper medical diagnosis rather than detective work.

Few cases involved doctors as the focus of Holmes's attention ('The Devil's Foot,' 'The Missing Three-Quarter,' and of course, 'The Speckled Band' come immediately to mind), though Holmes gravely remarked in the latter case, "When a doctor goes wrong he is the first of criminals. He has nerve and he has knowledge."

The similarity between medical investigations and investigations of crime was certainly evident to the Victorian and Edwardian reader. In addition to the stories authored by John Watson, the *Strand Magazine* featured 'Adventures from the Diary of a Doctor,' by L. T. Meade and Clifford Halifax. Dr John Evelyn Thorndyke, introduced by R. Austin Freeman in 1905, was perhaps the preeminent scientific detective of his day. Dr Petrie is the stalwart companion of Nayland Smith in the Fu Manchu series published by Sax Rohmer (beginning in 1913). Doctors also were often the principal investigators of supernatural or possibly supernatural mysteries. Dr Martin Hesselius, a German physician with a strong interest in the occult, appeared in a collection of tales, *In a Glass, Darkly*, published by Sheridan Le Fanu in 1872.

Dr Abraham Van Helsing is the lead detective in Bram Stoker's 1897 *Dracula*; he is assisted by Dr John Seward. Algernon Blackwood's collection *John Silence, Physician Extraordinary* appeared in 1908; and Dr John Durston appeared in William Le Queux's collection *The Rainbow Mystery: Chronicles of a Colour Criminologist Recorded by His Secretary* in 1917. Dr John Richard Taverner, assisted by Dr Rhodes, appeared in Dion Fortune's series of twelve short stories, collected in 1926. Dr Jules de Grandin featured in Seabury Quinn's long-running series of short stories, novellas, and one novel printed in *Weird Tales*, beginning in 1925 and ending in 1951. Medical doctors Herbert West and Marinus Bicknell Willett were the lead investigators in stories by H. P.

Lovecraft in the 1920s, and various professors (also termed 'doctors') were the principals in many others.

Finally, doctors were popular figures of mystery or villainy in literature. Of course, Dr Henry Jekyll was not himself evil, but his colleague Mr. Hyde certainly was, in the eponymous 1886 tale by Robert Louis Stevenson. Doctor Caresco, an insane surgeon, appeared in works by Andre Couvreur (between 1899 and 1904), and the misadventures of the equally insane Doctor Jack Quartz were written by Frederic Van Rensselaer Dey (1891-1925). Dr Moreau's egregiously cruel work is depicted in H. G. Well's *The Island of Doctor Moreau* in 1896, and the strange figure of Doctor Nikola first appeared in Guy Boothby's *A Bid for Fortune* (1895) and four sequels. Dr Mabuse, a master of disguise, featured in *Dr. Mabuse der Spieler*, a 1927 novel by Norbert Jacques, and a series of films. No list of villainous doctors would be complete without reference to the principal actors of the 'Yellow Peril,' Doctor Yen How, whose first appearance was in 1898, depicted by M. P. Shiel, and of course, Dr. Fu Manchu, mentioned above, who first appeared in 1913.

Holmes generally disdained his Continental rivals. Witness, for example, his harsh words about the Comte Auguste Dupin, the investigator Alphonse Bertillon, and the detective LeCoq (all French, it may be noted). Yet he had grudging respect for official colleagues like Stanley Hopkins and François le Villard and his friend and 'hated rival' Barker; and of course Holmes depended on his 'trusty comrade' Watson. It is not difficult to imagine him, then, working with other competent companions, as the writers of this collection have recorded, many of them physicians. It is also earnestly to be hoped that, as some suggest in the following tales, Holmes would have taken vigorous steps to oppose those doctors who were among 'the first of criminals.'

Sadly, despite handling over 1,000 cases during his career, only sixty stories of Sherlock Holmes's investigations were published prior to the death of Watson's friend Arthur Conan Doyle. For over one hundred years, readers have hoped that more tales would emerge. Now, this collection is at hand. Although the Bible advises against putting new wine into old wineskins, the

English novelist Angela Carter sagely wrote, "I am all for putting new wine in old bottles, especially if the pressure of the new wine makes the bottles explode." For a taste of explosively good new wine, read on!

The Final Prologue

CHRISTOPHER SEQUEIRA

From the handwritten Notebook of Doctor John H. Watson.

It began on a cold October morning. Holmes was seated at the breakfast table, smoking a cherrywood pipe and cutting pieces from *The Times* for his scrapbook. I was nearer the fire, scribbling notes for a paper I wanted to submit to *The Lancet* on some of the most interesting medical aspects of the Victor Savage murder that Holmes had solved with my help—the matter that saw print as *The Dying Detective*.

Victor Savage's uncle, the famous American doctor and adventurer, had corresponded with both Holmes and I and his additional researches on the deadly disease used to murder his poor nephew were very worthy of adding to the published lore on the illness, and with his consent I was readying an article.

Into this scene of quiet concentration a quick footstep was suddenly heard bounding up the stairwell leading to our rooms, and Holmes looked at me with a smile. I squared my papers away as I, too, recognised the signature of Inspector Tobias Gregson.

"Gentlemen. Good to find you at home," said the inspector, as his large frame entered our sitting room doorway.

"Ah, Gregson, equally a pleasure to see you—the last time was the Red Circle episode?" laughed Holmes.

"Very true, sir," said Gregson, doffing his hat and smoothing back his flaxen hair, and then helping himself to a cup of Mrs Hudson's coffee.

"And I'm afraid it's more of the same, Mister Holmes. Murder and mayhem. But there is a mystery solved at the same time as a mystery begun in the business I'm here about today."

Holmes had moved his chair and a third one over to the grate and gestured to Gregson to occupy one. "Excellent," he said. "Please explain, and we shall make a decision about whether to take the train to Endover this morning or this afternoon."

Gregson stared, then looked himself over, inspecting his coat, waistcoat and pockets, and the hat he'd laid down, then turned a steely eye at Holmes. "Not fair, Mister Holmes, I've no train tickets or letters sticking out of my pockets or hatband—how did you know my intentions?"

"The newspaper, Inspector. It contains a report of a body discovered in the West country, at Endover last night—not described as murder, but as 'cause of death—unknown, the matter having been referred to Scotland Yard'. You are here at eight in the morning, well before you normally arrive at your desk, ergo the matter relates to an issue from yesterday, or one you were urgently contacted about overnight. You mention murder, not mysterious death, so you do have information the paper is not privy to. Finally, Endover is normally outside your jurisdiction, unless of course it relates to some other matter, already in progress. I submit in the case of a newly discovered body that would then have to be a previously notified 'missing persons' matter. If you are here, you have not been to Endover, so I must assume you seek our company for the trip on either the morning or afternoon train that makes that run."

Gregson's blue eyes twinkled as he interrupted with a chuckle. "Very good, sir! Since May I have been trying to clear up the matter of a missing man—an engineer, a specialist in locomotive and engine design, named David Twykham. Only thirty years of age, he was a lecturer in engineering at Camford, too—quite brilliant, or so I'm told.

"Earlier this year Twykham left his house in Endover, in the West, to visit the barber, a routine occurrence, his family say. But he never arrived at the scheduled appointment and he never came back. A man of extremely regular habits, so the matter was exceedingly odd. However, there was some talk of a woman at the university he was overly-friendly with—so a scandal was whispered of. But when this woman—an assistant in the library—was questioned she went into shock—she knew nothing about Twykham's disappearance, and in fact had been planning to introduce him to her family as he wanted to broach the topic of marriage. Inquiries were made, his entire family and known friends were canvassed, but nothing was determined. A complete mystery."

"Was he engaged on any project of significance at the university?" said Holmes. "Perhaps in the military line—anything our friends in rival nations might either want to prevent this emerald isle completing, or which they would rather acquire first themselves?"

"Not as far as I can tell, sir. Twykham was working with the rail company on new engines, and even some track specifications, but nothing that would be confidential, as far as I can tell; just refinements of existing designs, as far as anyone can advise me."

"I see," said Holmes. "Now, Mr Twykham's body has been found, and by the circumstances murder is your straightforward conclusion, yet you have not seen the body, thus I assume a witness is involved? And as you are here in my consulting rooms, I assume some unusual aspect to this case awaits us?"

The big man grinned. "Indeed, there are features that suggest your 'unorthodox' lines of inquiry might be valuable, sir. Because the witness that you have correctly deduced exists, well, he has made quite a claim."

"Claim?" I ventured. "That suggests doubt, Inspector. What is this claim?"

Gregson placed his hat back on his head. "That David Twykham was shot in the back by a man who looked exactly like *himself*."

Holmes tapped his almost empty pipe into the grate. "I believe we should catch that morning train, Watson." he said.

Holmes always enjoyed travelling via the railway, as a first class carriage provided him both a comfortable situation and a place to smoke, as well as the sense of activity that his restless nature craved. He reviewed the facts with Gregson and I once more as the carriages rattled along, but for the most part he was silent—his grey eyes surveying the countryside outside the windows dispassionately.

I could only recall Gregson travelling with us once before—during the Adventure of the Cardiff Giantess—and it was clear he was still unaccustomed to Holmes's lack of effort to entertain or respond to idle social remarks. Eventually the Inspector gave up and directed his dialogue solely at me, and I must confess his interest in football matches tested me—as rugby was the only game that had remained important to me since my university days.

We eventually alighted at Endover and were met by a reedy constable named Kenners. I was anticipating a four-wheeler ride, but such was not to be as we simply walked a few minutes beyond the main train station platforms to a group of several buildings adjacent; the Endover Roundhouse and Repair Yards being the chief structures. Kenners began to explain, whilst Gregson headed off to see the Controller of the Yards, to make sure we could have access to all the grounds for our search, if need be.

"Endover Railyards ha' been built this past ten-year, big job war that, we are the top of the line, in more ways 'un one," he giggled, somewhat childishly, I thought. "Over thar,"—he pointed to the massive green roundhouse—"we set 'em oop and turn 'um through, and t'pride o t'coompany we be. This business, this murder business be a blight."

Holmes exercised that special capacity he had for putting a

person he'd just met at ease. "Mister Kenners, you have my sincere sympathies. An operation this size tells me much faith has been placed in the local community to support this operation, so, to suffer the grim occurrence of murder, well, sir that must be a shock."

Kenners nodded and launched into an almost incomprehensible listing of the functions of the different buildings on the allotment, which Holmes seemed keen to absorb, as Kenners led us to what was the key location. He then told us the strange tale of Twykham.

Kenners had been patrolling the Yard the previous afternoon when he saw a man leaning against a shed, arguing with someone who was on the other side—out of view. He got closer, saw the man was Twykham, and the argument seemed to have altered in tone; receded to calmer words. He decided it was not worth looking into further, and had walked away, when he heard a shot. He turned and saw Twykham had fallen and the man who shot him came out from behind the shed. He looked *exactly* like the dead man.

"It were his twin, no doubt—even dressed the same. I were a little bamboozled, I 'esitated—like, then rounded t'shed a minute later—and this be the hard part, sir—he war gone. Nowhere's tar be seen."

"Well, Holmes, a twin certainly narrows the field," I commented, a trifle obviously.

"Yes, Watson, except when he has no siblings. But why dressed identically? I—"

Gregson suddenly appeared and interrupted our discourse, looking strangely wild-eyed.

"Gentlemen, this is extraordinary!" he said. "Back at Endover Station, a train has pulled up—a Special, commissioned yesterday. It was apparently called for by David Twykham!"

"What?" I exclaimed. "The man found dead?"

"Indeed. It seems he organised it here and it was to run up from London—it must have been not far behind us! What's more, a number of parcels were placed on board at London."

Holmes was staring at Gregson's face; there was puzzlement in his eyes; an odd look.

"Well, Holmes, shall we go?" I ventured.

My friend suddenly regained his alertness. "Of course," he said, but again, I noticed him staring at the Inspector. Then he rubbed his hands together, briskly. "I daresay we have a look at such items as are on this train."

We arrived at the station shortly thereafter and saw the Special. It was a gleaming new engine, emblazoned with the word 'Pascal' on its cabin.

Gregson spoke to the engineer whilst Holmes and I boarded. We began an immediate search for the parcels.

We had covered the entire carriage when a violent lurch threw us to our feet. The train was leaving the station! With a suddenness that I was not anticipating Holmes sprung from his seat and darted to the compartment door. I followed as quickly as I could.

Out of the window the station was being left behind and I saw a disturbing sight—Gregson stood there looking at us—laughing with an expression of complete contempt. I was shocked.

"Watson," Holmes said before I could articulate my rage at what seemed to be a stupid prank, "what colour are Gregson's eyes?"

"Why, blue," I spluttered.

"Indeed," said Holmes, "they were blue at Baker Street. But when he returned from the Yard Controller's office they were dark brown."

"My, my word, you're right, I thought he seemed different. But eyes cannot change colour, though the pupils may dilate and give that impression, perhaps. Dilation of the pupils can indicate a drug has been consumed, Holmes. Gregson must have taken a drug of some sort or had one administered whilst he saw the Controller! What does it mean?"

"I suppose so. But yet I have a distinct certainty that his eyes were actually brown, not that his pupils were enlarged, though I could make no sense of observing that change in his appearance," said Holmes; then he fell silent, as we turned our focus to our current plight.

The train began to move faster, and faster, and it began to rock on the railings, the speed we were travelling seemed dangerously accelerated. Holmes and I ran to the external doors, but we discovered a weird sight—the doors were closed—and it was clear they would not open—they had been nailed shut!

We then ran throughout the carriage to the front-most part of the car, to where a door between carriage and engine was, and it was the same: the doors there were nailed shut. We went back to the doors whence we had originally entered the special, and though these were not nailed shut we found we were still in fact sealed in by an iron trellis that had somehow been deployed from doorway to floor, carefully hidden when we'd entered. This grate was a single piece of steel fabrication.

"We were brought here as part of a well-prepared plan." said Holmes.

I could only nod in agreement. The windows were all now barred from the outside; some similar ploy had been used that had allowed them to appear as ordinary windows when we boarded but allowed our captor—for that is what we were; captives—to surreptitiously lower the metal grilles that prevented escape whilst we travelled unaware. Had we been able to smash the windows we would not have been able to use them for egress; the bars left insufficient space. Whatever locking mechanisms were used were exterior to the carriage and my revolver would be no help on the iron.

Holmes began systematically battering the wooden panelling of the carriage's interior, quite methodically, even as I felt a sense of despair alternating with my anger.

"For the sake of Heaven! Will we die in a railway carriage? The prosaic nature of such a sinister campaign!" I said.

Holmes ignored this and began smashing the iron ferrule of his walking stick across the ceiling. When the stick did not puncture the wood he pointed to it.

"Quite amazing craftsmanship—metal painted as wood—what efforts have been made to keep us here! I am suitably impressed!" said Holmes.

I failed to share my companion's admiration, and I directed my attention out the windows, trying to discern our destination.

The train was getting faster and the scenery was blurring by. We seemed to me moving along spiralling tracks, splitting off from one junction point to another, then other, then another, nothing but rock and trees visible either side.

The view became hypnotic, frightening and compelling, the walls of the carriage were violently vibrating, the engine roared as we sped on, and on. I had a sensation we might be on some vast circle of track, perhaps some odd siding, as the view was monotonously unchanging as we continued, but we veered right as often as left—leaving me doubting we were simply traversing a loop.

Finally, a huge plume of steam painted the windows, throwing us into semi-darkness, and stirring me from what was almost a trance. The steam-cloud lifted, and I cried out aloud to Holmes, but he saw what I saw also—we were pulling into the Endover Roundhouse! As we rolled within its huge confines I peered from window after window, but I could not see a soul at work in the yards, although it was still day, though a fading day.

The train moved in and came to a halt. The iron trellis that had appeared over the door we'd used to come aboard rattled and by some hidden automation of gears it rose and disappeared into the door jamb.

Holmes pushed in front of me, gently. "Steady, old fellow," he said, and there was a tone to his voice I'd never heard before, one I did not care for—it sounded too like fear. He exited the door and I was directly behind him.

We left our carriage with the steam-clouds within it, like fog, making it hard to see, and giving the place an eerie atmosphere, save for the very centre of the Roundhouse which was brilliantly illuminated by gas-lamps on poles, arranged in a circle. I could see that all the berths of the Roundhouse contained carriages, just like ours, and I tugged at Holmes's arm—for I felt I was losing my mind, my sense of time and place—our carriage and all the others—none had engines in front of them! I could not see how we'd been shunted in here, our carriage prison uncoupled and wheeled away, without our being aware of it, but that was precisely what seemed to have happened.

"*He* will have the answers, though I am not sure I wish to hear them," said Holmes, as if to an unspoken question of mine, and he pointed to a doorway that faced us in a far wall on the opposite side of the circle of light. The door was open and a man was coming through it and towards us, walking at an almost jaunty pace, his feet ringing out in the stillness, his features slipping in and out of clear view as the steam—which emanated from nowhere in particular—roiled around. He reached the edge of the circle and waved at us, and seeing no reason not to, Holmes and I kept walking towards him. The man who stood waiting was tall and wiry, dressed in a dark suit of clothes. He looked anything between forty and sixty, for his face was smooth and unlined but he had completely white hair, receding. The features were sharp, and the eyes were clear and compelling. There was an energy about him, as with an athlete; he seemed coiled as if to move at any time.

I had never met him before, but I felt a dryness in my throat once I accepted that I knew him by his photograph all too well, except for one fact: The man before me, was, I had believed, been dead for more than a decade. He spoke, clearly, with a well-projected voice. "Yes, doctor, I am the man you think me to be. I am James Moriarty."

"Holmes," I exclaimed. "This man did not die at Reichenbach Falls? How could you conceal this from me? Why? I accepted all you had to say about your own falsified death, but this?" I looked at Holmes not angrily, but with pleading.

Holmes's expression was different to what I would have expected. He looked at Moriarty with contempt. Then he looked at me.

"Watson, I give you my word. I saw this man's body—*that is, some man's body like it*, in a mortuary in Switzerland, a week after he died—I was in disguise and wanted to be sure his menace had ended before I commenced my three year hiatus. Believe me, the ruined corpse…"

"Was not I, Mister Holmes," said Moriarty.

Holmes peered at the man and then was angry when he spoke. "I do not know what the nature of this farce is, but I shall let you know I have no time for this charade. James Moriarty died in front of my own eyes, when he fell after trying to kill me at Reichenbach. I have no remorse over acting in self defence, none whatsoever. I know not whether you be his twin or a look-alike effected through very impressive make-up, but you are not he. In any case, his criminal empire ended long ago. If this be about familial revenge, you may do your worst, although I would prefer you leave my friend out of such matters."

Moriarty spoke, again, as relaxed as if we were recounting the weather. "Dear me, dear me, Mister Holmes. No, no. My pursuits, since Reichenbach, have been directed away from crime. They have been in other fields entirely. Science. Transportation. And a unique nexus between the two, one might say.

"You remember my vast financial resources, and no doubt lamented the fact the authorities failed to get to my accounts in time to find all but pennies. Those funds were turned to good purpose. Through a series of proxies and agents all paid to carry out my strictest instructions, I have supervised the construction of this building we are now in, and more importantly the miles of track you rode upon to get here, and the Pascal Engine that pulled your carriage. It cost much, but it has been a profitable investment, too. Young Mr Twykham was my Chief of Construction, and he performed a marvellous job. His contract did have to end when he fathomed some of my purpose, but I blame his rather limited religious beliefs. He could not reconcile them with my employment, and alas, he had to be replaced. With someone *like* him."

The man laughed and the echoes of that outburst reverberated through the structure. I wanted to leave that building, I wanted to run from it, but Holmes was firmly planted, not taking his eyes off the man, who continued.

"You see, I redirected my entire criminal enterprise into transport and logistics; a wildly flourishing sector of business, let me assure you. The entire metropolitan railway network has been clandestinely suborned to my methods. I extract ten percent of all revenues of all goods that traverse it—a tidy sum. The simplest of accounting artifices ensure the funds are commuted to me without ever appearing on the ledgers of the railway institutions."

He continued, gesturing at our environment. "We stand, in many ways, at the centre of a vast web of commerce that brings me what I desire and allows me to move forward and seize what resources my goals require in order to be achieved. I believe, incidentally, I have made British railway systems more efficient by twelve percent since I took hidden control."

Holmes shook his head. "A colourful story. However, I fail to see the point of it, at all; despite its grandiosity. You claim to be Professor James Moriarty, you claim to have a new empire of illicit activity. Yet no shred of proof applies."

"No proof is needed." Moriarty said. "For the proof was in the journey you just took. The track-work you just traversed was designed to drive your train-carriage through what I refer to as a Moebius Point; an aperture in reality that allows one to journey to destinations that are normally inaccessible, but by dint of harnessing higher mathematics as a propulsive force, are at last attainable. You are now in the Roundhouse, and the Roundhouse is a nexus, where realities converge."

"Holmes, this fellow is speaking gibberish." I was annoyed that this self-confessed railways embezzler—if he was nothing else—was largely ignoring me in the conversation, as provocative as it was. "What does he mean, 'realities'?"

"I mean the answer to riddles, Holmes," said Moriarty, "and if nothing else, riddles will command your attention, your oh-so-weak attention-span. Answers to questions about how David Twykham could be seen to have killed himself? Why Gregson betrayed you? Why you saw my dead corpse in Switzerland, yet here I be? Why Professor James Moriarty had a brother, Colonel James Moriarty, who defended his academic sibling's name in the press vehemently, yet James Moriarty's birth records show him as an only child?"

Holmes looked at Moriarty. His voice was flat. "The binomial theorem."

"Yes," said the other. "You do comprehend."

Holmes nodded. "Your masterwork, the treatise on it. I'll admit

I could not understand the applications you made reference to. As with your other books, few actually understood the work you did with imaginary numbers—but now, now. It was this, wasn't it?"

Moriarty was shaking his head, side to side, a sadness in his eyes. "You, you are truly a marvellous, prodigious *natural* talent, Mister Holmes. My aptitudes were slow in developing, and required massive effort in childhood on my part, but you are like quicksilver. Such a shame, such a distinct shame I shall be terminating your existence. But I cannot allow my personal feelings to assail my plans."

Moriarty straightened his shoulders and looked at us both again. "I had divined that the multiplicity of realities are as real, as tangible, as iron and steel; but were separated by the most gossamer of divides, and that divide was a philosophical construct we call *choice*. Only we, only the one, thinking animal on this plane can exercise this capability; we generate the matrix for this in our brains and we even catalogue all its potential shades in memory and fantasy, and then we bring it into being. Thus, if we can create an infinitude of outcomes—"

"We might travel between those outcomes," said Holmes.

And the way Holmes made this last utterance made me feel very cold. He believed what Moriarty was saying, and because he did, I began to consider it possible, too.

"Yes, it is my belief that every thinking man, woman and child actually does travel from one world to the next whenever they exercise a choice. They can only travel, of course to a place occupied by themselves after making such a choice. The Pascal was my engine for making use of these principles to travel from one point to the other by another means, and to travel to universes where we had made other choices, lived other lives. Or even visit those worlds created by another's choices."

"Thus the three of you. Moriarty, the professor, who died at Reichenbach. The Colonel. And you, the Station Master of this little show," Holmes snapped.

"All James Moriarty, and all the same man, but from differing universae. Once I had fathomed the mechanism, I had no more to fear in this world of consequence. I could simply plot in my mind the action I wanted to take, such as chasing you to Switzerland where I might destroy you. I conceived that my plan *might* fail, thus the Special I engaged to follow you from London all those years ago was in fact the maiden journey of the Pascal, travelling to *here* before I left England, *and I brought one of my counterparts from the divide.* He was eager to risk death to face you; poor choices he had made in prior years had left him with advanced syphilis—his time was short and he was prepared to risk much. He openly wept for joy when he laid eyes on me, our plan was agreed to in minutes.

"He was reckless," said Holmes, "prepared to kill me in hand-to hand combat. I appreciate why now. And the third incarnation; the Colonel?"

"When you defeated my counterpart at the falls, I decided to avoid the temptation you would present me of revenge. I know my own mind, you see. The desire to settle the score would be a huge burden on me—I would be driven to act rashly, and think superficially, it would be difficult to concentrate on the development of my new sphere of influence—logistics—while you were in this world. So I vacated it for the place of my self-sacrificing doppelganger, and enjoyed the fruits of his labour for some time. His illness had prevented him advancing his criminal empire to the degree I had and as a result he was a Napoleon of Crime in theory only. You will be intrigued to hear your own counterpart had no interest in him, had not even been attracted to his few, profitable, isolated criminal ventures. But I could not leave you completely unwatched, so I travelled on the Pascal to a universe where I had made not a career decision to be an Army coach, but to be an actual military leader itself.

"That was from whence faux brother, Colonel James Moriarty, issued, and he was most supportive of the enterprise. In return I provided him some designs for army rifles that will likely deliver him a more obvious form of power, one that I will be keen to see how he has progressed should I visit him in five or six years—he may have annexed all of his Europe by then; such promise."

I decided to make another attempt at pushing away the absurdity of this subject matter that Holmes and his old enemy were discussing so calmly; I hoped I might be able to squash flat this outrageous raving, even though my friend was acknowledging it.

I barked "This is a ridiculous, elaborate hoax! Like that American Buffalo Bill, this is nothing but a cleverly arranged dramatic contrivance! I'm sure H. G. Wells and his ilk might write wonderful romances on the topic, but one *cannot* live in a world of one's imaginings."

Holmes was silent. I hoped he was preparing to challenge our adversary's madness after having lulled Moriarty into false confidence. I clasped Holmes's shoulder in a gesture of solidarity, with the intent we move against Moriarty. Then Moriarty held up his right hand in warning and using his other hand made a languid gesture at the carriages that surrounded us.

"Ah, Doctor, not only can one do just that, but this building we stand in and the methodology that brought you here was designed to do better. Not only can one journey to an adjacent reality, one can bring its inhabitants here, and if one gives the matter sufficient thought, one can invite inhabitants to visit that have the greatest desire to *replace the original inhabitant: permanently*. Haven't you ever wondered what would happen if you made the 'other' moral choice? And what if you did so in a world where the choices had been different for many, many people? With enough intriguing variances the nature of *being human* might even be different."

"The answer, my friend," he continued, "is in understanding *universae*, or what the American philosopher William James has termed *the multiverse*. But, again, for proof, don't ask me. I'd prefer you ask *them*."

Moriarty pointed at the dark, steam-clouded expanse behind us. As if by some pre-ordained signal the doors of the other eleven carriages in the roundhouse opened and from each one emerged people, in every case just two people. Soundlessly, in a way that was redolent of a dream—and, indeed, in many ways whatever one thinks happened that day, dream may be the right term—the couples came and stood surrounding us, on the exterior of the circle of light, all of them shrouded in darkness and steam.

I peered and I at last understood—even as I refused to accept. Holmes and I were surrounded by eleven pairs of men, and each one was a dark mirror of Holmes and myself; *they were Shadows of us.* Their aspect may have differed from pair to pair, but there was a common thread, a malevolent, hateful gaze at Holmes and myself that was disturbing. But as I studied these figures, as the dark and the vapour that swirled around that chamber allowed me periodically to see more details of them, the more I began to feel not just loathing, but horror.

"There are more things in Heaven and Earth, Horatio, than are dreamt of in your philosophies," said Moriarty. He laughed.

I had my revolver out, but the shadows remained outside the arena of gaslight Moriarty had arranged; I began to think there was some force that ensured that. If so, it was a blessed mercy, the only thing that stopped me from dashing in retreat from the Roundhouse. Instead I surveyed what I could of the Shadows:

Here was a Holmes and Watson who looked exactly as Holmes and I, save they seemed more 'brutish'; a nose flattened, teeth missing, small facial scar, and when I observed an obviously prison-made tattoo on my reflection's wrist the pattern was complete.

Another pair of shadows seemed less threatening at first glimpse, they even seemed somewhat frail and undernourished, until a curtain of steam in the room parted briefly and I noticed their eye sockets were black and oozing, the hands were rotting, and what looked like worms writhed in their hair.

Another pair were dressed in bizarre, torn clothing, their faces mutilated like some sort of primitive savages', with silver and gold rings and chains piercing their faces in the nostrils, cheeks and ears. Bizarre slogans and symbols were daubed in paint across their very clothing; the overall effect was of mad, self-vandalism.

Another two had skin covered in shiny black and silver scales that glinted in the darkness, their eyes were distended and round, as a fish's.

Two others at first glance seemed just like myself and my friend, yet when a ray of light pierced the atmosphere outside the gas-lit circle I saw their skin was etiolated, bleached white; the Holmes-shadow grinning in his dark purple frockcoat had hair that seemed acid-green, whilst his Watson, who glared at me evilly through a monocle, possessed a nose like a broken beak, and his hands that clutched an umbrella had suffered some deformity that had fused the fingers together.

I began to yell, before I even knew I was going to. "Impossible! A childish stunt. Do not think that we will cower, man, do not think we will! I faced worse odds in Afghanistan!" My head was pounding.

The Station Master raised his own voice to the Shadows. "You heard the man; he does not believe. You have received your invitations and accepted. The offer is valid. If any want the place of these two, now is the time to take it! I leave the outcome to you, all of you to determine!" yelled the Station Master. And a murmuring ripped through the shadows. Some voices muttered, so much like the sounds of my own and Holmes's; so, so terrifying because of that.

I turned to my friend. "A trick, a league of actors trained and prepared to frighten us, to get our guards down, before a genuine attack," I said.

Holmes looked at me. He was silent.

The figures waited, I could feel they wanted—that they *hungered*—for some event, as a crowd before a sports contest may be hushed but you can still feel their animal desire to witness a conflict, to see a party vanquished.

The Station Master withdrew, the steam parted for him and he disappeared into the doorway in the wall whence he had come originally. Strange light seemed to play from that open door as he slipped in, but my eyes could not penetrate, and my attention was on the threat around me.

Two figures emerged from the steam-shroud, and into the arena, only two. The first to become distinct was so like Holmes at initial inspection that I turned to where my friend stood beside me expecting to see him gone; but no, he was still next me, his face grim, angered. I looked back and saw why. The creature was like Holmes in build, height, even similar in clothing, sporting an Inverness cape—although this cloak was jet-black. But the face became quickly distorted—cruel lines stretched the eyes and mouth in a grimace, the eyebrows swept up wildly, the jaw was open and grimacing and sported enormous, snake-like canine fangs, and the eyes changed to become not cold gray but red; an almost phosphorescently glowing red. A stench issued from the thing; the vampire version of my friend.

Worse still was the mockery of me that accompanied the vampire.

Our wardrobes could might have come from similar sources but for the fact this shadow's suit adorned a figure much, much larger than mine. For it was near seven feet tall, and massively proportioned, it looked like some sort of walking corpse, with a hideous disfigured face; a face, I realised from hideous scars that adorned it, that was a patchwork of many faces, many swatches of human tissue. The head was lank-haired and the eyes watery, like a drowned man, the brow somehow exaggerated and distended as if bone and skin had been reinforced with more bone and skin, two odd metal plugs or posts adorned each temple, embedded in the flesh. The thing looked as if it had been strung together from disparate human anatomical parts like a mortuary jigsaw, the gray skin at the wrists and hands stretched over huge bundles of muscle and tendon, hands the size of hams clenched and unclenched. This, the hideous Monster companion of the Vampire Holmes, looked at me with heavy-lidded, pure hatred and I knew it would rend me if given the chance.

As the two nightmare distortions moved towards us in the light-circle the others outside receded into the steam, as if they had never been there. I knew that silent communion had been made somehow. If Holmes and I fell here, that would be an end to things, if we could survive, the others would make no attempt on us, but the reason for this chilled my mind; these two invaders were thought to be unlikely to be stopped. Our deaths were viewed as assured, not just possible.

The Monster lumbered towards me, quite slow, and I retreated as quickly as I could, trying to find my revolver. The thing made some strange, gurgling noises as I managed to get away from it and I thought to head to the doorway the Station Master had made his exit from. But as I darted that way I heard a creak and looked behind me, and that gesture saved my life. The Monster had hefted enormous broken-off sleepers from a pile of rubble at one side of the Roundhouse, one in each massive paw, and held them above its head! It threw them at me and I narrowly escaped them as they smashed against the wall and rebounded off in dozens of fragments—and I quickly noted the door remained un-breached. I turned and the monster was coming for me, another piece of sleeper held in its paw like a club.

Again it was slow, yet implacable; I knew if it got hold of me my life would be forfeit. I turned and braced myself and carefully took aim with my service revolver. I fired. Three times, aiming right for its head. The creature fell back into the steam clouds.

I glanced at Holmes, and his battle. The Vampire stood before him. The red-eyed face was animalistic; actual drool spilled over the open lips and out. But Holmes was surprisingly calm in the face of this nightmare; he actually lunged at the dark creature and grabbed its arm, and slammed his hip at the beast, a baritsu move I had seen him use once before in a street brawl when he was attacked by the John Clay gang. The Vampire was flipped up and over Holmes's body and I expected to see it fly crashing into the ground, but in mid air the thing tucked its feet under itself gracefully and performed an acrobatic roll that saw it land unhurt.

As it rose to its feet it smiled: it was clearly also a master of the fighting art.

Holmes however, had not waited for it to land. He had run for the wooden railing at the back of the carriage we had entered by and once there he kicked it with his foot, smashing it. I wondered why he might favour a piece of such kindling as a weapon, but I soon understood. Holmes extracted a broken railing and its broken cross-bar; he snapped off the ends, and suddenly was holding forth a make-shift cross or crucifix. He thrust it at the dark version of himself and muttered some word of blessing.

His adversary whirled away in a rage, shielding its face from the sight of the Holy object.

Holmes had his shadow at a disadvantage, he kept thrusting the cruciform at it, causing the thing to snarl and turn away, as if it were being lashed, but it would swiftly turn and try and attack him from another angle—its speed was amazing—and Holmes only narrowly was managing to keep turning and being able to brandish that cross in between himself and the Vampire. I could see that the creature was not without a strategy, Holmes was being backed ever so gradually into a corner where he would have nowhere to turn or flee if the vampire got the advantage. I could have fired my pistol but the risk with the two of them darting around was that I might hit my friend.

Then Holmes threw the cross *at* his foe! The Vampire flinched back and raised its cape to protect its face. Astonishingly, when the cross hit the Vampire the cape burst into flame and smoke and the creature howled in fear. But the moment was brief, for the cross then fell to the ground and when the fanged one raised its head now it showed a look of red-eyed triumph. Holmes had run across the chamber. The Vampire literally hissed with glee and when it leapt a distance no man could make, straight at my friend—who was stooped over—it was clear the vampire would be upon him.

But Holmes had a fragment of sleeper the monster had smashed apart, and he simply turned, reminding me of nothing less than a Spanish bull-fighter, and the Vampire was suddenly skewered right through the shoulder on the end of the broken shaft by its own leap at Holmes! The creature uttered a string of curses at Holmes, and almost fell to its knees; my friend had the beast at his advantage.

But before I could see how this would play out I heard a roar from the darkness and I looked up: The Monster that was my shadow was back, apparently unharmed. A few welts on its forehead were the only sign I had fired at it; clearly all I had done was temporarily daze it.

I did not have my revolver ready—I had returned it to my pocket and the thing was almost upon me—so I swung at the

Monster with my walking stick, which had the advantage of being a solid oak staff with a lead-filled head. The blow struck the thing soundly in the face. There was an audible thud, but the gray face was unmarked, it was like hitting stone; if a bullet hadn't killed it a blow like mine was a desperate move. I hit the thing again and again, and it moved somewhat slowly but I soon realised with horror it was amused, it watched me with evil mirth, not caring what I was doing. Then, suddenly, a black-nailed hand flicked out and knocked me to the ground, and, before I could rise, the thing picked up my stick and squeezed and snapped it into two like a pencil, ostentatiously letting it drop in two pieces to the ground. I saw then that I was a rat being played with by a cat.

So I withdrew my revolver, and fired at the thing's heart since the bony ridged face was too well armoured. The shirt the Monster wore exploded, but a gaping hole revealed more of the grey skin—and the skin was undamaged. I fired again, and nothing happened: this embalmed giant had a hide like some prehistoric beast.

It lunged and grabbed me. Agony fired through my ribcage as the thing crushed me in a sick embrace. I could barely breathe and I smashed my pistol at the thing's face, to no effect. It locked eyes with me and began to laugh, a horrible, nightmare sound issued between huge, uneven, broken teeth.

I do not know to this day what made me act the way I did then, perhaps wild desperation, perhaps divine insight. Where the idea came from I really cannot fathom. I raised my pistol and stuck it hard up against the side of the monster's head—right against one of the small metal posts that extruded from the side of the thing's temple—and I weakly squeezed the trigger on the final round I had in the revolver.

The sound of the bullet discharging was like a cannon in my ears—I was completely disoriented—and it took me a moment or two to appreciate I was no longer in the grip of the thing, but standing in front of it. The beast was standing, bellowing like a wounded bear. My shot had blasted the metal cap off, and taken a small chunk of the dead, leathery grey flesh, but no blood flowed. A gaping wound left a strand of wire exposed—and this began to issue furious, hot sparks. The Monster raised its hand to this and then screamed. Its hand seemed stuck at the side of its own neck, but did nothing to diminish the furious sparks which soon had its coat-sleeve burning.

The Monster jerked around like a macabre, gargantuan puppet being wildly tugged about by invisible strings. The air smelt of a lightning storm, and the sparks flew intermittently from the hole in one side of the neck and the still intact post on the other side. The horrible face writhed in grotesque transformation—agony, ecstasy, I could not tell, the contortions and twistings were hard to interpret in a face so misshapen.

The huge creature flailed about, then fell to its knees, then flopped sideways onto the ground. An arm spasmed out a few times, clutching at empty air. I looked at the features; the pitted and scarred face, and most of all, the dead eyes. I saw no reflection of myself—and wondered if one hid behind those eyes—and I said a silent prayer of thanks.

My prayer was premature. Something hit me and knocked me to one side—almost to my feet, and then the fanged Holmes-shadow had its hands about my throat and the immediate pressure was frightening.

I used all the strength I had to try and stop the Vampire's fingers from tightening, I had slipped my own fingers under its to try and save myself but I could feel the pressure increasing. I felt the bones of one of my fingers crack—but terror of death stopped me screaming and kept me struggling—futilely, I knew.

Then Holmes slammed the broken-off shaft of my stick into the fanged demon's back. It released its hands from my throat slowly and stepped back. It stared at the front of its body and the shaft protruding from its shirtfront. Black blood was oozing out of its chest around the stake—it fumbled with one taloned hand at the stick and I had a presentiment it would pull it loose and the black fluid would become a fountain, but it dropped its hands to its sides. It stared at Holmes and its features softened—for one terrible second they looked exactly like those of my friend, then a paroxysm of pain distorted the Vampire's face.

It resumed its inhuman cast and the creature fell to the ground, on top of the remains of its Monster companion.

"You once told me my taste in sensational criminal literature and natural history was unparalleled, Watson. I'm thankful it is. I would refer you to the case of vampires in the writings of Augustin Calmet; hysterical village criminal matters where the remedy is always the destruction by stake through the heart…"

"Really, Holmes," I gasped. "I thought you'd been reading Bram Stoker!"

"Who?" said Holmes.

The Vampire and the Monster were one, unmoving mass, and a change began to take place in that pile of remains. Both corpses—if that be the correct term—as one began to quickly liquefy into a huge, repulsive mass of whitish slime, which began to dissipate. It stunk in a way that reminded me of the dead corpses on a battlefield, and I moved away from it, even as the fluid sunk into the ground and became reduced to a stain, wisps of white gas coming from it.

The remaining Shadows could be heard conferring amongst themselves, each shade of me communicating in hushed, obscured tones with its counterpart of Holmes. Almost as one they could be seen faintly in the miasma again, but stepping back into their own carriages and closing the doorways. Holmes laughed, a touch of hysteria in his chortle, but he brought himself under control.

"Just what I would have advised. Time to return home."

I had been leaning on Holmes for support. My leg was aching, my blood was pounding in my ears, but I found I could ignore the feelings, the situation still seemed so unreal as to prevent me feeling panicked even though my heart was racing, my mind was calmer than it would normally be in this situation. I'd found my footing and Holmes, satisfied I was stable, had just let my arms and shoulder loose when the Station Master appeared before us, holding a pistol. He shouted at the Shadows in the carriages.

"Very well! I shall deal with this myself!"

Holmes spoke sharply. "They know, don't they? This is not the natural order of things? There is a risk, a danger of sorts in bringing…us together, isn't there? They don't want to end up affected by that danger, do they? But you don't care, because your obsession rules your mind, overrides even your sense of self-preservation—just as you yourself said you feared it would! In that sense, you *are* a madman."

"Irrelevant," the Station Master said, and he extended his arm and pointed the pistol at Holmes's face.

There was a noise and the Station Master turned away from us. There was someone standing behind him, presumably whomever it was had entered from the doorway behind him. It was clear from Moriarty's face as he turned that this visitor was a surprise to him, as much as to us.

I say this visitor was 'someone' but even as I do, I need to qualify the description. The new arrival to our scene was *not* a man, that much was clear. It was some sort of device, a construct, in the rough form of a man!

It had arms and legs and a torso and a head, but they were fashioned from a copper-coloured metal of some kind. It stood at about five and half feet in height and was very slender in shape, and it was terrifying.

I thought at once of the possibility that a man was concealed in some sort of burnished armour, but the legs were almost like thin brass pipes, they did not conceal a man, or even a child's lower limbs. The aspect of it that transfixed me the most was the thing's head. It was larger than an average person's, and had odd little metal flags and cones that were moving on it, like portions of a clock, or some small rotating weather vane. And the eyes were round and green, and a faint glow radiated from them, giving the thing a ghostly aspect. If I were not a man of the modern age I am sure I would have assumed the thing were some demon of the pit, some spectre, but there was something mechanical about the thing.

It spoke, the voice emanating from the head, but from no mouth I could discern. Its voice was male, clear and fluid, quite beautiful, in fact.

"No," it said, and raised one arm and hand. A puff of gas flew forwards and into Moriarty's face—his eyes bulged and his skin whitened, he screamed a horrible noise—then a rattle-like sound escaped his lips.

The Station Master died, but ere his body even fell to the ground, the thing caught it by the collar of the shirt, with swiftness and economy of movement so precise it seemed like a flywheel on a motor whirring into action, and held it, so that the dead man did not hit the floor, only his legs folded under him.

The thing held the Station Master's body like a doll, effortlessly. It turned its awful face at us, and shook the body as if gesturing with a toy.

"I can use bits of this," it said. It 'looked' at Holmes.

"We're not *all* like him," it said, "but too many of us are. I certainly *was*. Until someone like you made me see the error of my ways, made me see the misery I caused and how profoundly… *irrational* that behaviour was."

Holmes's mouth was open; not a word came out.

The creature held up its free 'hand' and a small aperture opened, from which a greenish light emanated, dim at first, then it became brighter.

"A pity I had to get thrown off a cliff over a waterfall to achieve that, but that's how these things go."

The light brightened, fiercely, and I had to shut my eyes.

I did not faint, I did not collapse. All I did, or at least all I remember doing, was close my eyes for a few seconds to shield them from the bright light. But when I opened them again it was clear that my recollection was false, or, failing that, some sort of transference of time and distance had taken place.

I was standing, dressed in exactly the same clothes as when I had shut my eyes, but I was outdoors and it was daylight! Holmes stood next me, in the same relative spot to me as before, and he looked confused: a rare sight, I must emphasise. Where we were was more incredible. We stood in the blackened ruins of some sort of wooden structure, some place that had been demolished or destroyed by fire. It was Holmes that spoke the impossible. He leant down and for some reason ran his fingers through the blackened earth we stood on.

"We're in the roundhouse, Watson, but it's been burnt to the ground—and these ashes are *cold!*" I imitated my friend's actions, and the pure insanity of what he was saying made sense to me! I looked around and could see, strewn here and there not far from us on the ground the gutted fragments of the walls, the blackened rails, the charred and crumpled sleepers.

"Halloa!" It was Gregson, strolling along, notebook in hand.

Holmes looked him dead in the eye. I started to speak, but my friend silenced me.

"Dreadful mess here, Holmes," Gregson said.

Then he turned to a passing worker, a scrawny old fellow with a wisp of beard pushing a trolley of grass cuttings. "This body you found, it was in this building, burnt, was it?"

"Yessir," the fellow said. "Sad it were, he were well liked."

Holmes and I looked at one another. "The engineer, Twykham?" Holmes said quietly.

The old man looked puzzled. "Engineer? No, sir, it were the local Station Master from Endover. Mister Moriarty."

Holmes and I were shaken—no—*profoundly disturbed* by these events.

We agreed to repair to a nearby public house, but, once we had settled there, Holmes became grim-faced, withdrawn; he was visibly pained, his hand rubbing his forehead. I wanted to talk about what we had seen, share our recollections, but he stared at me and shook his head.

"I require some…time to ponder what we have been through," he said.

He withdrew to a corner with a drink he didn't touch and began to smoke. I knew this mood, but for once felt just as *isolated* as my brilliant associate, isolated from the everyday ruminations experienced by my fellow mortals. For once, as I fancied Holmes feels often, I was in a stream of ideas so rapid, so vast, even frightening, that none could be trusted to hear them.

So, whilst Holmes smoked, I took out my journal, and wrote the account you have read above.

I do not know how to categorise it.

So Ends the Journals of John H. Watson

From the diary of Sherlock Holmes

Watson and I could not find the words to adequately communicate after the bizarre experience of The Lost Specialist. We returned to Baker Street with a black cloud hovering over us, spoiling that ease between us, that trust that respects silence. Now, the gulf without words was ominous; would one of us find cause to call the other a madman if we spoke of what we knew we had both seen and heard, however impossible it must have been?

This distraction was to be the cause of my terrible, terrible failure. We alighted from our cab and Watson unlocked the door to 221B.

A second too slow, I noticed a strange, stray shine of metal, a loop of copper-coloured wire poking out from under the front doormat! I tried to pull Watson back from the doorway—but it was too late—Watson had stepped through! An electrical connection was formed and a terrible pulse of force rippled through the doorway, and before my horrified gaze an aperture into black and purple, swirling voids appeared! A breathing maw of roiling nothingness, in a hole in thin air!

It sucked Watson in, before he could even scream! Then it closed in a blink, as if it had never been there.

I ripped up the doormat and uncovered a metal and glass plate over a bizarre, blinking, whirring device—an engine of some dark design! The finish of the craftsmanship reminded me of many of Moriarty's tools, such as those fabricated at his direction by the blind mechanic Von Herder, and for the first time, I wondered if this was why the professor's lead engineer had reputedly torn out his own eyes years ago, perhaps when the first work on this evil device had begun.

I believe the machine is a multi-versal transporter; a cut-down-in-size version of the locomotive we escaped. The perverse, but calculating, Moriarty's fail-safe: If he did not vanquish myself and Watson in the roundhouse he planned to dispatch us with this trans-dimensional booby-trap!

I pulled the wiring of the device open and saw a shimmering, perfect diamond powering the mechanism, and also saw it sparking and heating—smoke beginning to belch out of it. There was no time; I was not prepared to lose the only friend I have, the only friend a man could ever need, and so, I studied the arrangement of the device, and with no time to do anything but hope, and noting a congruence with more commonplace electrical and magnetic generators, I ripped two wires out, and exposed two bare ends, and connected the wires.

There was a boom and flash and I—well, to a passer-by, I imagine— it appeared as if I vanished.

Then I was back, standing on the doorstep to Baker Street, the front door now closed, as if naught awry had happened. I pulled my own keys out of my pocket and began to open the door, and just as I did so I felt my glance drawn to the brass doctor's plate on the outside of the building that reads 'JOHN H. WATSON, M.D.'; a plate Watson had insisted upon with his recent decision to make our address both his lodgings and consulting rooms since Mrs Hudson's other tenant had vacated.

The plate moved! It literally rippled, and I'm sure I frowned in puzzlement—and then, finally, it ceased wavering in form and cast, to reveal, to my gradually awakening understanding, the new name of the doctor that practises from these premises, living as my room-mate, friend, and biographer…Watson had been flung into the bridge between realities as it passed through this exact spot, at this juncture in the worlds of infinite possibilities, this spot where Sherlock Holmes dwells, and so, therefore a doorway opens to his residence; but beyond that fact, just WHO might I reside with, in worlds of infinite eventuality?

My mind became clouded, buzzing with visions of the ghosts of what might be, but this was no reverie; I could feel the thoughts solidifying; facts I knew to be were changing, my knowledge of my past, my future distorting. I tried to hang on, with all the concentration I have mastered my entire life, to keep hold of who I truly was and what I sought, of the friend I must rescue.

Though it seemed childish, I spoke aloud, in desperation: "Once I step through this door, the new reality beyond it will become mine. But if I can survive the experience of what lies beyond I can keep searching until I find the way to bring you back, Watson. For somewhere in my possible futures there is a way for me to pick the door that will lead me to home, and thence the scientific method to restore you. I just have to find it, though it takes me a lifetime, no, an endless array of lifetimes, old friend. I hope I will know when I have come to the right world, and surely will know when I am in the wrong one."

The End…

…of Only *One* Reality…

The Forlorn Death of Sally at the Crossroads

DENNIS O'NEIL

All this happened a while after that business with the Clantons in Tombstone. Wyatt's brother Virgil had gotten himself shot up and Wyatt asked me to help get Virgil and his family to California, where they'd likely be safe. I told Wyatt I would, but I didn't have much heart for it. Truth is, I was weary of politics and killing, and my cough was getting worse. I didn't like the color of what I was spitting up, either, and I was broke—being Wyatt Earp's friend brought me a certain amount of recognition, but it didn't put a thing in my pocket. So I told Wyatt that I'd meet him in Tucson in a few weeks and lit out for a town I'd heard about called Feeley, where a rail head they'd just built was bringing in cowboys and steel pushers with salaries to lose. I figured I'd help with the losing part while I got myself together, then head for Tucson.

I got off the stage round noon in a one-horse town called Keppel's Crossing intending to stretch my legs. I asked the driver when he'd be pushing on to Feeley and he said he wouldn't, not before the next morning at the earliest.

"Why might that be?" I asked him.

He told me that storms had washed out the trail between Keppel's Crossing and Feeley and nothing had passed between the towns for two-three days. He told me I was stuck and I couldn't argue, so I set out to make the best of it. There was no room at the local boarding house—seems I wasn't the only stranger who had gotten stuck. I finally found a stable with an empty stall that I could rent for the night. I wasn't happy about sleeping on straw with animals for companions, but I guessed it was better than spending the night outdoors.

Then I strolled out onto the unpaved main street and began seeking whatever fortune might be found in a place like this.

It was a quiet day, quiet and ugly. Fat, mean clouds were low in the sky, an ornery wind whipping the street. My best prospect seemed to be a salon called Yellow Rosie's and that's where I went. But I didn't get there right away. I got stopped twice, first by an old man, little fellow wearing ragged duds a couple of sizes too small and smelling like a charnel house.

"Mister," he asked, "have you seen my Sally?"

"Who might this Sally be?" I asked back at him.

Maybe he didn't hear me. "She run off again an' I don't know where she's gone," he said in a quivery voice.

I touched the brim of my hat and said, "I wish you good luck with finding her." I continued toward the saloon. A few raindrops fell around me and I started to run.

A big man with a belly the size of a bay window, driving a creaking buckboard with a canvas-covered load on the bed, halted his team alongside me. He called for me to stop and there was no reason not to. Wheezing and huffing, he climbed down; pulled a Spencer rifle from where it had been laying on the seat, pointed it at me, and gave me a hard look. Up close, I could see a star pinned to his vest.

"You'd be the sheriff," I said.

"Das'nt forget it. And you'd be?"

"I was born John Henry Holliday."

"The Holliday that was mixed up in the shootout down to Deadwood?"

"I wish I could say no, but that'd be a lie."

"You packin', Holliday?"

I hesitated, not wanting to surrender my meagre arsenal but not wanting to cross the local law, either, seeing as how I was new in town and didn't know how the game was played thereabouts. I reached under my belt and hauled out my derringer, a lady's gun I'd taken off a sharpie in Waco a while back.

The sheriff tucked the rifle under an arm and relieved me of the derringer.

"You shoot this? Looks to me like it wouldn't kill a butterfly."

"I'll keep that in mind next time I hunt butterflies."

He shoved the rifle into my belly and said, "You got a smart mouth. I come a long way and I'm dead tired and I'd sooner shoot you as look at you. Maybe you tell me where you was night 'fore last. Wouldn'ta been Feeley, would it?"

"Why?"

" 'Cause somebody busted into the bank and made off with a loada gold coins."

"Robbery's not in my line. But so you can be peaceful about it, on Tuesday night I was enjoying a game of cards with some lawmen in Tombstone. It's a story that'd easy to verify with an exchange of telegrams."

"Maybe I will."

"When do I get my property back?"

"Stop by my office on your way outta town if I ain't arrested you by then."

He mounted the buckboard and went to wherever he was headed and I dashed toward the saloon. Before I got there, the rain started.

That's how I come to be playing cards in a saloon called Yellow Rosie's late one Thursday afternoon. Yellow Rosie's was busy: couple of cowpokes at the bar, some farmhands, some laboring men, and a bunch in pricey clothes who, judging by their talk and accents, weren't from around these parts. The storm had made Keppel's Crossing pretty near a bustling metropolis. I got into conversation with two gents who'd made a bonanza selling ranch land to the railroad and mistakenly reckoned they knew how to play poker. We agreed on a few rules and the next thing I knew my new friends were sharing a table and a deck of cards with me and this other fellow, rail-thin, dressed in a grey suit he hadn't bought within a thousand miles of where we were sitting judging by the cut of it. He had the keenest gaze I'd ever seen, his eyes bright and as steady as nailheads. He watched for about an hour and then, as the barkeep was lighting the kerosene lamps, he asked if he could play a hand or two. From the sound of him, he came from England, but I figured that he had some American money and it'd be as spendable as what I was taking off the ranchers. I used my foot to push a chair away from the table and the Britisher sat down.

I had to figure him for a professional like me. He was good. A couple of hours later, one of the cattlemen said a few words his mother never taught him and stood and stomped away, and the other one was digging a coin from his coat pocket, maybe about to try one last hand before admitting he was beaten. But he never had a chance to bet. The door to the street slammed open and a gust of cold air blew in, followed by a man whose clothing was sopping wet. Even in the bad light from the kerosene lamps, I could see that he was pale and in need of a shave and that he was toting a double-barreled shotgun, a 12 gauge. He looked around and stopped looking when he saw me.

"Holliday!" he shouted and crossed the room, and I knew I had trouble. "I come for you, Holliday."

The odds were poor. I had a shotgun barrel four feet from my head. I considered trying to jump him, but I never got the chance. I began to cough, bad, my eyes watering and my chest heaving. Fighting was out of the question. But having my head blown off sure as hell wasn't.

Then I was looking at the underside of the table, cards and currency flying every which way. The edge of the table caught my would-be killer beneath his chin and the 12 gauge boomed and sent shot into the wall behind us. That was when I saw a grey blur and when my vision cleared, the shotgunner was lying on this back and the Britisher was standing over him, rubbing his right knuckles with his left hand.

I helped the Britisher stare down at the sorry lump on the floor.

"You kicked the table?" I asked.

"It seemed propitious."

"And you punched him?"

"That was perhaps unnecessary, but I thought it wise to err on the side of caution."

"Much obliged." I squatted and got a handful of shirtfront and hauled the Britisher's target to his feet.

He mumbled something and I told him to speak up.

"T'warn't fair," he said and I slapped him.

"Now I recognize you," I said. "You're one of the Clantons. A second cousin? You hightailed it when the fun started in Tombstone."

"I din't feel good."

"But you figured on evening the score today?"

The Clanton kept his mouth shut. I thought I saw a tear in his eye, but it might have been a raindrop.

I stepped close to him and said, "If I ever catch sight of you again, anywhere, any time, I will kill you."

"Does this town have a sheriff?" the Britisher asked.

"It does," I said. "Him and me had a little talk a while ago. We'll never be best friends."

The Britisher smiled which proved that he could and said, "I'll deliver our obstreperous friend to him and then perhaps we can share a meal."

I shrugged. The Britisher grabbed the Clanton's upper arm and steered him out into the rain. I set the table to rights and sat and shuffled cards to let any interested parties know that I'd be willing to play a hand or two. After a while that got boring and I was about to head back to my bed of straw when the Britisher came in and stood dripping water on the floor. He saw me and let go with another smile and walked over to the table.

"Allow me to buy you dinner," he said, and I nodded.

He bought two plates of slumgullion from the man behind the bar which we choked down because it was as close to dinner as we were going to get and then we settled in for what turned out to be a long talk. Seems I'd been wrong about him. He wasn't a professional gambler like me. Fact is, before he joined our game he'd never played poker before. He'd learned the game during the hour I was lightening the wallets of my victims by watching us.

"The tall chap had a habit of tugging at his ear when he was pleased with the cards and his friend stared down at the floor in similar situations," he said.

"Exactly right," I told him. "And what did I do?"

"Absolutely nothing."

"Glad to hear it. You didn't give anything away either. Mind telling me your name?"

"I am Sherlock Holmes of London, England. And you?"

I answered him and asked "What line of work are you in, Sherlock Holmes of London, England?"

"I am a consulting detective."

"Like the Pinkertons?"

"I fancy that my methods are a bit more refined than those of the estimable Mr Pinkerton and his colleagues and my clientele perhaps a bit more genteel."

"Not a whole hell of a lot of genteel folks round these parts. So if you don't mind my asking, what brings you here?"

"I am in the United States to conclude an assignment for someone in Buckingham Palace. I'm afraid I can say no more, except that my efforts have been successful."

"You headed back home?"

"If all goes as planned, and the weather permits, I will be on a schooner bound for the United Kingdom early next week."

"Well, Sherlock Holmes of London, England, I'm in your debt. Without you, I'd be splattered all over the wall. If there's anything I can do for you—"

"If you have an hour to spare, I would be grateful for more information about the American frontier in general and your profession in particular."

"Hell, I'll give you *two* hours."

I ended up giving him a lot more than that. While the wind howled and rain gusts slapped the roof, I showed Holmes how to cheat at cards—second dealing and bottom dealing and marking the aces with a thumbnail and a few other tricks—and how to win at poker *without* cheating and the fine art of killing the other man before he kills you and he told me about the difference between just seeing and really observing and how, when you've eliminated all the other possibilities, whatever loco thing is left has got to be the truth. It must have been near midnight when we decided we'd talked enough and I stood and looked behind the bar. The bartender was stretched out on the floor, on a blanket, fast asleep. I turned to Holmes, but before I could say anything, I commenced coughing and spitting blood. I went on for what seemed like hours with Holmes standing by, hands hanging at his sides, looking helpless.

When I finally stopped and wheezed, trying to catch my breath, he asked, "Am I correct in assuming that you suffer from tuberculosis?"

I wiped blood from my mouth on the back of my hand and said, "That's what they tell me."

The barkeep poked his head above the bar and said, "You wanna sit down?"

I did that and had another coughing spell.

Holmes put a hand on my shoulder and said, "I shall accompany you to your room."

"Won't be necessary. I don't much want to go out into the wet just now, so if our friend over there has no objection, I'll sleep here in this chair for a while."

"Don't see no harm in it," the barkeep said. He ducked behind the bar and probably got back to his snooze.

Holmes nodded, turned on his heel, and made for the door.

I closed my eyes. If I had any dreams, I don't remember them.

When I woke up, something was wrong. I sat until I realized what it was. No sound of rain and wind. The storm had quit and pale sunlight was streaming through the window. Morning in Keppel's Crossing. Time for me to get busy, but doing what? I began by walking around the room. My host was still asleep and nothing else was going on, so I strolled outside. Even before I felt the barrel of a Spencer repeating rifle punch into my temple I knew there was trouble. A body was lying face down in the middle of the muddy street and from the britches and boots I knew it was the Clanton, gone to meet his Maker. From the corner of my eye, I could see that the rifle belonged to the Sheriff.

"You gonta hang," he said.

"Any particular reason?"

He waved his gun toward the corpse. "Him."

"Hard to tell from here," I said, "but I'll allow that he's dead. But what makes you think I made him that way?"

The sheriff changed his rifle from pointing at my head to pointing at my belly as he moved around to my front. "For one thing, they was bad blood 'tween you. Six, seven men heard you say you was gonna kill him. An' that ain't countin' the furriner."

"I suppose you mean me," Holmes said, coming around the corner of the building. A few steps behind him, shuffling and snuffling, here came the raggedy, smelly little man I'd talked to the previous day on the way to Yellow Rosie's.

Holmes turned to him and said, "You seek the local sheriff? There he is."

The raggedy man stepped around Holmes and spoke to the lawman. "You the shurf?"

"You know I am."

"She's dead."

"Tell him *who* is dead," Holmes suggested.

The raggedy man stomped his foot and yelled "Sally, ya dang fool."

"Sally is, or was, his mule," Holmes said to both the sheriff and me. Some early risers were coming from the buildings that lined the street. A few were edging closer to us and the rest were hanging back, taking it in.

"How do you figure into it?" the sheriff asked Holmes.

"At times it is useful to be outdoors while considering a problem. I was having a stroll in the predawn mulling the circumstances that brought me to America when I encountered our friend here."

"He always talk like that?" the sheriff asked me.

I shrugged.

"Fella offered to help me look for Sally," the raggedy man said.

"I confess that I acted more from boredom than charity," Holmes said. "We found the unfortunate creature at the crossroads outside the town boundary."

"Shot dead," the raggedy man whispered, and then he snuffled. "She wuz my onliest friend."

"Pity," said a stout woman who had drawn near. "The Lord loves animals, too."

"Shut up," the sheriff said, swivelling his rifle so it pointed at her, which was a relief to me. "Get on outta here. The rest of you too. Ain't nothing to see."

"On the contrary," Holmes said. "If these gentlefolk do not mind lingering for a while, they may observe justice being served, which is always an edifying experience."

"They stay long enough they'll see this bastard hang." The sheriff swung his rifle until it was again aiming at me. I let loose a sigh. The respite was nice while it lasted.

"Highly doubtful," Holmes murmured. He moved closer to the sheriff. "We were discussing the evidence you have against Doctor Holliday. You mentioned the altercation between him and the poor fellow lying in the street. Is that all you have?"

"Hell no."

"Please! The language!" That was from the stout lady.

The sheriff ignored her. He was busy shifting the rifle and tugging a small pistol from his pocket and thrusting it under my nose. "You gimme this? Yours, ain't it?"

"Mine or one just like it," I admitted.

"Well, I found it layin' 'longside the body. You musta dropped it after you shot him."

Holmes nodded and smiled. "The game is afoot." He faced the crowd, which now numbered more than a dozen. "By any chance, were any of you people stirring during the middle of the night?"

"What you mean, 'middle'?" someone called.

"The dark hours. Three or four a.m."

The man who had spoken stepped forward. "I was down to the outhouse takin' care of business 'bout then."

"And what, pray tell, was the weather like?"

"The rain done let up some. Didn't last long, though. It comm-enced to come down again 'fore I got back to bed."

Holmes rubbed his hands together and his smile stretched into a grin. "Most satisfactory. Sheriff, may I examine the weapon?"

"You think I'm gointa hand you a gun—"

"No, no. By all means, keep it firmly in your possession. But I should like to see the ammunition."

"Nothin' doin'."

"Then will you kindly tell us if the weapon contains two bullets?"

The sheriff snapped open the derringer and then snapped it closed.

"You testify that the pistol contains *two* bullets?" the Britisher asked, loudly enough for everyone to hear.

"A full load," I said.

"What if it does?" the sheriff asked.

"Will you agree that if the weapon is fully loaded, the bullet that claimed the unfortunate Mr Clanton could not have come from it?"

The sheriff jabbed me with the Spencer for no reason and said, "He coulda reloaded."

"We shall soon see why that was impossible," Holmes said. He faced the crowd.

"Now, we come to the ugly part. I shall need the bullet which struck down the victim. Are there any physicians present? What about you, Holliday?"

"I'm a dentist, not a sawbones, but I watched an autopsy or two in my day, and I don't figure the corpse'll complain if I make any mistakes."

Holmes said, "Perhaps you'll accompany us, Sheriff?"

I noticed that a few of the crowd were departing as Holmes, the Sheriff and went to the dead man.

Holmes shouted to the crowd: "You'll note that there are no footprints in the earth around him and the ground is still damp from the rain."

"You don't haveta be standin' next to a man to shoot 'im!" said the sheriff.

"No indeed," Holmes murmured. "You most certainly do not. But it is useful to be close to a target if you plan to hit it."

I placed myself between the Clanton and the crowd, in case

any of them might be upset by a little butchery, opened my clasp knife and got to it. My slicing party didn't take much more than a minute. I handed what I'd dug out, a sticky nugget of metal, to Holmes. I'd begun to understand where all his might be going but I had no idea how it might get there.

We left the body and moved toward the crowd. The bunch that had gone must have gone to get friends because we were now facing a mob. Cowboys, merchants, a few laborers, ladies with youngsters and ladies without youngsters, overfed swells in fancy suits, farmers who were sitting on wagons and, standing off by himself, the raggedy man, owner of the late Sally.

"Can't we be more private about this?" I whispered to Holmes.

"The presence of witnesses will prove to be of advantage to us," Holmes said to me. To the sheriff, he said, "Will you kindly remove one of the bullets from the small firearm?"

"What the hell for?"

"Humor me."

The sheriff spat, took out the derringer, broke it open, picked out a shell, and gave it to Holmes.

Holmes turned to the crowd and raised his hands, displaying between thumbs and forefingers the slug I'd extracted from the dead man and the one from the derringer.

He explained what they were, his voice raised so everybody could hear him, and continued: "You'll observe that the bullets are noticeably dissimilar, different in size and color. Now, if the Sheriff will oblige me by firing the remaining bullet at…let us say, the bottom limb of the oak tree?"

"Hell no on this foolishness. We're wastin' time. Holliday's guilty and he's gonna pay the price."

"Perhaps, then, you'll allow one of your townsfolk to fire the shot?"

The sheriff looked ready to have a fit. His face reddened and that rifle of his was again pointed at me. "I tole you—"

Holmes interrupted him. "Will one of you gentlemen volunteer?"

A number of voices answered him all at once: "I'll do it"… "ain't gonna hit 'er "…"li'l sumbitch is useless…"

"They're right," I said. "The gun's maybe useful from across a card table, but best not try for something across the room."

"In that case, perhaps the sheriff will stipulate that the small pistol's range is limited to a few yards."

"What the hell's stippalate?"

"For 'stipulate' put in 'agree' and you'll get the sense of it," I said.

"And am I correct in positing that the crossroads where the unfortunate Sally meet her demise is much further than a few yards?"

Someone said, "dern tootin'" and someone else said, "gotta be near a half mile."

The sheriff prodded me with his Spencer and said, "I had enough. Holliday's going to jail."

"Excellent!" Holmes shouted. "We shall accompany you. I was about to suggest a visit to the jail. Come."

He marched across the street and the pack of us fell in behind him like the rats in that Pied Piper story I once read. We all stopped in front of the jail, which also housed the sheriff's office.

"I call to your attention the matter of direction," Holmes said, stepping onto the boardwalk that fronted the hoosegow. He looked out over the street. "I am now facing south, the direction of the crossroads."

There were grumbles of assent.

"Let us remember the small pistol. If fired from here it could conceivably hit something in the street, but could it hit something at the crossroads—could it, in fact, be the agent of poor Sally's demise? Surely not. I mention this only to put to rest, once and for all, the supposition that the small pistol was somehow involved in the murder. Now consider another possibility, which is that someone fired a much larger weapon from where I am standing, missed its intended victim, and fired again, this time accurately. The result you see sprawled in the dirt. All this may have occurred during the brief interval of quiet in the storm described by the user of the outhouse. What follows is the merest speculation, but let us conjecture that our murderer welcomed the interval as an opportunity to coax his victim outside. The storm may have begun again and an unexpected flash of lightning or rumble of thunder upset his aim."

"And on the second try, jackpot," I said.

The sun was well over the horizon and the day was beginning to bake. But nobody was leaving. Everyone wanted to see how this game played out, I suspect. They didn't have long to wait.

"We must now answer a few questions and then, I hope, our task will find an end. First, what manner of firearm is capable of being lethal over the distance between where I stand and the crossroads?"

"That Spencer the sheriff's got pointed at me would do," I said.

"And second," Holmes continued, "who might be standing here, in front of the sheriff's office, at three of a stormy morning?"

Everybody was looking at the sheriff, though I confess that I was paying more attention to the rifle digging into my belly than to the man.

"I din't have no reason, to kill Willy," the sheriff said in a voice that was somewhere between a yell and a growl. He was plenty agitated and I was wishing he could find somewhere else to aim his gun.

"We might ask how Doctor Holliday regained possession of the pistol when he gave it to you yesterday and you have it in your possession now," Holmes said.

The sheriff's face was flushed and he was shifting his weight from one leg to the other. "I ain't had no reason to kill Willy," he repeated.

"Interesting, that you call him by his first name," Holmes murmured. "Not conclusive, but interesting."

"I got an idea as to motive," I said. "I've not pieced it all together yet, but let me speculate a bit. Sheriff, you told me about a robbery in Feeley Tuesday night."

"I heerd 'bout that," a farmer said.

"My cousin says they was prob'ly two robbers," a shopkeeper said.

"The outlaws might have been stranded there, on account of the rain, particularly if they were headed this way. They might not hit Keppel's Crossing 'til...I don't know. Yesterday afternoon?

Might have split up to avoid attention. Or maybe one of 'em lamed a horse. Or got lost. Lotta reasons they might not travel together. Anyway, maybe one of 'em got greedy and decided to cut his partner out of the profits. If he just flat out killed 'im, maybe there was a reason folks would be suspicious. Maybe somebody seen 'em leave town together, maybe one had a change of heart and was going to inform on the other. Something like that, anyway. But if somebody else could take the blame…Now, along comes me, Holliday, a ne'er-do-well with a bad reputation. I'd bet that yesterday, when you and I talked, the loot from Feeley was in the back of your wagon, and that's when you got the notion to use me. You probably knew that the Clantons have no love for me and I'm guessing you talked Clanton into going after me with the shotgun. Maybe figured that if he killed me, you could go after him for murder and maybe have an excuse to shoot him for resisting arrest. If somehow I get hold of a gun and kill him, your problems are solved. Way it turned out, you saw a chance to frame me and that was just fine by you."

"Bravo," Holmes yelled, slapping his palms together.

"You could make me a liar by showing us what your freight and—"

The sheriff had heard enough. He twisted himself to the left and started to run. But I recalled all the prodding with the Spencer he'd given me, none of it necessary, and I wasn't of a mind to let him get away. So I shoved him and he fell forward, the rifle flying out of his grip. Then the townsfolk were clustered around us and Holmes was hauling me to my feet.

"You see why we needed spectators," he said. "We couldn't go to the authorities with our suspicions—"

I finished it for him: "—'cause the only authority hereabouts is the killer."

"He would have attempted to make us his second and third victims."

I heard someone say "Lemme see if I unnerstand," and the raggedy man pushed through the crowd, the sheriff's rifle in his hands. "The shurf killed my Sally?"

"That appears to be the case," Holmes said and quicker than

I would have thought possible, the raggedy man chambered a shell and fired and the sheriff acquired a red hole in the middle of his forehead and fell dead.

The raggedy man threw down the rifle and limped away.

Nobody else moved for a long time. Then the townsfolk began to drift away, not saying a word, until Sherlock Holmes and me and two bodies were all that was left in the street.

"Should we do something about burying them?" Holmes murmured.

"None of our business," I replied and went my way. I never saw Holmes again and once in a while I wonder what ever happened to him.

The Sign of Two: Sherlock Holmes and Dr Jekyll

PHILIP CORNELL

*From the journal of Sherlock Holmes as transcribed
and edited by his literary agent*

Having had the opportunity whilst still undertaking my University studies to exercise my aptitude for meticulous observation and deductive reasoning to unravel several problems brought to my notice by my fellows, I resolved upon completing my eclectic course of study to make my name as a Consulting Detective. I was living at the time in rooms near the British Museum but it occurred to me that if I could find someone with whom to share the rent I could afford more spacious accommodation. Consequently I made some inquiries and learned of a suite of rooms in Baker Street not far from the underground station. A meeting with the landlady, a Mrs Hudson, proved the rooms to be eminently suitable and, although several people had expressed interest, nobody had yet taken them. At that very moment the doorbell rang and a broad-faced, clean shaven, fair skinned gentleman of some fifty summers was ushered in by the pageboy.

"Why, Doctor Jekyll!" exclaimed the landlady "How nice to see you again."

"It's '*Jeekyll*', remember, Madam," replied the man amiably in an Edinburgh accent, "with a long *e?*"

"Yes, my apologies, Doctor," said the landlady "Have you come to inspect the rooms again? This is Mr...Holmes...who is also interested."

"How do you do?" said I. "You have been in Edinburgh I perceive."

"You can tell by my accent? Most English folk don't have such a finely tuned ear when it comes to the Scots brogue."

"It was partly that, but I observe that your tweed jacket is woven of that particular fibre that is unique to Edinburgh and its surrounds. It is a year old at most so I concluded that until recently you dwelled in that city."

"Why, that is extraordinary."

"Superficial."

I ventured to ask whether he practised in London.

"No," he replied, "that is, not yet. I have been conducting private research at my own expense, but needs must..."

"Might you be amenable to splitting the rent between us?"

"Possibly," responded Dr Jekyll, a little tentatively. "The size and location of these rooms would suit my needs well."

"Though not myself a physician, I studied several medical subjects while at the university. I too am interested in this suite but could not afford them alone."

Jekyll studied me pensively for a moment then said, "Perchance we could come to some arrangement to our mutual benefit. I have, at the moment, other demands on my purse."

He enunciated it "purrse" with the distinct burr I had noticed earlier though in other respects his brogue was not a pronounced one.

"That would be splendid," said Mrs Hudson. "You gentlemen strike me as the quiet, studious type and that would suit me admirably."

Without further ado we shook hands and arranged with the landlady to move our belongings in during the coming week. Jekyll and I descended to the street.

"Would you care for a libation?" I asked. "There is a public house at the corner."

"I...don't drink," said Dr Jekyll, "but a glass of tonic water would be most agreeable."

We adjourned to a corner table where we could talk undisturbed.

"I hope you do not object to violin playing," said I. "It is best for two fellows to know the worst about one another before sharing diggings. You don't mind the smell of strong tobacco, I trust, for I am an inveterate pipe smoker?"

"I am not myself a smoker but I don't dislike the odour. I find it quite pleasant."

"I generally keep chemicals about and conduct experiments."

"I conduct experiments myself so that would not cause me any problems. Quite the opposite."

"I get down in the dumps at times and don't speak for days at a time."

"I quite understand. I, too, have times when I am not quite myself."

"And what have you to confess, Dr Jekyll?"

"Well, let me think," said the doctor. "As I mentioned, I do not take alcohol nor do I smoke, but don't think me priggish. I come and go at odd hours at times. I had a period of ill health before coming to London and I believe I am past that now but I object to rows. I have another set of…vices…when I am well. But rest assured I do not consider the sound of the violin to be a row, nor cause for one, if well played."

"You must be the judge of that," I laughed. "Let us toast a satisfying future."

We clinked our glasses and drank to 221B Baker Street and agreed to book a removalist van to transport our belongings at the earliest opportunity, picking up my goods from Montague Street and then collecting Jekyll's chattels from his hotel.

We carried out the move of our respective belongings, and as we sorted our possessions into our respective rooms Jekyll asked me what occupation I followed.

"I am starting out in a trade of my own," I replied. "Just as a consulting physician is approached for his expertise by other medicos, I hope to be a consultant in the field of *detection*."

"Detection?" asked Jekyll, looking up from his unpacking.

"There are many official detectives in London," I explained, "and many private investigators. When these fellows are at a loss they can consult me."

"That sounds potentially a most interesting line of work," commented Jekyll. "Do you feel you can make a success of it?"

"Time will tell," I replied though inwardly I felt confident that I could indeed achieve some renown.

The next few weeks did not, however, bear out my optimism. Jekyll spent his days at the chemistry laboratory at London Hospital. I had offered him the use of the 'chemistry corner' I had set up in Baker Street but he politely declined, pointing out that a paper he had published had sufficiently impressed the Hospital board that they had allowed him to use their facilities. A succession of small matters, insignificant in themselves, gradually led me to believe that Dr Jekyll was being less than frank with me. Since we had not long known each other that was hardly surprising. I am not a terribly outgoing individual myself yet I instinctively felt that I should not advertise the extent of my deductive abilities until such time as my doubts took stronger form.

I was musing on these matters one day while filing my findings in my recent investigation into the murder of the cabman, Albert Gray. The case had enjoyed some notoriety in the press and gripped the city and when the official force made little headway beyond rounding up the usual suspects I had been consulted; leading to the arrest of Donald Fettes and Wolfe MacFarlane. What had initially seemed a rather commonplace murder proved to have a number of points of interest that set it apart. I heard footsteps mounting the steps from the street and Dr Jekyll returned from the hospital. He looked rather worn and tired, and a little dishevelled. I wondered whether the ill health he had mentioned at our first meeting was troubling him once more.

We were exchanging pleasantries when Jekyll's attention was arrested by the papers on my desk. He paused and looked up, seeming oddly disconcerted, and seeing my raised eyebrows he muttered something about having been acquainted with 'Toddy' MacFarlane.

His use of MacFarlane's nickname suggested something more than a casual acquaintance. I did not press the point but taking up a volume of legal history I removed a bookmark and endeavoured to give the impression I was merely resuming some earlier reading, but Jekyll's behaviour confirmed my resolve not to draw undue attention to my powers. We ate the dinner our landlady brought up from the kitchen in silence after which Jekyll excused himself and I adjourned to my bedroom and lit my pipe.

The following morning the boy in buttons knocked on the door to announce a Mr Newcomen to see me. I motioned to him to take the basket chair.

"What can I do for Scotland Yard?" I asked.

"You recognize my name?"

"No, but I see the official notebook in your waistcoat pocket and your police issue boots. These proclaim that you are a plain clothes police officer and the spatters of mud on those boots and on your trouser cuffs is that reddish soil surrounding the private rear entrance to Scotland Yard. The newspaper folded in your overcoat pocket is this morning's *Daily Mail* reporting the murder yesterday of Sir Danvers Carew. You have underlined certain passages and made marginal notations. Ergo, it is about this matter that you wish to consult me."

"I see the reports have not exaggerated your abilities," said my guest. "One of my colleagues at The Yard, Mr Lestrade, thought you might be able to offer some advice. Your comments reveal you have read of the murder of Sir Danvers."

"All the papers were full of it. When a man expected by many to be a future Prime Minister is bludgeoned to death..."

"Quite. Mr Lestrade tells me you have a knack when it comes to weapons. Identifying them, I mean. Our medical examiner confirms that Sir Danvers had his skull fractured repeatedly by some heavy club. If you'd be so good as to accompany me to examine the body I have a four wheeler waiting."

"My fellow tenant is a medical man attached to The London

Hospital. Perhaps he could accompany us? His expertise might prove helpful."

I knocked on Jekyll's door to briefly explain our mission. He leapt at the chance and we joined the Inspector outside.

The detective shook Jekyll's hand and began to explain the reason for our expedition.

"We have a witness to the murder. A servant girl. She describes the killer as a small man. Almost dwarfish. And of particularly repellent appearance."

"Would you have any objection to me interviewing her?" I said.

"She is has been sedated. The experience upset her greatly. But I'm sure it could be arranged for tomorrow."

Once we arrived the Inspector escorted us to the morgue where Sir Danvers lay on the examination table. The wounds to his cranium were extensive. I took out my magnifying lens.

"The weapon would appear to have been a heavy, bulbous-headed walking stick. Probably of the type known as a 'Penang Lawyer'. More interesting are these splinters caught in the crook of his elbow which suggest that the blows were so violent that the stick actually broke. I would also suggest that when you undress the body—and I appreciate that you left it fully clad to permit me to examine it just as it was found—that you will find the right collar-bone broken, as well as broken bones in both hands beneath his gloves."

"Yes. Doubtless incurred as he tried to shield his head from the blows," said Jekyll.

The mortuary attendants proceeded to undress the M.P.'s body and we found in addition to the other wounds that there were two fractures to his spine. For my part I continued my examination but my lens did not reveal anything pertinent to identifying the murderer. While Jekyll took an interest in the matters he had little to add to the proceedings beyond confirming the cause of death as multiple fractures to the parietal bone.

We concluded the interview and set out for our lodgings, but something the Inspector had said awakened a half-forgotten memory in me that I could not bring into clear focus as we travelled. Arriving back in Baker Street Jekyll excused himself saying he had to be off to the hospital to further his experiments. There was little else I could do pertaining to the Carew murder until I had a chance to speak to the servant girl, and this was dependent upon requests I sent being responded to.

Jekyll did not return until evening and we sat in silence over our meal; I because I was deep in thought about the Carew killing and wracking my brain to summon whatever latent memory Newcomen had jogged. Jekyll just appeared rather distrait after our trip to the morgue.

The following morning I left early to pursue some research at the British Museum, not returning until mid afternoon. I then settled myself into the wicker chair and took out the packet of papers relating to the Gray murder. I suddenly froze because it was clear to me that Jekyll had been examining them again in my absence. So, I had been right about Jekyll having secrets. This was patently something more than morbid curiosity. As though to punctuate the realization the front doorbell sounded.

"I'll get it, Mrs Hudson," I called. It was a middle-aged, sombre-looking man. I observed that his top hat, while elegantly polished, was slightly misshapen. I recognized that this could only be the result of a medical man keeping his stethoscope therein.

"Come in, Doctor..."

"Lanyon, Hastie Lanyon," said he to my unspoken query. "I am an old friend of Harry Jekyll. Is he at home? A mutual friend, Gabriel Utterson, told me I might find him here."

"Alas, I must disappoint you. I don't expect him home until about five this afternoon. Could you call again for him then?" Lanyon agreed, seemingly quite happily, and departed.

I could of course have directed Dr Lanyon to the London Hospital laboratory but my interest was piqued and I felt I could learn more if I could observe the two of them together. In the meantime it seemed to me no bad thing if I were to find out a little more about what Jekyll was up to in that laboratory. I have some proficiency in the art of disguise, having taught myself the use of greasepaint whilst at the University where I undertook classes in drama for that very purpose.

Accordingly, I applied a false, bulbous tip to my rather aquiline nose, affixed a 'handlebar' moustache and side whiskers with spirit gum and gave myself a slightly more ample, and, I hoped, prosperous looking figure with some padding. I keep a range of spurious visiting cards and found one in the name of "Doctor Shaw Higgins - F.R.C.S." and hailed a cab to take me to the London Hospital. The cabby left me about a block away and adopting a pompous posture I sauntered to the porticoed front door. It was no difficult task to bluff my way to the chemistry laboratories on the pretext of replicating an analysis I had previously undertaken at Bart's of certain blood samples which I had in a Gladstone bag.

"My name is Dr Shaw Higgins," said I, presenting my card. "I have been conducting research at Saint Bartholomew's on a test which I confidently expect will supersede the old guaiacum test. Some question has been expressed in certain circles and I should like to conduct similar analysis here."

"Certainly," came the reply. "I shall see that one of the junior doctors shows you to the laboratory."

I was duly escorted to the lab and, thanking the young doctor, I set about looking busy with vials and test tubes while unobtrusively observing Jekyll. He was earnestly occupied filtering a greenish liquid into a glass beaker. He then dipped a wooden tongue depressor into the vial and proceeded to taste it with the tip of his tongue. He shuddered involuntarily and made a few hasty pencil notes. I waited a few moments and then walked over, confident that my disguise would stand close scrutiny. Continuing the pompous pose that had gained me entry I introduced myself.

"Doctor Shaw Higgins. I am working on a new blood test. Mark well the term "Shaw Higgins Test", it will one day soon be a standard in our profession. May I ask what you are working on?"

"You may not," said he. "My research is my own business.

Good day, sir!"

With this curt dismissal he packed up his accoutrements into his medical bag and walked to the sink to wash his hands. I had just enough time to surreptitiously remove the next blank sheet from the notepad he had been working on, and I memorised the odd assortment of chemical bottles he had been working on before he made his disgruntled exit. Then, allowing Jekyll enough time to clear the building and pausing just long enough to remove my makeup in the hospital lavatory, I departed myself.

Returning by cab to 221 Baker Street I mounted the stairs and with a brief greeting to Jekyll replaced my Gladstone and taking an innocuous volume by Eckermann on the religions of the West Indies settled into the basket chair. After about three quarters of an hour Mrs Hudson knocked on the door with a pair of partridges for supper which we ate in comparative silence. I made a couple of token efforts at conversation to maintain my façade of a harmless eccentric with a preoccupation with criminal studies but met with little response from Jekyll. After lingering a while over my coffee I excused myself and retired to my room. I still sought the elusive half-memory, but neither tobacco nor quiet contemplation illuminated it.

The next day provided progress as I was asked to return to Scotland Yard and rejoined Newcomen to interview the servant girl who had been witness to the murder of Sir Danvers Carew. She gave her name as Molly Riley and explained that while walking home late one night she had seen the attack.

"He was an 'orrible little man," she said. "Quite turned my blood cold just to look at 'im."

"You describe him as 'little'. How tall would you say he was?"

"No taller 'an me," she replied, and she would have been barely five feet in height.

" 'Orribly ugly too," she continued, "like some kind of wicked gnome."

"And of what age?" I asked.

"Youngish. Five an' twenty p'raps."

Inspector Newcomen summoned a police sketch artist but despite her best efforts Miss Riley seemed curiously unable to describe the man she had seen in any specific detail despite saying that his " 'orrid face" filled her nightmares. There seemed little point in continuing the interview further.

"At least she should be able to identify the rogue if only we can find him," said Newcomen as we parted.

In the cab back to Baker Street the nagging memory that had been bothering me at last took proper form. It is my practice to docket references in newspapers and journals to criminal activities that I might need to refer to in future. The girl's description was strongly reminiscent of a report which I had noted a year earlier of a youthful female who was trampled by a young man in Cavendish Place. The assailant simply walked right over the young girl, who had been rolling a hoop, rather than deviate from his path. Beyond the physical description there also seemed the implication that this strange young man possessed an ungovernable temper.

I expected Jekyll to be out when I returned home but found him on the chaise longue cradling his forehead.

"You look unwell, Jekyll," said I.

"Yes…I am rather. Besides, I am expecting my friend Lanyon momentarily."

I politely excused myself to allow him exclusive use of the parlour and retired to my bedroom where I prepared to eavesdrop using an empty tumbler pressed to the wall as an ear trumpet. I hardly needed to have done so, for after his arrival Dr Lanyon's voice became quite loud and heated.

"You know I considered your theories preposterous and your experiments upon yourself positively dangerous!" said he.

Dr Jekyll seemed unmoved.

"You made your feelings perfectly clear."

"And now," continued Lanyon. "Utterson tells me you have

altered your will to make some total stranger heir to your not inconsiderable assets. Have you taken leave of your senses, man?"

"Mr Hyde is an old acquaintance," replied Jekyll, in tones of reason, "and he has my complete confidence."

The next comments were then delivered by Jekyll in a tone of utter coldness. "It is none of your concern nor Utterson's. I'd thank you both to keep out of my affairs."

I heard Lanyon gasp.

"Good day to you, Hastie," said Jekyll, unmistakeably dismissing Lanyon. I could make out Dr Lanyon sputtering unintelligibly followed by the sound of the door being firmly shut.

I allowed half an hour during which time I took the unused top page I had taken from Jekyll's note book and by gently rubbing a soft-leaded pencil across the impressions I was able to make out some of Jekyll's words, "...*refined solution...why disparate personalities exist...side by side...turn back...*" I pondered on these tantalising snippets until I heard Dr Jekyll's tread mounting the steps to his bedroom. I gave him a further five minutes before returning to the sitting-room to consult my legal directory. There was only one Utterson, J. G. of that ilk, and his practice was in Gaunt Street.

Once again I employed my talent for imposture. Disguised as a cleric I approached Utterson on the pretext of wishing to consult him about a client of his, a Mr Hyde, whom I wished to thank for a good deed. Utterson explained to me that Edward Hyde was not a client of his but that he was not at liberty to reveal his address. It was obviously absurd to expect Utterson to divulge the contents of Jekyll's will or why he had chosen someone like Hyde as his heir but now I had Mr Hyde's forename; "Edward": Whatever secret Jekyll was keeping or how it related to the mysterious Mr Hyde I was at least making some progress. But as I left Utterson he muttered Hyde's name, and added a phrase that absolutely startled me, and I realized the visit had delivered far more than incremental progress.

"Little gargoyle!"

My concerns about my fellow tenant's behaviour were second-ary to my investigation into the Carew murder, yet now my instincts were increasingly leading me to wonder whether there might not be some connection between the two matters.

I resolved to telegraph Newcomen to ask whether the Yard had any record of Edward Hyde. The reply came back that Mr Hyde of Soho had been named as a suspect in the Carew murder case following information from lawyer Utterson. It was encouraging to have my suspicions about a link between Hyde and the Carew murder confirmed.

I consulted a Post Office directory to ascertain the Soho address of Edward Hyde, hailed a cab and made my way thither without delay. I had no trouble finding the unprepossessing two-storey house, for a milling crowd of onlookers immediately marked the spot. I paid the jarvey and leapt down. Two uniformed constables were without, one calming the crowd. I presented my card to the other and asked to see Inspector Newcomen and was shown up.

The inside of the first floor rooms could not have offered a greater contrast to the mean, shabby exterior. It was tastefully furnished with fine paper on the walls and a number of framed paintings hung from the picture rails. It seemed clear to me that Mr Hyde was a man of some culture rather at odds with the effect he had on others.

Newcomen showed me a closet in which he had found the heavy stick with which Sir Danvers had been brutally done to death. "As you can see, you were quite right about the murder weapon. And that it was broken in the attack."

I nodded my appreciation of the implied compliment to my powers and asked the Inspector how Utterson had been able to direct them to Hyde's abode.

"Utterson, who is a respected Prosecutor with whom the Yard has had frequent dealings, had reason to suspect this Hyde of being a blackmailer in consequence of past dealings they'd had. The description of both Hyde and the stick used to murder Carew led Utterson to contact us."

"I see."

"A number of Hyde's papers have been found burnt in the fireplace. We found the butt of a green chequebook…"

"And a few charred corners of letters in Hyde's hand," I observed.

"We looked at those but there's not enough there to make any sense."

"There would also seem to be the remnants of some publications of a rather lewd nature."

"Very racy stuff from what we can make out. There's a call for these from among the servant classes."

And not only among the servant classes, I thought.

"Is there anything to indicate this Hyde worked as a servant?"

"We have no notion as to his employment."

I investigated the rooms further, finding nothing of note save some medicinal bottles and a jar of powder I recognised as cocaine. I suggested to Newcomen that he might find it worth his while to have the contents of the bottles analysed.

"You mean if we find out what ailments Hyde suffered from it might help us to trace him?"

"Something of the sort."

There being little more for me to do, I thanked Newcomen and returned to Baker Street.

I have made a study of graphology and am guilty of a monograph on the topic. I took out the notepad sheet with the impressions of Jekyll's writing and recalled the charred remnants Newcomen had showed me of Hyde's script. There was a marked similarity between the two, notably in the extended tail of the letters 'y' and 'k' and the construction of the lower case 'x'.

I mused as to whether both Jekyll and Hyde shared the same teacher or even more likely, given their apparent ages, they could possibly be father and son despite the lack of physical resemblance.

Could this then account for the secrecy Jekyll maintained about the other man to his friends? Worse, was Mr Hyde mentally ill? This might explain his reputed violent behaviour. I strongly suspected that the solution to the Sir Danvers Carew matter would lead me to also resolving the strange case of Dr Jekyll and Mr Hyde.

The next morning, again without eating breakfast, Jekyll left early. Leaving a note to Mrs Hudson apologising for the uneaten meals I set out after Jekyll. I soon spied him a short distance in front of me so I slowed down, allowing me to duck out of sight should he look around, but he seemed so single-minded that he never once glanced behind. It had snowed overnight so following his footprints was simplicity itself. Jekyll soon turned aside from the thoroughfare and took to the laneways and alleys. Following his footprints I became aware of a gradual change in his gait. His stride grew shorter and his footprints became more splayed; it appeared Jekyll might be feeling ill.

Another change in his footprints was more inexplicable. They seemed to grow shallower, although a quick peek over my shoulder showed no similar effect on my own. I was in the process of reasoning a cause for this effect, as I turned a corner into a courtyard, and I was stopped in my very tracks by the sight, not of Dr Jekyll—of whose foot prints I did not believe I had once lost sight—but of a small, misshapen man who could only be the mysterious Mr Hyde.

He sat, his head slumped in hirsute hands, his clothes oversized and loose on his diminutive frame. I could only conclude that I had somehow lost track of Jekyll, perhaps when he had turned aside from the main road, but perhaps Jekyll had been meaning to meet this other individual. Hyde's odd appearance was likely due to his being unable to return to his rooms in Soho; he had been compelled to steal the clothing of someone taller.

Be that as it may, if this were indeed Hyde, then it behoved me to hold him for the police. I walked over to the little man and said, "Edward Hyde?" He looked up in surprise, then his eyes narrowed. "I have reason to believe, Mr Hyde, that you are sought by the police. I propose to hold you until the constabulary arrive."

I always carry a police whistle and I gave a short blast but before I could give a second Hyde sprang at me with a speed for which should not have given him credit.

But that was nothing compared to his unexpected strength. I am no weakling and an amateur pugilist but Hyde knocked me off my feet with little effort. He aimed a kick at my head but my reflexes were quicker than those of the aging Carew had been and I just dodged his boot. I was grateful that he no longer had a heavy stick for though I am accomplished in singlestick I would still have been hard pressed to hold my own.

In any event, the blast of my whistle had brought a pair of constables with truncheons drawn and Hyde took to his heels. One of the constables took off after the shrunken brute but the other stopped to check that I was unharmed.

"After him!" I bellowed. "He is wanted for the Carew killing!" as I struggled to right myself on the snowy footpath.

The second constable took off after the first and I eventually was on my feet and forging ahead when the constable reappeared supporting his fellow who was now without his helmet and bleeding from a wound in his scalp. Winded though I was, I set off in pursuit of Hyde but lost his trail when it rejoined the High Street. He had vanished.

Somewhat dispirited I returned home—after pausing for a small brandy at the first hostelry I found—to find Jekyll in the parlour; looking pale and a little dishevelled.

"Are you all right?" I asked.

"I have had bad news," said he. "That friend of mine, who visited earlier, Lanyon, is dead. His heart suddenly failed him. Some shock triggered it."

I offered my condolences but Jekyll waved them aside.

"I must see Utterson," said he, more to himself than to me and walked out the door.

This was possibly my best chance to answer all the questions surrounding Jekyll. I had no time to adopt a disguise so I clad myself in as anonymous an outfit as I could find, grabbed a scarf of neutral hue and tied the flaps of my travelling cap over my ears to obscure my features. Jekyll was hailing a cab. "Gaunt Street," he called to the driver. I have trained myself to perch on the back of a Hansom cab and this I did, jumping down before the cab pulled up.

Stepping into a doorway I wrapped the scarf around my lower face, it still being wintry though the snow had stopped. I could not use impersonation to trick my way into Utterson's office as I had done on my previous visit so I trusted that my own card would be sufficient for me to at least gain entry.

Utterson's clerk showed me to a small antechamber outside his office. I could see Jekyll's shadow pacing to and fro and could make out snatches of what Jekyll was saying, for his agitated state had caused him to raise his voice. Utterson seemed to be attempting to placate the doctor. "A letter? What letter?" cried Jekyll. Then spoke Utterson again to which Jekyll responded in tones of greater reason.

"My death or disappearance? What did Hastie mean by that…I know I made clear in my will…"

Another pause followed, after which Jekyll's voice concluded "Goodbye, Gabe. I doubt that we shall meet again."

I held a newspaper to obscure my face though Jekyll, when he emerged, was so distraught that he gave me no heed. I waited as long as I could lest he turn on the stairs and see me, and hurried down the steps, taking them two at a time, but Jekyll was already off in a cab this time and I was not close enough behind him to jump aboard and cling on the rear of the vehicle as I had before.

The frustration of the moment was punctuated by a newspaper boy crying "Carew killer eludes police!"

My best course seemed to be to return to Baker Street post haste, so I hailed a hansom. In the cab I had the opportunity to try assembling the various pieces of the puzzle, though the resulting picture seemed to defy all reason. It was clear that Jekyll had been doing experiments upon himself. I have done so myself on occasion but only when I was fairly confident of the outcome. Henry Jekyll seemed to have no such certainty but rather was using himself as a human lab rat. His incredible motive appeared to be the goal of attempting to take the conflicting tendencies in all men for good and evil, for virtue and vice and to isolate in his own body all that was noble and selfless and to confine all that is licentious and vicious in his associate, the young Edward Hyde. Yet how could he treat the young fellow in such a way if he himself embodied nobility? Such behaviour was selfishness itself.

My cab pulled up outside number 221B just as the cab that had been Jekyll's drew away. I tossed the cabby some coins and rushed inside. "Jekyll!" I called, "Jekyll!" as I mounted the stairs but halfway up I encountered Mrs Hudson coming down.

"Dr Jekyll's just gone to your rooms," said she. "I trust you'll both be dining tonight—"

I worked my way around the landlady as gently yet swiftly as I could and hurried to our rooms. Jekyll was not in the parlour but I could hear sounds coming from his bedroom.

"Jekyll!" I called. "I must talk with you, Jekyll!"

"Not now, Holmes," came the voice of Henry Jekyll.

"Jekyll, this is urgent," I persisted.

"Go away!" he countered.

"Jekyll," said I. "I know about Hyde."

There was silence and, to be frank, I was by no means sure in my own mind the exact nature of the relationship between Dr Jekyll and Mr Hyde. Again there was silence for several moments and then there came a guttural rasping hiss. *"Go away!"*

I tried the door to Jekyll's room again but it was locked.

"Mrs Hudson!" I called downstairs. "I need your key to Dr Jekyll's room."

While she took out her keys I grabbed my singlestick.

"Is something the matter?" called the landlady.

"Now, please, Mrs Hudson!"

Mrs Hudson duly produced the duplicate key and waited,

peering in, partly curious and partly concerned.

I unlocked the door and looked inside. The room was in darkness for Jekyll had not lit the lamp. The strange voice that had issued from the room told me Jekyll was not alone.

"Mrs Hudson," I said. "Send someone for a policeman."

"What?!" said the poor lady, more than a little startled.

"Now, Mrs Hudson!"

I gripped the stick and stepped into Jekyll's room. My senses heightened I peered around the room for the two men for it seemed clear that Edward Hyde had somehow gained access to our rooms and had been waiting for Jekyll. I could just discern the sound of breathing. It was measured and calm.

The sound of an intake of breath gave me the split second I needed to block the blow that came swinging at me. My stick and the cudgel clashed together with a resounding 'thwack'. My height gave me an advantage for Hyde had aimed his initial blow at my skull. I knew his second would be a low blow and so it was. My eyes were now accustomed to the darkness and I could just make out the diminutive figure of Hyde. He swung a blow at my knee but I avoided it and simultaneously aimed a sharp direct thrust to Hyde's breastbone. A hissing exhalation told me I had succeeded. We traded blows and counter blows, Hyde's reactions seemed somewhat hampered on occasions and at one point I heard the sound of fabric tearing leading me to deduce that his clothing was somehow hindering him. Our contest was as much a question of strategy and tactics since I could not match my opponent's ferocious strength. As his fury grew his attacks became less considered and it increasingly became a contest between brute strength and intellect. Hyde's growls became increasingly animalistic until I landed blow upon his head which I followed instantly with a sharp jab aimed at his jawbone.

I heard his cudgel strike the floor. A gargling, rasping sound however told me that I had instead struck him in the throat. Then all was silent. I stepped back and pushed open the door allowing the light from the hallway to flood the room.

It was not the sudden, brighter light that caused me to blink but disbelief. I had expected to see Henry Jekyll behind Hyde in the room but there was only the one prone body on the floor. The sole body on the carpet was that of Mr Hyde: Clad in Jekyll's suit! Of Dr Jekyll there was no trace! I searched to be sure.

Jekyll could only have escaped out the window. Yet a quick check showed the window was securely latched, so clearly he had exited and his friend, whom he had lent clothing to again, I realized, had latched the window behind him. I kept a close eye on the prone Hyde, wary lest the powerful man stir, but I already thought this was beyond him.

I could hear outside the sound of the policeman arriving with the boy in buttons. Mrs Hudson was tearfully telling them that I had been attacked by Dr Jekyll. He entered and we both looked at Hyde's still figure with greater scrutiny, now I was no longer fearful of being sprung at alone.

"This man is dead," said the policeman.

"Yes," I replied. "He attacked me with that cudgel."

"Is this that Jekyll bloke?"

I did not answer immediately but advised the bobby to send for Inspector Newcomen.

"Tell him this is the man sought for the murder of Sir Edmund Carew."

The policeman's eyes grew wide. "Yes, sir," said he and rushed out.

While I awaited the Inspector I asked Mrs Hudson to make us both a cup of coffee.

I turned the afternoon's events over in my mind attempting to make sense of an irrational situation. I had been only moments behind Jekyll. Although Mrs Hudson was already accustomed to my strange and diverse clients she had said nothing of admitting so bizarre a figure as Hyde. And what in the world had become of Jekyll?

In a flight of imagining induced by narcotics one might even conjecture whether Jekyll and Hyde might have been one and the same, but such a preposterous premise flies in the face of every principle of scientific observation and rationality upon which I have built my life. I dismissed the idea as beyond fanciful. It was nothing less than insane. Yet there was *some* sort of relationship between the two men that was eluding me, and discovering such truths was my very vocation.

For the first time in my life I found myself utterly perplexed. And if it takes me the rest of that life I *will* solve the strange case of Doctor Jekyll and Mr Hyde!

Literary agent's postscript

It is a matter of public record that Mr Sherlock Holmes failed to solve to his satisfaction the riddle of Dr Jekyll and Mr Hyde despite grappling with the problem for many years. He eventually filed it away as "insoluble".

The Adventure of the Madman

Dr John Seward

Together with an addendum by His Wife

Transcribed from wax phonograph rolls found among the belongings of the former Mary Holder, ancestress of

NANCY HOLDER

6 December, 1901

I am quite insane.

I have deceived all who love me of it, save one.

My mentor, the good Dr Van Helsing, could not be fooled by that King of the Undead, Count Dracula. He knew the lordly vampire for what he was, and was never dissuaded to do what must be done because others could not believe. But where the Count failed, I have succeeded. Through our ongoing exchange of letters, the good Dutch doctor thinks that all is well with me, but in truth, I am a drowning man, as I was last summer when we reunited to remember what we must not forget: that a vampire tried to destroy us all, and that Quincey Morris, our American friend, died so that we might live.

Yes, it has been seven years and one month since we destroyed the Count. Those years have been good to Mina and Jonathan Harker, as they have had a child. Lord Godalming (Arthur Holmwood) and I are both counted as happily married, but I thought surely they would see through my polite lie during our reunion, when I explained that my wife could not join us because she was visiting a sick aunt. Of course that was not true.

You may recall that I reside within the walls of the asylum of which I am director. It is an institution for the insane, those poor, tormented souls whose inner ravings dictate and shape the nature of their outer reality. They see ghosts and monsters where there are none.

Except...that my madness has progressed to the point where I see the monsters, too.

It is not that unusual for the unafflicted to live within the walls of a madhouse. Indeed, the Harkers and Dr Van Helsing stayed here on the night Count Dracula murdered his poor minion, R. M. Renfield. Dear Mrs Harker was already under the thrall of the accursed vampire, and I must say that my admiration for her has steadily grown through the years. She is a most singular woman, a lady whose fortitude surpasses even that of many men. Had I endured the vampire's assault as she had, I am sure I would have gone mad much sooner.

My wife Eliza is a more usual lady, having come into my life innocent of the horrors of the rough wide world. My profession caused her much anxiety, and because of it, she hesitated for quite some time to marry me. She feared that insanity was a disease that one could catch, such as the plague, and that setting up house within my asylum might lead to infection.

I was in an agony of waiting! I assured her that diseases of the mind do not travel on the wind, but I see now that that was not precisely true. The Count had flown in bat form through the casement to destroy Renfield's body, mind, and soul. Mrs Harker was horribly used by the Count within these walls, slowly draining her of life and making her his own.

However, these injuries were of the past, and I had thought them buried forever. But after Eliza and I returned home from our honeymoon (going on six years after we had vanquished the Count), she discovered my phonograph diary quite by accident and listened to all my entries concerning these dark times without consulting me. She was furious with me for withholding this story from her—indeed, for speaking not one word of my past adventure, ever. I told her that I had kept the subject closed because

I wished to spare her. But she likened this omission to that of Mr Rochester in her favourite novel, *Jane Eyre*: he concealed the secret that he was already married…to a madwoman. Rochester imperiled Jane's very soul, as they came very near to committing bigamy.

Then Eliza claimed not to believe anything in my diary, declaring that I had been infected with madness, having caught it from my tormented patients as she had first feared should happen to her. That I was insane and the story of Count Dracula was the proof.

I offered to have the others speak on my behalf. I begged her to attend our approaching reunion and listen to the story and then judge for herself, for then she would know that I was as sane as she.

Alas, that was entirely the wrong thing to say. For she told me that if she had to choose between marriage to a madman or to a sane man who had truly done the unspeakable things I had described in my diary entries, she would not choose such a man at all. She would leave him. And she did.

And God help me, now that the summer is gone and the winter snows bar my doors, I agree with her decision. She is better without me. I was sane then, but I have lost my sanity, of that I am certain. The horrible dreams…they are *not* dreams. *They are not dreams.*

I *have* become infected.

3 January 1901

It happened thusly: two months ago, there came to us a man quite destroyed by his fears to the point of near-catatonia. He was a gentleman whom I shall call "M," brought in by a man claiming to be his brother (although they didn't look like each other at all. I believe the brother was actually his manservant. As we in this country do not recognize voluntary committal, I believe this "brother" was created solely for the purpose of committing "M" into my care.)

"M" allowed as how he had been doggedly pursued by a venomous foe, robbing him of home, hearth, and sanity. This fiend was determined to put an end to "M" by any means necessary.

He wept at our first interview. "I see him everywhere. I turn a corner and he is there. I gaze through a window, and I see his narrow face and piercing eyes. He is a demon! A devil! He will be the death of me for I cannot elude him any longer!"

I believed him, and I was much dismayed. I am in charge of one hundred inmates and staff. Their care devolves to me. I should not ever allow harm that I was utterly able to prevent to come to them.

"Then this is a matter for the police," I said. "I shall summon them at once."

"No, no," he said quickly. "I speak in metaphor, good doctor. In madness." He seemed to get hold of himself, even managing a small, mortified smile. "For parts of every day I am a rational man. I know that my delusions are only that—delusions. But when the megrims are upon me and I can no longer shore up my defenses against my fears through the application of my reason, I see him in my mirror. I see him in the shiny wax polish upon the floor. He is insubstantial like a ghost, and I tell myself that he simply cannot be there…and yet he *is*. It is from this horror that I seek relief."

Thus I admitted him, and as he is a gentleman, of fine education and breeding, I set him apart from the other inmates. He is a singularly aristocratic fellow, possessed of a high, domed forehead and intelligent eyes. Within days, he settled into the routine of the asylum quite naturally, save for terrible nightmares that still call me to his bedside at all hours of the night, during which time I administer laudanum. That quiets his nerves, as it is wont to do, and he thanks me profusely and begs me to station an orderly by his bedside, to guard him during the night.

In the daytime, however, he is in command of himself, and so I permit him some liberties not extended to the other inmates: for example, the freedom to go on long walks in the fresh air, which I deem beneficial to his convalescence. I confess that I am a bit house-proud, as he observes all the niceties and modern conveniences with which I had equipped the asylum. He marvels at our extensive vegetable garden and our fruit trees, and is most astonished by the giant cisterns I have employed for the storage of our water.

"What indeed is this about?" he asked me today. "Have you not a well from which you can draw water when you require it?"

I explained to him that I subscribe to the notion that one ought to drink plain water—a good quantity, every day. Having read the medical and scientific journals of the day, I refined my theory one step further—that this water should be boiled, to destroy any lurking impurities and keep the drinker safe from attendant disease. He finds my notion somewhat radical, and asked why I did not simply stick to serving tea and spirits, as most households did.

"See what a tremendous amount of work you make for yourself," he observed, gesturing to the immense stores of firewood I had laid on beside my cistern. "There is enough wood cut here to warm three asylums!"

Indeed there is, and soon enough, he has seen proof of that. This morning marked the second month and a week that he has been with us, and though the day grew very cold, "M" stomped about the grounds like a fire-breathing dragon, so white and billowy were his exhalations. It was time to light the fireplaces, and I ensured that we had laid in sufficient stores of wood and of coal to keep us warm for the winter. "M" was interested in our preparations, asking many questions, and I began to form the opinion that he once owned an estate.

This afternoon, at tea, my head nurse, Miss Mary Holder, privately expressed grave reservations about "M". She tells me that "M" follows her every move with a keen eye, as if memorizing her routine, and that at no time does he appear witless or troubled. His eyes are cold and his manner detached, giving off an air of ruthlessness so palpable that she is afraid of him. Additionally, he requests of her all the newspapers, most especially *The Times,* and his conversations with her centre quite frequently on the activities of the police.

Taking together the timbre of his discussions, his actions, and his manner, Miss Holder has deduced that he is not in need of our help at all, and never has been. That he was brought to us so that he could hide from the authorities, and they are closing in. That his nightmarish adversary is more likely a constable, and that in addition, he is only biding his time until he can commit an offense against us before he takes flight once more.

I did listen to her, as she is my head nurse, but I also note that she is a woman, and therefore given to some timidity when confronted with a forceful personality. Rather above the middle height, slim with dark hair and eyes, Miss Holder came to me shrouded in something of a mystery herself. Her letters and certificates were all in order, and yet when I interviewed her, I sensed that she was holding something back. There was a deep sorrow about her, and an anxiety not unlike "M's." Her behaviour betrayed a story I had yet to hear. However, I do count myself a good judge of character, and I have found her to be intelligent and capable, and unruffled in the face of madness. I must admit that it is difficult finding stalwart nurses to attend the insane, and for this reason I perhaps did not investigate her history as much than others would have.

I wonder too, if she unconsciously projects her own secrecy upon the cipher that is "M." While it is true that she is surrounded by madmen every breathing second of her life save for days-off, church, and holidays, still, we have not had the likes of him before (save, perhaps for poor Renfield). He is clearly of a higher class than she is accustomed to among our sufferers, and I am certain that the habits of civility and good manners frequently cloak the ferocity of his mental imbalance—thus persuading her that he is not unbalanced at all.

What I cannot tell her, of course, is that I have begun to see what "M" fears so keenly. I catch little sidelong glimpses of a strange man's long, pale face in the windowpanes; when I glance into mirrors, I think I see him there, too. A tall man, keen and vigorous. A man who wants something from me. Something dear, which he seems to assume I will fight to keep. He is appearing, too, in my dreams! I hardly sleep one night in seven, and yet I stifle myself from crying out for the same succour I bestow on "M." The saying goes, "Physician, heal thyself." But I cannot. How he plagues me!

Who is he, this shade, this figure of doom? He cannot be the Count returned, for I know that the vampire cannot show in a reflection. But I see so much of him! Much distressed, I have no one to speak to of my plight, but seek solace in listening to "M" describe his haunted mind. *Yes*, I want to say to him. *Yes, that is my mind, too! I am not the only one. I am not alone! I share your illness!*

4 January 1901

But I am alone. "M" has gone.

He came to me this morning and told me that he felt quite himself again. The fresh air, rest, and brisk exercise had quite recuperated him, and he wished to re-enter society. I confess that for my own sake I was overwrought, but for his sake, I acquiesced. He spoke of wishing to leave us in haste, as snow flurries had begun to fall.

"Your fires shall burn brightly tonight!" he said.

I granted him his liberty immediately. His "brother" arrived to convey him away, and he left as he had arrived, a nameless gentleman, and I had thought the matter concluded.

How wrong I was! For tonight it is as if all his fixations and tremors attenuate themselves to me! Where before I suffered nightmares, now I am in an absolute terror, and so have turned on my phonograph so that I may record my state of mind. As I stare into the flames in the grate in my rooms I *see* the figure in the crackling waves of heat! Now I turn my head and see him looming upon my threshold, arms extended as if to choke the very life out of me!

"Back, demon! You are but a figment of my imagination!"

But my imagination has the best of me. Images churn before

me—the Count and my poor Lucy Westenra, a full vampire bride; impalements, beheadings, blood gushing everywhere! And in the midst of it *that man*, eyeing me curiously through a glass he holds to his eye, as if I am a specimen!

"Begone! Demon, get thee to hell!"

And now he comes!

5 January 1901

I awoke to find Miss Holder's pale white face staring past the shoulder of my strongest orderly, Mr Driscoll, who was tying me to my bed. *Me!* Dr Adams, my assistant, was preparing for me a syringe—of laudanum, I determined—and the flames of my fire seemed to reach for me like the long fingers of demons! I stared at all in utter horror.

And then I saw the face of the man. In the window, and in the mirror above the fireplace mantel, and then in the very flames themselves!

"He is coming for me! He is coming!" I cried.

And then, as one, they began to scream, too! Miss Holder shrieked like a banshee and tore at her hair, her dress. Mr Driscoll left off tying me and wove back and forth, back and forth like an automaton, gibbering and laughing. Dr Adams stabbed himself directly in the forehead with the syringe, and fell down in a quivering heap beside my bed.

As the imp approached, his face *melted* and great fangs protruded from the mess. A caul swallowed up his head and tiny winged things capered and danced upon it! The clanging of church bells and ship bells and the great chittering of a thousand starving rats filled my ears. I saw them coming at me, *creatures* and *monsters* and the thing that held sway over them all!

I shrieked and flung myself at him. I had patients and staff to protect. I could not let him take me.

I railed at him, at *it*. I flailed, arms like windmills, legs like the great pistons of a train! I tried to bite it; I would do anything to save the world from it, *anything!*

I do not know how long I battled thusly; but at length I heard an English voice saying, "No more of this! No more!"

And then I became aware that I was being dragged from my asylum, which was heaving with smoke and screams of panic. I fought and strained, but to no avail. We moved past the cells and out into the receiving room, my kidnapper and I!

"Get thee behind me, Satan!" I implored.

"*Satan?*" the figure roared, as if with great good humour.

I saw his crazed smile, and then he flung me into a snow bank. The shock stunned me into silence and I began panting, sucking in large gulps of icy night air.

Fire and brimstone ebbed from my sight; and demons and rats; and I beheld the tall man I had often spotted in the periphery of my vision.

So now I die, I thought, bracing myself. *I die at the hand of the phantom that haunts me.*

But the man held a handkerchief over his mouth and was fiercely coughing. He seemed to have no fear of violence from me whatsoever.

Surely the Devil does not cough, I told myself, though I could not inhibit my reaction as he reached toward me. I scrabbled backwards away from him, commencing to shriek once more.

And then I saw Miss Holder standing beside him, gazing at him for the all the world as if he were her protector. He, and not I.

"Dr Seward," he said, "you have been poisoned, and it is playing tricks on you. Pray draw in as much fresh air as you are able or you will surely go to Bedlam."

"Please, Doctor, do as he says," Miss Holder implored me. Orange flames were dancing on her face and hair, and tears shimmered like jewels upon her cheeks.

As I exerted myself to strenuous breathing, I turned around in the snow. The shock that grabbed hold of me was as overwhelming as those which I had felt when we had beheaded Lucy and dispatched Count Dracula to hell.

My asylum was going up in flames! The walls and parapets

were ablaze; smoke boiled to the moon, and the roof crashed in as I watched. Years of investment, and toil, my fears and hopes for the minds of our sufferers, rushing to destruction!

My staff was surrounded by our madmen, some of whom were capering and dancing, rejoicing in their freedom. Others were crying like widows, and still others, like tiny, heartbroken children.

"My asylum!" I protested. "I am ruined!"

"No," said the man. "You are alive, and that is enough to ask for in a misadventure such as this."

"How dare you, sir," I said, though I was mortified to speak so to the man who, clearly, had saved me. "You know nothing of my fortunes, nor of me."

Nor I of him, for of a certainty, he was *not* Satan.

"I know plenty." He regarded me once more, studying each detail of my person. "Miss Holder wrote to me of you and described you to a T. Nicely done," he said, and she flushed and curtseyed. "I know that you are Dr John Seward, more familiarly called 'Jack.'

"I know that you offered hospitality to one who would have me believe he is dead from our encounter at the Reichenbach Falls of Switzerland. His name is Moriarty, and I know that he poisoned you with *radix pedis diaboli*, or Devil's Foot Root, which he sprinkled liberally on your woodpiles, in hopes that when you lit logs in your grates, you would release its noxious fumes and perish, or at the least be rendered so mad that no one would believe any tales you had to tell of a gentlemen called "M."

"Forgive me, sir," Miss Holder said to me, sinking to her knees in the snow beside me. "I knew things were not right. And I so wrote to Sherlock Holmes, and asked him to come."

I blinked. I knew the name, of course. He was the world's greatest consulting detective. Was it actually true that he stood before me? Or had I gone mad indeed?

As if in answer, Sherlock Holmes smiled faintly at Miss Holder, and inclined his head in her direction.

"It was very brave of you to send for me, my dear, seeing as you left my company under rather...compromising circumstances."

"What sort of circumstances?" I asked sharply. "Would you be so kind as to elaborate?"

"I would never be so *unkind*," Holmes replied. "All that you know of Mary Holder is all that you need to know. Item one: After she had raised the alarm and implored me to help you, I wrote back to her and advised her to quit your employ to save herself any mortification. But she refused to be parted from you. She is utterly devoted to you, and it appears that you have been quite unaware of it.

"Item two: Mrs Eliza Seward has obtained a writ of divorcement on the grounds of insanity, and you, sir, are a bachelor."

6 January 1901

And thus it was that as Jack's asylum burned to the ground—in the same manner that Mr Rochester's mansion burned in that dreadful novel—his feeling for me was kindled. And I felt myself to be free of the terrible consequences that a single occasion of momentary madness had wreaked upon me. For I am—or I was—Miss Mary Holder, the niece of the banker Alexander Holder, from whom I attempted to steal a priceless beryl coronet—one of the treasures of the realm—for the man I had believed to be my lover, the insidious blackguard, Sir George Burnwell. I knew when I met him that Mr Holmes suspected me, and that I had to run away.

As soon as I left my beloved Uncle Alexander and my cousin, Arthur, who loved me, I knew that I had made the worst mistake. I wept bitter tears, but there was no going back. I had made my bed, to be quite coarse, and I must lie in it.

Of course Burnwell threw me over. That was to be expected. I came to understand that that was how he treated all his "darlings." I was forever soiled, and therefore had no expectations of marriage. I had no idea what I should do…save what other fallen women have undertaken to survive. But I thought that I should rather die, and began to contemplate the manner of my self-murder.

Strangely, at the soaring height of my desperation, a sum of money came to me by post. I thought it might be from Uncle Arthur.

I know now that it was a gift of mercy from Sherlock Holmes.

With the funds I secured a place in a nursing college, and from there, I came to work for Jack. He was such a caring, dear man, deeply scarred by his tragic marriage and the torments that had led up to it. My heart beat only for him, and I determined to be useful to him until I could no longer be of service, and to love him from afar forever.

Then Professor Moriarty came, and hid himself among us, a wolf among sheep. I knew that our "M" was a *wrong* man, but I did not know how wrong until Mr Holmes answered my summons and revealed all.

It is Mr Holmes's birthday tonight. And while he is far away from us—he being in England, while we have settled in Texas, the family seat of Quincey Morris, who gave his life so that my Jack might live—we have had a party in his honour. The cakes are made, lemonade and candies laid on for our little son Sherlock, and we are a jolly party of four: Jack, Sherlock, I, and dear, sweet, Dr Van Helsing, who as you may imagine, is quite old and frail. The dear man lives with us now, and we love him with all our hearts. He tells the story often of his and Jack's foray against Count Dracula.

In turn, I recount some of the many adventures Jack shared with Sherlock Holmes until such time as we decided to make our way to America. Perhaps you would like to hear some of them as well, you who are listening to my phonograph diary. I have recounted them all on these wax disks, and I do hope they will outlive us. No; I do not hope.

I am certain of it. For like my love for Jack Seward, our story will last forever.

Mary H. Seward
Discovered in Nancy Holder's attic April 7, 2019, San Diego, California

Sherlock Holmes and Dr Nikola: The Adventure of the Empty Throne

BRAD MENGEL

As I look back over my association with Sherlock Holmes, I find nothing on that day we met many years ago that would have suggested that he and I would become friends, or that we would still be sharing rooms in Baker Street together. I cast my mind back over the adventures we shared over the years, the villains we foiled such as Professor Moriarty, Klimo, and The Devil Doctor from China.

The year 1892 was a particularly fruitful one for The Holmes Consulting Detective Agency. There were many cases of note; *Wisteria Lodge*, where my step-brother, Don Jose De Martinos, 'The Tiger of Equinata' was discovered after fleeing a revolution; *The Sign of The Three*, which led Holmes and I to Tibet to investigate the murder of the High Priest of Hangkow by the criminal conspiracy known as The Three; and *The Baritsu Master*, an exploit that delves deeply into that Japanese system of wrestling that only few in the Western world fully comprehend. But perhaps the most intriguing and interesting case of the year began on a cold evening in early January.

Holmes and I had just returned from a concert given by The Australian Songbird, Miss Hilda Bouverie. We had just turned into Baker Street, when one of the many street urchins that populated London came up to us.

"Mr 'Olmes! Doctor Nikola!" greeted the young boy as he saw us. "Mrs 'Udson said that you might be 'eaded this way when she chased us out of 'er parlour."

I immediately recognised young Wiggins, the leader of the group of scalliwags and larrikins that Holmes had hired to act as his eyes and ears throughout London, his own Irregular network of informants.

"Well, you shouldn't have wiped your mouth on your sleeve after eating the carrot cake, young Wiggins," greeted Holmes after making the same identification.

The young lad's jaw dropped in amazement. "I don't know 'ow you do it, Mr 'Olmes."

I have to admit that I was in no mood for Holmes' theatrics as I was keen to return to my cat, Apollyon. "Holmes knew Mrs Hudson had baked a carrot cake and that Mrs Hudson would offer you a slice. The fact that there are crumbs on your sleeve tells us that you wiped your mouth with it. Although I admire your restraint, waiting for the third slice to do so. Now I take it that you have a reason to be looking for us other than to be amazed by Holmes' deductions? I take it that it has something to do with the letter in your pocket." I snapped, knowing it would irk Holmes.

Wiggins stood looking even more dumbfounded as he reached into his pocket and pulled out an envelope. For his trouble, I plucked a half Crown out of mid-air and handed it to him as Holmes took the envelope.

"Thanks, Doctor," Wiggins said, as he disappeared into the teaming throng that is London.

Holmes looked at me with annoyance. "Let's return home and read this letter from my brother, Mycroft."

"Obviously, it's important, or he would have waited for the post, or used a telegram," I replied as we continued down the street in companionable silence.

We soon reached the door of 221B, to be greeted by Mrs Hudson. "Mr Holmes, did that lad find you? The little terror took three pieces of my carrot cake, so there'll be no supper for you and the doctor."

Holmes assured her that we had no need for cake and would most likely be heading out again shortly. That did little to placate the long-suffering woman, as she bustled to her room muttering all the way.

Holmes and I soon mounted the seventeen steps that lead to our rooms. Holmes grabbed the jack-knife from the mantle and sliced open the envelope.

I sat in the chair on the left side of the fireplace and Apollyon took his usual place on my shoulders. I could see that Mrs Hudson had given him a saucer of milk while we were away, the fact that her arms bore no scratches meant he was getting used to her. Holmes read the letter and snorted before handing it over to me.

It was a short missive. "Meet me at Diogenes. M."

"Typical of my brother, too lazy to even write his own name," Holmes declared.

"I would think that a man who is sometimes the British Government would have access to more resources than one of the Irregulars to deliver such a simple message," I declared as I stroked Apollyon.

At that Holmes' face turned a most intriguing shade of red. "How on earth did you know that?"

I steepled my fingers and smiled at the Great Detective. I had, as a matter of course, compiled a complete file on Holmes and his family when I moved into 221B, but I wasn't about to tell him that. "Perhaps I'm a psychic."

At that, Holmes turned purple. "This agency is founded on the principals of rational scientific investigation, and we do not deal in spiritualist mumbo jumbo!"

It was a long running debate between us. Holmes refused to acknowledge anything that was impossible to his rational mind. I gave him some peace before he might have a heart attack. "Or maybe I deduced it from the letterhead and the watermark on the paper."

Holmes' face returned to normal as did his breathing. "Of course, that's what it is."

I caught him glancing at the locked draw which contained his cocaine; I had weaned him off that poison when I moved in. While he might be more pliable on the drugs, with the dangerous men that we often faced it was not wise to have any of his faculties impaired. I quickly diverted his attention by rising, as Apollyon leapt from my shoulders, and taking my hat off the hook. "Let's visit your brother."

Holmes was a few steps behind me as we entered the street. I signalled for a cab, and one soon came along. The driver was Baxter, one of my own agents, responsible for keeping tabs on Holmes's movements. Holmes gave the address of the Diogenes Club.

During the trip Holmes explained the unusual nature of the Club. "The Club was founded by Mycroft so that men who were otherwise unsuited to traditional clubs through either misanthropy or shyness would have a place to go. Silence is strictly enforced in the Diogenes. We will be taken to the Stranger's Room, which is the only place in the club where one may speak."

As predicted, on our arrival the doorman silently ushered us to the Stranger's Room. There we found Mycroft Holmes. Where Sherlock was tall and lean, his older brother was still tall, but much stouter.

Mycroft offered his hand. "Doctor Nikola, so nice to finally meet you. I enjoy reading your accounts of my brother in *The Windsor Magazine*; it's the only way I can discover what he is doing."

I shook his hand and returned the greeting. I could see that Mycroft was worried. While he looked the typical civil servant in government employ, there were very subtle clues he was far more than that. His right cuff was more worn that the left indicating that he was right handed and had been doing much writing lately and that he had not changed cuffs for a least a day. The slightly longer right sideburn confirmed that he was, indeed, right handed, and that he shaved himself. The tiny nick just below his right ear indicated that he had been distracted whilst shaving. The slight trickle of blood told me that he was shaving to meet his brother this evening. The 'stiff upper lip' was not just an expression for men like Mycroft. Clearly, there was a problem. It could only be professional, as Mycroft worked just around the corner from his club and his home, and he had no personal life to speak of. The fact that the Holmes brothers did not communicate was evidence of that. One does not become as important to the government, as my file indicated Mycroft was, if you were not dedicated to the job. The fact that Mycroft did not use his official resources for this problem, instead, using Wiggins to summon his brother was very suggestive.

Holmes and I took the glass of brandy offered by the club's waiter and sat in the leather chairs and waited to hear from Mycroft. He paced a little around the room before turning to us. "I'm sure that Sherlock told you that I hold a significant and fairly unique role in the British government. I hold no official job title and I draw a wage that covers my expenses only, yet I am privy to everything that occurs in the government. I make the connections that others are unable to, as they are fettered by the concerns of their department. As in the nursery rhyme, the want of a nail leads to the fall of a kingdom; my role is to ensure that a missing nail doesn't cause the fall of The British Empire."

Mycroft paused and paced some more. "I have noticed a pattern that shows that someone has been deliberately removing nails, if I may continue the metaphor, to bring about the end of the reign of Queen Victoria and the House of Saxe-Coburg and Gotha."

As someone who had been involved in several revolutions around the world, the idea wasn't as inconceivable to me as it was to the Holmes brothers who had lived all their lives under one monarch who had ruled for fifty-five years. Indeed, for an unemotional man, Sherlock Holmes was able to display a great deal of emotion for the Queen, as he'd once demonstrated to me via by the 'VR' he had shot into a wall in our Baker Street suite in bullet pocks. "Surely, this is impossible!" Holmes declared jumping to his feet, proving his respect for Her Majesty was still strong.

"Not impossible, just improbable," I replied, after taking a sip of the excellent brandy. "The Queen has more children than the little old woman in the shoe."

"As you keep saying, Sherlock, once you have eliminated the impossible, whatever remains, no matter how improbable, must be the truth," Mycroft stated. "I fear that the recent death of the Duke of Clarence was the start of the next phase of a plot. It was reported that he died of influenza but the truth is that he was assassinated."

"Assassinated? But how?" I queried.

"The Royal Physician reports that he was poisoned," Mycroft answered.

Holmes lit his pipe and began to puff. "If memory serves, the Duke had just become engaged, and was going to become the Viceroy of Ireland. He'd come a long way from the scandal at the Cleveland Street male brothel, and his sending compromising letters to prostitutes, a few years back."

"It was his rehabilitation that led to his death," agreed Mycroft, "for, as long as he was a potential embarrassment to the Royal family he was safe. My reports are that his parents are distraught and that his father, The Prince of Wales, is contemplating renouncing his succession rights."

"That would not be enough to dethrone Victoria and end her line. As I said, she has many children and grandchildren." I ventured.

"Quite right, Doctor," said Mycroft. "Prince George would ascend to the throne upon the death of his grandmother in that event. But I have just been informed this evening that he has been struck down with typhoid and confined to bed and there is grave fear for his life."

"Surely not another poisoning attempt?" asked Holmes. "That would be far too obvious."

"No, he has the disease but it would be easy enough to infect him at a public event."

"While the death of two heirs, and another renouncing the

throne, would be tragic, it wouldn't be enough to cause the fall of the Empire," I pointed out.

"True, but I have had reports that dissent is being sown throughout the Colonies. There is a push for independence by the Australians, Maoris in New Zealand are openly calling for the revocation of The Treaty of Waitangi, and there is dissent being sown in South Africa, Rhodesia and our other African colonies. If these become open rebellions, paired with the succession issues we just discussed then the British people will call for the removal of the Monarchy and we may be faced with a Protectorate with a new Cromwell."

Holmes and I sat for a moment and digested that information.

"There is no-one with the reach or planning ability to pull off such a plot since the late Professor Moriarty danced the Newgate jig at the end of the hangman's noose," Holmes said gravely.

"Perhaps we did not sweep away all of the web that Moriarty wove as thoroughly as we thought, and a new spider is sitting in the centre of this web and plucking at the thread of a plan that offers the ultimate punishment against the government responsible for his death?" I suggested. "Colonel Moran, for one, evaded our broom, and fled to the Continent."

"After Moran's escape, I contacted several of my colleagues throughout the Continent to keep watch for him but no one has reported anything, as you well know," Holmes rebuked me. "There have been no murders with his signature weapon—an air gun—reported anywhere."

Mycroft cleared his throat. "No, not on the Continent, but there was a report last month that a Maori chieftain was murdered with an air rifle, which helped stir up unrest in Tahupapa, New Zealand. Also, the irregularities of the death of the Earl of Maynooth in one of our Australian colonies are suggestive of an air rifle; as is the dissent that the Governor's recent death has raised. And I have an unconfirmed report that an air rifle might have been used to spark a riot in Kabul just last week. So it seems that Moran is involved in this. Sherlock, I need you and the doctor to locate the puppet master pulling his strings."

The large man moved closer to his brother and put his flipper-like hand on Holmes' shoulder. "You are the only one I can trust with this. I have no idea just how far this corruption is spread throughout the civil service and the military. There will be gratitude and honours from the Empire if you are successful."

Holmes smiled. "This is a mess of my own making, as I did not properly finish the Moriarty organisation the first time. To be of service to Her Majesty is honour enough for me. Come, Doctor." With that, Holmes walked out of the Stranger's room. I took a moment to compliment Mycroft on the brandy, then followed.

As we walked out onto Pall Mall, Holmes stopped to look back at his brother watching us out of the window of Diogenes Club. It was at that point that one of the ground floor windows of the club shattered. Had Holmes not stopped to look back, he would have been directly in the line of fire.

The fact that there was no sound of a gunshot meant that the bullet had come from an air rifle. That suggested that Colonel Moran was most likely the shooter. In any case, the only conclusion was that the shooter had been assigned to watch Mycroft Holmes, to see what counter-measures were being taken by the one man with both the access to the large tapestry of information needed as well as the requisite intellect to discern the common disruptive thread to the Crown's interests. The one man who might be able to prevent the unravelling of the British Empire.

My files told me that Mycroft Holmes was a man of fixed habits, only leaving his flat to travel to his office around the corner, and the Diogenes Club across the street. As I mentally followed the bullet's path back to Mycroft's rooms I could see the air gun being pulled back into the window. I could tell that Holmes had matched my deductions as we both sought cover. I could hear him cursing his brother's laziness from my vantage point. Mycroft had uncovered this vast conspiracy, and his idea of a safe house was one of his usual haunts directly across the road from where he lives!

While there was an element of laziness to Mycroft hiding at the Diogenes Club, the truth was, he was a thinker, and a planner, who left the practicalities to others, and when he was threatened, took to the place where he felt safe. As a founding member of the Diogenes Club, it was a niche that he had made for himself. I suspected that were Holmes thrown into the byzantine political waters that his brother effortlessly sailed he'd make equally embarrassing mistakes, although perhaps not as potentially permanently fatal.

I yelled to Holmes that the gun had been taken from the window, and together we raced across Pall Mall and into the building where Mycroft lived. I was very keen to make the acquaintance of the shooter, but as we raced up the stairs I could hear a door slam shut. By the time Holmes and I reached the back door, our assailant was long gone, and it defied even Holmes's deductive abilities to track the shooter. There seemed not a trace of evidence.

We returned to the stairs to determine if any clues had been left in Mycroft's rooms. In his haste to flee, the shooter had left the door ajar. Holmes pulled out his magnifier and inspected the lock.

"It's been picked," he declared as he showed me the minute scratches; an expert job.

As we entered Mycroft's rooms, another sign of the differences between the Holmes brothers became apparent. Where our flat in 221B Baker Street was a miscellaneous collection of curiosities haphazardly decorating our living space, Mycroft led a more Spartan existence with few personal items; in the event of Mycroft's death the landlord could rent the room fully furnished after removing only a couple of items. The only two items—aside from the obvious toiletries that showed that Mycroft Holmes lived here—were a cameo of a woman in a sitting room; Holmes' reaction to it told me it was their mother, and another picture. This other was a portrait of the Queen.

I could see that Holmes's eyes were darting around the room looking for any detail that was out of place. I looked around, but with so few items there was nothing that seemed out of the ordinary. There was a comfortable chair beside the fire with a folded paper placed on it. Much to my surprise, it was that very paper that Holmes seized and began to frantically look through. I said as much to him.

"Mycroft takes his papers at the club, there is no need for him to have one in his rooms. Also this is this morning's paper, and, as we know Mycroft has not been here for the last two days," Holmes snapped as he returned to the paper.

I could see that he was furiously scouring the agony columns, I suspected this was for some message that had been sent to those watching Mycroft. Holmes was muttering as he read the notices, so I took the opportunity to peruse the headlines on the front page. "ROYAL FUNERAL TOMORROW" the headline screamed at me.

I pulled out my pocket watch and saw that it was past midnight. "Holmes, let's take this back to Baker Street, and get some rest. The Prince's funeral is later today, according to the paper."

With that Holmes leapt to his feet. "That's it, Nikola! You are a genius; you never fail to show me a new perspective on a case. Our mastermind hid his plans in plain sight. If he plans to overthrow the monarchy the death of Her Majesty at this time would be particularly disastrous, especially if the Prince of Wales steps down. Come, Nikola, there is much to do."

We hastened across the road and again spoke with Mycroft. Security at the funeral was already high but Mycroft promised to do what he could.

Later that morning saw Holmes and I, in disguise, amongst the crowd at the funeral to pay their respects to the late Prince. I looked for any threat that the very prominent police presence might overlook. I looked around and saw Holmes wandering through the crowd as an elderly clergyman rattling a donation can for the needy orphans at Saint Simon's Orphanage. While Holmes walked through the masses I was hobnobbing with the elite of London posing as Sylvester Wetherall, the Colonial Secretary of New South Wales.

Nothing untoward happened at the funeral and there was barely a dry eye in the house when the Prince's fiancée placed what was to have been her wedding bouquet on his coffin. The funeral procession left the church to take Prince Albert Victor to his final resting place. I made my farewells, and found my way to Holmes.

To say that Holmes was disappointed there had been no attempted act of violence was an understatement of the first order. As we made our way back to Baker Street, he expressed how he sought to understand why our mysterious nemesis had not struck at the most opportune moment.

"These are most deep waters, Nikola," Holmes exclaimed. "Our mystery villain is playing a deeper and longer game than I first thought."

In some perverse way, Holmes was taking delight in being stymied. Since the demise of Professor Moriarty, however, I had noted he was prone to fits of despair. He would sprawl over the easy chair with his long leg draped over the arm and play the most maudlin music on his violin. When he spoke it was only of the lesser calibre of criminal left in London, declaring that the police no longer needed to consult him. Each new mystery would temporarily break him out of his mood but after the solution of a case a dark cloud would settle over his head and he would return to his melancholy.

He had seemed to delight in explaining this mastermind's recent plan. The public assassination of any member of the royal family would serve to make them martyrs in the eyes of the public and gain them further sympathy. A case worthy of his mind, I realized.

It was during his explanations and hypotheses, as we turned into Baker Street, that a cabbie lost control of his hansom taking the bend. Holmes was so engrossed in his deductions that he was oblivious to the danger. It was only the fact that I was alert that spared our lives. I shoved Holmes out of danger, and leapt after him. The cabbie did not stop his horses and instead continued on his journey. It happened so quickly that neither Holmes nor I was able to recall any specific details of the cab.

The attempt on his life delighted Holmes! It told him that we were considered a threat by a foe perceptive enough to penetrate the disguises we were still wearing. We hastened into our rooms. We made sure to stay away from the windows as we removed our disguises; a sound precaution knowing that there were assassins on the loose.

"Our enemy has failed twice to kill us now and I'm sure that they will try again," said Holmes as he lit his pipe. "We can use this to draw them out when *we* want."

"I have just the thing," I said. I went to the storage cupboard and pulled out two boxes. "You may recall the gift from John Theodore Tussaud when we solved the mystery of his moving waxworks?"

"And prevented the robbery of the Bank of England by John Clay," Holmes added.

I reached into the boxes and pulled out wax replicas of both Holmes and myself. We soon had them set up so that the silhouettes could be seen in the window once the night had fallen. Holmes and I sat in silence as he puffed on his pipe and contemplated the case. Apollyon rubbed against my legs and I stroked him as I waited.

The night wore on, and I was just about to turn off the light, when the window shattered and the bust of Holmes fell to the floor. Holmes and I were soon out the door and heading for the origin of the shot. By the time we arrived in Camden House, the building opposite 221B Baker Street, the shooter was long gone, but Holmes was immediately on the scent for any clues, and moved to the open window that was best located for a weapon used to shoot at us. Holmes's nose came close to the windowsill, and he took a deep breath.

"Nikola, come smell this, and see if you match my conclusions."

I walked over to the window and duplicated Holmes's actions. I smelt tobacco, a particular blend unique to the Indian sub-continent, particularly favoured by members of the British military; a blend we both had familiarised ourselves with when hunting the late Professor Moriarty's lieutenant, Colonel Sebastian Moran. Combined with the fact an air gun shot at us, doubt was removed that we had been attacked by any other man.

But with that tobacco scent, I caught a hint of another scent. I took another deep inhalation, and allowed the smell to trigger my olfactory memory. It took a couple of seconds to recall the exact location that I had come across the smell.

It was the unique, spiced rum served in a waterfront pub, the Green Sailor on East India Dock Road. About three years ago, Holmes and I had come close to capturing Moriarty when he had been running his operations from the back room of that establishment. It took all of my powers of persuasion to convince the barman to let us into the back room and I had ample opportunity to smell the house speciality at that time. The barman was resistant to my pleadings, and Holmes and I were regrettably to later find that Moriarty and his lieutenants had made their escape through an old smuggler's tunnel. It took much further investigating but we were eventually able to track the Napoleon of Modern Crime down to his new hideout and send him to his deserved fate at the end of a hangman's noose— but that is a case fully documented in a one of my published accounts in the *Windsor.*

I told Holmes of my observations. "Excellent, Nikola, you have exactly replicated my findings. It seems that the man responsible for resurrecting the Moriarty organisation has returned to one of the professor's old haunts; I think I feel like a hot toddy of spiced rum."

With that we returned to the street and soon hailed a cab. I noted that Pendergast had relieved Baxter as we hopped aboard. We were soon headed to the Green Sailor. Holmes once again resorted to his infuriating habit of talking on esoteric subjects instead of informing me of his plans. This time it was the embalming processes of the ancient Egyptians upon which topic he was planning on writing a monograph. Even if Holmes refused to believe in telepathy, he had inadvertently discovered the perfect technique to divert my psychic abilities!

We soon arrived at the inn and entered. Neither Holmes nor I—fairly well-known figures—were best prepared for an 'incognito' arrival without wearing any form of disguise, but the urgency of our mission precluded taking the time to adopt any such measures. Instead, we entered the inn as bold as brass. The barman was the same as on our last visit and he visibly blanched at the sight of us, and fled.

Holmes and I went to the back room that was the subject of our previous visit. I heard a high voice speaking in what might be considered a falsetto as we went down the hallway; I could not make out words but the elevated pitch of the voice carried some distance. There were moments of silence that must have been the responses of the Voice's companion. As we walked through the door I detected a strange popping or cracking sound.

"Welcome, Mister Holmes and Doctor Nikola," the high pitched voice greeted us. "I have been looking forward to meeting you both for some time."

There have been very few times in my life when I have been taken completely by surprise but the man sitting behind the table in the back room certainly warranted same. The first thing I noticed was that he had the most severe case of albinism I'd ever seen: his skin was as pale and as delicate as a piece of China. His hair looked like thousands of spiders had spun web from his scalp, so fine and pale was it.

His head was so disproportionately large that if skull-size was a true measure of intelligence he would be more intelligent than Holmes and I combined. I stared into his feral pink eyes and was reminded of a white rat that Apollyon had captured and brought to me one time. The eyes of that rat had glared at me with the same hatred as Moriarty's disciple did now.

"Permit me to introduce myself, my name is John Macklin." The albino stood and walked around the table and for the first time I saw Macklin in full. His body was dwarfish in configuration; it most closely resembled that of a four year old child except for arms that seemed to belong to a member of the great ape family. He stretched one of these limbs out to offer his hand which Holmes and I declined to shake.

Out of the corner of my eye I could see that Holmes was tensing to strike at the albino dwarf.

"I wouldn't do that," came a stern voice from behind us. In our surprise at the appearance of Macklin, Holmes and I had both forgotten that this new criminal mastermind was not alone. Colonel Sebastian Moran had the drop on us.

"Excellent work, sir," Macklin complimented as he began to crack his knuckles one by one. The smug satisfaction in that falsetto voice and the eerie pops from his finger joints put my teeth on edge. "You both, of course, know the Colonel? As I said earlier, gentlemen, I've been looking forward to meeting you both. Although, after spending some time with the late professor's dossiers on you, I feel as if I already know you.

"James Moriarty, my mentor, knew that the end was coming and so he made a plan to gain posthumous revenge on you. I have modified that plan to one in which I bring down the throne of the British Empire."

Macklin reached into the pocket of his vest and pulled out a fob-watch. "Your capture means that my operation can continue. Poor Prince Albert Victor has been laid to rest and the Prince of Wales has called a special sitting of Parliament, and—with the exception of poor George on his deathbed—all members of the House of Saxe-Coburg and Gotha will be there. I'm sure that the Prince of Wales's tearful renunciation of his succession rights will be remembered for eternity."

Macklin pulled a revolver from the waistband of his trousers. "Colonel, would you please ensure that our guests didn't bring along any of their friends from the police force? I can keep an eye on them."

Moran made a hasty exit. The albino gave a high pitched giggle. "The turmoil that will follow if Eddy tries to climb back on the throne! Every royal bastard from the last century will make a claim for the Crown. Republican sentiment will grow in the period of uncertainty. England will look to a strong man for leadership."

"You?" I asked, even as I knew what the answer would be.

"You flatter me, sir. No, while I would be an excellent ruler, my unconventional appearance would go against the populace accepting me as their emperor. Besides, it's easier to be the power behind the throne. Moran's military service makes him the ideal man to become the Lord High Protector and he will make a perfect puppet ruler," the albino gloated.

The sound of police whistles suddenly intruded into Macklin's speech. The albino was distracted and his gun began to waver away from Holmes and I. I saw Holmes leap!

I reached for the pistol I had put in my pocket earlier in the evening, but did not make it to the weapon before I heard the gunshot and felt the burning sensation of a bullet grazing my right bicep. Holmes was upon Macklin and applied a baritsu throw that disarmed and incapacitated the man.

I was groaning in pain as Holmes came to my side. He quickly removed my coat and tore my sleeve off, examined me and bound my arm with his pocket kerchief. "It's just a flesh wound," he declared tersely with obvious relief in his voice.

It was at that point that the police burst into the room lead by Inspector Peter Jones.

"Who do I arrest?" Jones boomed.

Holmes indicated where he had left Macklin, but much to his irritation the dwarf had recovered and taken advantage of the chaos and utilised the smuggler's tunnel that his mentor had used three years ago. Inspector Jones commanded his men to take the tunnel but they reported that the criminal was nowhere to be found.

The Inspector told us that Pendergast had arrived at the Yard with the note I had slipped him when I paid him for our cab ride. While the Inspector was disappointed that he was too late to capture Macklin, he was pleased that Colonel Moran was in his custody.

A medico was called to treat me more thoroughly. He introduced himself as Dr John Watson and confirmed Holmes's initial assessment, as he cleaned and bandaged my wound.

The next morning saw Holmes and I again in the Stranger's Room of The Diogenes Club, where we joined Mycroft for breakfast. The elder Holmes looked more relaxed than the last time we saw him. He was wearing a different suit and new cuffs and collar.

As he offered us a hearty English breakfast Mycroft informed us that the police were searching for John Macklin and that he was sure that such a distinctive individual would be easy to find. Holmes merely smiled, for, upon our return to Baker Street the evening before Holmes and I had discussed the escape of the deformed genius; we'd agreed a man so distinctive in appearance was sure to have planned for such a contingency and would be able to travel incognito.

Mycroft then reported that, based on information that Moran had given to the police after his arrest, one of the Queen's ladies-in-waiting had been caught preparing to smother Her Majesty in her sleep. Moran's confession at the eleventh hour was considered the only act that could have saved the rogue Colonel from swinging from a noose. In any event, according to a Royal Physician's report that Mycroft read from, Her Majesty was merely shaken. The report also contained an encouraging prognosis for Prince George who was starting to rally from his bout with typhus.

As Holmes added to his breakfast plate, he asked about the Prince of Wales's address to Parliament that Macklin had mentioned the previous night. Holmes was rewarded with news that the purpose of the speech was for the Prince to address and deny the rumours that he would be relinquishing his succession rights. Mycroft assured Holmes and I that we had saved the British Empire, and, as the news of Edward's speech spread through the colonies, the unrest was sure to resolve itself.

As I look back knowing what I know now, we three might have been more concerned about the escape of the deadly dwarf.

For, the next time we faced the albino genius Mycroft Holmes himself was accused of the murder of Colonel Moran. The matter is recorded in my notes as *A Study in White*.

The Adventure of the Reckless Resurrectionist

WILL MURRAY

The events that I am poised to relate transpired late in that terrible summer of the year 1918. The Great War, then at long last lurching to a satisfactory conclusion, nevertheless began exerting its toll upon our civilian population.

The scourge commenced with an outbreak that spring of what the French called *La Grippe*. The "three-day fever" was the name we gave it. In its earliest manifestations, it was unremarkable, for most patients recovered. There came an interregnum of several months. After that merciful pause, the revitalized virus reappeared in late summer, vastly more terrible than heretofore.

Before long, newspapermen had dubbed it the "Spanish Influenza", owing to the fact that our war censors had forbidden the press from reporting its true and terrible extent for many months—except in the case of neutral Spain, which was ravaged by the modern plague most mercilessly.

I had been called out of retirement by the war. Not that a physician ever truly retires, but as the war-wounded streamed into London hospitals, I feared that I worked far harder in those awful months than in all the busy years of my previous practice.

It was during the treating of the casualties lately arrived from the Battle of Saint-Mihiel that September that I found myself treating an American doctor with the portentous name of Dr West. It was portentous only in the fact that American Expeditionary Force soldiers had cultivated the habit of referring to comrades who had been lost in battle as having "gone West"— in the direction of sunset, one assumes.

This sinister connection was lost upon me during our first meeting, I must confess, but in subsequent weeks I had reason to mentally refer to Herbert West as "Dr Death". But I get ahead of my story.

I was examining Dr West at the Brook War Hospital—formerly the Brook Fever Hospital at Shooter's Hill—on a very quiet Monday morning. Traffic had been rerouted around the great array of brick buildings, and only the luffing and chattering of a great outside banner exhorting "Quiet for the Wounded" came in through the open windows. West's head was bandaged, but his limbs proved to be sound and, more importantly, whole. I had grown numb of performing endless amputations upon otherwise healthy young men that year.

The report said that Major West and an assistant had been working in a field hospital in Saint Eloi when it had been struck by a German shell, making the spot an unsightly charnel house of a blast crater—for the greater portion of Dr West's work had to do with the surgical removal of traumatized limbs. The assistant, whose name I never did learn, had been conveyed to the King George Hospital in Waterloo.

"Miraculous that you survived," I remarked to the man, not only out of conversational necessity, but to ascertain if he suffered from shell-shock, a common enough malady among those brave soldiers who survived German artillery attacks.

The major's response was clear and pithy.

"Pray tell, where is this wretched place?" he demanded coldly, donning a pair of wire-rimmed spectacles.

After I informed the major that he was safe and secure in a London military hospital, our conversation grew professional.

"Have you...many dead?"

"None as yet. But expectations are optimistic in that regard," I told him bluntly. "Why do you ask?"

"My professional interest lies in that direction..." he said vaguely.

"What direction?"

"With the...dead."

This naturally quickened my interest, for I am also keen to learn about the experiences of my American colleagues across the pond. But when I pressed Dr West, he grew surly and evasive; a fact I attributed to the extreme hardships he had lately endured.

Changing the subject, I formally introduced myself.

"I am Dr John Watson, in charge of this ward."

The curiously blue eyes, which had been wandering about the room as if in search of something unguessable, suddenly careened in the direction of my own frank gaze.

"Not the Dr Watson who had been in service to the famous Sherlock Holmes?"

"I confess a certain portion of my younger years were so occupied," I said, wishing to change the subject. But West would have none of it.

"I should like to meet this outstanding man, about whom so much is written."

"I am afraid that Mr. Holmes has been retired some years now, and passes his remaining time comfortably on a farm near Eastbourne these days. He does not often receive visitors."

Dr West grew coldly insistent. "Still, I would very much like to meet Holmes. My work would interest him greatly."

"Precisely upon what lines do you work?" I asked.

"That," Dr West responded, "is only for the ears of Mr. Holmes himself. And no other."

I ignored the veiled slight, saying only, "Perhaps when you are better, such a meeting might be arranged."

Dr West tore his gaze from mine, but not before I detected a flash of ill-repressed anger toward me. In this rude gesture I took it that the tow-headed medical man was rarely refused a request.

Returning to my rounds of the convalescent ward, I recorded that Dr West had suffered a moderate concussion, but showed little sign of shell-shock, although I reserved the right to alter my initial diagnosis at a later date.

In the days that followed, the curious American physician grew stronger, and my diagnosis held unaltered. In less than a fortnight, Dr West was up and about, assisting the staff in the caring of the sick and wounded; for I had requested and received permission to reassign him to the hospital, he not yet being fit enough to return to the field, but very sorely needed here.

By that time the ill were threatening to push the war-wounded out of their cots. For the first wave of severe influenza victims began to accumulate, baffling and frustrating all efforts to administer to them.

Although ours was now a military facility, its past as a sanatorium where victims of Scarlet Fever were treated, naturally came into play. Those of you familiar with this scourge that had been spawned by the foul conditions of trench warfare in Europe need no reminders of its horrors. But for those who have been spared the details, I will write only that the poor victims often exhibited mild symptoms in the morning, only to expire by early evening, their skins turning a cyanotic blue, with a bloody froth upon their lips as they suffocated.

The progress of the new disease was shocking in its mortality as well as its unheard-of rapidity. The healthiest were hit hardest, contrary to earlier such plagues, to which the young and elderly alike typically succumbed. Pneumonia was the ultimate cause of death. Nothing could be done for these unfortunates. There appeared to be no cure discoverable. Had any remedy existed, the unchecked speed with which the infection overwhelmed its victims would surely have outpaced any antidote applied in the early stages of the progress of the disease.

Soon, the contagion became an epidemic. They perished by the hundreds, then by the thousands. It was appalling.

The epidemic was so ferocious and all-consuming of civilians that it was initially thought to be a war-weapon unleashed by the Central Powers to forestall its increasingly inevitable defeat. But the Germans and their allies were likewise affected, so that theory was soon dismissed out of hand.

During the first weeks of struggle to deal with the crisis, Dr West turned his attention to the conundrum.

"It may be possible to save some of these," he remarked to me one day.

"By what means?" I blurted out.

"The dead succumb to pneumonia of the lungs. The remainder of their tissues and vital organs remain unravaged, and presumably undamaged."

"I do not follow your trend, Dr West."

Dr West eyed me with his uncomfortably direct, unblinking gaze. "I had been conducting experiments upon the worst of our casualties in the field, Dr Watson. Some of my discoveries might be applied here. I will need access to a pharmacological laboratory."

I was hesitant, but the chorus of gasping and choking victims punished my sensibilities most vexingly. The pleas for respite, the remorseless cyanosis creeping over previously healthy features, overwhelmed my reluctance.

I saw to it that Dr West had access to whatever he required.

That first night, the American major worked feverishly as I slept on a cot, exhausted from dealing with suffering and unbelievable horror as I did for days upon end. Days with no end. And no end in sight.

The next morning, Dr West awoke me rather roughly, displaying a hypodermic needle which he had charged to capacity with a potion of his own concocting.

"My chemical exciter is ready for testing, Dr Watson."

"Whatever is it?" I demanded, getting up.

"Watch, and learn."

"Dr West, I cannot allow you to experiment upon my poor, suffering patients. It would be wholly unethical."

Dr West quirked his self-satisfied mouth in a matter I grew to loathe.

"What about those who have already passed?" he countered.

"What would that accomplish, man? The dead are dead—most profoundly so."

"Permit me to prove you different," he said in an unctuous tone dangerously close to a sneer.

Had the situation not been so horrific, so maddeningly dire, I would of course have refused. But all hope had been lost. The influenza was ravaging the hospital, contaminating its overworked staff, and crossing over to the war wounded, decimating them.

I nodded my assent, unable to give voice to permission that would have poisoned my tongue in a less extreme time.

Smiling thinly, Dr West took his instrument to the morgue where the dead were stacked under white sheeting, awaiting the trucks to haul them away for burial, much as the victims of the Black Plague were removed by carts in a bygone era that now seemed no less terrible than ours.

West went among them, lifting soiled sheets, feeling the cooling flesh with the touch of a man accustomed to such charnel work. I began to think of the American major as an undertaker or embalmer, not a physician of the living.

At last West found a specimen that seemed to meet with his professional, if ghoulish, approval. Without hesitation or preparation, he plunged the needle into the forearm of a strapping young man the colour of pale clay.

Then he stood back, the corpse sheet clutched in one pale hand. In that fearful moment, I was reminded of Shelly's supremely arrogant Dr Frankenstein.

Not a minute passed, when the bare chest of the wretch gave a spasmodic jerk. Suddenly the dead face commenced twitching, eyelids fluttered alarmingly.

I gasped out an inarticulate word, my mouth gone bone dry. Then to my utter and unbounded amazement, the cadaver sat up, looked around and croaked out a macabre but perfectly natural question.

"Where—am—I?"

He no more uttered those baffled words than a great bloody

froth rushed up from his lungs and was violently expelled by mouth and nose.

With that, the poor beggar fell back with a sickening thud.

I checked his heart and pulse. Both still. But the formerly cold flesh was strangely warm. As I felt about for other vital signs, the corpse again began cooling.

"Dead," I told West hoarsely.

"Again!" snarled the man, pale eyes searching the sheeted remains. "I must find a livelier specimen."

As it happened, a fresh victim was wheeled in and deposited on the floor. I signalled the curious ward maid—all men suitable to perform the duties of an orderly having naturally gone off to war—to depart and Dr West knelt before the new arrival.

Again, that foul needle found its way into a sluggish vein.

And again, life was revitalized, only to come smashing down again.

Three times Dr West worked his scientific sorcery. And in each instance, he succeeded, only to crash into the abyss of failure once more.

"You are on to something quite remarkable, Dr West," I admitted at last. "But I fear that your solution is not quite up to so formidable a task."

"It is a reagent," West flung back in frustration. "Please call it by its proper name."

I ignored the outburst, recognizing it as a nervous reaction to the horrid moment. It was clear to me that the American was deeply frustrated by the limitations of his serum, and had been for some period of time.

Reluctantly, Dr West surrendered his vial and needle and looked me dead in the eyes, saying, "One man alone possesses the mentality to assist me in perfecting my elixir," he said gravely.

He did not have to speak the name, for I took his meaning.

"Sherlock Holmes?" I returned.

Dr West nodded. "Take me to him." It was almost a command.

We were not able to get away for another week—a week in which the combined horrors of war and the unstoppable influenza filled our wards beyond capacity, and tried our souls beyond endurance.

Through it all, Dr West moved as a machine through the dead and dying, taking equal interest in both. He appeared, to all objective scrutiny, uninterested in the maimed survivors of battles in Europe. The dead or near-dead alone fascinated him. I shudder now to contemplate the why of it all...

Finally, I was granted my leave and with Dr West formally but temporarily placed into my custody, we trained up to Sussex Downs, where we found a motorcar for hire to take us to the charming villa of Mr Sherlock Holmes.

I had telegraphed Holmes in advance of my arrival, and received a friendly if curt reply. I failed to apprise Holmes of my travelling companion, for I felt strongly that no one could do justice to Dr Herbert West and his intrigues than the remarkable A.E.F. major himself.

Arriving late in the afternoon of a unreasonably warm Saturday, I paid the driver and escorted Dr West to the modest home of my old friend and former benefactor—for I have always considered Holmes as such—a man whose keen intelligence and sterling presence had immeasurably enriched my otherwise humdrum existence.

"Hulloa! Watson!" cried Holmes. But it was not the hale call of yore. There was a bit of a croaking of age-stained vocal chords in his timbre. I saw also that his complexion had attained a greyish pallor that concerned me.

I said nothing of my observations, of course. "Holmes, dear fellow! Jolly good to see you after these long months."

"How fare the gallant fruits of the war?" he asked, shaking my hand firmly.

"If you mean the maimed and worse, this conflict has borne England more bitter fruits than any in its bloody history," I told him gravely.

"Ah, but it will be over with soon. Mark my words. Now, who is this fellow?"

In typically American fashion, Dr West spoke over my attempted introduction, impetuously thrusting out his pallid but eager hand saying, "Dr Herbert West. At your service, Mr Holmes."

This last took a bit of the sting out of the *faux pas.*

"What brings you here, Dr Herbert West?" inquired Holmes.

"I have a proposition that may interest you."

"Indeed?"

West got right down to brass tacks, as Americans so often do. "I propose, Mr Holmes, to raise you from the dead."

"Good heavens!" I gasped.

An eerie twinkle flickered in and out of Holmes's canny grey eyes. "Might I point out that although I am obviously at an advanced age, I have not yet passed over into the great unknown."

"But you do admit that this event looms on your personal horizon?" countered West.

"It appears to be unavoidable," allowed Holmes rather diffidently. "Now, how do you propose to create such a Biblical miracle?"

"Are you familiar with the so-called Arkham Atrocities?" inquired West.

Holmes gave that only passing reflection. "Indeed I am. Although many of those foul events actually took place in surrounding towns, such as Bolton."

West nodded, evidently pleased to find Holmes in possession of his old faculties, despite his wrinkled and rheumy appearance.

"I," proclaimed Dr West with a touch of maniacal pride, "am the author of those atrocities…"

Holmes lifted his tangled eyebrows. "You are? I should like to hear more of your career, morbid as it promises to be."

We adjoined to Holmes' spacious if cluttered study, where a woman I did not recognize served tea. As the water was being boiled, Holmes regarded Dr West in a profound silence.

"You are obviously an American, but I take it you have served in France, as an officer. A major, I should judge."

"Very astute, Holmes," West acknowledged.

"By what deductive wizardry did you arrive at that correct

assessment?" I asked grandly.

I fully expected a recounting of clues and other minuscule trivia, but Holmes, as always, baffled me. He said, "I now recall reading in the *Times* of an American major, Dr Herbert West by name, who had his field hospital blown to flinders by a German shell."

"The very same," said West, inclining his blondish head so that the light momentarily made the lenses of his spectacles opaque.

Turning to me, Holmes smiled and said, "It is no more remarkable than an attentive eye coupled with a retentive memory."

Tea was served and, after his third thoughtful sip, Holmes addressed Dr West by saying, "Now, you were going to recount for my edification your rather sordid career."

"I hardly call it sordid, for I have been engaged in the remarkable enterprise of unlocking the secrets of bodily reanimation."

"As I recall, the press accounts that reached us here implied grave-robbing as a prelude to the atrocities themselves," commented Holmes.

"One cannot reanimate cold clay without suitable raw material," insisted West, his voice skittering in the direction of *High C*.

"Your theory then is that life is but a series of chemical reactions, and by the application of the proper chemistry, whatever processes have been interrupted may be restored to full vitality?"

It was such a penetratingly accurate summation of the man's true thinking that Dr West sat blinking, incapable of answer.

Finally, he stammered. "How-however did you deduce that?"

Holmes remarked simply, "You do not strike one as a man who credits the existence of the human soul."

"A damned myth!" snapped West.

"Permit me to point out that there exists no credible scientific literature addressing the question one way or another, so the issue must remain an open one. Now, as to your goals in this seemingly unsavoury enterprise," pressed Holmes. "For how long do you propose to sustain your Lazarus-like subjects?"

"Indefinitely."

"Do you speak of immortality?" asked Holmes, dreamy eyes alight.

"Precisely. I have devised an injectable reagent by which a recently deceased cadaver may be restored to full vitality."

This bald statement was met by no outward display of emotion, nor any comment on the part of my friend. I took this to mean Holmes maintained a studied scepticism, restrained only due to necessary politeness toward a house guest.

I hastened to add, "Holmes, I beg of you to hear this man out. While working in my ward, I witnessed him inject no less than three deceased victims of the so-called Spanish Influenza. All were resurrected, although for mere moments. One spoke distinctly, wondering aloud as to his present whereabouts, before death reclaimed him."

"So the solution is not permanent, then?" inquired Holmes, a trace of disappointment threading his wavering voice.

"Not *yet* perfected," insisted West. "But I am edging closer to perfection. I had thought a man of your intellect might assist me in this great endeavour."

Again, this absurd suggestion was greeted by no outward enthusiasm on the part of Sherlock Holmes, yet I, who had known him for so many years, could detect a trembling interest. It shocked me. But then I recalled how many years-prolonged my friendship with Holmes was, and the traces of rheumatism that wracked that spare and fleshless frame suggested that his own mortality weighed heavily upon him in as this new century advanced through its present stage of global war.

Momentarily, I yearned for the grand old days, and the Sherlock Holmes I once knew — young, keen of wit and impossibly vital. He had been a man of electricity in those former days. A dynamo of sheer, unsurpassed brilliance and robustness. No more. Alas, no more.

I turned my head away for a moment in order to compose myself.

Holmes finished his tea and launched into a series of penetrating questions.

"The Massachusetts phase of your researches. Tell me of them."

There followed a recounting as grisly as it was improbable.

Poe himself might have penned such a monstrous account. I began to apprehend why they had come to be known as the Arkham Atrocities. For Dr West had been a cold-blooded and unrepentant grave robber; disinterring and reanimating corpse after corpse—always successfully at first, but never vindicated in the final results.

"Your degree is from Miskatonic University Medical School?" Holmes asked at one point.

West nodded. "Class of '05."

It seemed a minor point, for the man's credentials were not in doubt, but Holmes seemed to derive special meaning in the American's alma mater. I, for one, knew only of its reputation as a seat of rather arcane, if not eccentric, learning.

The unsavoury discussion ranged far into the evening, and, as the hour approached ten, I could see that Sherlock Holmes began to shows signs of fatigue, especially in the unsettlingly grey cast of his craggy features.

Abruptly, he declared, "It is my intention to retire early, for I have absorbed much that interests me this evening. I beg you both to be my guests overnight, that we may discuss this further in the morn."

Dr West nodded eagerly. He seemed to think that he was getting somewhere with Holmes. For my part, I rather doubted it, but as we repaired to our guest rooms, I began to grow unconvinced of my own convictions.

The summery night passed fitfully for me, and I found myself tossing and turning, opening the windows to let in the night air, which was so stifling hot that I could scarcely breathe.

I am by nature and professional temperament an early riser, but on this fateful morning I slept late. I awoke with a queer sensation in my throat, and rather a gurgling from within my own larynx. My head muzzy with sleep, at first I did not take any particular meaning from these sensations, unaccustomed as they were. Then, before conscious thought could form, my heart started pounding and I struggled for my breath. With a slow dawning of dread, I began to suspect that I had come down with the thrice-accursed Spanish influenza. There was a servant's bell at my bedside, and I floundered about until I had grasped its mahogany handle. I began ringing it vigorously, having discovered that I could not organize my feeble powers into understandable speech.

Sherlock Holmes promptly threw open the door, and cried, "Watson, what is it?"

I could manage only the most spasmodic of gasps, and the alarm on Holmes's sharp features merely added to my floundering consternation.

Herbert West made his appearance next, and the eyes behind his spectacles grew rather round, but otherwise did not reflect any deep concern, as one might expect of such a cold-blooded adventurer into the macabre.

Both men rushed to my bedside, one on either side of the four-poster. West made a cursory examination, and spoke to Holmes as if I were not present, "All signs point to the flu."

Holmes seemed at a momentary loss for words, then drew back a measured pace, as if instinctively fearing the pathogen I now knew was harboured within me.

"Terribly sorry, old man," he muttered, his gaze shifting this way and that.

He stamped his foot once, in a gesture of baffled frustration.

West continued speaking in his confoundedly detached manner. "If the disease progresses as expected, the virus will run its course approximately four PM this afternoon."

Holmes made a clucking sound deep in his throat, and shook his head sadly.

"There is no medicine suitable for this case?" he asked.

"None," replied West.

"Then there is no hope for him?" murmured Holmes, closing his eyes. "That I would live to see such a sight, witnessing a dear friend approach such an unjust end," he murmured.

Dr West stated firmly, "Just because there is no hope in the view of conventional medical science, does not mean that none exists."

As I struggled to make my malfunctioning lungs process revivifying oxygen, a strange conversation ensued, which I overheard in fits and starts.

"Speak, man," Holmes demanded of West. "I implore you."

"As Dr Watson has testified, I have brought back from the brink three victims of the Spanish influenza. That they did not persist in their revival was only because they had already passed beyond this mortal gate."

"What do you mean?" Holmes asked.

"What I mean, Mr Holmes," Dr West said with a fever of excitement trembling in his voice, "is that we do not wait for death to settle in before injecting Dr Watson. We inject him while he trembles on the brink of eternity."

"I see," said Holmes softly. "You propose to make an experiment of my dear friend, Watson."

I heard these words as if eavesdropping from some far-off listening-post, remote in time and space from earthly concerns.

"Exactly," said West.

"I do not think I should allow this," snapped Holmes. "It is against the natural order of things."

"What is natural about a damn disease taking a man before his time?" West retorted hotly.

The vehemence of the American major's assertion was electric. It suggested a man riding hard toward the edge of madness, but also an individual possessed of the firm conviction of his own Olympian powers. I have seen such mania as this amongst other members of my profession. Never on quite this order, but the flavour was the same. Place the power of life and death in a man's trained hands, and he begins to think as if he stands above all other mortals.

West continued in that vein. "If we do not intervene, Dr Watson dies a horrible death, his face turning blue, his lungs filling with blood and fluid."

Holmes hesitated, his gaunt facial lineaments resembling the strings of a violin being plucked by unseen hands. Even in my torture, I could see the play of conflicting emotions passing over his features.

After several moments of these alterations in my friend's facial expression, the emotional tremors appeared to subside, and once again the cool intellect of the Sherlock Holmes of years gone by reasserted itself like an eagle awakening to take flight.

"If you inject Dr Watson with your solution before his untimely passing, how can you justly call it a resurrection?" he demanded.

"By virtue of the unavoidable fact that if we do not arrest the progress of this disease, Dr Watson will inevitably perish before the sun sets on this day."

This struck Holmes most forcefully. By now, he had out his pipe and was charging it with tobacco, as if to mask his inner agitation. Setting the bowl aflame, he took several puffs, watching me gasp like a floundering fish through his hooded eyes, which age had barely dimmed.

Presently, Sherlock Holmes said, "I commend my dear friend into your peculiar, if capable, hands, Dr West."

"Thank you," said the other, evidently pleased with his triumph over a man of equal if not superior will. For I recognized in the American major a steely intellect which mirrored Sherlock Holmes's alone, but of a more depraved character.

"What do we do in the meantime?" asked Holmes. "For, poor Watson is clearly suffering tremendously."

"There is nothing we can do but make him comfortable, and see to his minor needs. This is a death-watch, Mr. Holmes. A death-watch in which we hope to pluck out a victory before the black wings of death smother your companion."

My eyes were upon Sherlock Holmes at that point, and I would have sworn that I detected something akin to a shudder pass through his gangling body. But I cannot be certain, for my own pain and hardship were rapidly consuming me.

Abruptly, Holmes threw the windows fully open, to allow in the suffocating heat. But it did no good. He paced endlessly, smoking furiously, and finally, overcome with inner turmoil, Sherlock Holmes departed the room, to leave me in the hands of the uncanny American physician.

Hours passed during which I suffered the torments of a very airless Hades. There was no respite from my struggles. No breath of air seemed cool enough or fresh enough to do me any good. Nor could I gain sufficient oxygen to appease my ravenous needs.

I had closely observed these early symptoms in others, and as the morning progressed, they worsened. I could feel the pneumonia clutching at my struggling lungs like a tropical python wrapping its inexorable coils around my heaving ribs.

I do not recall how long I tossed and turned, trapped in a body consumed by rebellion against the virus which had invaded it. But I fear I was not strong enough to withstand and stave off the inevitable for as long as Dr West had predicted.

It was sometime in mid-afternoon that awareness fled, and I entered a blackness that seemed then to be irredeemably absolute.

When consciousness returned, I was astounded to discover that it was morning. I sat up in bed, and found myself alone. The door was wide open. My first sensation was that my lungs were heaving with fluid, and I began coughing, expelling their contents in wave after wave of torrential fluid.

This ugly chore left me racked and depleted; then I found that I could breathe more normally.

Fumbling for the servant's bell, I tried to ring it. My strength all but failed me. The noisy device fell to the floor, making a discordant clatter. This brought Sherlock Holmes and Dr West immediately.

"How are you feeling, old man?" asked Holmes in a solicitous tone.

"Beastly," I replied frankly, my cough returning, but without its former violence.

"You look all in," agreed Holmes, nodding.

Dr West had been a silent witness to this brief exchange, but now he spoke.

"You succumbed more rapidly than I expected," he said rather clinically. "It was difficult to determine when to inject you, but evidently my timing was impeccable."

To which Holmes added, with a trace of competitive spirit, "I hasten to add that I was consulted in the matter of timing, and my will ultimately prevailed."

A flash of something like anger crossed Dr West's pale features, but he held his quick tongue.

"What matters is that you have been preserved from one of the most lethal scourges ever to strike mankind," said Holmes.

I struggled with my words, my brain rather fagged from my ordeal. "Did I...expire?"

Sherlock Holmes and Dr West exchanged acute glances, neither man seemed willing to offer a firm opinion.

Instead, Holmes asked, rather pointedly I thought, "What do you recall of your most recent slumber?"

I had not given the matter any thought heretofore, as I readily admitted. Searching my memories, I offered, "I recall vaguely strangling in my sleep, then a warm blackness, followed by the most inchoate dreams."

"These dreams," probed Holmes. "Kindly enlighten us as to their exact nature."

I struggled to assemble my words. "They were rather kaleidoscopic, and I can derive very little meaning from them, except that I felt as if I was wandering through what might best be described as a maze composed of my own past recollections. My entire life, as it were, began unreeling before my eyes as though a motion picture were playing haphazardly."

"I see," mused Holmes. He grew very thoughtful of countenance.

Dr West regarded him speculatively. "Dr Watson may well have been reliving his life on earth, which he now remembers imperfectly, owing to his difficult translation from this world to the next and then back again."

"Both are rank speculation," retorted Holmes. "The facts as presented to us do not perfectly fit your theory as broached."

"They do not contradict it!" retorted the American, rather forcefully for a guest in another man's home, I thought.

After a pause, Holmes said reluctantly, "No, they do not precisely contradict it. They fit only in the manner that sackcloth fits a man's form—in a rather makeshift way."

"I do not see Watson's dream memories as cheap sackcloth," countered West rather darkly. "Perhaps as a shroud, which I have helped him cast off."

"Perhaps," allowed Holmes. "Perhaps."

I did not personally care for the trend of this conversation, and made to sit up on the edge of the bed, asking in the most polite tone I could muster, "Would a spot of tea be too much to ask for a man who has been brought back from the brink of eternity?"

This seemed to snap the two intellects out of their verbal conflict, for Holmes immediately called down for tea, as well as toast and eggs.

I consumed this unsurpassed breakfast in my bed, as a wolf might devour the chicken. Sherlock Holmes and Dr West left me to my repast, and were gone over an hour. Their arguing voices beat against the closed bedroom door, but I could make out none of it.

When the two men returned, they gave me a thorough examination, with Dr West taking the part of the attending physician, and Sherlock Holmes that of a clinician studying a rare case. They traded observations, contradicted one another at different points, agreed on others, and came away of one mind.

"Watson, I congratulate you," said Sherlock Holmes. "For you may be the first human being in history to recover from the ravages of the Spanish influenza in its latter, terminal stages."

I pushed away my plate, and asked in the spirit of honesty, "Are these laurels truly deserved, or do I have others to thank for my resurrection?"

Dr West seemed on the point of claiming full credit when Sherlock Holmes murmured, "Whenever a patient recovers from an illness, his attending physician must be credited. Yet his own vitality cannot be dismissed from consideration. There is no doubt the Dr West's alkaloid solution played an immeasurable role in arresting your mortal dissolution. But even at your age, your robust physique cannot be dismissed out of hand."

Turning to West, he added solicitously, "Do you not agree, Dr West?"

"I do not disagree," snapped the other, refusing to surrender the point entirely.

"The question as to whether Watson has been truly resurrected or merely reanimated at the brink of his last breath remains an open one, then," murmured Holmes.

Dr West said nothing, but his face fumed to the point that I feared that his smouldering blue eyes might ignite. But they did not. Nor did his obvious temper.

With that, the discussion wandered into fresh and frightening territory. To my utter astonishment, it was Sherlock Holmes who opened up the Pandora's box of the subject unspoken.

"Dr West, as I recall yesterday you made me a proposition."

"I did," returned West.

"Are you still game to go through with the test?"

"Are you up to the challenge?" countered West.

"I do not know that I am up or down," remarked Holmes coolly, "only that I am intrigued by the possibilities."

At this point, I was forced to interject, "Whatever are two of you rattling on about?"

Holmes gave me a thin smile, saying, "Do you not recall Dr West's kind offer to resurrect me upon my demise, Watson?"

It all came rushing back to me. The sheer audaciousness would have been difficult to forget. I can only ascribe my failure of memory to my overnight ordeal.

"Good heavens, Holmes!" I cried aloud, sitting up sharply. "You do not mean to entertain this man's offer of a scientific resurrection?"

Holmes had again dug out his pipe, and was puffing away at it. His eyebrows hooded his grey orbs like those of a hawk frowning down upon prey. At length, Sherlock Holmes uttered these unforgettable words. "I fear I am coming to the end of my days; the usefulness of this body is growing thin. Yet for all that, my mind balks at the thought of being extinguished like a common candle. Still, I must face up to facts. I am mortal, as much as any other man."

A thin smile crossed the delicate features of Dr West. I knew from the weird light in his eyes that he had Holmes under his scientific sorcerer's spell. There was nothing I could do about it. Holmes was a man of mental activity. That his body was slowly succumbing to the ravages of age was undeniable. That his brain remained lucid in the face of advancing years was also beyond doubt. I did not often peer into the man's mind, despite its crystalline clarity. But in that moment, I knew what Sherlock Holmes was thinking. He was a solver of many mysteries. Uncounted crimes had been laid at his table. And he unravelled virtually all. Had age not overtaken him, Holmes would still be about that business. For its fascinations, its appeal to his thirst for intellectual variety, and the manner in which puzzles seized upon his mental machinery, had been his meat and drink. Alas, after a lifetime of such pursuits, he had had more than his fill. His appetite for novelty, as it were, was off.

To Holmes, only one compelling mystery remained. The riddle of death. The fate of consciousness. The chance, however remote to his way of thinking, of an afterlife. More to the point, Sherlock Holmes was pondering the possibility that while his body would ultimately fail, his mind might persist in some other vessel, or perhaps no vessel at all.

Standing at the edge of his mortal span, the great Sherlock Holmes keenly wished to know what lay beyond this earthly vale. More than that, he desired to bring that knowledge back to the earth, as if to show mankind one final time that Sherlock Holmes was the greatest the solver of conundrums the world had ever known.

All this I understood in a flash briefer than a watch-tick.

"Holmes!" I implored. "This is madness! You cannot subject yourself to this inhuman monster's experimentations! I forbid it!"

Dr West favoured me with his jaundiced eye, but Sherlock Holmes looked upon me with a mixture of sympathy and dark humor.

"I daresay I should be the final judge and arbiter of my own fate," said Holmes dryly. "Do you not agree, Dr Watson? Should not every man, or any man, be the ultimate decider of such business?"

"Under ordinary circumstances, of course I would be in complete agreement with you. But you have life yet within you, Holmes, and your years may yet number a score or so."

"Perhaps," allowed Holmes. "But there is something else, a singular fact which you do not yet know."

"And what is that?" I demanded.

"That I am, and have been suffering for the last several months, from a rather difficult progressive disease. My days are numbered, not in years, nor necessarily in months, but in actual fact, mere weeks are left to me."

"Say this is not so!"

"Alas, it is so. And Dr West was good enough to diagnose my present situation, and agrees with my own personal physician. I spared you this awful knowledge, for I knew you were busy with your medical duties at this terrible time. I did not want you wasting a shred of thought or regret on my inevitable fate."

I was struck speechless. My mouth worked, but it was filled with dryness, my throat parched by emotion while the tongue in my head felt like an alien organ placed there by some mad surgeon—something not even my own.

My stricken gaze went back from the faces of these two singular men who had discovered common cause, despite the very different paths they had walked in life. I knew that a solemn compact been made, and once made, brave Holmes would see through to its conclusion, regardless of consequences.

Thus, I had no other choice but to surrender to his decision.

There in the room where I had expired—or nearly expired and returned from wherever I had returned from—the three of us entered into a rather grim understanding.

We would remain with Sherlock Holmes until the end came, and then we would attend to his transition, and if practicable, his resurrection. During that period, Holmes would apply his considerable knowledge of chemistry and botany to the problem of perfecting Dr West's unique serum—it having been agreed by all that the dose which had plucked me from the certain jaws of death was not necessarily efficacious in all cases and circumstances.

Over dinner, the conversation was restrained and limited to the calamitous events that had seized the world. Holmes continued to insist that absolute victory for the Allies was near, and a matter of a few months. No more. I did not doubt him.

Then, over apple pie, Holmes turned to Dr West and remarked, "Your arrival was timely indeed."

"Fateful, at any rate," concurred West, somehow implying that the mechanisms of Fate were definitely aligned to his fortunes and no other's.

I laid down my fork, suddenly losing my appetite in the face of the morbid trend of the dinner talk.

Holmes remarked suddenly, "I keep bees, Dr West. Do you know that the properties of raw honey have a peculiar restorative quality?"

West blinked behind his spectacles. "I confess I do not," he admitted.

"My thinking is that we might apply some of my apiary knowledge to the problem of your reanimating mixture. Are you familiar with the substance known as royal jelly?"

West's blue eyes took on a distinctly intrigued quality.

"I see that you are," continued Holmes. "I have long been fascinated by this singular secretion of the honey bee. It is packed with nutrients, and so powerful that when fed to a common bee larva, it transforms the specimen into a queen, thereby insuring the continuation of the hive. All of that may already belong to your storehouse of knowledge. But consider this: certain experiments have shown conclusively that the introduction of the royal jelly nutrients stimulate the growth of *glia* cells of the brain."

A flash of light came into West's eager eyes.

"You are suggesting, Mr Holmes, that my revivified subjects have failed to thrive owing to deficiencies in their brain matter?"

"I do," admitted Holmes. "As you are well aware, Dr West, the brain is the first organ to putrefy at death. If that highest of organs can be fed the proper nutrients via your serum, this decay might be reversed, and the deceased may well be persuaded to remain among the living far longer than your previous experiments have thus far permitted."

I failed to follow it all, but Holmes had the man spellbound, as it were.

We stayed only five days in the farmhouse of Sherlock Holmes—five days in which I watched the singular man fade away. As if given the sublime opportunity to match his wits against the unknown, he at last willingly released his hold on life.

All during that difficult passage, Holmes directed Dr West to reformulate his dubious elixir of life time and again, displaying a chemical knowledge that deeply impressed the American experimenter, for Sherlock Holmes, once he had grasped the essential alkaloid formulation, seemed to comprehend it as fully as its creator, and readily identified the weaknesses in its composition. In truth, he had already done so, for both men seemed satisfied by the introduction of a solution of royal jelly into the mixture.

Much of it was, frankly, beyond me. But the confidence with which the two intellectual giants spoke of the new formulation gave me faint hope.

By the fourth day, Sherlock Homes was bedridden. There were few outward symptoms of his condition, only a deeper greyness descending over the pale parchment of his face.

By the morning of the fifth day, the end was near. A persistent rattling emanating from Holmes' throat told me so. I did what I could, saw that the wasting man was kept well hydrated, but Holmes refused all other nourishment, and his eyes became heavy of lid while his face grew rather spectral and carven, as if composed of bone covered in parchment.

The stark aspect of the man I once revered grew unpleasant

beyond endurance. But I thrust my personal feelings aside, and administrated to him as best I could.

Dr West took little part in this routine. As before, his interest appeared less about making a sick man well as it was in plumbing the depths of dissolution in the mortal destruction of flesh and bone.

Holmes began slipping away at the noon hour, which I thought rather odd. He seemed more the type to pass in the night. Perhaps this was due to his often nocturnal habits. But when midday struck, my friend began to fade.

I called Dr West to the room urgently.

The American physician had prepared a fresh vial and hypodermic needle and was prepared to do what he had come to do. I thought again how the Fates had conspired to bring these two men together at this dreadful hour, and it seemed to me that the universe showed a greater intelligence and careful planning than men of science gave it credit.

As the dying man began to breathe his last, Dr West charged the needle, then drove it straight into Holmes' heart.

I was shocked by the feral manner in which he did this. It was as if the doctor were mad, and was attempting to destroy life, not protract it.

Wheezing, Sherlock Holmes gave a convulsive jerk; his fingers began fluttering, features now grey and sere, if already interred.

West stepped back while I plunged in, seizing Holmes' wrist, groping for the thready pulse, watching his thin nostrils for signs of the resumption of respiration.

Timing his pulse by my watch, I began to despair. Then, suddenly I felt a surge pass through that lank body, and the dying pulse began to hammer and hammer as though adrenaline had been introduced into the heart.

Suddenly, Sherlock Holmes sat straight up, grey eyes flying open, strange gleams in their cloudy depths.

His magnificent head swivelled about the room, and it seemed as though his brain was groping for understanding. I was reminded of the poor wretch who had cried out "Where am I?" in that brief period when he was neither man nor corpse.

I snapped my fingers in Holmes's face, trying to bring him out of his apparent daze."Holmes!" I called out to him. Seizing shoulders, I shook him. "Holmes, you have come back from the brink of eternity! What have you to say?"

A light leapt into Sherlock Holmes's eyes, and a calmness came over his agitated face. He looked to Herbert West, and lips like parchment seemed to compress into a smile. "Congratulations, Dr West. Apparently success is yours. You have my unbounded admiration."

"But, Holmes," I cried. "Tell us what you saw when you were no longer present on this earth."

Sherlock Holmes was a long time in replying. Perhaps he groped for the words. Possibly his mind needed time to sort out the thought impressions that had been placed into it during his celestial interregnum.

Nodding to Dr West, he turned his dreamy grey gaze to me, and spoke these words."The universe is like a great, unfathomable machine. And we mortals are but tiny gears in that immense mechanism. When we break down, the engine of eternity continues to grind on—but not without us. For, when a solitary gear loses its teeth and ceases to function in the mighty engine of the All, it perforce finds new expression through and in other forms..."

Holmes paused. His words struck me with great force, even though I was not sure what to make of them.

"Did you see the Almighty?" I pressed eagerly.

But Holmes failed to offer any response on that critical point. Instead, he murmured, "My gratitude to you, Dr West, for this grand opportunity, and to my good friend, Watson, for enabling me to plumb successfully this final enigma. Having done this, I see no further reason to persist as a corroded and toothless old gear in an infinite construct that constantly replaces and replenishes its own mechanistic parts. Thus, I insist upon going forward into my new form—the present one having served me admirably during my allotted lifespan. Thank you again."

With that, Sherlock Holmes closed his eyes and fell back upon the pillow, expiring for a second and final time. The expression on his features, haggard as they were, was one of supernal peace and contentment.

I stood awestruck in that moment, my mind a mad whirl.

I turned to Dr West for understanding, but the American had taken himself and his monstrous past out of the farmhouse and into the astringent sunlight, apparently crushed by yet another failure of his fiendish aims.

I never saw him again. I never wished to. West was charged as a common deserter, but never found. One imagines he made his secretive way back to the United States, where he continued his ghastly career.

As for me, although my own years now grow short, I think often of the final words of Sherlock Holmes, and ponder their existential meaning. That he had stared into eternity and carried back a shred of understanding seemed to me beyond all doubt. But the words Holmes had employed to convey his insights were insufficient to the task. I imagine that whatever visions he perceived in his mind's eye, they belong to the category that more learned men than I call the *ineffable*.

That said, I look forward to the day that I see my close friend again in whatever far vistas he sought, and is presumably now exploring to the full extent of his unsurpassed ability...

The Angel of Truth

I. A. WATSON

I

"Jane…I need you."

My heart lurched. It was a long time since Dr John Dee had said that to me.

I blinked sleep out of my eyes and peered across my bedchamber. My scholarly husband stood in the doorway, candlestick in hand, but he was not undressed for bed. Nor did his eye gleam with desire, or even droop with wine-lust. His face was pale beneath its greying beard. He looked scared.

I sat up quickly. "What's wrong? The children…?"

"Sleeping in peace," my husband assured me. "I…need you in my workshop, Jane."

I shuddered. It was nearly two years since I'd last heard those words from him. Those words had preceded the effective end of our marriage.

Yet I'd seldom seen John so white with fear as he was now; certainly not since that last shattering night in damned Trebona.[1] His hand trembled, quivering the candle to send crazy shadows

---

1. Dr Dee, his associate Edward Kelley, and their wives visited Třeboň, German Wittingau, in southern Bohemia in what is now the Czech Republic, intermittently from 1556-1559. Dee recorded the alchemical experiments and séances they undertook there in his diary — and their eventual conclusion.

spidering across the rafters.

I glanced across at the cot-bed where month-old Madina slumbered. The other children slept in a nursery under the attic eaves.[2] I looked back at John. I tried to keep my voice steady. "What must I do?"

He heard the tremor. "Nothing like that," he frowned. We never now discuss my part in his former experiments. "It is—Jane, I have *succeeded!*"

"Succeeded at what?" I began, but some nuance of expression in his face warned me of his meaning. "You mean you have *found* one? *Brought* one?"

My husband nodded. "At last. In greatest need. Perhaps that was what was lacking before—need. Need most dire!"

I misunderstood him then. I thought he referred to our reduced straits, near-bankrupt after our long sojourn overseas, returned four months since to a house burned and plundered by the ignorant and the jealous who thought Dr John Dee a sorcerer or necromancer. I even dared hope he was speaking of the parlous state of our marital relationship, so sundered that we merely staggered through the motions of matrimony. I did not yet know of the darker problem with which he wrestled.

His beard was matted, I noticed irrelevantly, and his garments were creased with many hours of uninterrupted labour. I reviewed when I had last seen John, and wondered that a time had come when his three days' absence from our board could pass without my notice.

"You're saying—claiming—that your experiments have worked?" I clarified. "That you have summoned…"

"An angel," John insisted. "I have summoned the Angel of Truth."

He swallowed hard. So even my brilliant husband had doubted whether his rites and calculations would ever bear fruit.

John pressed a night-robe at me. "Hasten. There isn't time for…for anything! He is come—*it* is come—but who knows how long the bindings will hold? I need your aid, to shore up the

---

2 This detail indicates a narrative date of early April 1590, since Jane's second daughter Madina was christened on 5th March of that year. Jane's older children at that time were Arthur, Katherine, Rowland, Michael, and Theodore.

circle, to take notes as I question the being. Please, Jane…I really do need you. Please?"

As long as it was since John had come to my bed, how much longer since he had allowed me at his work? Perhaps he wouldn't have called upon me now had not our fallen circumstances robbed him of all other assistance.

I almost turned him down. Bitter words rose at the back of my throat. And yet—an angel! And John, shocked and vulnerable as I had not seen him for so long. John, needing me.

I dragged the robe over my shift. "Show me your angel."

John led down the narrow staircase to his workroom. A complicated chalk circle etched with seven names of God warded the door. The threshold was scattered with salt.

"John, these are serious precautions for an angel."

My husband winced. "We are beyond what we know here, Jane. Beyond aught I have achieved, even with…" He fell silent. He would not name his former associate in my presence. "What is in that room, inside a diagram of conjuration, is far from anything in our experience. Every precaution is necessary."

He did not mention his old experiments in an Essex graveyard, nor the Reichstein scryings in which he had involved our son, Arthur. He would never remind me of the Uriel rites in Trebona. He did not need to. I knew how seriously he took precautions in his conjurations. I knew what happened when those precautions failed.

"He may try to escape," John warned me. "He may seek to beguile you to breach the circle that confines him. Remember that he is more than he seems. His mind is not as ours. He is dangerous."

I wanted to protest. Had John learned nothing? To bring such an entity into our home, where our children lay sleeping? To leash such a thing behind some flimsy line of chalk and salts?

My husband must have seen the criticism in my scowl. "There's good reason for this risk, Jane. I swear it. There are… matters of state, of high policy. Matters concerning the fate of nations."

I recalled the stream of visitors we had received these past bleak months at Mortlake. I had naively assumed that they were well-wishers, greeting our long-delayed return to England, perhaps bringing comfort and assistance in our reduced straits. I should have known that privy secretary Sir Francis Walsingham, England's spymaster,[3] would never call on the Queen's astrologer from mere courtesy.

"What matters?" I asked John.

He shook his head. "No time now for that. We must enter my workshop and reinforce the bindings. Paint an outer ring with tincture of hyssop, whispering the Paternoster—Greek, not Latin. Beware answering the creature's questions. Do not tell him your name."

We paused at the threshold. "An Angel of Truth, you said."

"Yes. And do we not know, Jane, that there are some truths which must be feared?"

He had the right of it. I nodded. He clasped my hand—his touch was cold and unfamiliar, a stranger's grip. He unlocked his workroom door.

There was light within. Five lanterns were positioned at the points of the pentacle drawn in the centre of the floor. A diagram was inscribed in careful detail across the polished oak, like the sigil upon the portal but much more complicated. Supplementary lines etched out to five smaller circles, each containing a small dish, variously filled with water, incense, flame, iron, and coal. John had bound his guest with the five elements and the secret names of the Creator.

I gasped. Right until then I had not really believed. A delusion, it might have been; John was well able to fool himself into believing his results more than they really were. Or a trick, to lure me back to his experiments and more vile degradation. But there, inside the magic circle on a high-backed wing-chair, sat a

3 Walsingham's titles do not immediately indicate the power this political insider possessed. As Privy Secretary he set the agenda for the Queen's Privy Council, her most intimate circle of advisors. He was also referred to as Secretary of State, in an era long before there was a role of Prime Minister. Walsingham effectively set the nation's foreign and domestic policies and ran its civil service. He was instrumental in thwarting several plots to displace or kill Queen Elizabeth I. It was his support that sent Sir Francis Drake on his circumnavigation of the globe. He was probably the driving force behind the 1586 entrapment for treason and subsequent execution of Elizabeth's Catholic cousin, Mary, Queen of Scots.

creature unlike any I had seen.

He seemed almost human. Tall he was, a head higher than most men, thin faced with sharp cheekbones, a hawk-hooked nose, hair drawn back revealing widow's peaks. His eyes glittered in the lantern-light, sharper and cleverer than anything I had ever seen in mortal man.

He stirred as we entered, looking up from a contemplation of his long, delicate hands. His fingertips were pressed together, but it did not look like prayer.

He spoke. "Good evening," he bade us, "Doctor John Dee. And..." Those narrowed piercing eyes ran over me, "...Mistress Jane Fromond Dee."

John gasped. "An Angel of Truth," he breathed. "I did not tell him..."

The Angel tutted. "Come, come. If I'm to be plagued with hallucinations, at least allow that my deeper mind will provide me with signs and hints as to what vision I am to experience."

John's hand still gripped mine. It tightened as the Angel spoke. The creature's voice was deep, masculine, cultured. A scholar's speech, yet without deference or humility. A cold voice, devoid of emotion or humanity.

The Angel gestured around the workshop. "Construction, décor, and furnishings bespeak of sixteenth century, yet the items here are not of three hundred years vintage but new. The smell, I may note, is particularly authentic; and the stench, some dried clay upon that matting, and certain sounds beyond your house, suggest a Surrey location close to the Thames. The clutter of your study indicates travel and scholarly endeavour. I perceive you have lately visited the Continent—Nuremburg, Frankfurt, Prague, Cracow and elsewhere. The volumes on your desk..."

John looked to the content on his table. A new-printed copy of Hariot's *a briefe and true report of the new found land of Virginia* lay there, carefully bookmarked where John had reached in his studies.

The Angel made a wide gesture with those artistic fingers. "Those calculations on the chalk-board refer to a revision of the calendar in line with Gregorian principles, making use of the controversial Copernican theories of your correspondent Tycho Brahe. That partially-assembled device on the tool-bench is a replacement sea compass for one recently looted from this study during your European absence."

His gaze fixed upon my husband. John shied back a step.

The spirit leaned forwards. "Your hands display the callosities of a constant writer, a scholar given to using a goose-quill judging by the ink-spots on your cuff. Old acid burns on the backs of your hands suggest a practical chemist. Your dentistry and complexion speak of primitive medical practices. In short, my delusion insists that you are John Dee, Elizabethan mathematician, navigator, astronomer and alchemist. Fascinating."

John gestured for me to begin my work reinforcing the circle. He picked up his hickory stave, to command the Angel if he could. "You know much that no mortal could," he told the spirit, "but I charge thee now to speak thy name!"

"Holmes," the Angel replied, without hesitation or chagrin. "William Sherlock Scott Holmes."[4]

"Homes?" John puzzled. No book I had ever seen, nor any of my husband's reading judging by his expression, chronicled an entity of such a name. And there had once been many volumes of angel-lore on the shelves of Mortlake, before our house had been plundered in our absence and damaged by fire. It was not only our personal relationship that was wrecked and gutted on our return to England.

"Sherlock Holmes," the Angel corrected us. "From the Old English *holm* and the Norse *holmr*, meaning holly tree. But this is irrelevant. I note from your easel that you are studying a manuscript which I have seen before—or later, might perhaps be a more accurate tense."

The spirit directed our attention to the vellum codex that John had left open on his writing slope. I had not seen this document before, but was amazed and enthralled by it. A fold-out triple page was rendered with beautiful depictions of plants and

---

4 At no time in the Canon does Watson or Doyle record Holmes's full name. The information is revealed in W.S. Baring-Gould's definitive 1962 biography, *Sherlock Holmes*.

animals, accompanying a text in some coded language that I did not recognise.[5]

John's brows rose even further. "You...know this tome? I have only recently acquired it. It is said to be the work of Roger Bacon."[6]

"I am intimately acquainted with it, my dear doctor," the Angel replied. "Indeed, I suspect it to be the primary and immediate cause of my remarkable current delusion."

John brandished his hickory wand. "I charge you, explain!"

"I was retained by representatives of the Society of Jesus from the Villa Mondragone at Frascati, Italy.[7] This document had been extracted from their archive. They believed the thief had brought it to London, and therefore sought out my assistance in recovering the codex. This I did—the problem was elementary. Having recovered the tome I naturally inspected it in my Montague Street chambers[8] to verify that it was the stolen item and to study the remarkable cypher it employed."

John looked uncertainly at the thick volume with its narrow

---

5 Jane describes here what would be known in modern times as the Voynich Manuscript, a mysterious tome "discovered" in 1912 by book dealer William Voynich. He claimed to have purchased the volume in a lot of books sold by the Jesuits from their great Collegio Romano library at Villa Mondragone. Carbon dating has placed the book's paper to the fourteenth century but doubt remains as to whether the content is authentic or a brilliant hoax. An accompanying letter claims its provenance from Holy Roman Emperor Rudolf II (1552-1612) then through the hands of Johannes Marcus and Athansius Kircher. Tradition has attributed the coded—or nonsense—volume to Roger Bacon (see footnote 6), with Dee selling the book on to Rudolf. The manuscript is now in the care of Yale University. Reproductions of it are available online.

6 Roger Bacon (1214-1294), English philosopher and Franciscan friar, was accorded the title of Doctor Mirabilis—marvellous teacher—for his erudition and research. His 840-page *Opus Majus* covers optics, mathematics, alchemy, and astronomy. He may have been the first European to describe gunpowder. As with many middle ages scholars, he was also popularly attributed with occult learning and magical powers.

7 The Jesuits' distinctive, historical, and beautiful headquarters outside Rome housed their greatest library. The former papal residence was sold in 1981 and is now part of the University of Rome Tor Vergata.

8 Holmes's move to his more famous Baker Street address depended upon him finding some flat-mate with whom to share the cost.

strange-charactered script. "You...decoded this?"

The Angel looked rueful. "I had scarcely begun when what I assume was some fungal toxin dusted onto the sheets took its effect and triggered this remarkable sensory delusion. I posit an interaction with other chemical agents which I have utilised of late to direct and divert my cognitive capacities. A fourteen percent solution of...[9] No matter. It seems the most rational response to my hallucination to treat it as real until my mind resolves itself to conventional reality once more."

I did not understand Holmes's words, though he spoke them as if they had sense and meaning. I am not sure even John followed, though his is the most acute mind I have ever known.

"I am John Dee," my husband admitted to the spirit in the circle. "Late of John's College Cambridge and the University of Louvain, Fellow and Under-Reader at Trinity, Dean of Gloucester, Freeman of the Mercers' Company..."

"Yes, yes," the Angel interjected. "I am somewhat familiar with you and your work. *Mathematicall Praeface to The Elements of Geometry of Euclid of Megara* laid down some basic principles of calculation. *General and Rare Memorials Pertayning to the Perfect Art of Navigation* pioneered some excellent practical applications of science and mathematics. I was not so impressed with *Parallaticae commentationis praxeosque nucleus quidam* — too much superstitious astrological nonsense without clear evidence."

John frowned. "The work was well received in several European courts. Prince Laski, King Stephen Batory, Emperor Rudolph himself..."

"There will always be fools to admire foolish unsupported theories," Holmes snapped. "Your *Heparchia Mystica* - On the Mystical Rule of the Seven Planets — was confounded nonsense.[10] Your Paradoxal Compass, however, was an admirable advance

---

9 In the Canon, Watson chronicles Holmes's occasional use of a seven percent solution of cocaine, then a legal drug. This is quite a mild dose. A fourteen percent solution used by a Watsonless Holmes bespeaks of a more serious addiction.

10 This work, written "under the guidance of the angel Uriel" from a series of séances in 1582-3, contains diagrams and instructions for the summoning of spirits.

in polar navigation. You should have refined your studies to the geo-mathematical and astronomical, where they would have been much admired."

John advanced as if to remonstrate with the Angel's brutal critique. I caught my husband's shoulder. "He goads you to cross the circle, John."

The spirit mused for a moment. "An occasional correspondent of mine even dedicated his volume *The Dynamics of an Asteroid* to you."[11]

"He is testing you, John," I warned.

My husband looked closely at the gaunt figure that regarded him across the enchanted circle. "Not testing me," John reasoned. "He is reading me, as a man might read a text. See how he scans the room, every book and paper, every instrument, missing nothing. If he provokes me it is to observe my reactions and learn from them."

"Most perspicacious," the Angel of Truth remarked. "However... our encounter, ephemeral as it might be, is clearly for some purpose. If one follows the logic of the situation as it presents itself, you have gone to remarkable lengths to obtain a consultation on some problem that perturbs and perplexes you, doctor."

John raised his stave again. "Yes. I charge and conjure thee, Angel of Truth, to answer fully and freely in revealing the plot aimed against Her Majesty, Queen Elizabeth."

The spirit snorted. "You don't require an Angel of Truth, then, Dr Dee. You require an Angel of Detection." He seemed amused.

I turned to John. "What's this? There is some conspiracy afoot against the queen? Is that why Walsingham came to Mortlake of late?"

There was a time when I would have recognised my husband's intense concern at some intractable problem. There was a day when he would have told me about it. Even now he looked a little shamefaced. "Walsingham came to me in confidence, to see if I could explain..." He paused, unsure how much he should tell me.

---

11 This would be the scholarly and controversial work published by Professor James Moriarty, "a book which ascends to such rarefied heights of pure mathematics that it is said that there was no man in the scientific press capable of criticizing it."

Holmes sat back in his chair, leaning on one arm to cradle his long forehead. "If I am to be presented with a case, Dr Dee, pray use that well-regarded intellect and impart the information as precisely and cogently as you are able. Spare no detail but include no editorial. Above all, let your account be interesting. Begin."

John looked at me. "You will record the conversation, Jane? Make notes as you used to?"

I stuffed down my first responses and assented. Most people assumed that it was for my looks that the widowed and eminent scholar had wedded a wife twenty-eight years his younger. I always suspected it was because I was literate and could record his experiments as he made them.

The Angel settled back in his chair, folding his hands on his lap and giving John his full attention.

My husband began. "This matter was brought to me by Sir Francis Walsingham, Secretary of the Queen's Privy Council. It is a matter of national security." He reached for a small wooden case and hinged it open to show Holmes the contents. "On Christmas Day, one of these ornamental pins was discovered in Her Majesty's clothing, threaded into the fabric of her day gown."

I craned to look into the box. On a padded cushion lay six straight silver pins, three inches long with ornate moulded heads. They were the kind of fashion accessory that a lady might use to fasten hair, scarf, or veil.

"Little was thought of it," John went on, "until the first day of January, when a second was similarly discovered. That evinced some concern, for none were seen close by the queen to thread such a pin into her mantle. Indeed, one who was close enough to slide the pin into her dress was surely close enough to slide a dagger into her back."

I could see why Sir Francis, always Elizabeth's first protector, might be alarmed.

"A third pin appeared on Twelfth Night,[12] but this time on her

12 The 6th of January, the twelfth night after Christmas, was the end of medieval Christmas revels, remembered now in vestige as the date by which trimmings and trees should be cleared away.

majesty's night-gown. Her Majesty's lady-in-waiting, Lady Elsbet FitzHammond, was closely questioned but would not confess to planting it. Lady Elsbet is rumoured to have been a mistress of disgraced Sir Francis Drake.[13] In any case, she was removed from her position."

"Who undertook these investigations?" demanded the Angel.

"Walsingham himself, assisted by some gentlemen of the court. Depositions were taken, witnesses of high degree. Many were…"

Holmes waved John on. "The other pins?"

"This fourth on February 1st, discovered by Her Majesty's new lady in waiting, Jenet Hastings, when she disrobed the queen at night. It was threaded into some concealed undergarment, where none could possibly have placed it. The fifth appeared on March 16th on Elizabeth's pillow, stitched there as she slept. You will imagine that the sovereign of England is well guarded in these times of Papist plot, and yet…"

"Who discovered this pin?" the Angel interrupted.

"Her Majesty herself. It was the first thing she saw when she awoke. There was a considerable stir."

"I imagine so," I interjected. A shudder ran through me.

John saved the most spine-tingling event for last. "This sixth object was discovered only two weeks ago, on Lady Day…[14] in her majesty's hair!"

"Detail," insisted our consulting spirit.

"Coming out of chapel, the item was noticed by William Cecil,

---

13 Drake (c1540-1596) was the archetypal English privateer explorer, second man to circumnavigate the world, wanted pirate to the Spanish fleet, second in command of the English force that had broken the invading Spanish Armada, and general swashbuckler. King Philip II of Spain placed a bounty on his head of 20,000 ducats — US$6.5m in modern money. Drake fell out of favour in 1589 when his mission to Lisbon to follow-up the English triumph over the Spanish Armada went wrong, costing 12,000 English lives and 20 English ships.

14 March 25th, one of the old English "quarter days" on which rents and taxes were due and wages were paid. The other quarter days were Midsummer's Day (24th June), Michaelmas (29th September), and Christmas Day. March 25th converts to April 6th under the current Gregorian calendar, and that revised date still marks the beginning of the British tax year.

Baron Burleigh himself, the Lord High Treasurer of England. Good Queen Bess[15] was much alarmed. As you can imagine there had by then been much gossip and speculation about the appearance of these talismans."

"Cries of witchcraft," I supposed.

"Most certainly, and of Papal devilry. Many observed that witches stab pins into poppet dolls to work malice on their enemies. Some hold it to be a work of vengeance for the execution of Scots Mary[16] - or even divine judgement for it. Accusations abound. A dozen great men have been arrested, questioned, their estates seized."

"Indeed," muttered the Angel. "And you, Dr Dee, do you attribute these pins and their appearance to some supernatural agency?"

John paused. He smoothed his beard as he often did when thinking. "I am loath to resort to crying deviltry until I have exhausted the possibilities of human agency. I have read the depositions that Walsingham took. There are still possibilities for mortal intervention. However, mundane or mystical, if the queen is in danger then nothing must be stinted to save her." He gestured to the circle where the remarkable creature he'd conjured listened to his account.

Holmes held out his hand for the pins. My husband shook his head. "Do you think me a novice, that I will break the binding circle? Make your observations from there, Holmes. I charge thee!"

The Angel growled. "Have you tested the pins? Analysed their composition, the silver content therein? Are all of them of the same minting, or are some created separately from others? What of the heads, those ornately carved decorations, each

15 A colloquial term for Elizabeth I.

16 Mary Stuart, (1542-1587) Queen of Scots and dowager Queen of France, was Elizabeth's first cousin once removed and had a strong claim on the English throne. Elizabeth kept her imprisoned for eighteen years before Walsingham's entrapment garnered enough evidence to compel her execution. Baron Burleigh later criticised the Queen very strongly for allowing Mary's death. Mary's son became King James IV of Scotland and succeeded Elizabeth I to also become James I of England and Wales, uniting the kingdoms into Great Britain.

slightly different from the rest? Under a lens it might be possible to discern any meaning those imprints bears." He glared at John. "You can either be a sorcerer or a scientist, Dee. In this matter you cannot be both!"

A great hammering at our outer door interrupted John's answer. The thumps made us both jump. "Who could that be at this time of night?" I asked, trying to keep my voice calm. Had the ignorant fools who had broken in and wrecked John's workshop in our absence returned to finish us, too? Or did soldiers bear some arrest warrant to drag John away for diablerie or too-close association with Catholic scholars in Europe?

"Stay here," John instructed, passing me the hickory wand. He set the box of pins down beside the Bacon manuscript. "Keep watch." He hastened out of the room to attend the urgent knocking.

I turned back to guard the Angel—but he was gone from his chair!

Holmes was out of the circle. He had stridden across it to pick up the pin casket. Now the Angel was examining the items with a tiny lens from his pocket.

I raised the hickory stick faintly. A spirit escaped its bonds can be cruel and dangerous. I knew that to my cost. Memories of that night in Trebona—when Uriel and Madimi had entered Kelley and convinced John that Kelley should lay with me—set me trembling again.[17]

"Your husband loves you," the Angel told me, absently. He continued his inspection of the pins as he spoke. "It is evident from your body language that the two of you have been distant of late, since well before the birth of your recent child. Your glances around this workshop indicate that you have been excluded from this place since your return to England. Your reaction to my simple perambulation across a scribble of chalk suggests some disturbing experience with Dr Dee's previous researches. I

---

17 Dee's partnership with medium and alchemist—and convicted fraudster— Edward Kelley, ended abruptly shortly after Kelley relayed the spirit Madimi's command that the two men should lay with each other's wives. Dee records the "cross-matching" on 22nd May 1587; Jane's son Theodore was born nine months later.

assure you, madam, that I mean you and your spouse no harm, and that that your current estrangement is as avid a source of grief to him as to you."

"You...you know this?" I gasped.

"The signs are evident to any who will take the trouble to observe them." He laid a long hand on the illustrated page of Bacon's codex. "There is a subtle genius in this code. It requires certain modes of thought which predispose one to creative illusion. This is a most remarkable experience."

"If you will not harm us, will you help us?" I asked. "John is wise, and good, but not always worldly. He thinks Sir Francis Walsingham his friend, but Walsingham would sacrifice any man in service of the state. If John cannot solve this problem..."

"Sir Francis is first amongst those I must interview," Holmes declared.

"You...will assist? At what price?"

Holmes snorted. "The uniqueness of the experience pays for itself, Mistress Dee. The problem and context are sufficiently engaging to divert. And now, I suspect, comes a further complication."

He looked to the door as John returned. My husband was so pale and shocked that he did not even react to the spirit's escape. He clutched me and broke the news that had come so suddenly by urgent courier. "Walsingham...Walsingham is dead! He was discovered so in his bed—a silver pin pressed into his heart!"

I had not previously been to Hampton Court, that great cardinal's palace built by old Thomas Wolsey, stolen by Henry VIII, expanded to be the largest royal dwelling in England. At another time I would have thrilled at the barge-ride along tidal Thames, at our arrival through Anne Boleyn's gate—she was executed before the chambers prepared for her there were completed—at the great hall with its carved hammer-beam roof, at the sheer pomp and majesty and bustle and intrigue of Elizabeth's court, so well-remembered from my younger days at Windsor.[18]

John was familiar with the site. He paused in the inner court to point out to Holmes the astronomical clock that showed time of day, moon-phase, month, quarter-year, sun and star sign, and the state of the tide at London Bridge.[19] I was too concerned about the abrupt summons that had dragged us from Mortlake at dawn to take in the details.

We entered a royal palace in mourning for one of the queen's mainstays. Few could remember a time when Walsingham had not held a subtle and near-silent grip on the nation's governance. Yet already there were whispers, ambitions, changing allegiances, to fill the power void that Sir Francis' passing had left.

John and I were led into that court—and an Angel of Truth walked beside us!

Spirit Holmes might be, dragged by John's arts from some other place, but he strode as confidently as any man of mortal flesh, his odd quilted robe billowing behind him, his legs clad in cloth tubes over short boots, his shirt of odd design and material, stiff-collared and studded. His hands were rammed into capacious pockets.

Beyond the great hall were privy chambers, smaller but equally ornate. We were led to one such room where a dozen or more courtiers gathered round a table. The only one I recognised from scant acquaintance was sat in the tallest and most elaborate chair, at the centre of the huddle: William Cecil, Baron Burleigh himself.

The Lord High Treasurer looked up from the volume he'd been

---

18 Hampton Court remains one of the stateliest of all England's stately homes even today. Little of the complex as laid out by Cardinal Wolsey around 1514 or massively extended by Henry VIII from 1528 survives unchanged. The palace and grounds were thoroughly overhauled and rebuilt in the 1600s.

Anne Boleyn was the second wife of Henry VIII, for whom he broke England from the Catholic faith and instituted Protestant Anglicism. She was executed in 1536 on charges of adultery, incest, and witchcraft.

Hampton Court is now open to the public. A visit is recommended.

19 This massive 1540 timepiece, built into the gatehouse tower wall in what is now called the Clock Court, still functions. Its display of the tide's condition was a practical one at a time when most traffic to Hampton Court came by Thames; at low water there were dangerous rapids under the arches of London Bridge.

consulting as we entered. "Ah, Dee," he muttered. "And...?"

"My lord," John replied, "may I present my wife, Jane Fromond, formerly lady-in-waiting at court to Lady Howard of Effingham.[20] And this is my associate, Master Holmes of..."

"Mycroft," the Angel supplied.[21]

"I am consulting with him in my inquiries."

"Your *inquiries*," said Lord William. From what I'd glimpsed of him and heard back in my Windsor days he had always been a sour man. Years had not improved him, though his political stature had grown and grown. Surely it was he who would replace the late Sir Francis as Secretary of State.[22] If any had cause to celebrate Walsingham's death—or arrange it—then it was Baron Burleigh. "You are summoned here, Dee, to testify as to why Sir Francis Walsingham visited you some days ago."

My husband clutched the lapels of his court gown and addressed himself as if to a Star Chamber.[23] "Sir Francis has long been a patron of the sciences. On many occasions he referred some question to me, and found me to be of full use."

"He used you as a spy, you mean," one of the young men flanking Burleigh snorted.

"I am a loyal and patriotic Englishman," snapped John. "If

---

20 Lady Howard was wife to Lord Admiral Charles Howard, who had commanded the fleet that repelled the "invincible" Spanish Armada. She remained a good friend to Jane and her husband throughout their lives.

As a minor lady of court, Jane would have required royal assent to wed Dee, and Dee's diary describes his visit to court at Windsor at the end of November 1577 and several conferences with the queen and "Mr Secretary Walsingham", one of which must have broached the subject. Jane married Dee on 5th February 1578.

21 Again according to Baring-Gould, Holmes' birthplace in the North Riding of Yorkshire supplied the names of both Holmes's paternal uncle and his elder brother.

22 Cecil had actually already held the post from 1550-53 under King Edward VI.

23 Jane shows some political naiveté here. The Star Chamber was a court convened from the 15th century in the royal palace of Westminster, made up of privy councillors and common law judges. It took its name from the painted roof of the court-room, which represented a night sky so the accused could look up and consider his place in the universe. Tasked with trying those deemed too powerful for conventional courts, it met in secret without indictments or witnesses, relying upon written evidence alone.

I visit abroad, in company of kings, princes, and prelates, it behoves me to communicate any matter of national interest to the man entrusted with preserving our nation's security. It was in this vein that Sir Francis visited me at Mortlake a short time ago, to lay before me the problem of the silver pins."

"A sorcerer for sorcery," the youngster sneered.

"A scholar for a task not fitted to the ignorant," John barked. His glower quelled the bravo; perhaps the young toady had sought to please his master with his impertinence.

"That is a concern that has occupied much of our thought at court," the Lord High Treasurer admitted. "There have already been many accusations, some arrests, even duels over the matter. Superstition runs rife, and yet—when the Privy Secretary dies of such a tine to the heart, one begins to fear the devil's hand."

I noted the volume that the men were consulting. *De la Démonomanie des Sorciers* was French philosopher Jean Bodin's seminal condemnatory work on witches and witchcraft.[24] And we brought with us a spirit conjured by arcane art!

Burleigh suppressed a shudder at his own words then asked, "Have *your* researches suggested any conclusion, Dr Dee?"

John glanced at Holmes before replying. "Well, my first observation is that each of these pins is slightly different. See the embossed heads? Close examination under a lens of magnification reveals that each has a different sigil engraved upon the knob. This first is Venus, then Mars, Jupiter, Saturn—I shall return to describing the fifth—and the pin found in her majesty's hair carries the symbol of the Moon. In short, this set includes each of the planetary bodies that orbit our Earth excepting the Sun— unless we choose to dare follow Copernicus and place Sol at the centre of our cosmology."[25]

---

24 *De la Démonomanie des Sorciers* (On the Demon-Mania of Sorcerers) by jurist, political philosopher, and French MP Jean Bodin (1530-1596) was a very popular tome, published in ten editions from 1580 to 1604. It cited cases of demonic pact, lycanthropy, and intercourse with devils, and argued for legal exemptions when dealing with witches from the usual judicial requirements of physical evidence, witnesses, and confession without torture. It was influential in developing the climate of inquisition which led to thousands of convictions and executions for trafficking with the devil in the years to follow.

25 The ancient Greeks knew of the planet Mercury, although they mistook its

"Have you the pin that was taken from Walsingham?" the Angel asked. Such was his authority that an attendant handed over a linen-wrapped object without question.

"What of the fifth pin, then?" Burleigh asked John.

"Closely examined, chemically tested, the silver is of a different mint," my husband reported. "Somewhat more mixed with tin, antimony, and bismuth than the others. The head appears to be copied from the fourth pin, representing Jupiter. In brief, this pin is not part of the set. It came from another source, for another reason."

"The dates!" I realised. "John, the fourth pin came on the first day of February, you said. There was a gap, a long gap, before that fifth one appeared in mid-March. Suppose someone felt that the scare was dying down? That her majesty was getting over her fright? Maybe someone took matters into his own hands?"

"Someone with access to the real pins to be able to mould a copy," John reasoned.

Holmes turned on us all angrily, waving the Walsingham pin. "This item has been cleaned! The blood stains are wiped away. It has probably been washed! How am I expected to deduce anything when idiots have tidied away the evidence and destroyed any clue?"

Baron Burleigh frowned. He did not like being barked at. "Of what use might a blood-crusted shaft be, sir?" he demanded gruffly.

Our Angel answered to no Earthly authority and feared none. "It might tell everything. Whether the victim was alive or dead when the pin punctured him. Did he die of a pierced heart, or was this placed there afterwards? If the wound was fatal, what effusion of blood occurred to suggest whether the needle-point

---

morning and evening appearances as separate bodies (the morning version was named Apollo). It was also part of ancient Chinese and Indian astronomical lore and was known to medieval Islamic stargazers. It was not recognised in the west until Galileo's 17th century observations. Uranus was considered a star rather than a planet until the 18th century.

Nicolaus Copernicus (1473-1543) was the Renaissance astronomer and mathematician who posited a heliocentric model of the universe. The idea was not well received by the Catholic church on doctrinal grounds and was still a point of contention in Galileo's time.

was withdrawn to let its puncture do its work and then replaced later? Useless to ask now. Where is the corpse?"

"It lies in state in the lady chapel here at Hampton," the Lord High Treasurer revealed. "Sir Francis had been unwell for some time and had repaired again to his own estates. When he died, Her Majesty attended on him immediately and had him brought back in her own cortege. There will be a full state funeral presently."

"And I suppose the corpse will have been washed and cleaned," Holmes objected. He turned to John. "Carry on, doctor. Sift what you can from these ignorant fools whilst I inspect this seventh pin with my lens."

My husband hastened to mollify the powerful men whom Holmes had insulted. "We can perhaps get to the truth of all this without having to resort to cries of witchcraft," he offered. "The fifth pin might be the key. The different pin. That was the one discovered on the queen's pillow. Who had access to her chamber that night?"

"Very few," Lord William deemed. "We can send for the waiting lady, Jenet Hastings, and ask her."

"Send for her," commanded the Angel, "but do not remain for the interview. I shall conduct that. What became of Elsbet Fitz Hammond, by the way?"

"After she was put to the question she was sent home to her father," John recalled from the testimony. "Whatever else she had done or not, she had disgraced herself over Drake."

Holmes dismissed adultery with a wave of his eloquent hands. "Was she put to torture?"

"No," insisted Burleigh. "There was scant evidence to warrant it. Even Francis Walsingham, anti-Papist terrier that he was, would baulk at using such cruelty on a noble lady without some cause."

The Angel of Truth paced the chamber. "I will see Lady Jenet first," he announced. "Then I must view Walsingham's body. Then speak to some other witnesses—*you* noticed the pin in Her Majesty's hair, I understand, Lord William? And after that I shall need to interview Elizabeth Gloriana Regina herself."

"That is not possible," Burleigh objected.

"Make it possible, Lord William," Holmes demanded. "If you want this murky business resolved, if you would not have it hanging over the court while Sir Francis is buried, if you do not want rumour and panic spreading like wildfire, accusation on accusation and suspected traitors everywhere, get me my interviews."

John interceded. "Her Majesty has always been pleased to entertain me before when I have something of import for her." It was true. Her Majesty even set the date of her coronation by Dr Dee's astrological calculations.

"Very well, I shall see what may be done," the Lord High Treasurer conceded.

"We shall take this chamber," Holmes told him. "Dr Dee will bring you a list of our requirements shortly."

I had never thought to see Baron Burleigh and his toadies hastened from a room as Holmes did then, yet swiftly the Angel was alone with John and I. He brandished the seventh pin at us. "The last of the set," he announced. "See the engraving on the head, doctor? A sun! The pins were placed in order from the centre of a Copernican universe, then moon and sun to finish all. A minor detail, except to tell us that our perpetrator is an educated person, who either believes in a heliocentric creation or else has a sly sense of humour."

"A nice detail," John agreed. "There are astrological significances to the celestial bodies and their corresponding metals and notes which have occult significance also. A practicing magician might elect to use such symbols in this progression for some malefic purpose."

I saw Holmes' expression sour at this suggestion of necromancy. I hastily intervened. "A man need not be able to perform magic to believe he does. The perpetrator surely knows that these signs will add to a general rumour that the queen is plagued with sorcerous malice."

"The progression was completed with *sol*," reflected my husband, England's greatest astrologer and celestial philosopher. "Certainly it is with that symbol that the supposed curse bit. Unless one assumes that *terra* forms part of the set too, and a worse final stroke is still to come?"

"The hint of occult trappings is significant," the Angel conceded without emotion.

"However, it cannot lead us to whoever placed these items, nor tell us how. Or why? There are so many suspects it is impossible to even guess. How many arrests did Walsingham make these last few weeks as fear mounted? How many loyalties have been tried? How many secrets betrayed? If these pins are indeed cursed, they scatter their malediction far and wide."

"They do," Holmes agreed.

The door rattled. A young girl peered timidly round the timber. She wore a sombre, high-necked dress with no jewellery; court mourning garb. She was surely no older than I was when I first went to Windsor, a tender seventeen. "I am sent to Doctor Dee?"

The child was frightened. "Come in, Lady Jenet," I requested as kindly as I could.

"Yes, come in," Holmes told her. "Come and tell us why you slipped a fake pin into the queen's pillow that night. Or better yet, let me tell you."

Jenet's brows rose. "What? No. I never..."

"Observe the tiny bulge beneath this girls neck-hem," Holmes advised John. "The faintest rattle of muffled beads?"

John quickly followed the Angel's reasoning. "Lady Jenet conceals a Papist rosary under her clothes! The Hastings must be secret Catholics, I deem—and as such have ample reason to wish Protestant Queen Bess an uncomfortable fright with silver hatpins."

Jenet backed away. Her eyes were wide with horror at her discovery. Catholic plotters went to the gallows, the headsman, or the stake. "No!" she told us, desperately. "They never—they wouldn't! It was me that bethought of it, none other. Only me."

John accused her. "You forged, or had some helper forge, a copy of the genuine fourth pin you had discovered before as you undressed the queen. Why?"

The maid-in-waiting dropped to her knees. "I'll confess. Anything you want. It was me. I am a witch! I am possessed of a demon! No other helped. No other instructed. It was me, all me. Burn me—but blame no-one else!" She began to sob.

Holmes was relentless. "Mistress Jane, you hypothesised that our fifth, anomalous pin was planted after so long a pause to keep her majesty and the court disturbed, to fan fading rumours of divine displeasure against queen and administration."

"I was five years at Windsor Castle. I know how court gossip works," I replied.

Holmes stalked round the weeping girl, lunged suddenly, and hooked the concealed prayer beads from the girl's neckline.

"Give those back...!" blurted Jenet. She reached futilely for the confiscated necklace. It occurred to me how unwise and foolish it was to wear a rosary at Hampton Court, however well concealed beneath formal mourning dress. Surely the girl did not wear her talisman always? Had she donned it before her interview in the hopes of divine protection? To prevent its discovery in its usual hiding place if her chamber was searched? Or was I missing something?

Holmes lifted his lens to inspect the rosary clasp. "I see now that Lady Jenet had another motive for her deeds. Observe the engraving, doctor. *E F-H*. Might we posit Elsbet FitzHammond, this lady's predecessor-in-office, who was dismissed on suspicion of planting the pins?"

"How came you by this necklace?" John demanded of Jenet.

"A gift!" she whimpered, kneeling almost double now in her fear and distress. "Given to me as a remembrance."

"You claim to have this from Lady Elsbet?"

"I...no, of course not."

"Then how do you explain the inscription?"

Jenet reached the end of her resources. She lost all power of coherent speech and collapsed weeping, sprawled across the tiled floor.

"Lady Elsbet would only own such a dangerous item if she were Papist," my husband argued. "To pass it to you would be to deliver herself into your hands, for this rosary's discovery would betray her to those who hunt such secret Catholics—Walsingham, for example."

I had to intervene, to save the sobbing girl from her implacable interrogators. "John, Holmes, you don't understand how it can be at court. When a young girl comes to such a great household to serve a high lady, shyest and least at first amongst so many noble retainers, that newcomer can be overawed. It is easy—and common—for such an impressionable girl to develop an admiration, a devotion, to some older and more experienced courtier. As Lady Elsbet once did with Drake." I dared a glance at John. "As I did with the queen's astrologer."

My husband blinked and did not meet my look.

I went on. "As I think Jenet did with Lady Elsbet."

Now John stirred. "You think the girl had a passion-crush for the former senior lady-in-waiting?" John knew well that women can couple together amorously in their own fashion to the release of pleasure—another lesson we had learned at Trebona under Madimi-Kelley's malefic carnal guidance.

"Poor Jenet may have placed the fake fifth pin to 'prove' that her object of desire was innocent of the charges that had cast her from court," I reasoned.

Holmes regarded the quivering, hysterical mass that had been his suspect. "Nothing more can be got from her for now. We will return to this witness later. Let her be placed under watch, but say nothing of what she's confessed to Burleigh or any other. Our investigation has scarcely begun."

The Angel of Truth led us on to the chapel where Sir Francis' body lay. No sombre choir monks interrupted our study. In these Protestant days such indulgences smack of Papery. John, Holmes and I were left alone with the bier and coffer that held the fallen Secretary of State's mortal remains.

The spirit wasted no time in niceties but immediately stripped open the corpse's tunic and began an inspection of his wounds. To my dismay, John peeled down Walsingham's hose.

"Here is the pin mark," Holmes noted. "It penetrated the heart well enough, but as best I can tell—after these benighted fools have sponged and scented away the evidence—there was no great effusion such as a beating organ would have gushed from the lesion. A stiletto prick could kill a man, but with a three-inch pin it requires proximity and absolute accuracy."

"Here," John beckoned the Angel to the dead man's nethers. "Walsingham's balls. Feel them."

Holmes did so without demur. "A great lump," he found.

"Like unto a third testicle. When Sir Francis visited me at Mortlake he was much changed from the hearty man I had known before my Continental sojourn. He'd came to consult me on the witchcraft pins, of course, and to thank me for certain intelligences I had conveyed to him during my travels by means of coded letters. He brought a sum of gold to assist Jane and I in repairing our home after its vandalism and looting, and passed to me the names of certain men to whom I might look to find my missing books.[26] In return I consulted on his failing health. He confided that he was having gut pains and difficulty pissing."

"A testicular tumour such as this one could certainly impede his passing water," agreed the Angel. "One might wish for the opinion of a reliable modern man of medicine but…it is entirely possible that Walsingham's deterioration and death could be attributed to blockage and infection of the urinary tract. Or this growth might be one signifier of many other malignant tumours beneath his flesh."

"Caused by sorcery?" I ventured.

"Caused by nature," Holmes scorned. "If we could cut open the carcass…"

"I beg you not to try," John told the Angel hastily. There was a limit to the license we might claim. "Is there aught else to see here? If we are not to desecrate the flesh of England's spymaster and the queen's favourite?"

There was not. Holmes led us back to the room he had commandeered for interviews. Weeping Jenet had been cleared away to some annex. The Angel demanded, through John,

---

26 Thieves who benefited by acquiring books through the Mortlake villagers' arson attack on absent "magician" Dee's house included Dee's former pupil John Davis and Catholic polemicist Nicholas Saunder (or Sanders). Ironically it is Saunder's loot, now lodged at the Royal College of Physicians, which forms the majority of the surviving part of Dee's collection today.

conversations with an eclectic roster of men.

First was the Master of the Queen's Wardrobe. "Who had access to Her Majesty's gowns before she dressed? How were they stored? How were they guarded?"

The portly gentleman stuttered out his information. The monarch's gowns were very valuable, kept in locked storage in the privy wardrobe safe from men and moths. A guard stood sentry in the lobby outside. The Master and some few ladies-in-waiting had keys. When her majesty dressed there were always several ladies in attendance. It was these women's duty to see that Gloriana appeared immaculate. An unauthorised addition to her underclothes or outer mantle would most certainly be noted before she was allowed to leave. Her senior Lady in Waiting, formerly Elsbet, now Jenet, was responsible for a final check.

"It is impossible that those pins could have been there when her majesty left her dressing rooms," the Wardrobe-Master insisted. "The only feasible way would have been for her senior lady to affix the pin during final inspection, and Sir Francis — God rest his soul after his long labours — put Lady Elsbet to the question and found her innocent."

"Say rather he could not prove her guilt," John clarified, then thought again. "Walsingham was ruthless enough to wring the truth from any man or woman, though. If he released Elsbet FitzHammond he must have been satisfied."

Next was the Warden of the Queen's Bedchamber. I recalled this fussy little man's counterpart at Windsor, a sly grabby fellow we ladies took good care to avoid being corned by. This specimen was altogether different; I doubt whether ladies interested him at all.

"The queen's private chambers are guarded at all times and points," this functionary assured us. "There are many plots against her majesty's life. Security is vital. None may enter without permission. Few have that privilege." He reeled off the names of ladies in waiting, some more common maids and footmen, and certain trusted guards who had permission to intrude.

"On the night when the pin appeared on her majesty's night-gown, the 6th of January, I believe, did the queen receive any visitor to her chamber by night?" Holmes enquired. "A suitor, perhaps?"

The Warden of the Queen's bedchamber spluttered at the suggestion that the Virgin Queen might receive a midnight caller in her bower. Yet even in my day at Windsor there were certain rumours repeated to me by Lady Howard that...

But this is not relevant to my present account. The Angel demanded and received assurances that no stranger had violated the monarch's room that night. Only Lady Elsbet and three other maids had attended her.

Walsingham's private secretary was a cultured, well-spoken man with a fashionable forked beard. He never met Holmes' eye. The Angel questioned him on his former employer's business. "Sir Francis was said to be the best-informed man in England," our spirit noted. "What happened to his files and notes after his death?"

"All my master's papers were bundled together and dispatched to the Tower of London for the queen's pleasure."

"Nothing abstracted? Nothing burned?"

"In the last days of his illness Sir Francis disposed of certain documents himself, feeding them to his bedroom hearth."

"He was a knowledgeable man. Well read?"

"Yes. He corresponded with many of the great thinkers of our day." The secretary's shifty gaze flickered over John for a scant moment.

My husband chimed in with questions. "When was the pin in his heart discovered? At the moment of his death?"

"It was concealed beneath his outer jacket. It was only when he was stripped for his shroud that the item was first seen."

"There was not enough blood to betray the wound?"

"Underlinens were soaked, but the lining of Sir Francis' mantle had absorbed the effusion so it was not evident to the eye. The discharge was not great."

I remembered Holmes' earlier comments. "Not enough for it to have spurted from a beating heart?" I checked.

"I would have thought not," the secretary opined. "Of course, some thought the spirit that had murdered the Secretary of State might have feasted upon his blood."

"The stains were discovered was after he had been laid out at his home and the queen and court had hastily visited to pay their respects?" Holmes checked.

"Yes. When he was brought to the chapel here and stripped in preparation for his shroud-clothes. Though even before that some cried poison and others cried witchcraft. Sir Francis Walsingham has been England's bastion against black magic and Spanish and French aggression for many years. Even in these last few weeks that her majesty has been tormented by the curse-pins he rooted out many traitors. He has cleaned England of those who seek our ruler's harm. Countless enemies would wish to see his death."

The Angel was tireless. He continued on until night fell and sconces were lit to illuminate his interrogation room. Humbler servants were summoned to add their testimony: guards, serving girls, footmen, coachmen, butlers, heralds, scrubbing women, sweeps. Each lady in waiting was questioned without knowing what the others had said. Even the scullions charged with laying out Sir Francis' corpse were called to speak.

As the night ground on I found a moment to break from taking notes and speak in undertones with my husband. "It's close now to twenty-four hours since you conjured the Angel of Truth. How long can he continue to manifest?"

John shook his head. "In truth, wife, I am still not certain *how* I brought him to us, or what I did differently from any time I have performed the rites before. You know that I have enjoyed some success in bringing forth spirits..."

"Enjoyed?" I challenged the conjurer's choice of words.

"Well, Madimi was...You know I am sorry for Madimi, Jane."

"So you have said," I answered bitterly. "You have rarely shown it, though."

John swallowed. "I have taken Theodore for my own, raised him in my household."

"Theodore might be your own. Not Kelley's—or whatever demon he claimed rode him as he tormented me."

John glanced at Holmes as the Angel interrogated the Keeper

of the Queen's Jewel Box. "This is not the time to speak of such things, Jane."

"No, the time was long ago, John. Before you avoided my bed. Before that one drunken night when you got me with child again. Before you closed me from your heart and counsel as a soiled thing unworthy of your regard — soiled by *your* consent and command, John, never by any will of mine."

I saw the guilt in my husband's stare. The rite of Uriel still cast its shadows over his heart.

I took a deep breath. "The Angel of Truth…Holmes…He said that you still had regard for me. Still loved me."

Dr John Dee looked away. "I will need to make a careful study of Bacon's manuscript. The Angel was somehow brought here by that."

There was to be no answer to my deepest question.

"I have surreptitiously appropriated certain artefacts from the Angel," John whispered. "A hair, a thread of his gown, a cup he touched which bears the grease-imprint of his fingertips. From these I can perhaps devise the alchemy to treat Bacon's codex so it will bring Holmes to me."

"Holmes is already here."

John rubbed his forehead. "This Angel comes from outside time. Outside our time anyway. If I prepare a summoning for him over the months to come then it may bring him to us last night." He reached out and touched my cheek, a gesture of affection that was strange and alien in our cold contemporary lives. "Keep careful note of everything he speaks and does, Jane. There is no other but you I can rely on for this…and none I would rather have at my side to rely upon."

We were interrupted. Holmes dismissed the jeweller and rose to stalk the room.

"Have you concluded your interviews?" my husband ventured.

"Not quite," the detective spirit replied. "There are three more people I must see, and such is their importance that I deferred their questioning until I was fully informed of the detail our minor witnesses could afford. Now I am prepared to speak with William Cecil."

It was perhaps a sign of Baron Burleigh's worry that he consented to meet with Dr Dee and Sherlock Holmes as the clock bell tolled eleven. He came alone and found my husband and our angel awaiting him at a writing table. I shall never forget that image of those two brilliant men, painted by candlelight, seated side by side in rapt attention. Holmes' gaunt, hawk-like countenance and John's wise intent gaze both focussed on the Lord High Treasurer.

"What have you discovered, astrologer?" Lord William demanded. He may have sneered.

Holmes pressed his fingertips together. "We are close to revealing our conclusions, but some few anomalies must still be explored. You opposed the late Sir Francis's recent policies regarding the appearance of these pins, I understand."

"Of course," scorned Burleigh. "Any rational man must see that England's future depends upon a balance of interests. We are, and shall remain, a Protestant nation, but we *must* have relations with Catholic Europe. Perhaps, had Drake's foray prospered to punish the Spanish for their Armada, it might be different; but with religious war in Holland[27] and our queen expelled from the Catholic communion by the Pope we cannot afford to be so broad and blatant in our persecutions."

"Walsingham arrested several people these last few weeks, as concern for the queen's wellbeing mounted," John observed.

"And left me with the mess to clean," the Lord High Treasurer spat. "Sir Francis was apt to become so enamoured of his tangled plots that he forgot their wider consequences. He entrapped poor Scots Mary with his Babington conspiracy and had her head.[28] With one blade-stroke he inspired a hundred counter-plots

---

27 Burleigh's role in the Dutch Protestant rebellion was to finance it enough to continue but not so much as to allow it success. In this way religious concern was diverted from England and a potential rival nation was weakened and distracted.

28 Elizabeth I imprisoned Catholic Mary, Queen of Scots, also a viable claimant for the English throne, for eighteen years. Idealistic recusant Sir Antony Babinton was recruited into a poorly-thought-out Papist plot to rescue Mary and place her in power with military support from Spain and the Catholic League of France. One of Walsingham's double-agents uncovered the plan. Babinton was "turned", forced to lead on the conspirators so that there was clear evidence of their guilt. This included corresponding with Mary until she wrote ordering Elizabeth's assassination. This

against Elizabeth and her state. I do not wish to malign the dead, but the man was an adventurer—irresponsible and heedless of the collateral harm his exploits caused."

"Did you attend upon Sir Francis' body as he lay out at his estates before the queen brought him to Hampton Court?" Holmes enquired.

"When word came of his death my place was here, to ensure the smooth transition of responsibilities to other hands."

I well understood what those words really meant. No man would benefit more from Walsingham's passing than William Cecil.

"Were you present at the interrogation of Elsbet FitzHammond?"

"As if Sir Francis would allow any to contaminate his questioning! Look to Walsingham's smooth-tongued secretary for an account of that event—if you can get any word of sense from his conspiratorial lips."

Holmes deferred to John for a turn at the questions. "It was you who first spotted the pin in Her Majesty's hair, I believe," my husband began. "Please describe the occasion."

"We had heard an early morning service on Lady Day. Her Majesty was attended by her usual retinue. She bade me walk beside her as she left the church. We progressed down the nave aisle and emerged from the eastern porch. A pale sun glinted off something in her majesty's hair. Not in her wig, but the natural locks that emerged beneath it, just below the left ear. I looked more closely, and there was one of those infernal pins, thatched into the queen's plait!"

"How did her majesty react?"

"She was much distressed. Each pin's appearance has alarmed her more. She must have heard by then the court gossip that the witchcraft was growing stronger, that each pin came closer to piercing her heart. She tore the item loose and hurled it in the mud. I retrieved it for Walsingham's investigation. I understand

---

final proof was enough for Walsingham to bring down the whole conspiracy. Sixteen principal plotters were executed. Babington was disembowelled before death. Mary was tried for treason (without legal counsel, access to the evidence, or the right to call witnesses) and eventually beheaded on 8th February 1587.

he subsequently passed it to you."

"That's correct," John confirmed. "Sir Francis, though ill by then and withdrawn from court, made a personal visit to Mortlake. You summoned me to ask about it."

"He wasn't there on Lady Day," Lord William declared. "Walsingham's malaise was already taking a grip by then. If... if there is some sorcery directed against her majesty and her principal ministers..."

"The truth will be discovered," the Angel assured him. "You may go now, my lord. You have been moderately helpful."

It was close to midnight when Holmes again summoned the unfortunate Jenet Hastings. The lady in waiting had endured long hours under guard, knowing that her secrets were discovered. She entered timidly, supported by two soldiers whom John dismissed.

"It is time to reveal the truth," the Angel warned her. "Dr Dee, Mistress Jane and I are not a court. We owe no duty to the Lord High Treasurer, or to Sir Francis Walsingham's faction. We are not here to catch Catholics nor to punish affections. But we *shall* have a full account from you before you leave this room."

There was no doubt in the spirit's voice. Jenet trembled and shrank back in her chair, but from Holmes there was no escape.

"The rosary. Did you steal it or was it given to you?"

"It was a gift. Truly, sir, it was given as a keepsake."

"From Lady Elsbet?"

Jenet squeezed her eyes shut and nodded.

"You were fond of her?"

Another nod, and a deep blush.

"You idolised her."

"Yes."

Holmes pushed the beads across to the young woman. "Pray with it now," he instructed. "Out loud. Show us how it works."

Jenet faltered. Her hands clutched the necklace. "H-hail Mary, full of grace..." she began.

The Angel shook his head. "The Lord's Prayer, then ten Hail Marys, then Glory Be To the Father," he corrected the lady in waiting. "You are no Catholic. That was Elsbet."

"She gave you the beads for affection," John suggested to the girl. "As a sign of trust."

"Or as a final coercion to carry out a task that Elsbet was no longer able to perform," Holmes accused. "There are a strictly limited number of people who could have placed the pins about Her Majesty. Of them, her lady in waiting is the one who could have done so the easiest. Most often the logical suspect is the correct one. Catholic Elsbet was slipping those pins into the Queen's garments—until she was suspected and taken for questioning. Did she leave you that fourth pin to plant after she had gone, to suggest supernatural occurrence rather than human agency? To offer her an alibi?"

Jenet hesitated to surrender up her friend.

"And the fifth," the Angel persisted inexorably. "When no new instruction came from close-watched Elsbet did you decide by your own initiative to forge another pin, modelled upon the one previously left in your charge, to continue the deception, to protect your idol and further her plot?"

Jenet gasped. The spirit had hit upon the exact truth.

John saw the problem, though, and spoke it before I could. "Elsbet could have placed the first three talismans, and Jenet the fourth and fifth, but what of the sixth that appeared in church? Or the seventh in Walsingham's dead flesh?"

Holmes took up quill and scribbled some words on a scrap of parchment. "For that," he replied enigmatically, "we require one final testimony." He handed the paper to Jenet. "Take that and deliver it now. Go in haste."

The lady fled from the room, trailing guardsmen. John and I regarded the Angel of Truth with surprise.

"You see now how it came to be, and why?" Holmes asked us.

"I confess to still being puzzled," my husband regretted. "What have you seen that mortal eyes cannot discern?"

"Nothing that mortal eyes cannot perceive," Holmes snorted. "You are blinded by your training, doctor, by your prejudices and preconceptions. Free yourself of these things and you will excel. Your name will resound down history as a thinker, a scholar, a seeker. Merely *look* at what you see!"

John hesitated. "My name will be remembered? Is that prophecy or...?"

"Care not so much that it will be recalled as for what it will be recalled, Dr Dee," the Angel advised.

"Are we close, though?" I had to ask. "Close to penetrating this terrible mystery?" I missed my children, and my exchange with John earlier had left me raw, unsettled, hurt, as I'd not been since those weeks recovering from Madimi's ministrations.

Holmes interlaced his fingers save for two pointed indexes which he directed towards the door. The portal opened. Elizabeth Regina swooped into the room.

I had seldom seen the queen so close. She must have been approaching sixty, old King Harry's daughter who had reigned these twenty years with absolute power, who had survived her mad, bloody sister and executed her cousin, who had loved Dudley and destroyed him,[29] who had defied Spanish Philip and the Pope himself and forged a new England.

Holmes eyes sparkled.

Her Majesty held the parchment he had sent by Jenet. "What is the meaning of these words?"

John winced. Our monarch has a tendency to have men beheaded if they catch her ire.

"I believe the message was quite legible, ma'am," Holmes responded. "However, there are a few points I should like to clear up before I am satisfied that I have fathomed the case."

"A few points?" the queen repeated.

"Indeed. When did you first deduce that Lady Elsbet was placing the pins upon your person?"

An invisible contest seemed to be going on between ruler and

29 The other of Elizabeth's three greatest courtiers alongside Burleigh and Walsingham was Robert Dudley, 1st Earl of Leicester (1532 or 3—1588), who was widely rumoured to be her lover. When Dudley's first wife died suddenly of a fall downstairs it was bruited that he had murdered her to be free to marry the queen. The resultant scandal killed off any chance for such a wedding, but Dudley and Elizabeth remained close all their years. Dudley refrained from other marriage until very late in his life; the queen reacted badly when she learned of his secret wedding to Lettice Knollys, Countess of Essex, and banished the lady from court. Dudley died unexpectedly two years before our present narrative. Elizabeth kept to her chambers and admitted no-one for six days until Baron Burleigh had the door broken in. She retained Dudley's last letter to her in her bedside treasure box all her life.

spirit, some wrestling of mind and character beyond the outward show that we could see. Queen Bess elected to answer the question. "It was self-evident. The simplest explanation. When Elsbet was exiled and Jenet attempted the same ruse it became clear what was going on. Jenet is not so clever as Elsbet."

John stirred. "You were distressed."

"I certainly appeared so. Why spoil a perfectly useful plot?"

Holmes's face lit with admiration. "You also discerned, then, that Elsbet and her Catholic contacts were not the originators of the scheme?"

"Of course. Elsbet is smarter than Jenet, but not so clever or well read as to devise the astrological symbol sequence on the pin-heads. It was clear that she had a backer."

"So there was a Catholic plot?" I blurted, then regretted it. "Um, Your Majesty."

"No, Jane," Holmes told me. "What value would there be in stirring up anti-Catholic sentiment by so public a resort?"

"Would Walsingham have allowed a secret Catholic so close a place in the monarch's intimate household?" John objected.

"He would certainly have known," Holmes confirmed. "That is presumably the hold he had over the lady, to force her to plant the pins?"

"And so alarm me and my court into allowing his Papist-cleansing?" the queen suggested. "Francis knew of his illness. He knew he had not long to finish his work for me and leave me a kingdom secured from treason and treachery. Hence his Byzantine plot to nudge my hand against my enemies, or potential enemies, while protecting me from opprobrium at court and amongst the general masses. Who objects to defending the queen from foulest black witchcraft?"

"You allowed Jenet to continue Elsbet's—Walsingham's work!" John exclaimed.

"And continued it yourself," Holmes observed. "No other could have placed that sixth pin whilst you were at prayer in church but you."

"I sent a trusted messenger to Elsbet in her exile," Her Majesty revealed. "At my letter the girl confessed all and yielded up the remaining two pins from the set that Francis had given her. One I used to complete Francis's plot; his weeding out of future threats was a useful last gift to me. I wonder if he realised by whose agency his pin was placed? I imagine he did. He was a subtle man."

"On this occasion he was mystified. For evidence I offer Dr Dee's involvement. Your ailing spymaster would hardly have made the journey to Mortlake to recruit Dee's help in discovering who placed the first five pins. It was that mysterious sixth that troubled him."

"And the final pin you reserved for Walsingham himself, majesty," John concluded. "You visited him as he lay out at his estates. You paid your last respects there."

The monarch inclined her head slightly. "The old scoundrel had gone behind my back before, for my own good as he saw it. He and Dudley used a warrant of execution for poor Mary that I had signed on condition it would not be delivered without my further consent."

"His behaviour in the current matter was not uncharacteristic then," surmised the Angel.

"Characteristic but irking. His final gambit used even my own superstition to further his ends. I felt a little bit of posthumous payback was in order. I returned his final pin to him." Queen Bess snorted. "Perhaps the myth-makers will decide that Francis's last loyal act was to draw upon himself the supernatural end that would otherwise have befallen me?"

"Burleigh does not know," John realised.

"Burleigh is a fine man and a good servant. He does not need to know everything. England is *mine*, and only I keep all its secrets." Walsingham's papers had gone to the Queen's own Tower of London.

Holmes was satisfied. "Then the problem is solved. It was hardly a challenge once the obfuscations of royal etiquette were dismissed. Walsingham never prosecuted Elsbet nor put her to torture because she was his agent all along. You never confronted him because he was doing your business for you in a way you could forever deny.[30] The plot had just enough macabre touches to draw idle attention from the likely and correct solution. My congratulations, Your Majesty. A neat and professional gambit."

Elizabeth shifted her head in the barest motion of acknowledgement, of one master to another. Without making any other gesture she somehow caused her guards to re-enter the chamber.

"Now that you know the truth, you must also know that you cannot take it beyond this room," regretted the Queen. "I am sorry, Doctor Dee, Mistress Jane. You have never done me harm. You come to this end through your loyal endeavours to serve me."

I gasped. "We are…to die?"

John folded me in his embrace. "There's no other way," he recognised. "Jane—my beloved Jane—I am so sorry. All my arts and cunning have led you to torment and shame and…this."

"Not only to this," I assured him. "To enlightenment and joy and travel and the society of kings, to poets and wonders and our children. And to love!" I swallowed back sobs and clung to him. "I would not change the bad if it would also take away the good."

He held me tight. The dark spirit that had lain on us ever since the Trebona rite could not endure that affection. I felt it lift from us, cast back to sinister shadow from whence it could not return.

"I love you, my wife," John told me. "*You* are my angel." In the end he too had discovered truth.

"Ah, angels," Holmes interrupted, rising from his chair to his full impressive height. "Remarkable things, those. Do you believe in angels, Your Majesty? You're not shackled by superstition, as is clear from your part in our recent conundrum. But do you believe there is a greater truth?"

The queen looked at John and I, together at the last, clinging to each other. She faced our detective Angel with a quizzical regard. "There's no trick can save you. I'll see that your ends are quick and merciful. Dee's children will be maintained."

Holmes chuckled then, the only time I had heard his mirth. "Dr Dee and his good lady wife will swear an oath to silence on

---

30 One of Queen Elizabeth's mottoes was *Video et taceo*—"I see and am silent."

this. Better, he'll pronounce the conclusion about Walsingham taking your supernatural doom on himself and so further cover your trail. He is a man adept at secrets, visionary, gifted, and loyal; and Jane is his true match."

"I am sorry," good Queen Bess mourned.

"Don't make an error now," Holmes advised her. "Watch." He turned to John and I. "Dr Dee, you conjured me here to solve your mystery. It is now revealed. My work is done. Release me. I need to rouse in my own rooms and return to the waking world."

Comprehension dawned on John's face. "Yes," he breathed. "Thank you." He raised his hand. "Sherlock Holmes of Mycroft, Angel of Truth, Spirit of Detection, your labours are done. I charge thee depart without malice. By rod and rood I dismiss thee! Avaunt!"

Holmes disappeared. Only a pungent scent of Virginian tobacco remained where he had stood.

Her Majesty saw him vanish in plain sight. "Remarkable," she whispered to herself.

John and I had the sense to stand silent.

"A spirit," the queen recognised. "Conjured by your art, John."

"At mighty need only," my husband cautioned prudently. "At unique cost."

Gloriana turned to us. She was England. "I will take your oaths and command your service as the Angel suggested. No man so clever as to associate with a creature of that kind should be wasted to the headsman's axe."

We made bow and curtsey. "He brought the truth," John acknowledged, clasping my hand tight. The Angel had brought truth to us too.

John needed me.

The Locked Cell Murder

RON FORTIER

D r. Van Helsing was late as usual.
Not that that was any real surprise to me. Despite her magnificent credentials as one of the world's leading authorities on secret cults and rituals, Amelia Van Helsing was still a female and suffered from the same inability to make rendezvous with any modicum of success as the rest of her fair sex.

Normally I wouldn't have minded all that much, but the situation before me was precarious to say the least. Hiding in an old storage warehouse on the shores of the Charles River, that cold November evening of 1898, my only concern was for the poor young woman strapped to the altar at the center of the massive building about to be dispatched as the fifth and latest sacrificial victim to the Egyptian *Cult of Kemk*. Kemk was a male fertility god who supposedly bestowed on his followers extreme sexual vitality.

Which was why the twenty men surrounding the raised platform on which the altar was constructed were naked under the dark green robes they wore. According to Dr Van Helsing, after the female sacrifice was murdered, her blood would be drained into a large bowl and then the High Priest would pass it around so that each participant could wash his genitalia with it.

I'd never witnessed the actual event, but trusted in the good doctor's knowledge of such macabre and unholy practices; after all, she was the expert and yours truly but a humble Inspector of Police with the Boston Colonial Constabulary.

When the first victim, a Charlestown prostitute, had been discovered, my colleagues had begun investigating the killing as a random act of violence. Two weeks later a second body washed ashore near Plymouth mutilated in the same manner as the first poor girl. My superiors feared we had a madman on the loose and a special unit was formed with the sole purpose of hunting down this fiend; whoever he was. Whereas the similarities in how the women had been stabbed and the complete draining of their blood was enough for me to call upon Dr Van Helsing.

At my request she visited the city morgue and personally examined each body. Almost instantly she claimed we were dealing with a cult and listed three that performed ritualistic slaughter similar to that evidenced on the remains she had studied.

When the fourth young woman disappeared off the streets of Chelsea, the good doctor and I set about hunting the people behind this cult and the location in which they conducted their gruesome rituals. By the time we'd learned about the Cult of Kemk and the man who led them, the body of the fourth girl was discovered; again near the ocean shore.

Our suspect was an export-import trader named Josiah Sparks who, as our investigation revealed, had spent a great deal of time in Egypt as a lad and was now very influential in Boston society. A bachelor, he maintained a home on Beeker Street and owned several dockside facilities in which clandestine meetings of large groups could easily be held. Thus did Dr Van Helsing and I begin shadowing Mr Sparks on alternating days. We did this with the aid of several uniformed officers we'd come to depend on in past cases.

That had been a week ago and now victim number five was tied, hands and feet, to the stone altar awaiting a similar fate unless we could stop the cultists. Although she twisted and fought against her restraints it was to no avail and the poor girl couldn't scream, as a gag had been tied over her mouth. Yet even at this distance I could see the terror in her crying eyes.

Where the hell was Van Helsing? If she didn't arrive in the next few minutes I would be alone to face the Cult of Kemk and their mad leader.

Standing next to the altar, Josiah Sparks was a remarkable sight, all seven feet of him adorned in a feathered girdle, with gold sandals on his feet, and intricate, Egyptian hieroglyphics painted over his naked torso. He was powerfully structured, with a barrel-like chest, and massive arms, now clutching a foot long dagger. His dark complexion told of his years under the hot, desert sun and his face was stony in appearance like a very Sphinx. Over his long, black hair he wore a head-dress of white fur shaped like a lion's mane.

As I said, a remarkable, daunting sight to say the least.

His followers had been chanting ever since the poor girl had been dragged into the place and tied to the blood-stained stone. When they suddenly ceased, I knew it meant I had run out of time.

Sparks raised the dagger up over his head so that its sharp, silver blade sparkled beneath the kerosene lanterns hung overhead.

I stepped out from behind the pillar and raised my Colt .45 pistol, and fired at the weapon in his hands. Being a crack shot, it wasn't a difficult mark at all and I took great pleasure in seeing the knife knocked forcibly—and hopefully painfully—out of his grasp.

He screamed out and turned in my direction.

"The next one I will put between your eyes," I said calmly.

It took him only a second to recognize me. "The illustrious Inspector Sherlock Holmes. We are flattered by your presence."

His people were shuffling about, still surrounding the altar, but all eyes were locked on me and my gun. How much longer I could forestall them was the question of the moment.

"Josiah Sparks, you and your men are under arrest," I kept my tone confident. "The building is now being surrounded by a dozen armed officers. If you refuse to surrender peacefully, then I cannot guarantee any of you will leave the premises alive."

At that Sparks laughed aloud. So much for my bluffing skills.

"I doubt that very much, Holmes," he said, upon catching his breath. "In fact I believe you were foolhardy enough to come alone—like some gallant knight of old; Hell-bent on rescuing the fair maid.

"Well, my dear Inspector, she is clearly anything but a fair maiden," he pointed to the trembling, bound girl. "But you are indeed bound for Hell. Of that I can assure you."

He pointed at me and bellowed. "Destroy him, my loyal apostles. Rip the very flesh from his body!"

And just like that the agitated devotees of Kemk charged for me, yelling and screaming, bloodlust in their eyes.

I shot down the first three, holding my ground, but realized my plight was untenable. Some had produced blades and hatchets from their cloaks, and as they encircled me the chances of my survival dwindled rapidly.

I determined that if I must fall, then they would pay a heavy bill and I brought down two more of the blighters who, in falling, caused those behind them to stumble and fall. One wiry devil managed to leap over this pile, and—swinging what looked like a butcher's cleaver—sliced open the jacket sleeve of my left arm and the skin beneath it. The stinging pain registered as I clubbed him on the back of the head with the butt of my Colt.

At which time there was a loud crashing noise and tiny shards of glass rained down from above as Dr Amelia Van Helsing came plunging through the skylight above us. Holding on to a rope, she slid down behind the main group of howling cultists and landed gracefully on her feet; which, by the way, were encased in crepe-soled black boots. In fact, her entire outfit was black, from the hood over her head, to the tunic and loose, baggy pants she wore.

You see, while growing up in the east, Abraham Van Helsing had seen to it that his one and only child was to be skilled in all the exotic martial arts known to that part of the world. When Amelia had reached the age of seventeen she was one of the only white women to have been taught the assassin skills of *ninja-jitsu*.

Therefore, by the time any of the howling mob had noticed her timely arrival, it was too late for most of them. With one easy motion, she reached up and pulled out two short *Wakizashi* blades from the crossed leather scabbards on her back and went on the attack. The twenty-four inch long, razor sharp swords are the shorter version of the better known samurai *katanas.* Whereas, in this close-up combat, the shorter blades were far more lethal and effective.

Watching Van Helsing hack and slash her way through the now disorientated rabble was like watching a ballet of death-dealing. She moved through them like the lithe killing machine she had become and her long knives sliced through limbs and torsos with bloody efficiency. In fact, within seconds of her assault, more than half the cultists were down; their life's blood pouring out and covering the floor like a quick spreading carpet of slippery, red goo.

Momentarily happy at the realization I was not going to die, I started shooting again until my hammer clicked on an empty chamber.

Suddenly, two huge hands grabbed me and lifted me off the floor. I was staring into Josiah Spark's crazed visage, then he hurled me through the air with a maniac's cry.

I landed on my side almost ten yards away. The impact knocked the wind out of me but I somehow managed to maintain my grasp on my gun.

"You will die for this!" Sparks declared as he then turned his attention to Dr Van Helsing and what remained of his followers.

With no regard for his own people, he shoved those still standing aside to confront my partner. To her credit, Van Helsing chose to twist herself out of his frontal charge and missed being punched in the head by mere inches. As she glided around the maddened giant, she cut him with a back slash across the ribs.

Sparks roared in pain and whipped his left arm around, catching her in the small of the back and knocking her off her feet. That such a large man could move so fast amazed me and I knew it would take our combined efforts to defeat him.

I hurriedly got to my feet again, holding tightly to my empty revolver. If nothing else, it would make an effective club. Van

Helsing had leaped back onto her feet by performing a backwards somersault just as Sparks came for her again. With his back to me, he was now vulnerable and I raced at him, flipping my pistol so that I was holding the barrel, and, without hesitation, I jumped up and smacked him on the back of the head with the butt. He was jolted and stumbled a few feet forward.

And that was the extent of his reaction. It was as if he'd been struck by a fly. Turning on me while massaging the knot forming on the back of his skull, he smiled cruelly.

But only for a second.

Dr Van Helsing, using my futile attack as a distraction, had managed to launch herself at him, her entire body flying through the air, and, at the last possible moment, she snapped out her right foot and kicked Sparks in the chest. He fell backwards and toppled over like some mighty oak in the forest. Dazed now, he tried to sit up only to have me drop down on my knees beside him and this time smash my pistol butt into his forehead with all the strength I could muster.

Sparks's eyes rolled up in their sockets; he groaned and then his head fell back. He was unconscious and no longer a threat.

Dr Van Helsing approached him from the other side, her blades held before her in case he was merely faking. When he didn't move, she sighed and straightened up.

From my knees, I looked up at her. "What the bloody hell kept you so long?" I inquired.

Shrugging, she pulled back her hood to show off her lustrous brown hair, tied in a bun, and smiled, "My dear inspector, a woman must take care of her appearance before going out. I'd have thought you would know that by now."

There is no need to bore you with the minutiae concerning the aftermath of that evening. Sparks, and those of his followers who survived Dr. Van Helsing's wrath, were arrested and brought to trial. As the leader of the cult, Josiah Sparks was sentenced to be hanged at the Lexington State Penitentiary three months hence. That should have been the end of the story. It was not.

The days went by and I confess to forgetting all about Sparks and his sentencing date. The Commonwealth has no shortage of crime. I was kept busy protecting the streets of our fair city while the good doctor signed on to teach a class at Harvard on Secret Cults of the Middle East for a semester as a guest lecturer.

The three months passed as time always does.

I was nearly finished shaving when the knock on my front door interrupted me.

"Van Helsing?" No reply. Sometimes, I think the woman could sleep through the Second Coming.

Cursing, I put down my razor, wiped away most of the white foam off my face and tossing the towel around my neck, jogged down the stairs to the front door.

"Good morning, Inspector," a nervous Officer Robert Muldoon greeted as he handed me a telegram. "This arrived at the station a few minutes ago. Superintendent Lestrade said to get it to you at once."

"Hmm." Naked, except for my pants and slippers, I tore open the envelope and read its content. It was more than enough to ruin my day permanently. Muldoon kept fidgeting.

"Is there a reply, sir?"

"Yes, tell Lestrade to wire the prison that I'm on my way."

"Yes, sir." He started to turn.

"And find a hansom cab on your way. Have the driver here in ten minutes."

At that, he tapped his hard cap, "Will do, Inspector. G'day to you." Then he was rushing off down Boylson Street.

As I walked back up the stairs I re-read the telegraph from Warden Horatio Alper. It was a puzzle, the kind I am incapable of ignoring.

Back in the bedroom, I started towards the bathroom, setting the telegram on the bureau beside the door. Of Dr. Amelia Van

Helsing, all I could see was a very shapely leg emerging from a tangle of blankets and pillows.

"Amy, wake up," I said in a loud voice.

"Huh…wha…?" A lovely, round face, hair all a-mess, rose up out of the concealment. "What the bloody hell time is it?"

"Just after seven."

The head fell back on the pillows. "Aggh. Leave me alone."

"Can't; we've got a case."

"I don't care."

"Josiah Sparks…"

"I don't give a shit about Josiah—"

"He's been murdered."

"**W**hy would anyone want to kill a man who was scheduled to hang in two days?" Van Helsing asked as we rolled towards the prison complex in nearby Cambridge.

"An intriguing question, Doctor. One I am most anxious to discover the answer to."

It was a cool fall day and the leaves were changing their colours so that the sombre, dark, gray edifice at the end of the long boulevard—which was our destination—was surrounded all sides by trees of red, yellow and orange. The scene was like a surrealist painting. The guards stopped us at the gate to confirm our identities, then another pulled back the massive bars, and our cabbie urged his horse to continue on to the main building on the opposite side of a long courtyard.

Stepping out of the hansom, we were greeted by Warden Alper, a portly man with graying hair and a thick, walrus-like moustache of the same hue.

"Thank heavens you're here, Holmes," he blurted, not bothering the formality of a hand shake. "Please," he swung his arm to the main entrance hall and the staircase along the right wall. "The Final Corridor is located on the second floor. I believe you've been here before?"

"On several occasions," I confirmed. "This is my consulting

assistant, Dr Amelia Van Helsing."

"Yes, yes," he looked back at her sheepishly. "Please excuse my lack of manners, Doctor. This entire affair has me quite flustered."

"I'm sure," Van Helsing politely said. "When was the crime discovered, if I may ask?"

"Only a few hours ago when Guard Edgar Tennant went to his…ah…Spark's cell to deliver his breakfast. He found Sparks on his bed: dead."

We reached the second floor landing and Warden Alper, while holding onto the banister, took a second to catch his wind. By his girth, it was obvious he did very little in the way of physical activity. Taking a silk handkerchief from his coat, he mopped the perspiration from his forehead.

"And who was the last man to see Josiah Sparks alive?" I asked while Alper regained his breath.

"The same fellow, Tennant." He pointed to a door at the end of the hall. "In there is the guard station which is manned by two men at all times. Last evening's shift consisted of Tennant and Guard Leo Bailey. They are both awaiting us now."

At the door, the warden rapped his knuckles under the eye-slot. It opened, someone peered out and then it closed; followed by the sound of a lock being slid back. The door opened and Van Helsing and I went in after Warden Alper.

There were actually three people awaiting us in the square room; the two prison guards easily identified by their dark blue uniforms, and my old friend, Dr Nigel Pettibone, the county coroner.

The room had a single window to our right that overlooked the main courtyard and high prison walls beyond. In front of this were two small desks set side by side and to right was another door appropriately marked 'LOO'. There were several hard wood chairs scattered about, a clothes rack, and to the left of the window a tall medicine cabinet. Directly across from the entry door was a matching door which I easily assumed led out to the so-called Final Corridor; the place where condemned men were quartered five days before their appointed executions.

While I was taking all this in, the warden was introducing everyone. "This here is Edgar Tennant," he said indicating the shorter and older of the two guards. Tennant was balding with patches of gray hair over his ears, a button nose and wire-rim glasses covered two brown eyes. He could not have been more than five feet, five inches tall.

"And guard Leo Bailey, two of our finest men." Bailey was average height, maybe five feet, ten inches, with fine, straw coloured hair and a razor thin moustache barely visible over his upper lip. Both men, standing behind their respective desks, nodded to us politely.

"I'm sure you know Doctor Pettibone," our host concluded, pointing to the beefy pathologist in the brown tweed suit. A dapper fellow, with slick, black hair, my friend looked more like a barrister than a medical man.

"Hello, Inspector and Dr. Van Helsing," he smiled. "Good to see you both." Pettibone was enamored of Van Helsing and could never quite hide it completely; whereas she often flirted with him unmercifully. Women are by far the crueller sex.

"Pettibone," I returned his greeting, while eyeing the closed door behind him. "I take it you have not yet examined the body?"

"What, and incur your wrath, old boy," he chuckled. "Heaven forbid, Holmes, I do know you that well by now."

"Yes, I dare say you do." I turned my gaze to Warden Alper. "Shall we proceed?"

Alper in turn gave Tennant a hand wave and the small man hustled over to a wall mount to retrieve a set of keys. He reached up; grabbed them, and then, circling around us, went over to the locked door and opened it. He backed up to let us pass.

"It was you who discovered Sparks dead?" I asked Guard Tennant.

"Er...yes, sir, Inspector, when I went to bring him his break-fast."

"Very well, you will accompany me and Dr. Van Helsing." I looked back at the others. "The rest of you will kindly remain here while we examine the crime tableau."

Knowing they would comply with my wishes, I then allowed

Tennant, still clutching his keys nervously, to move past me into the adjoining corridor.

The Final Corridor is a long, rectangular, windowless hall through which extends a small aisle for approximately twenty yards. At the end of this aisle was a door secured with a chain and lock. To either side were two fairly large cells, each of which contained a seven foot cot, with a pillow and rough, coarse blanket. At the centre of each cell, against the back wall, was a white porcelain toilet.

In the exact centre of the aisle was an old, cast-iron, pot-bellied stove; its flue-pipe rising up through a fitted hole in the ceiling. We could feel the heat emanating from it as we approached the first cell on our left. It was the only one of the four cells currently occupied.

Looking through the equally spaced bars, I saw the late Josiah Sparks lying half on the floor in a diagonal position, his thighs and legs still on the cot where he supposedly had met his demise. Something, or someone, had caused his body to slide off the bed during the commission of their foul deed. All imposing seven feet of him; although no longer menacing.

"Is this how you found him?" I asked Guard Tennant as he slid the proper key into the cell locking mechanism.

"Aye, sir. He was just like you see him now, Guv'nor, half in and out of his sack."

"Did you enter the cell?"

Tennant pulled open the door. "Yes, sir. I did."

"What did you do with the breakfast tray?"

"The wha…oh, right. Yes, sir. Well, when I sees him stretched out like that, I set it down on the floor slot next to your foot there. It's against orders to open the door without an armed guard present, he being such a monster and all."

"Did you call out to Sparks?"

"Well, no, sir. I mean, I could see by the blue colour of his face he was a goner."

"Continue, Mr Tennant. What did you do next?"

Tennant looked at Van Helsing and then back to me obviously fearful of what he was about to confess. "I was scared and all, not thinking right. As I said, I set the tray down and I unlocked the door to go in and check on 'im."

Then Tennant, having opened the cell door, entered and moved to the body and demonstrated what he had done. He pointed at the dead man awkwardly. "I knelt right here, Guv'nor, and leaned over his face to see if he were still breathing. He weren't."

"And then?"

"Well, then I run to fetch Leo Bailey, I did. Told him what I'd found is what I did."

"Did Mr Bailey come back with you to see for himself?"

"Yes, sir. He did. Then he left to go tell Warden Alper while I stayed in the hall there, waiting."

The poor fellow looked as if he would be physically ill. I was almost finished with him.

"Just a few more questions, Tennant, if you don't mind."

"No, sir. Whatever it is you need."

"Excellent. Who was the last person to see Josiah Sparks alive?"

"That would be me, sir. When I brought him his dinner last night."

"What time was that?"

"Shortly after six, sir. The kitchen had made up a lamb stew, sir. Our cooks do a fine job of it, they do. We get no complaints from the inmates cause of the grub."

Dr Van Helsing was doing her best not to chuckle.

"Was that the last time you saw him alive, when you brought him this meal of lamb stew?"

"Well, yes, sir."

"Then where is the bowl and serving tray upon which you delivered it?"

Edgar Tennant's eyes widened like a trapped rabbit, then he shook his head. "Forgive me, sir, I misspoke. I did return later to remove those items."

"Which would have been what...about six-thirty?"

"Yessir."

"And did Sparks appear well and healthy when you returned and removed those items?"

"Yes, sir, he did. He shoved the empty tray through the floor slot, said to give his compliments to the chef like some fancy big-wig and then returned to his bunk. That was how I left him. Sitting there, with his back against the bars."

"Thank you, Guard Tennant. You may return to the guard station now while my colleague and I examine the body."

As soon as Edgar Tennant was gone, Dr Van Helsing came into the cell and stood beside me. I could see her own eyes flicking back and forth as they took in every single detail before them. Van Helsing's memory is nearly as sharp as my own.

"Do you believe him?" she finally asked, referring to the guard's story.

"Do I have a choice?" I went down on one knee and carefully took a hold of Spark's right wrist. Even through my kid gloves, I could feel its coldness. "Rigor has set in. He's been dead for most the night."

"Look at his throat," Van Helsing directed as she leaned over my left shoulder. "Those are fingers marks about his neck. It appears his larynx has been crushed."

Staring into the face of a dead man is not pleasant but in dealing with murder one must endure such discomfort in seeking out the truth.

There were indeed ligature marks on Josiah Sparks' neck, rough, red bruises like those left by human hands. His mouth was open and his tongue, now gray in colour, stuck out from it like some devilish slug attempting to rise from its hole. The pupils of his eyes were dilated and there was blood around them; evidence of ruptured capillaries. The human body undergoes many violent changes when violent death attacks it.

It was then that my nose detected a faint, sweet odour. I titled my head closer to that awful, gaping maw and sniffed.

"You smell something?" Van Helsing is also very good at stating the obvious.

"Perhaps. But it's too faint and I cannot quite identify it."

Having observed all I needed to, I rose to my feet and said,

"I'm done here. You?"

She made a point of walking in a tight circle around the small cell then copied my own inspection of the corpse to include smelling the area about the mouth.

"Hmm…the only odour I can smell is foul; from whatever he ingested last. Nothing overly peculiar in that regard."

Thus we concluded our tableau investigation and returned to the guard station. There I informed Dr Pettibone about our surmising that death was by strangulation. Pettibone picked up his medical bag and went to make his own determination.

In the meantime, I turned my focus on the second guard; Leo Bailey. He was standing beside his desk, having given over his chair to Warden Alper.

"Now, Guard Bailey," I began. "If you would be so kind as to answer a few questions, just as your associate has done."

"Anything, sir. I am at your service."

"**O**ne of them did it," Van Helsing said matter-of-factly as we were jostled up and down in the hansom cab.

"Or both of them," I returned as we rode through Boston and to Constabulary Headquarters. There was a fire in her eyes indicative of the puzzle's challenge.

"But bloody how?" she slapped her hands together. "Together, Tennant and Bailey wouldn't pose a problem to a normal back alley ruffian. One is no more than a bean stalk and the other an overgrown dwarf! It is physically impossible for either of them, alone or together, to have gotten the best of a giant like Sparks; overwhelmed him and then successfully strangled him."

"But we are left with the fact that it did happen, my dear. There is no denying the man is dead, the very life choked out of him, while he was incarcerated in a cell where the only two people having access to him were George Tennant and Leo Bailey."

I tapped the two slim folders on my lap; the prison's personnel records on both men which Warden Alper had been kind enough to let us borrow. "I believe the answer...or part of it, lies within these pages."

"How do you mean, Holmes?"

"Considering the absurdity of the murder's timing, I've ruled out any thought of a third party having hired Tennant or Bailey to commit the act."

"Because if that were the case, they most likely would have accomplished it weeks ago."

"Exactly, Doctor. With only two days remaining before Sparks' public execution, all of this smacks of a final, desperate act meant to thwart the cold and unemotional sentencing and replace it with an act of obsessed, violent passion."

"Meaning one of them wanted to personally bring about Sparks' death with their own two hands."

"So I surmise, until we have facts to prove otherwise."

"But damn it, Holmes! Which one of them?"

"And thus the carousel turns, Van Helsing. Let us forego any further discussion until we are back in my office. Allow our minds to work in silence for a while and enjoy this splendid autumn day."

"For a copper, Sherlock, you have a great deal of the poet in you."

"One of my many fine qualities."

"Of course," she laughed. "Humility being another."

Once back at the station, we went directly to my office. Van Helsing removed her jacket and hat and made herself comfortable on the settee while I took a moment to glance into the open squad area. It being long after noon, both of us were hungry and I sought to remedy that situation by sending Officer Donald Smite to Jake's Tavern at the end of the street to procure us sandwiches and several bottles of his finest ale.

That settled, I returned to my cluttered desk, took hold of the guards' folders and handed them to my colleague.

"I want to you read these very carefully, Doctor." Amelia Van

Helsing's mind is as brilliant as my own and anything she reads is instantly committed to memory; a trait most useful in our line of work.

"And what will you be doing, Sherlock?"

I returned to my desk and there, amidst the several layers of paper debris, withdrew four police folders and held them up for her to see. "These are fact-sheets on our Sparks' victims. I believe somewhere in these records and those of the two prison guards there is a connecting thread. If we can uncover it…"

"It will reveal a possible motive for the murder."

"Affirmative."

"Then let's get to it." She leaned back on the padded sofa, opened one of the folders and began to study it while I made myself comfortable in my swivel chair behind my desk and proceeded to do likewise with my own records.

Smite returned twenty minutes later with two meatloaf sandwiches and four brown bottles of strong beer. We continued our reading while enjoying this late but tasty lunch. The clock on the wall over Van Helsing's head was tipping two o'clock when I finished perusing the last of the four reports of Josiah Sparks' sad victims.

I looked up to see Van Helsing starting to sip on her second beer, both prison folders closed on the cushion beside her.

"So, are we ready to continue?" I asked, wiping my mouth with a paper napkin.

"Fire away, old boy."

"Alright then." I pushed away from my desk and turned to stretch out my legs while extending my arms over my head to relax the muscles in my back. "Why don't you start by telling us who the two guards are." I brought down my right hand and put it over police folders. "If any single item is repeated in the dossiers I've just read, I will stop you."

"Very well, let's begin." She took one more swig from her

beer, adjusted herself on the sofa and then laying her head back, began her recitation.

"Leo Hiram Bailey was born in Saco, Maine, fifty-eight years ago. He went to the Saco Peremptory Academy. Upon graduation enlisted in Her Majesty's Navy and served for eight years aboard the gunship, Excelsior. Upon his discharge, here in Boston, he entered the Cambridge Police Force and shortly thereafter met his wife, Maude Mary Daniels. They have two children, Walter Riley and Alice Kay…"

"How old is the girl?"

Without opening her eyes, Dr. Van Helsing, counted the fingers on her left hand and then said, "She would be twenty-nine at this time."

All the victims were no more than twenty, according to the coroner's reports. Still, without proof of documentation, which was unavailable for three of the four deceased women, affixing an age to a lifeless body is in the end mere guess work.

"Continue, Doctor."

Without skipping a beat, she did so. "And they currently reside at 27 Westchester Avenue, in Cambridge proper. Bailey left the police department ten years ago receiving several citations of merit upon his departure and an enthusiastic letter of recommendation which he used to gain his guard position at the prison."

She paused. "That's all we have on Bailey. Shall I go on to Tennant?"

"Please."

"George Arnold Tennant, born in Quincy, attended public schools and then enlisted in the military; the Colonial Forces to be exact. Served with distinction in the Western Territories Uprising where he was wounded and later discharged with the Victoria Medal for Meritorious Service. Became a constable in the Chelsea Police Department, and while there married one Grace Ann Dupris of Mantapan…"

"What was that maiden name again?" I cut in.

"Dupris, she was of French Canadian ancestry."

"Was?"

"She died four years ago."

"Does it state a cause of death?"

Van Helsing opened her eyes and sat up straight. "No, it does not. Is there something here?"

I tapped my victim's reports. "The name of the fourth and final victim was Helen Dupris. No known address or other vital information."

Van Helsing picked up one of her folders and opened it on her lap. "George and Grace had two daughters; Samantha, now age twenty-two and...Helen. She would be nineteen."

"Then it is possible she is our fourth victim and sometime in the past, most likely after becoming a prostitute, adopted her mother's maiden name."

"That's rather flimsy at best, Sherlock. It could merely be a coincidence."

"Balderdash, Doctor; you know my feelings about coincidences."

"The sheerest veneer of any lie," she recited, having heard me say it repeatedly. At the same time she pulled a small pack of cigarillos from her vest pocket along with a wooden match.

I wrinkled my nose watching her light the foul thing. "Must you?"

"Don't start," she countered blowing out a puff of smoke. "You have your vices and I have mine. If it bothers you so much, crack open the window."

I spun about in my chair and was just about to do as she had suggested when I inhaled a small whiff of her tobacco. I instantly forgot about the window.

It was the smell of the tobacco that had finally triggered what I had barely picked up in Josiah Spark's cell.

"Laudanum!" I blurted out, slapping my hands together.

"What?"

"My lovely, sweet Van Helsing. I could kiss you."

"Contain yourself, dear boy," she blew out another puff of smoke. "What the blazes are you getting at?"

"I know how he did it!"

The young woman who answered the door at the Tennant residence the next day was plain in appearance but had lovely blue eyes that hinted at a warm and loving soul.

"Yes?" she smiled at us; curiously wondering who would be calling on such an early hour on a Saturday morning.

"Miss Samantha Tennant?" I politely removed my derby and bowed slightly.

"Yes, I am she." Spoken like the prim and proper elementary school teacher she was.

"Inspector Sherlock Holmes," I announced. "And this is my associate, Dr Amelia Van Helsing. I was hoping we might have a word with your father."

Her confusion expanded and she was about to question us further when George Tennant's voice was heard from within the small cottage home. "It's alright, Sammie, dear, I've been waiting for the Inspector's visit."

Ushered into the main parlour, we found it both quaint and neatly kept. An old, worn, Persian carpet of faded colours covered most of the hardwood flooring. There were potted flowers everywhere and a large over-stuffed sofa facing several padded chairs over a small coffee table.

George Tennant appeared from a connecting hallway which I surmised led to the kitchen and dining area at the back of the house. Upon seeing us, he stiffened his resolved and confronted me in the middle of the room, head slightly bowed.

"Please forgive me for lying to you," he began in a soft voice. "After what I'd done, my nerves got the best of me, Guv'nor, and for that I am deeply ashamed."

"Father, what is this all about?" Samantha Tennant was shaken by her father's words and I hoped Van Helsing and I could continue in a delicate manner. Neither of us wished to cause these people any further pain and suffering.

Tennant started to reply but I quickly touched his arm and said, "Why don't we all sit down and sort all this out quietly."

Assayed for a moment, the school teacher and her father sat down on the sofa while Van Helsing and I sat in the matching chairs.

"Very well, let us start at the beginning, shall we, Mr Tennant?"

He merely nodded.

"I take it Helen Tennant was your youngest child?" Samantha's eyes reacted to my use of the past tense. "Is that correct?"

"Was?" she couldn't help but utter, turning to the little man beside her. "What does he mean by that, Father? Has something happened to Helen?"

"Miss Tennant," Van Helsing, God bless her, spoke up, realizing that what was needed here was a woman's touch. "When was the last time you saw your sister?"

Detoured from questioning her father, the now perplexed school teacher nervously touched the back of her brown hair and a sad look came over her face. "Let me see, it must be over three years now. Helen took Mother's passing so hard and no matter what we said, she wouldn't be reconciled with it."

"May I ask how your mother died?"

"It was consumption. Mother was always a fragile person and she'd suffered several bouts of pneumonia in the past. The attending physicians said it was the damp and cold of our New England winters that brought on her early...passing."

"Helen always blamed me," George Tennant added, taking hold of his daughter's hand. "You see, it was suggested we move to the dry climates of the southwest to help Grace's condition. But we couldn't, don't you see. What with my meagre salary..."

"Stop that, Father, you know full well Mother never entertained the idea. Even had you been able to gather the funds, she was determined to live out her life here in the Commonwealth."

"But your sister did not share that opinion?"

"No, I'm afraid not, Doctor." Samantha Tennant was doing her best to keep herself composed. "After Mother's passing, she became sullen and moody, staying out at all hours of the night and eventually she fell into the wrong crowd.

"When she was arrested with a group of her peers for vandalism, Father brought her home and did his best to correct her, but by then Helen wouldn't listen. She accused him of being responsible for…for Mother's death, and that very night she fled; never to return again."

And there it was, in so short a tale. Van Helsing nodded to me. Now it was upon my shoulders.

"Miss Tennant, it is my sad duty to inform you that your sister has died."

She released her Father's hand and brought it up to her mouth to stifle a gasp. "How?"

"She was murdered several months ago in Boston, the victim of a sadistic killer named Josiah Sparks."

"Josiah Sparks? The cult leader I read about in the papers." She turned to her father again. "Wasn't this the man who was to be executed tomorrow?"

George Tennant's eyes began to water. "Yes, my dear. He was the monster that killed our sweet Helen."

"And how did you learn of this?" I asked, doing my best to keep things moving forward. "From the papers as well?"

"Yes, Inspector. An edition of the Gazette published a photo of all the victims shortly after Sparks had been apprehended. Of course it was hard to recognize her after all these years and… the picture of her…body…was so horrible to look upon," said George Tennant.

"So what did you do?"

"I visited the morgue by myself, sir. I know a few of the blokes that works there on the graveyard shift. They let me take a look at her."

"Thus confirming she was in fact your lost daughter."

"Yes, sir."

Samantha Tennant began to sob and her father put his arm around her. "There, there, Sammie. I'm sorry, I just couldn't tell you before. My heart was broken and I feared I would lose you as well."

"Oh, Daddy." She hugged him all the tighter.

I pressed on. "And so the man who had murdered your daughter came to be in your charge at the prison for the last week prior to his sentencing."

"Yes, sir." He looked at us over his daughter's shoulder. "You can't imagine how hard it was to look at him every day, Inspector. He and that smug attitude of his. Always laughing and jeering as to how he'd done in those poor girls…as if it all were some silly joke and all."

"Never realizing he was confronting the father of one of them."

"I never told him, Inspector. No, sir."

"But ultimately you came to desire revenge."

"Yes, sir. As much as I prayed, the anger in me would not be denied."

"And it seemed unfair to you that this fiend should meet his end at the hands of an unfeeling, court appointed executioner. Is that the gist of your reasoning?"

"It wasn't right, sir. That he should die laughing about it all. Where was the justice in that? As the days grew closer to the hanging, I determined I couldn't let that happen. I vowed that this foul creature would die by my hands."

"Which is when you fell upon the idea of using the laudanum to incapacitate him."

Samantha Tennant stopped her crying and took the white linen handkerchief I leaned over and offered her. "Laudanum? Isn't that a drug of some kind?"

"Yes, Miss Tennant. It is a tincture derived of opium," I explained. "When Doctor Van Helsing and I examined the body of Josiah Sparks, I detected a trace of its odour about him. Then, later in my office, I recalled that the prison kept a supply of laudanum on hand in their medicine supplies to be used on those inmates to help steady them before their fateful encounter with the gallows."

"And my father administered this drug to this Sparks fellow?"

"Yes, Miss Tennant," Van Helsing picked up the narrative. "Josiah Sparks was a giant of a man and the Inspector and I were at a loss to understand how someone of your father's stature could possible overcome him. Until Inspector Holmes fell upon the idea of the laudanum. He surmised your father had laced Sparks' evening meal with a higher dose of the drug and it acted as a powerful sedative making him virtually helpless."

"That's what I done, Doctor. Just as you say. It was easy enough to pour almost an entire bottle into his lamb stew when old Leo Bailey was in the Loo."

I rose to my feet and slowly walked behind the sofa while still addressing the Tennants. "So that by the time you returned thirty minutes later, Josiah Sparks was in a drug induced stupor and you murdered him in his bunk."

"Yes, Inspector, that's what I done. Afterwards, I made sure to keep Leo out of the corridor so that I was the only one making periodic rounds."

"On a dead man."

"Yes, sir. After I'd done it, I didn't feel right. All night long, whenever I went in there and saw him, I knew there would be no escaping my punishment. By the time our shift ended, I acted as if I'd only then discovered the body and…well…you know the rest, sir. That's how it all happened."

A thick silence fell over all of us. With the story told, all that remained was to arrest the man and bring him into custody.

Samantha Tennant got to her feet and stood before the crumbled old man behind her. "What are you going to do now?" she asked me. "Are you going to lock him up too? Must I lose all of my family, Inspector?"

I began to reply when I caught Van Helsing's look. It was one I'd grown quite familiar with over the years.

I looked back at George Tennant's remaining daughter and sighed. Maybe in a perfect world, perfect justice exists. This is no such world.

"Mr Tennant." I looked past his daughter at where he sat. He lifted his tear-stained face.

"I'm ready to go with you, Guv'nor."

"That will not be necessary."

"Sir?"

"Josiah Sparks was sentenced to death by the Commonwealth of Massachusetts and for all practical purposes, that sentencing has been carried out. Regardless of the circumstances, the court order was executed."

"But, sir…"

"Allow me to finish, Mr Tennant."

"Sorry...sir."

"You will report to work on Monday and there submit your resignation to Warden Alper. From your file, I see you are eligible for a fair retirement stipend."

"That is so..."

"And you will never again make mention of this to another living soul. Nor will you ever seek employment elsewhere. Is that absolutely clear, Mr Tennant?"

"Ah...yes...I...yes, sir. I understand."

I looked to my associate who had gotten to her feet. "Then we will bid you both a good day. Our business here is concluded."

We had just started through the front door when I felt Samantha Tennant's hand on my elbow.

"Inspector Holmes...I...don't know what to say?"

I nodded to the little man still seated on the sofa. "Take care of each other, Miss Tennant. Simply take care of each other."

She closed the door and Dr. Van Helsing and I started walking down the street looking for a cab. She slipped her arm through mine and smiling said, "You old softy."

I did my best to ignore her. Honestly, she will be the end of me some day.

The Adventure of the Slaughter Stone

RAFE MCGREGOR

I

On glancing over my notes of the seventy odd cases in which I have, during the last eight years, studied the methods of my friend Sherlock Holmes, I find many tragic, some comic, a large number merely strange, but none commonplace; for, working as he did rather for the love of his art than for the acquirement of wealth, he refused to associate himself with any investigation which did not tend towards the unusual, and even the fantastic. Of all these varied cases, however, I cannot recall any which presented more singular features than that which was associated with the well-known Wiltshire family of the Rosses of Salisbury Plain. The events in question occurred in the early days of my association with Holmes, when we shared rooms in Baker Street as bachelor and widower. It was early in April in the year eighty-three that I woke one morning to find Sherlock Holmes standing, fully dressed, by the side of my bed. He was a late riser, as a rule, and as the clock on the mantelpiece showed me that it was only a quarter-past seven, I blinked up at him in some surprise, and no small amount of resentment, for I was myself regular in my habits.

"Very sorry to knock you up, Doctor," said he, "but it's the common lot this morning. Mrs Hudson has been knocked up, she retorted upon me, and I on you."

"What in God's name is it, then, a fire?"

"No, a client. It seems that a young lady has arrived in a considerable state of excitement, who insists upon seeing me. She is waiting now in the sitting-room. Now, when young ladies wander about the metropolis at this hour of the morning, and knock sleepy people up out of their beds, I presume that it is something very pressing which they have to communicate. Should it prove to be an interesting case, you would, I am sure, wish to follow it from the outset. I thought, at any rate, that I should call you and give you the chance."

"Seeing as I am already awake, there seems little point in missing it."

"Quite so."

I had only one pleasure keener than following Holmes in his professional investigations, and in admiring the rapid deductions, as swift as intuitions, and yet always founded on a logical basis, with which he unravelled the problems which were submitted to him. I rapidly threw on my clothes and was ready in a few minutes to accompany my friend down to the sitting-room. A young lady dressed in green, wearing a velvet hat adorned with an ostrich feather, who had been sitting in the window, rose as we entered.

"Good-morning, madam," said Holmes cheerily. "My name is Sherlock Holmes. This is my intimate friend and associate, Dr Grimesby Roylott of Baker Street."

II

The lady was small and slender, with fair hair, blue eyes, and ruby lips. A beautiful creature and rare too—unlike most pretty young things she held my gaze when I feasted my eyes upon her form.

"Ha! I am glad to see that Mrs Hudson has had the good sense to light the fire. Pray draw up to it."

"I am quite comfortable where I am, Mr Holmes."

Sherlock Holmes gave her one of his quick, all-comprehensive glances. "You have come in by train this morning, I see."

"You know me, then?"

"No, but I observe the second half of a return ticket in the palm of your left glove. You must have started early, and yet you had a good drive in a dog-cart, along heavy roads, before you reached the station."

The lady gave a violent start and stared in bewilderment at my companion.

"There is no mystery, my dear madam," said he. "The left arm of your jacket is spattered with mud in no less than seven places. The marks are perfectly fresh. There is no vehicle save a dog-cart which throws up mud in that way, and then only when you sit on the left-hand side of the driver."

"Whatever your reasons may be, you are perfectly correct," said she. "I started from home before six, reached Wilton at twenty past, and came in by the first train to Waterloo. Sir, I have need of your assistance. At present it is out of my power to reward you for your services, but in four weeks I shall be married, with the control of a large income, and then you shall not find me ungrateful."

"My professional charges are upon a fixed scale," said Holmes. "I do not vary them, save when I remit them altogether and leave matters in Dr Roylott's hands. Now I beg that you will lay before us everything that may help us in forming an opinion upon the matter."

"My name is Flower Dalrymple. I spent my early days on the Continent, travelling about from place to place learning much of Bohemian life and Bohemian ways. When I was eighteen years of age my father got an appointment in London. We came to live here—my father, my mother, two brothers, a sister, and myself. Before I was twenty I was engaged to David Ross. David is a landed proprietor. He has very good means, and is a most suitable match. His father died when he was a baby and he has spent all the intervening years, except when at school and the University, with his mother. His mother's name is Lady Sarah Ross. On her own mother's side she is of Spanish extraction, but she is the daughter of Earl Reighley. She is a great recluse, and David gave me to understand that her character and ways of life were peculiar.

"Unfortunately, she is rather more than eccentric and the relationship between mother and son is very strange and very deep. Lady Sarah is entirely opposed to David's engagement and it was only with some difficulty that I was able to persuade him to set a date for our union. Two weeks ago I received an invitation to their place, Longmore, for Easter, and I remain a guest until the end of this week. Longmore is a rambling old estate situated on Salisbury Plain. The house is built in the form of a cross, with a turreted roof, and a tower at one end. The centre of the cross, which forms the body of the house, is very old, but modern and well-appointed. I look forward to making it my own. Lady Sarah keeps a curious house, which includes a native butler, an Aboriginal from Australia whom she prefers to dress as if he was an Indian. Her taste in pets is even more bizarre, and she has a horrible collection of reptiles which she keeps in a specially-fitted greenhouse across the yard. She has some two or three dozen snakes collected from all over the world in this menagerie. She feeds them live pigeons and rabbits, calls them her beauties, and has given each a pet name. The woman is not in her right senses."

Sarah Ross sounded like a lady after my own heart. If I'd had enough loot I'd have taken my animals with me when I left India.

"On the first morning of my stay I was awoken by the lady's-maid pouring hot water into a bath for me. She came quite close and said, 'I am very glad you are going to marry Mr Ross, and I am very glad that you will be mistress here, for if there was not a change soon, I could not stay.'

"'What do you mean?' I said.

"She shrugged her shoulders and replied, 'This is a queer house. There are queer people in it, and there are queer things done in it, and—*there are the reptiles*! There are the reptiles,' she repeated, 'and Lady Sarah plays tricks with them at times. Samuel has a stuff which drives them nearly mad. When Lady Sarah is at her wildest she uses it. I have watched them when they didn't know I was looking: half a dozen of the snakes following Samuel as if they were demented, and Lady Sarah looking on and laughing! He puts the thing on his boots. I do not know what it is. They never hurt him. He flings the boots at them and they are quiet. Yes, it is a queer house and I am afraid of the reptiles. By the way, miss, would you not like me to clean your boots for you?"

"'Why so?' I asked.

"'I will, if you like,' she said. 'Samuel will not have them.' Then, with a 'Now, miss, I think you have everything you want,' she left me.

"Samuel is the Aboriginal butler and I could think of only one reason why he would be cleaning my boots. Later that day I asked the maid if any of the snakes were ever allowed in the house, but she seemed aghast at the idea. Nonetheless, I have been on my guard ever since and been especially careful to check my boots before putting them on."

Sherlock Holmes had been leaning back in his chair with his eyes closed and his head sunk in a cushion, but he half opened his lids now and glanced across at me.

Miss Dalrymple continued. "On Monday David was called away to London on urgent legal business. I did not see Lady Sarah until dinner, which was taken in complete silence. Samuel stood behind his mistress glaring at me throughout and although I had no appetite, I ate as quickly as courtesy would allow. Lady Sarah disappeared before the last plates were removed and I was about to escape to the sanctuary of my bedroom when Samuel escorted me to the morning-room. It is a somewhat dismal apartment and Lady Sarah was waiting for me.

"'Come here,' she said, 'I want to speak to you. So, you are David's choice! Now listen. The aim and object of my life ever since I lost my husband has been to keep David single.'

"'What do you mean?' I asked.

"'What I say. I love my son with a passion which you, you little white creature, cannot comprehend. I want him for myself *entirely*. You have dared to step in—you have dared to take him from me. But listen: even if you do marry him, you won't keep him long. You would like to know why? I will tell you. Because his love for you is only the passion which a man may experience for a pair of blue eyes, and a white skin, and childish figure. It is as water unto wine compared to the love he feels for me. Be warned in time. Give him up.'

"'I cannot,' I said.

"'You won't be happy here. This life is not your life. My fortune is not yours to take. My son is not the right sort of man for you. In some ways he is half a savage. He has been much in wild countries, in lands uninhabited by civilised people. He is not the man for you, nor I the mother-in-law. Give him up. Here is cheque for one thousand pounds. Here is paper and here is pen. Write him a letter. Write it now. The carriage is at the door to take you to Wilton. From there you can get the train to London, and you will be safe, little girl, quite safe. A small fortune is better than no fortune at all, which is what you will have if you stay.'

"'You ask the impossible,' I replied, 'I love your son.'

"She had spoken with earnestness, the colour flaming into her cheeks, her eyes bright. Now her face grew cold and leaden in hue. 'I have given you a way of escape,' she said. 'If you do not accept the offer, it is not my fault.' Once again, she rose and left without a word.

"Yesterday, I did not see Lady Sarah until lunch, when she was smiling and agreeable, as if the conversation of the previous evening had not occurred. Samuel was absent and my worries eased until Lady Sarah spoke.

"'I have had a busy morning,' she said. 'Little Blackie is ill.'

"'Little Blackie?' I asked.

"'My beloved *Pseudechis Porphyriacus*. Blackie is the biggest in my collection and his bite can kill a *man* in six minutes. Samuel and I have been giving him some medicine.' I made no remark. 'I'm afraid you must amuse yourself as best you can this afternoon,' she continued, 'for Samuel and I will be engaged with the snake.'

"I thanked Lady Sarah for her concern, somewhat relieved that I would not have to endure her company, but my spirits sank again when I received a telegram from David saying that he would not be back until Thursday—tomorrow. Lady Sarah made only a brief appearance at dinner, and has invited me for an evening stroll tonight. She said that Stonehenge is particularly pleasant under a sickle moon and that she wants to show me the Slaughter Stone. David has already given me a tour of the stones and the one to which Lady Sarah referred is where the Druids used to conduct their human sacrifices. I have absolutely no wish to be there at night, let alone with Lady Sarah, but I cannot refuse. When I retired last night, I was informed by the maid-of-all-work that the lady's-maid has been granted a leave of absence to visit an ailing relative. The scene has been set for a tragedy I wish to avoid, which is why I have returned to London with the one object of seeing you and seeking your assistance."

"You have done wisely," said Holmes. There was a long silence, during which he leaned his chin upon his hands and stared into the crackling fire. "Lady Sarah is still in possession of the Rayleigh tiara?"

Miss Dalrymple's eyes sparkled. "Oh, yes, Mr Holmes, David is going to have the jewels re-set for me once we are married."

"The tiara will be my fee. Or a cheque for the equivalent. I have no preference."

Our visitor nodded. "You will have the cheque when I am married."

"Protection is not my usual line, but given the financial incentive which you have so graciously provided, I have several most able agents whom I should be glad to oversee. If you would prefer someone to accompany you back to Longmore today, I am sure Dr Roylott will oblige. Otherwise, I shall have an agent in place on Salisbury Plain this evening. As to the term of engagement, will you be requiring the service for the duration of your stay at Longmore or until the happy day of your union?"

"Mr Holmes, I am disappointed."

"I can assure you that I select my agents with great care. It is not for nothing that I am the last and highest court of appeal in crime."

"Then I fear I have not made myself clear. I do not seek your assistance as a bodyguard."

"No? Pray be precise as to the details."

"I want you to kill Lady Sarah."

III

"What do you think of it all, Roylott?" asked Sherlock Holmes once Miss Dalrymple had glided from our sitting-room.

"That I should like to acquire whatever it is the Aboriginal puts in—or on—his boots. It could be most useful in future."

"Exotic animals are your department. What game do you propose that Lady Sarah intends to play at the Slaughter Stone this evening?"

"She will see that this mysterious substance is applied to our client's boots. I have never been to the stones, but I have seen a photograph. There are places aplenty to hide. Lady Sarah will have the Aboriginal set an ambuscade with the snake. All she need do is draw Miss Dalrymple close enough for the snake to smell her and it will be yet another unfortunate accident of the type you are so fond of creating. A pukka death by misadventure."

"I see many objections your theory, but they may not be fatal. But what in the name of the devil!"

The ejaculation had been drawn from my companion by the fact that our door had been suddenly dashed open, and that a tall and stately woman had framed herself in the aperture. Her costume consisted of black velvet and the finest Brussels lace, with diamonds glittering on her fingers. She had almond-shaped eyes and an unnaturally swarthy complexion. Her hair was abundant and white as snow, and her very black eyes, narrow-arched brows, and dark skin were brought into sharper contrast by this wealth of silvery hair. There was something wild about her and she must have been a fine figure of a woman before her youth faded and withered.

"Which of you is Holmes?" she demanded.

"My name, madam; but you have the advantage of me," my companion replied quietly, without rising.

"I am Lady Sarah Ross."

"Indeed," said Holmes. "Pray take a seat."

"I will do nothing of the kind. Flower Dalrymple has been

here. I have followed her. What has she been saying to you?"

"It is a little cold for the time of the year," said Holmes.

"What has she been saying to you?" screamed the old woman.

"But I have heard that the crocuses promise well," continued my companion.

"Ha! You put me off, do you?" Our new visitor entered the room. "I know you, you scoundrel! I have heard of you before. You are Holmes, the pilferer."

My friend smiled.

"Holmes, the blackmailer!"

His smile broadened.

"Holmes, the common criminal!"

Holmes chuckled heartily. "Your conversation is most entertaining," said he. "When you go out; close the door, for there is a decided draught."

"I will go when I have said my say. Don't you dare to meddle in my affairs. I know that Miss Dalrymple has been here. I *followed* her! I am a dangerous woman to cross! See here." She stepped swiftly forward, reached into her reticule, and hurled a snake onto the floor.

Holmes leapt to his feet and seized the poker.

"Leave it, Holmes," I said. "It is a carpet snake, harmless, like this old crone." I leant forward and rubbed my thumb back and forth over my fingertips to attract the snake, which slithered towards me.

Lady Sarah snarled and strode from the room.

"She seems a very amiable person," said Holmes, laughing. "Fancy her having the insolence to confound me with a common criminal! This incident gives zest to our investigation, however, and I only trust that our client will not suffer from her imprudence in allowing this harridan to follow her. And now, Roylott, I was speaking of fatal objections—or, more to the point, fatal snakes. Is *Pseudechis Porphyriacus* as dangerous as our client has been led to believe?"

I picked up the carpet snake, which curled around my cuff. "To Miss Dalrymple, no."

Holmes put his fingertips together. "Pray explain."

"The Red-Bellied Black Snake is fatal to small mammals, but not humans and certainly not quickly. Its bite would be a most unreliable manner in which to remove a prospective daughter-in-law. I suspect that the good lady intends to frighten her to death. The snake can grow to more than six feet in length and would make a fearful predator if it could be induced to chase her among the standing stones. But Miss Dalrymple is quite obviously made of sterner stuff, so perhaps Lady Ross is doolally tap."

"Perchance, but the care of her calculation suggests otherwise. Consider the steps she has taken to plan this evening's theatre, and her concern to avoid any charges of assault we might bring against her. I shall handle her—can you do the same for *Pseudechis Porphyriacus*?"

I stroked the head of the snake, now wrapped around my forearm. "My riding crop would suffice in normal circumstances, but not if the Aboriginal's trick is as effective as Miss Dalrymple claims."

"Then why don't you order breakfast while I send for Parker. Afterwards I shall take a cab to Fitzroy Square and see what Von Herder can do for us on short notice."

Von Herder was a blind German gunsmith. I was pleased that it was going to be one of Holmes's hands-on cases.

IV

Sherlock Holmes and I had no difficulty in engaging a bedroom and sitting-room at the Bridge Inn in Upper Woodford. He had selected the village over Wilton or Amesbury as it was located a mere mile and a half from Longmore. Our rooms were on the first floor, and our window commanded a view of the avenue gate to the estate with the naked eye, and of the cruciform manor house with my field glasses. It was a perfect evening, still and cold. The sun was near the horizon and would soon set, but there was no sign of the waning moon yet. Holmes and I sat together in the gathering darkness.

"Do you know, Roylott," he said, "I have really some scruples as to taking you tonight. There is a distinct element of danger."

"There always is."

"Yes, but the danger in this instance is the unpredictability of the situation. There are a large number of variables in play and the most important of them all is simply too capricious to second-guess."

"Lady Sarah?"

Holmes nodded. "Leave her and her butler to me. You shall take care of the snake should it appear. You have your Eley's No. 2?"

I patted my pocket.

"Capital. Take these five rounds. I suggest you load three of them, no more."

Holmes dropped five bullets into my hand. I picked one up and examined it closely. The brass cartridge was identical to my other shells, but the lead had been replaced by a glass bullet, inside of which were half-a-dozen tiny pellets. "Shotgun rounds for revolvers?"

"The principle is the same. I anticipate that a frenzied snake playing amongst the stones of the Henge under a sickle moon will make for a difficult target. You can wound it with Von Herder's snakeshot and then finish it off with your regular shot. He warned me that the snakeshot is only effective at very close range, but I expect that's obvious. I have my own revolver to hand for our human antagonists."

I began reloading as instructed. "What's your plan?"

"We will leave as soon as you are ready. Proceed to the stones and take up our position before the curtain rises."

"What if the Aboriginal joins us before the crone and our client?"

"Then," said Holmes with icy calm, "we shall re-christen the Slaughter Stone before we begin our commission for Miss Dalrymple. Leave that to me. Your job is to ensure that the snake does not obstruct my movements."

"What about Miss Dalrymple?"

"You have said yourself that the snake's venom is not fatal. If you must let it bite her in order to get a better shot, do so. If she is wounded by the snakeshot, the damage will be no more than cosmetic. Just make sure you don't injure her right hand. We don't want the handwriting on the cheque contested by the bank."

I snapped the cylinder of the Eley No. 2 closed. "I'm ready."

V

The plain looked weird in the moonlight. Weird and unfathomable. It was easy to imagine the howls of prehistoric savages and their victims in the wind whipping across the earth. It was some distance to the nearest copse so the broken ring of stone afforded the only shelter from the intermittent gale. Despite the absence of trees and the flatness of the ground, I could see very little in the faint illumination of the moon, even with the assistance of my glasses. I could spy a faint light from Upper Woodford to the south, but not Longmore which, although much closer, was invisible behind a screen of trees. The view above was more revealing and the canopy of stars added to the eerie atmosphere of our hide. Holmes and I had been waiting for two hours and he had forbidden me to smoke in order to preserve my night vision.

I passed the time by pacing to and fro instead, stomping the springy turf and alternating between slapping my riding crop against my gaiters and peering into the night with my glasses. Holmes sat on one of the fallen stones, displaying the red-Indian composure which had made his reputation as a machine rather than a man. Patience is one of the many virtues I lack and my mood soured at the start of the third hour of our vigil. Irritation gave way to anger and I began to worry about controlling myself when the action started. Anger provides me with a satisfaction that no other experience has afforded and I have little incentive to restrain myself, even had I the temperance.

Holmes rose and stepped forward, pressing against one of the standing stones. "Roylott!"

"What?"

"The wind is in our favour. I hear a carriage in the distance. Can you see it?"

I couldn't hear anything, but I squinted out across the plain through my field glasses. At first, I saw nothing, then the outline of a human figure—a woman, about two hundred yards away. "A woman, running, either towards us or in the opposite direction, I can't tell yet."

"Our client. She will be making for the stones."

Holmes was right. I couldn't discern the details, but the form fitted Miss Dalrymple perfectly. "It's her. She has stopped. She is looking behind her. Now she is running towards us again."

"Can you see the carriage yet?"

I scoured the plain behind Miss Dalrymple and made out a dog-cart, about a hundred and fifty yards behind her and gaining rapidly. "Yes. Two people. One has white hair, the other is dark." I heard the crack of a whip. "I think it's Lady Sarah and her Aboriginal."

Miss Dalrymple stumbled and I started forward, but Holmes held his arm across my chest.

"Wait."

I raised the glasses again. "Miss Dalrymple has fallen...she is back on feet, running again. I can see Lady Sarah and the Aboriginal clearly now. They will be upon her before she reaches us."

I threw down my glasses and reached for my revolver. "Let me get rid of Von Herder's cartridges; we can ambush the dog-cart together!"

Holmes gripped my wrist and the strength in his fingers was even greater than my own. "No!" I nearly seized him by the collar, but my fury was not sufficiently fuelled to risk death for no good reason. "Listen, Doctor, listen!"

Miss Dalrymple reached the Slaughter Stone, some twenty yards from us, and collapsed upon it with a cry of despair. I could hear the gasps of her breath, the thudding hooves of the horse, another crack of the whip, and...*hissing*. A low, continuous hiss. There was a shout from the cart and Holmes leapt forward, dragging me with him.

"The snake, Roylott, the snake!"

We ran at the Slaughter Stone, revolvers at the ready, but the dog-cart reached it first. Holmes stopped and took aim. I saw the snake rear up to about two feet in height, its long body glistening in the moonlight. I stood over Miss Dalrymple, cocked the Eley No. 2, and took aim at the big black head as it drew back. A loud report rang out across the plain and Miss Dalrymple screamed. Lady Sarah had climbed from the dog-cart—she fired a second shot at the snake. She missed, its head lashed forward, and I fired. The head snapped sideways and I fired the rest of the snakeshot into it. The poor creature fell, now writhing in agony, and I administered the *coup de grace* with one of my own rounds.

Lady Sarah stared at me, dropped her revolver, and ran to Miss Dalrymple.

"Stay right where you are," Holmes told the Aboriginal, who was still atop the dog-cart. He turned his revolver to Lady Sarah, who was now bent over our client.

"Flower!" Lady Sarah's face was very white and had a peculiar expression about it. "He is dead. I tried to shoot him with my own hands, but Dr Roylott succeeded where I failed. You have nothing to fear from me or from Little Blackie. Come!"

The madness I had seen in her eyes in Baker Street had gone and she did not look unkind. "You are a plucky girl, and I respect you, but you do not need Mr Holmes anymore."

"My snakeshot is finished, Holmes, do you want me to take care of the Aboriginal?"

"Do nothing."

Lady Sarah drew Miss Dalrymple to her feet and held her in both hands. "Hear what I have to say. Long ago I made a vow. I solemnly vowed before Almighty God that as long as I lived I would never allow my only son to marry. He knew that I had made this vow, and for a long time he respected it, but he met you and become engaged to you in defiance of his mother's vow and his mother's wish. When I heard the tidings I became wild with jealousy, rage, and real madness. I would not write to you, nor would I write to him."

"Why did you write at last, why did you ask me here?" asked Miss Dalrymple.

"Because the jealousy passed, as it always does, and for a time I was sane."

"Sane!" cried our client.

"Yes, little girl, *yes, sane!* But listen. Some years ago, when on the coast of Guinea, I was the victim of a very severe sunstroke. From that time I have had fits of madness. Any shock, or excitement, brings them on. With madness in my veins I watched you and David during this last week, and the wild desire to crush you to the very earth came over me. David went to London, and I thought the opportunity had come. I spoke to Samuel about it, and Samuel made a suggestion. I listened to him. My brain was on fire. I agreed to do what he suggested. My snake Little Blackie was to be the weapon to take your life. I felt neither remorse nor pity. There is a certain substance extracted from a herb which the Aborigines know, and which, when applied to any part of the dress or the person of an enemy, will induce a snake which comes across his path to turn and follow him. The substance drives the snake mad, and he will follow and kill his victim. Samuel possessed the stuff, and from time to time to amuse me, he has tried its power on my reptiles. He has put it on his own boots, but he himself has never been bitten, for he has flung the boots to the snakes at the last moment. This afternoon he put it on the coat which you are now wearing. He then terrified you and induced you to run away across the Plain, whereupon he let Little Blackie loose. Little Blackie followed you as a needle will follow a magnet. Samuel called me to the wicket-gate, and showed me his handiwork. As I looked, a veil fell from my eyes. The madness left me, and I became sane. I saw the awful thing that I had done. I repented with agony. In a flash, I ordered the dog-cart and followed you. I was too late. Had it not been for Mr Holmes and Dr Roylott you would be dead." Lady Sarah wiped the drops of perspiration from her forehead. "You are quite safe," she said, after a pause, "and I am sane. What I did, I did when I was not accountable. Are you going to tell David?"

"How can I keep it from him?"

"It seems hard to you now, but I ask you not to do it. I promise not to oppose your marriage. I go meekly to the Dower House. I am tired of the reptiles; my favourite is dead and the others are nothing to me. They shall be sent as a gift to the Zoological

Gardens. Will you tell David?"

"Miss Dalrymple," Holmes interrupted, "would you be so kind as to take a pace to your right. I am an excellent shot, but I am sure that you would rather avoid adding blood to the grass stains on your ensemble."

"No!" Miss Dalrymple jumped in front of Lady Sarah, her arms outspread. "No, please, Mr Holmes, there is no longer any need. I have succeeded in my goal and you will be rewarded for your services as agreed."

Holmes and I locked eyes. "You are certain, Miss Dalrymple?"

"Yes, I am certain. Lady Sarah has tried to save me, now I shall save her."

"The Aboriginal," I snarled, "let me have him!"

"We have no commission for Samuel, although I am prepared to make an exception for our client if she believes her life is still in danger. Miss Dalrymple?"

"No, I shall deal with him myself," she replied.

Holmes nodded. "Very well. We do, after all, aim to give satisfaction." He turned his revolver on me. "Roylott?"

I replaced the Eley No. 2 in my pocket, disgusted at the turn of events.

"Thank you, Mr Holmes." Miss Dalrymple embraced Lady Sarah. "I will never tell him, if you will never tell him about Mr Holmes and Dr Roylott."

"You are worthy to be his wife," replied Lady Sarah, her voice hoarse.

"A charming domestic scene," I spat.

"Indeed," said Holmes, "and one to which our presence is now entirely supererogatory."

VI

Two months later the case had almost passed from my mind. In the interim, Holmes had received a handsome cheque from Mrs David Ross, I had been amply rewarded for my services on the plain, the newly-wed couple had gone abroad on their honeymoon, and Lady Sarah had repaired to the Dower House of which she had spoken. The affair had, in short, proved yet another startling success for my friend. Then one morning there came one of the enigmatic notes which appeared in our letterbox from time to time, usually anonymous and always in cipher. Mrs Hudson brought up the message with the first post and I watched Holmes page through *Whitaker's Almanac* and scribble the results of his deduction with a pencil. I waited without word until he tossed the paper over to me.

"There you have it," he said, knocking the ashes from his after-breakfast pipe.

On the reverse of the message, Holmes had written:

DEAR MR. HOLMES,

Lady Sarah Ross committed suicide last night. She had spoken of it several times to her lady's-maid. She appears to have used her own pistol to shoot herself in the temple and death was instantaneous. The case is cut and dried. There is no doubt what the coroner's verdict will be.

FRED PORLOCK.

Porlock was one of Holmes's many agents, but I couldn't fathom why he'd have thought Holmes would be interested in the old crone's fate. "I thought you had been paid," I said. Holmes nodded. "Then why did Porlock waste your time with this intelligence? For that matter, how did he know of your involvement with the Rosses at all? I thought you used Parker for the commission."

"And what was the commission?" he asked, refilling his pipe from the Persian slipper.

The commission had of course changed that night on the plain. "I don't know. To protect Mrs Ross? To make good her marriage? I'm not sure."

"I am a scientific criminal, Roylott. When I accept a commission there is neither margin for error nor room for ambiguity. My commission was to kill Lady Sarah Ross. That commission has been fulfilled."

"This was your work?"

Holmes nodded again as he picked up a glowing cinder with the tongs and used it to light his pipe.

"But why go to the extra lengths? You had been paid: Mrs Ross was content." I said.

"How long do you think I should last as the highest court of appeal in crime if it became known that I had accepted a commission for murder, and that the victim was alive, awaiting her natural end in the comfort of Longmore's Dower House?"

I considered for a moment. "Then you were lucky that she decided to keep her revolver with her."

"She decided no such thing."

"I don't understand."

"I slipped it into my pocket at the end of our adventure on the plain. You were too enraged to notice."

"And rightly so, there was precious little reward in it for me, beyond the financial."

"That's not entirely true," Holmes pointed his pipe at my recent acquisition, which was coiled near the fireplace.

"It was always your intention to kill her?"

"Of course. In this way Mrs Ross is no doubt indirectly responsible for Lady Sarah's death, but I cannot say it is likely to weigh very heavily upon her conscience. A failure would, however, weigh very heavily upon my reputation, which must be preserved at all costs. You should guard yours with equal care."

"What's that supposed to mean?" I demanded.

"Your new pet is a *swamp adder*. I have been reliably informed that its bite can kill a man in *three* minutes. My informant tells me that the brown speckles on the yellow scales are unmistakable."

The blood drained from my face. "Good God!"

"Not to worry; it seems to have taken a liking to you, and may, as you remarked some time ago, prove useful in the future."

The Adventure Of The Walk-Out Wardrobe

JULIE DITRICH

There are two colours I will always associate with the formidable Sherlock Holmes. The first colour is yellow but I will touch again on that presently. The second colour is luxurious purple, which had nothing to do with his leanings towards the arcane, simply because he had none. For he was the personification of a skeptic who had no time for fanciful notions about Fourth Dimensions or the Greater Mysteries. Indeed the doorway to his third eye and the majestic amethyst vibration that lay beyond that could have connected him to the Invisible Forces, was well and truly bolted and, despite my gentle rattling of it, he chose never to pry it open. No. The purple I will always associate him with came very much from the physical plane when I first spotted him from afar—his tall frame leaning into the doorway of his lodgings, puffing on a pipe, and completely oblivious to his natural surroundings, which underscored the grape-purple robe he was wearing.

It was late autumn 1907. I was living in Hindhead, Surrey—some forty miles south west of London. I had left my understanding wife and two children behind in South Africa for a six-month sojourn in England so I could concentrate on furthering my esoteric studies in seclusion. For that purpose, I had rented a cottage in the woodlands not far from the local hospital where I volunteered several times a week. I had made the acquaintance of the hospital physician, the bespectacled and rather proper Dr Alexander Lambert, who recognised me at once as brethren. He had invited me to observe his varied approaches to conventional and holistic medicine. After a day of rounds attending to convalescing patients who had brought on their afflictions through misadventure, madness or microbes, I would need to flick off the pernicious psychic residue that settled on my skin like iron filings on a magnet. A ritual cleansing took care of that, preventing it from permeating deeper into my being and disturbing the balance I strove hard to maintain. Strenuous exercise often achieved the same results.

In the evenings I would don my flat cap and hiking boots to explore the trails and pathways that criss-crossed the terrain. Oftentimes, I would meander around the eerie heather-and-gorse covered landscape up as far as the Devil's Punch Bowl. Local folklore had it that Satan had slammed his fist into the earth, creating this basin-shaped valley. Although I detected all manner of nocturnal spirits and pagan mischief-makers, at this moment in time I sensed no malevolent presence or the dregs of devilry and black magick.

One day by coincidence or grand design—some would argue they were one and the same—I took a new route at the western juncture of the road from Haslemere with the Portsmouth Road only to discover a three-storey red brick home built into a natural alcove on a landholding of several acres. The house was asymmetrical, flush with mullioned windows, and capped by a steeply angled roof. There was a grove of trees and shrubs in its surrounds and a magnificent south-facing outlook of the undulating South Downs vista.

I had heard of this house but couldn't remember its name. I had thought it to be vacant until recent idle village chatter informed me it had been leased to a retired headmaster. It was now clearly occupied because one of its chimneys was smoking and the aforementioned man with angular features and a rather patrician bearing who looked to be in his fifties, stood staring into nothing. Even though it was on the cusp of sunset, from my vantage point I could see lines in his forehead etched into a grimace as if he had retracted his consciousness into a tight ball in his brain matter and was pondering some inevitable "why". I did not want to linger for fear of intruding so continued on my way.

I was to find out later he was certainly no schoolteacher. Rather, he was a detective and that our paths were about to cross on a criminal case that teetered on the edge of being unsolvable had he not been called in to consult on it.

The Haslemere and District Cottage Hospital had been set up to tend to the poor in the parish. It was a small building nestled in a copse of thin pines. It had ten beds and two cots, as well as a large operating theatre the resident country surgeon had deemed to be scientifically sound and functional.

On the morning Holmes and I first made our official acquaintance, I had arrived in the middle of a great commotion. A motor car was parked outside the hospital entrance. It was an unusual sight and still warm to the touch. I walked inside and hooked my hat and coat onto a rack. A nurse came scurrying around the corner—her apron flapping and her young, roundish face puckered up in obvious distress. She gesticulated to me to follow her into the main ward, which doubled as casualty.

Dr Lambert was checking the vital signs of a young woman who lay limp and supine on the cast iron bed closest to the door. Her limbs were unceremoniously splayed out as if she had just been dumped there. Her carefully coiffed and pinned up auburn hair was in complete disarray. Her complexion was rosy and flushed. She also had blue circles under her eyes, which contrasted with her dry and blistered lips.

Now, I am not customarily one to notice women's garments, but in this instance her blue satin ball gown was rumpled and had edged up so much I noticed tears in her stockings; at the knees. The ward sister hastily pulled down the skirt to preserve the young woman's modesty while I averted my gaze.

A fresh-faced young gentleman was pacing backwards and

forwards at the foot of the bed. He looked to be in his early twenties, and his thick, russet hair was sweat-stuck to his forehead. He wore a double-breasted driving coat, and was twisting a bowler hat in his hands.

"Quick. The facts!" demanded Dr Lambert as he felt for a pulse on his unconscious charge.

"The patient's name is Sophie Brackenridge," said the nurse, "She's four-and-twenty and—"

"And I found her just like this, slumped on the floor of her private quarters," interrupted the young man, biting his lip. "There was nary a breath. Can you help her?"

"I won't know until I make a proper assessment…" mumbled the doctor, but the young man continued on in agitation, as if the words tumbling out of his mouth would somehow impact positively on the diagnosis, "I've never driven so fast in my life."

"May I inquire as to your name and your relationship with the patient?" I interceded quietly to divert the young man's attention. The doctor trusted me in these instances as I often had a seemingly unnatural ability to calm people down.

"Toby Brackenridge," replied the young man whose breathing was beginning to slow. "Sophie's my sister. Is she dying?"

"I think the doctor needs some time to examine her more closely. Come…" I said pointing to the far wall, "…and help me fetch those partitions over there."

"Of course. Of course," stammered Brackenridge. Before I could muster a step, he had walked over to the wall, hoisted up a folding screen under each arm and tottered back.

"Where do you want them?" he asked.

"To the side and foot of the bed," I answered and he set them up promptly after which we positioned ourselves behind the side screen with our backs to the other patients in the ward.

I could see that taking action on what even appeared to him to be a benign task helped him feel he was being useful. But there had been a practical goal to this enterprise. Creating a barrier also prevented other patients from seeing what was going on. Out of the corner of my eye I had caught them craning their heads to peer at the unconscious newcomer since it appeared by all accounts that rather than treating a charitable case, Dr Lambert was ministering to the local gentry. And one thing I had learned from my time as an observer of human nature was that no matter how many maladies a person was suffering or indeed what strata of society or part of the world they came from, when there was scandal to be had then they suddenly developed an added sensory capability that caused them to focus their attention with remarkable acuity.

Brackenridge must have caught the other patients staring too because he lowered his voice and quietly pressed me, "Please, sir. I must speak to the doctor at once on a most confidential matter. Would you be so kind as to arrange it?"

By then the senior nurse, Mary, a plump middle-aged woman who was exceptionally competent, had joined the medical team. I guessed they were disrobing the poor girl because a moment later the aforementioned blue dress was tossed over one of the screens. The entire process was laborious and seemed to take an eternity.

"I don't know why these swan-bills are legal," murmured Nurse Mary from behind the barrier. She emerged a moment later, holding up the offending corset with two fingers and then tossed it with contempt into a receptacle on the floor, "They should be criminalised for the harm they do.

"More often than not this hospital has become a fainting room for young ladies who lace themselves too tightly," she nattered on to anybody who was listening, "Is that what you think has happened in this case, Doctor?"

"I'm not sure yet," came the reply, "I give no credence to the theory that young women swoon because they're all hysterics. But I do fear that fashion dictates the female body be forced into this unnatural S-shape, thrusting the chest forward like that of a courting pigeon…"

"Faut souffrir pour etre belle," proclaimed a strange man's voice from the doorway. The words were articulated precisely and with supreme condescension. Both startled, Brackenridge and I spun our heads in the direction of the voice's possessor, although from our vantage point we could not see who it was.

"Only the French and their obsession with fashion would make up an inane utterance like that," continued the soliloquy, "But I've always thought it counterproductive to the human condition. It wouldn't be necessary to suffer in order to be beautiful if we'd concentrate on cultivating our intellect instead."

The nurses tittered.

"I don't know who you are, sir, but you're intruding," said the doctor from inside the partitioned space, "Please leave at once."

"That's not possible," replied the disembodied voice, "I'm here on official business."

And with that, I heard the man stride up, and saw the two screens being pulled apart with great indiscretion.

I recognised him at once.

Backcombed hair the colour of onyx inter-mixed with streaks of grey, the sharp profile, the grandiose manner. The man in the purple robe, only this time he was dressed in a tweed day suit and coat that had the lingering scent of tobacco trapped in its fibres. In his hand he held a gold-tipped black cane that I suspected was less a walking implement and more of tool to brandish when making a point.

He leaned in and peered at Sophie Brackenridge with his dark eyes. There was no latent significance—carnal or otherwise—to his gaze. It was more a measured inspection from head to toe as if he was gleaning information.

Sophie now lay on her back, dressed only in a muslin shift. The doctor lifted her eyelids to reveal misty, dilated pupils. Indeed, her irises were practically obliterated so I could barely discern their bluish-grey rims. Her skin appeared scarlet, as if she had been sitting too close to a fire. There were also abrasions on her hands and knees, and her fingers and toes were twitching. The doctor then began raising her gaunt arms above her head and pushing them down and then back up to stimulate the muscles around her chest to force air into her lungs.

"Get out!" he said plainly with a fierce look on his face.

The intruder did not budge.

"Now look here, man, step aside," said young Brackenridge, pushing his way in and positioning himself between the visitor and the bed, "Who are you anyway? And why are you here?"

"I'll answer your second question first, my dear fellow," said the stranger, leaning in to examine Toby's face closely. "You're the young woman's brother, I take it? I can see the family resemblance." He gently thrust Toby aside with his cane to reposition himself so he could observe everything that was happening, "I'm actually here by your invitation..."

I saw Toby relax.

"And to answer your first question," he said, looking young Brackenridge straight in the face in a supercilious manner, "Since you have so shockingly forced me out of not only my bed but also my so-called retirement to hire me... I'm a consulting detective and my name is Sherlock Holmes."

Miss Brackenridge had stabilised somewhat after the doctor had given her an injection of a pharmaceutical he later told me was derived from the leaflets of a South American shrub. It reversed some of the effects of her ailment because her breathing became steadier, although her pulse still remained rapid and weak, her skin hot and dry, and she lingered in a state of unconsciousness. The doctor wore a worried look as he placed her dress, shoes, petticoats and stockings into a box that was to be sealed and made available for later inspection. He had also insisted that Holmes get out; even though it appeared for all intents and purposes that Brackenridge had hired the detective to stave off trouble for his sister. The problem at this point in time was that I had no inkling what that prospective strife could be.

I was given the task of escorting Holmes out of the premises and, as I was in the process of complying, he extended his hand to me in a grip I instantly recognised as that of the London lodge. I reacted almost by instinct and sought to respond with the corresponding token but suppressed my inclination just in time when I glanced at him and saw his eyes alight with mischievous glee. He had set a trap and I had well and truly nearly walked into it. Holmes then accompanied an agitated Brackenridge into the grounds where they had an intense but muted conversation I was not privy to.

Dr Lambert emerged for a brief period drying his hands with a cloth and then took me aside and whispered something in my ear.

"I don't know whether she is readying herself to walk out to death or to walk back in to life but there's something peculiar about the manner in which she was brought here and the cause of her condition," he murmured, "Perhaps you'll be able to shed light on the matter."

He could not be spared, as he needed to monitor his patient's progress. Instead he asked me to accompany Holmes and Brackenridge to the family estate—he had a theory as to what might be keeping his patient non-responsive but it needed confirmation. He had already sent a messenger to report his suspicions to the police. Beyond that I knew nothing more except that I was to provide an account on any findings that could have a direct bearing on his treatment regime.

Holmes and I were now travelling in a hansom cab, as Holmes had refused to step into Brackenridge's "infernal metallic wheeled contraption" as he had put it. I did not take him for a Luddite but I suspected the familiar rhythm and sway of our current mode of transportation would have been more conducive to deliberation. However, as it was, young Toby was forced to follow us in his automobile, albeit at a pace that must have seemed ponderous for him.

Holmes turned his attention upon me, as soon as we sat down in the carriage.

"I understand your name is Moriarty..." he said, with grit in his voice.

"Yes, indeed; Dr Theodore William Moriarty, to be specific. I'm pleased to make your acquaintance, Mr Holmes."

He seemed bemused.

"Not related to any criminal masterminds I gather...unless, of course, you're the single white sheep in a notoriously black flock."

"I have no idea what you're talking about," I responded in exasperation.

"No, I suppose you wouldn't. For one thing, you have a very obvious Irish accent that instantly sets you apart from your namesake. Furthermore, a long sojourn in Africa would have meant you're not always privy to sensational news from home."

I turned to him and stared.

"Let it further be said, Dr Moriarty, that I don't subscribe to spiritualism," he continued contemptuously, "It is a prestidigitation, sleight of hand, a mere conjuring of a speckled band."

I absorbed what he had to say for a moment but chose not to be insulted or provoked. Nor did I attempt to remain hidden in the shadows as others of my kindred might have done because I unequivocally understood there could be no subterfuge with him… his sense of observation was so acute that he could see hidden truths as plainly as a red fox on virgin snow.

"That's your privilege, Mr Holmes," I said, "My earthly calling is not to convince you as to the veracity of what I do nor what beliefs I subscribe to."

He didn't say a word, and sat there rather smugly knowing what he had revealed to me about myself had been verified by my response. I sensed him waiting for the subsequent question that he invariably must have heard a thousand times before, "Oh, my goodness. However did you figure that out?"

But I could not give it to him. It was not that I wanted or indeed needed to compete with his expertise—that was not my modus operandi nor my intention—but I did not want to play his game, either. I grasped he was a master manipulator…setting up bait in the form of a curiosity trap that inevitably his audience would walk into and whereby he could bear witness to them gasping at his cleverness. I already knew him to be exceptionally intelligent and a rationalist. The yellow told me so. I also sensed his vibration and empathically understood that despite his condescension and superior manner, that I had a most rare opportunity to take on a role of student; for I had an inkling that what he could teach me would prove important in my later career. In order for this to happen, I needed to earn his respect. In order to earn his respect and perhaps give him an insight into my world, I had to answer with something from my own repertoire of skills. But before I drew breath, he continued.

"How did I deduce that, might you well ask?"

I cocked an eyebrow and listened without responding, as the cab continued clattering over the road towards its destination with the clip clopping of hooves.

"Well, it was really a simple matter.

"Your Celtic complexion is sun-bronzed but not sun-roasted. It is not a mere tint from a sunny picnic by the riverbank, rather the deep lines around your eyes and mouth give you the appearance of somebody older than your biological age of... hmmmm...thirty-five or thereabouts. This suggests a long stay in a hot climate. Australia, perhaps, where the Irish are prone to emigrate either as freemen or in shackles in its not-so-distant convict past? No; too hot and extreme. Your face would have been even more degraded and be covered in cancerous growths by now. Much closer to home...Africa; but not the desert. A more temperate clime.

"And before you protest, I will confess when I entered the hospital I took the liberty of poking my head into an office to look for a person in authority before finding my way to the ward. There was an ostrich feather quill with an engraved bronze tip together with an inkpot on a writing desk. Too frivolous and feminine to be used on the job but sentimental enough to remain in plain sight every time its owner—you—would sit down. A gift from your wife, I suspect, to remind you she's waiting your return.

"Now tell me, are you partial to mussels?"

"Yes...with stout and black pepper," I replied, more in fascination than resentment at his impertinence. He gave me a self-satisfied look that I was to see again and again during our acquaintance. He gazed out of the window and then inexplicably began whistling a tune that I was more than familiar with. The lyrics tumbled over in my head.

> In Dublin's fair city,
> Where the girls are so pretty,

I first set my eyes on sweet Molly Malone,
As she wheeled her wheel-barrow,
Through streets broad and narrow,
Crying, "Cockles and mussels, alive, alive, oh!"

I spontaneously began singing the chorus and it brought yearning for home into my heart. His whistling was unexpectedly melodic.

"Alive, alive, oh,
Alive, alive, oh,"
Crying "Cockles and mussels, alive, alive, oh".

There was a pause while I collected myself, and then he said, "Only a Dubliner would sing this with such passion…dare I say it, you settled in a location not far from the sea. The fading scars from rope burns between your thumb and forefingers, as well as your jacktar stained hands, attest to a seafaring life in your younger days. You would have settled near a port where ostrich feathers are plentiful due to the export trade, and where bivalves are there for the taking…Mossel Bay in South Africa."

"Well done, Mr Holmes," I answered simply.

"Furthermore, my extensive study of candle wax—that I documented in my folios—exposes your occult training. There are small drops of blue wax on the cuff of your trouser leg. Blue candles are used ceremonially to enhance healing and to seek truth and wisdom, are they not?"

He did not wait for an answer.

"Moreover, the fabric on your trousers is thin and worn at the knees, suggesting you either spend a good deal of time crouching or in cross-legged repose with an inclination towards the meditative practices.

"I have already uncovered you as a Freemason…oh, don't tut tut me or be embarrassed for inadvertently revealing yourself. I have my ways of uncovering rituals and understanding symbols. You mustn't be concerned. I won't reveal your wretched secrets.

"But it is your study of theosophy that intrigues me most. What is it that you subscribe to? One almighty and Great Architect of the Universe?"

Again, I realised it was useless to deny it. Although I did not confirm his exposition through my words or gestures, I am sure my countenance betrayed me. In a strange way I felt liberated that a little piece of my usually shielded but genuine self had been revealed.

I was in no mood for further discussion and we were coming closer to our journey's end so I decided he should answer as well.

"I'd ask you what brings you to these parts, Mr Holmes," I said, rapidly changing the subject, "Except that I already know."

"Aaaah…a reversal of roles. Splendid. So what is it exactly that you think you know?"

"A friend or companion in the medical sciences has urged you to come to Hindhead to seek the air for your lung complaint brought about by too many years of pipe puffing."

He snorted. "Doesn't every tourist…" he said, overemphasising the 'tourist', "…come to Hindhead for the air? It is, after all, known as 'Little Switzerland'. Long-stay visitors who come here for their convalescence have even been known to recover from phthisis. You yourself have also suffered from this particular complaint have you not, Dr Moriarty?"

"Yes, indeed."

"One doesn't have to be a medical practitioner to discern that."

"Yes, that's why I moved to Africa; but other people suffering from your affliction rarely come to Hindhead with your particular combination of complaints."

"Then please enlighten me. What do you observe with your… sixth sense?"

"Energetically I can feel pulmonary congestion. It's like a jungle swamp in your lungs."

"Phewy."

"There is a tightness and lack of mobility in your right shoulder. Be wary. If you don't warm up your musculature, you'll tear it when next you practice your swordsmanship.

"The scornful way you treated the nurses suggests you have little sensitivity towards women."

"Correction. I dismiss or ignore anyone who doesn't pose a challenge, not merely women," said Holmes.

"I sense desolation…I discern the letter 'M'. A rival, but yet a fraternal and maternal connection…A brother perhaps? But there is another 'M' who has featured in your life…Departed now but brought you to the brink of destruction. Your lung complaint is more than the accumulation of toxic ash and debris. I sense your lungs filling with water…you gasping to breathe. A struggle. Perhaps a bout of pneumonia brought you to the brink? But there is something perilous about *this* M. His psychic venom has permeated you. If you don't release him from the entirety of your body you'll still bestow him with power over you, and I can see a future of crippled hands, hooked over like raptor talons, and throbbing joints, and you writhing to suck air into your bronchial tubes as you drown: not from your physical afflictions but from adverse feelings trapped in your mind and body."

"Balderdash…" he replied, "I've never had pneumonia in my life."

He did not change his expression. He merely glared at me. I felt a subtle energetic shift as if something I had said had connected but it was gone in an instance. And as a consequence, he battle-hardened again and so I was unable to probe anymore.

"Not that it is any business of yours, Dr Moriarty, but I give you that seven per cent of what you said had some truth behind it. The other ninety-three per cent is pure conjecture and unadulterated fantasy. You are nothing but a terrible fortune-teller. All academic pretentiousness and pretence. You're not a real medical doctor by any means, and to remind you of that I think I shall call you "Dr M."

"If you must. I'll answer to that."

I refused to be baited for I perceived this interaction with him as an opportunity. I was being tested and he was the vehicle of that test. The Invisible Forces were using him for their own means, as well as to assess my conviction to the path I was resolved to walking.

The cab rounded a bend, slowed down, and passed through the stone pillars of a gateway.

"Oh, look. We've arrived, and not a moment too soon, I see," Holmes said, glancing at a small but elegant, two-levelled sandstone Georgian house. Small droplets of rain started to descend. He poked his head out of the window to get a first impression and, once we had clattered to a stop outside the entrance, he looked at me and said, "Ahah. Now let the fun begin."

Police Sergeant Ingram and Constable Bennington—with whom I was already familiar—greeted us at the doorway. They were dressed in full uniform with custodian helmet, belt and baton. Brackenridge pulled up and then paled when he spotted them.

"Are you the man of the house?" Ingram called out brusquely.

"Er...yes," said Toby, clambering slowly out of his vehicle. He looked up at the heavens and his face became splotched in the drizzle.

"It seems you and your sister are in a spot of bother. We'll need to question you both."

"I'm afraid my sister is lying unconscious in a hospital," answered Brackenridge.

"Perhaps I can be of service?" interrupted Holmes, stepping out of the cab and tipping his hat—more to deflect attention away from his charge rather than from respect for the police I suspect. "The Brackenridges are my clients and I'll be consulting on this case, Police Sergeant..."

"Ingram," said the policeman suspiciously, "A solicitor already, Brackenridge? Something to hide have we?"

"Oh, no. Nothing as unseemly as all that. My name is Sherlock Holmes."

There was a pause. The policemen glanced at each other and their expressions changed rapidly.

"Not 'the' Sherlock Holmes?" asked Bennington.

"I didn't know there was another."

"Well I'll be..." said Ingram, striding forward and offering up his hand. "We know you by reputation from our fellow bobbies in London. We've also been hearing how you've been solving little Hindhead mysteries for our townsfolk. Now the case of the suiciding dogs…that was a tricky one. Never would have picked that myself."

"And what about the mystery of the kidnapped garden dwarves," said the constable with sheer delight, "Who'd have thought that holidaying on the continent would be the answer!" They guffawed simultaneously.

"You look as if you know nothing about this, Moriarty?" said Ingram, glancing in my direction as I paid the cab driver and then walked towards them, turning up my coat collar to avoid getting completely wet.

"You're correct in your assertion," I answered, feeling rather stupefied by their rapid shift from suspicion to mirth.

Ingram slapped me on the back and replied, "Mr Holmes has been keeping himself busy solving our country shenanigans. Modest by London standards I'm sure. Buy me a pint at the pub after we've closed this case, Moriarty, and I'll tell you all about it."

"What case is that?" I asked.

"I'm afraid we have our own little murder upstairs," replied the constable.

I flinched. This had taken me by surprise. Brackenridge, however, lowered his eyes and shuffled, indicating he probably already knew and established why he had urgently sent for Holmes.

"Let's wait to determine if it is indeed a murder or mishap," replied Holmes, "And as to your contention about the modesty of crimes in the boroughs, let not the guise of an idyllic country town pull the wool over your eyes. I've attended the scene of many a county homicide and oftentimes they're even more diabolical and gruesome than anything I've witnessed in the city."

"We've got our theories, Mr Holmes, We'd be honoured if you could put forward your own extrapolations. Yours may very well tally with ours."

An elderly butler, introduced as Hobbes, opened the door to let us in. In the midst of unnerving joviality, Brackenridge remained quiet and anxious. He seemed perturbed that Holmes appeared to be aligning himself with the police and their dark comedic jesting. But I understood this to be more tactical than anything else. Holmes could glean more information in the spirit of cooperation rather than in an adversarial relationship. And, as it was, once we entered into the household, the frivolous mood turned to one of grimness and authority.

"We've questioned all the servants, Mr Holmes. None of them saw or heard nuthin', save the cook who mentioned the only deviance from her daily pattern was discovering the side door flapping open at midday. But that timing doesn't concur with our reconstruction of last night's events," said the police sergeant. "We'll show you to the deceased now."

We followed him up the several flights of a sweeping staircase to the top floor then walked down a corridor towards a locked room. The constable produced a key from his pocket, inserted it into the keyhole and opened the door to reveal Sophie Brackenridge's bedroom. We remained in the doorway while further discussion ensued.

"The body was discovered in the walk-in wardrobe, Mr Holmes, after Brackenridge here took his sister to hospital," said the constable, pointing to second closed door in the interior.

"Has anybody been in here since you arrived?" asked Holmes.

"Nobody in and nobody out."

"What have you done with the body?" asked Holmes.

"It's still where the maid found it earlier this morning. She's in a state of shock and sniffing smelling salts downstairs."

"Excellent. I'll interview her later. I don't want anyone else entering the crime scene until we've had a proper opportunity to thoroughly examine it ourselves."

We stepped inside the bedroom and quickly surveyed it. Nothing appeared to be untoward. It was rather charming, actually. It contained a four-poster bed that had obviously not been slept in and an open marble fireplace with slate hearth. There was a sash window with interior shutters, and the walls were covered with romantic paintings of slumbering women and dead heroines inspired by poetry and prose. On the vanity cabinet, there was a vase of flowers, an empty glass water pitcher, as well as a knife and a lemon on a silver tray. Holmes sniffed the air and slowly dropped to his knees beside the bed. He peered underneath but his expression did not alter.

"Mr Brackenridge, this is where we need you to tell us everything that happened? And I do mean everything," said the police sergeant.

"Everything that is relevant to ensuring your sister remains safe," added Holmes cryptically.

Toby Brackenridge hesitated, caught Holmes's eye, and then launched into his story.

"Last night after dinner when we were sitting in the drawing room, we heard a knock at the door and a messenger delivered a letter addressed to Sophie. When she opened it she went pale, as if that is at all possible because for the most part she walks around as white as a ghost anyway."

"What was in the letter?"

"I don't know. All I know was that it contained some sugar."

"Interesting," said Holmes, "And where is that letter now?"

"I've no idea."

"Continue," said Ingram.

"I asked her if she was feeling all right, and she made a feeble excuse and rushed upstairs. I took no more notice of it because Sophie...well, you see...Sophie has piques and can be temperamental and belligerent at times. When she doesn't want to talk she just withdraws from the world and sits in her wardrobe."

"Keep going."

"This morning the maid came to wake her at eight with a breakfast tray but the bed hadn't been slept in. She called me up at once. I promptly sent the servants to search the rest of the house and the grounds. I noticed the door to the wardrobe was closed but didn't think anything more of it. Sophie always keeps it under lock and key even when she's in there."

"Why would she feel the need to do that?

"Sophie wants complete and utter privacy. Even I'm not allowed inside. She brings her clothes out herself and leaves them on the bed for her maid to dress her. The one time she forgot to lock up the wardrobe, she found a maid in there, trying on a pair of Persian slippers."

"Where is that maid now?"

"She was dismissed on the spot."

"Would you say this maid harboured a secret resentment and wanted to exact revenge?" asked the constable.

"I don't think so. I gave her a good reference and helped secure a position for her in a nearby town. By all accounts she's happy there. But after that incident Sophie kept her key on her person."

"Hmm..." said Holmes, "So, what happened next, young man?

"Well, after I sent the servants away I knocked on the wardrobe door. I didn't hear anything but turned the doorknob expecting it to be secure but instead I discovered it to be unlocked. I found Sophie unconscious on the floor. I also saw a man's body lying near the window. He was already dead."

"How do you know that?"

"It was pretty obvious from all the blood."

He paused and then said, "That's when I picked up Sophie and rushed her to the hospital in my motor car. Clocked up forty-five miles an hour."

"What state did you leave the room?" asked Ingram.

"I locked the bedroom door again to avert any scandal but one of the servants must have entered and saw the body and called the police."

Ingram nodded subtly at Holmes to indicate what had just been said had indeed transpired.

"Now for an examination of the wardrobe," said Holmes. "That includes you, Dr M. Do not touch anything unless instructed. Be cognisant of where you walk. You're here merely as an observer. As for you, Brackenridge, I'm sure I'm speaking on behalf of our fine British police force when I insist you not accompany us beyond the threshold but continue your narrative from the door."

"Yes, most assuredly, that's our position," said the police sergeant.

Brackenridge nodded and complied.

Holmes and I walked tentatively inside accompanied by Ingram.

The wardrobe was no armoire that could hold eight small men. Instead, it was a small room attached to Miss Brackenridge's bedroom and was spacious enough to have held at least forty large men. The walls were painted forget-me-not blue. It was also surprisingly intimate and ladylike. A keyhole into this young woman's secret life. But that was not what drew my attention.

My immediate thought was to reach the dead man who was lying face up on the floor near the sash window. I automatically took a step towards him but Holmes blocked me with his arm and said, almost kindly, "The instinct that has you rushing forward, no doubt from keeping company with physicians, is admirable but there's nothing more you or anybody else can do for him. You'll merely corrupt the crime scene. I ask you to switch into another mode and adapt to a new way of thinking…Become a detective while you're here with me, for at this moment I have need of you. You're a proxy for another and your observations will offer me a unique perspective."

"Very well. What must I do?"

"Follow me as I make my way through. Tamper with nothing. This is a methodical and practiced art."

We proceeded, and Ingram and I stepped where Holmes stepped.

"Right where you're standing is where I found my sister," said Brackenridge from the doorway.

Holmes dropped to one knee and examined the oak floorboards for a few minutes.

"Yes, I see," he said mysteriously. Then he stood up again.

On the left wall was some shelving, containing a large collection of women's shoes. He picked up several pairs seemingly randomly, scrutinised their soles, sniffed them and returned them to their place. Beside that was another shelved compartment containing millinery boxes and a jewellery case. In the corner was a full-length standing mirror.

On the right hand side were several garment racks full of ladies day, travelling and dinner dresses, and evening gowns. Holmes's gaze lingered there for a moment longer than necessary. One thing was obvious, even to me. Half of the garments hanging together were multiple colours but the second half was entirely blue.

"Tell me, Brackenridge, when did your sister start wearing blue?"

"About eighteen months ago," he answered, "It was quite peculiar, really. She travels to London by steam train on her own once a month to visit the art galleries, as she had a particular fondness for paintings of the Pre-Raphaelite Brotherhood. She would take an empty portmanteau with her to shop for garments. That particular morning she left miserable as usual but returned positively ebullient. I've never seen her like that, as her propensity is to exist in a permanent state of enmity. It was after that trip she began wearing only blue."

"Your sister fritters away her allowance does she not? Her wardrobe is full of unworn clothing and shoes."

"Quite correct, Mr Holmes. She rarely seeks society but is still rather vain. Despite the fact there is no one to impress here except the servants and me, she still always dresses for dinner."

"My dear fellow," said Holmes, addressing Ingram but staring at Brackenridge, "If I am to make sense of what happened here I'd like to examine the evening dress she was wearing last night."

Brackenridge gulped.

"We'll inspect it together at the hospital where it's my understanding it has been secured," said Ingram, "No doubt it'll provide crucial evidence of what happened here."

"No doubt indeed," said Holmes.

He moved on and then stopped at a dresser, opened a drawer and peered inside. All the while I was feeling most uncomfortable...the dead man's corpse was calling to me to attend it. It was nearly beyond toleration and I had to restrain myself from bursting forth and seeing to the poor fellow.

"It would be more seeming, Dr M, for you to search amongst these undergarments as you are here as a representative of the hospital. Run your hands over the back and underside of the drawers and tell me what you discover."

I slid out each drawer one at a time, glanced inside and gently ruffled everything with my hand to see if there was something present that should not be.

"Corsetry and other undergarments and nothing more..." I replied, "...but, what is this?"

I pulled out a cosmetic palette, containing a white powder. I carefully prised open the lid but before I knew it, Holmes had leaned in, and touched the substance. I saw a momentary gleam in his eyes...a sense of exhilaration. I began to understand.

"This may explain why your sister always looked like death," said Holmes, "Rice powder. "Tell me, Brackenridge, do you have a herb and vegetable garden?"

"Oh, yes," said the young man from the doorway, "I'm a keen gardener. We have some beautiful trees on the estate and oh so many birds...I do my best to attract them. We have nightjar and stonechat, pheasants, quail and lots of other game birds, although I baulk at hunting...and, oh, we still even have a nesting robin in the chestnut tree so late in the season..."

"Yes, yes, but did your sister ever accompany you?

"She rarely ventured outside during the day unless it was overcast or dawn or dusk. She was sensitive to light you see."

"Tell me, did she ever eat beets?" asked Holmes.

"I spotted her carrying a beet in a basket once. I asked her why she hadn't asked the cook to make a salad for her for luncheon, and she mumbled something unintelligible. I didn't pursue it."

Holmes whispered to me, "I occasionally inhabit the thespian world and am familiar with stagecraft and theatrical makeup. It's considered most improper for respectable women to use cosmetics, as it remains the domain of prostitutes and actresses. Where young women cannot access them freely, they create their own. Young Sophie has been using lemon juice and rice powder to obtain a pale complexion, and red beet juice to emphasise the lips without appearing obvious or garish. The blue circles under her eyes are an affectation as well. It's considered highly fashionable in some quarters to look like an ailing woman with consumption."

Holmes seemed satisfied and then strode towards the raised wooden platform in front of the window. Now we could finally see everything in close detail. And by everything I meant the blue-faced, dead-eyed man lying in a pool of blood around his head underneath a heavy ornamental mahogany cabinet with shattered glass and *objets d'art* scattered all around.

Holmes gave the body a cursory glance then exclaimed, "It's a very irregular way to arrange furniture would you not say, Dr M?"

"I suppose."

"Look at the chaise longue…"

I turned my attention to the sofa, which sat in the middle of the raised platform. It was covered in a delicate, pink flowered and blue bird patterned chintz. A fringed wrap was draped over it. There was a circle of beeswax votive candles and strewn rose petals around the exterior that had been disturbed and trampled.

"It's facing the window, which is nothing strange in itself, as a *méridienne* is intended for day rest and its directionality would mean there was ample sunlight across the seasons," continued Holmes. "But if she was sensitive to light, why would she place it here? A conundrum."

"Our theory is that she let in this stranger for an assignation," said Ingram. "It was to be all romantic like. That's why she locked the room all the time…she sneaks him in while everybody is either at dinner or serving dinner. She sneaks him out in the wee hours of the morning and nobody would be the wiser."

"That's simply not true!" protested Brackenridge from the door. "I'll ask you to withdraw that statement. Sophie had no interest in the young men who came to court her and, dare I say it, she considered them all without exception to be frightful bores."

"Well, something interested her in this one," continued Ingram, "She must have met him in London. I'd say she's known him for eighteen months to be exact. Blue must have been his favourite colour. He rejected her and then she stabbed him. As he fell, he grabbed onto the edge of the cabinet and it toppled on top of him."

"There are more subtleties to this case than a simple intrigue gone wrong," said Holmes, "Besides…there would have been a deep incision in the palm of her hand had she been the perpetrator."

He suddenly slid his hand along the lengths of the *chaise longue* and withdrew not the expected coin or hairpin but two objects—a letter in a crumpled envelope and a small vial with a stopper that only had a few drops of liquid remaining in the bottom.

He opened the letter carefully then gently shook out some of the contents onto his palm. Grainy. Crystals. Sweet. Sugar.

He read out the scrawling on the correspondence which said, *"I know who you are and what you done and have took back what is mine."*

The letter lacked a signature.

"Fascinating wouldn't you say?" said Holmes, "This letter was enough to panic her and have her dash upstairs but what was it of value that would cause her such consternation?"

"Seems like we may have another theory," postulated Ingram, "This man is either a blackmailer or dare I say it…something worse. It stands to reason that whatever happened, it happened either last night or eighteen months ago."

"Now, look here," cried Brackenridge in a pained voice, "I told you before. My sister did not keep the company of men."

"But perhaps last night this one kept company with her," replied Ingram.

Brackenridge emitted another howl of protest.

"This case is getting more intriguing by the minute," said Holmes, holding up the vial to the light. "If I'm correct, she's been using belladonna drops to dilate her pupils to give them that misty-eyed look. It's a common tool used for the purposes of seduction. That's why she finds it difficult to be out in bright sunlight."

"There…it's just as I said before," insisted the police sergeant, shifting his ever-malleable theory with every revelation of a clue.

"Ingram, you'll need to send this to Dr Lambert at once, as its contents will impact on Miss Sophie's treatment; if she hasn't already passed away. She is most certainly the victim of a poisoning—now all we have to deduce is whether it's self-induced or administered by a third party. For I believe she swallowed the entire contents of this bottle."

"What did I tell you!" exclaimed Ingram, "He either tried to hush her up and forced it down her throat or she did it herself out of shame. We'll get it examined at once, Mr Holmes. Constable?"

Bennington stepped inside the wardrobe, pocketed the vial and then walked out.

Brackenridge had now slumped to the floor and was holding his head in his hands in obvious distress.

"I see your sister never finished anything she started," Holmes called out to Brackenridge without any thought to comforting him.

"Yes..." stammered the young man, "How did you stumble on that?"

"My dear fellow, I stumble on nothing," said Holmes caustically, "I painstakingly deduce as you also could you if you paid attention."

"Oh, come, Holmes. The man's in shock," I said. "Anybody's attention span would be compromised in circumstances such as these."

"But you're not in shock. Your faculties are uncorrupted and yet you've not gleaned an iota of detail from this crime scene. Take this, for example," he said, indicating a stack of books by the chaise longue, "There are seven books here. Each one of them has a bookmark that extends no further than a quarter way through. There's a thick layer of dust on the top book and any other covers that protrude out from underneath. This indicates they've been here for some time and that she has not been compelled to either return them to her library or to finish reading them."

"You're right, of course," I replied with a sigh, "You make it sound so easy in hindsight but it evidently is not."

My capitulation seemed to satisfy him momentarily, and then his features took on that hard edged look again as he moved carefully from here to there.

"Miss Brackenridge would lie here, staring out of this window. What is out there that could be so enchanting?"

He inspected the sash windows. It also had interior shutters like the bedroom window and was similarly locked from the inside. I followed his gaze. Outside in the drizzle, stood a chestnut tree. Its branches extended from the trunk like the long necks of a Hydra. The foliage was yellowing and the leaves were dropping to the ground. Beyond that was a sunken garden.

"Come now, Holmes, isn't it time to address 'the elephant in the museum', if I were to invoke Dostoevsky?" I said, pointing to the dead man.

"And he was invoking Krylov, yes, Dr M? So, perhaps it would be apt to let metaphors flourish…Our dead man is not quite 'a skeleton in the cupboard' but he could very well be the 'skeleton in HER cupboard'," said Holmes wryly. He did not appear to accord any sympathy to the young woman who lay in the hospital, possibly dying.

I didn't laugh but turned my attention, at last, to the deceased man.

The glass doors in the cabinet had shattered—he was lying in a puddle of coagulated blood that had pooled and spattered around his head. A shard of glass penetrated the side of his neck, dividing the jugular vein and the carotid artery. His bald head and his puffy blue-tinged face were clearly distinguishable. There were haemorrhages on the surface of his blue vacant eyes. I couldn't see anything below his throat.

His life force had corroded but I still felt a tingling sensation and I saw something that Holmes didn't—a faint glow, like a will-o'-the-wisp. It stayed for nary a second then faded away like water droplets rapidly evaporating into the atmosphere. I also felt an energy signature of another sort that made me stop in my tracks. *Wickedness.* It bore investigating, but not now.

In the interim, Holmes had been examining the back of the cabinet with a magnifying glass he had withdrawn from his coat pocket.

"Ingram, has the crime scene been sketched and photograph-ed?"

"Yes, Mr Holmes. We've been quite thorough."

"So we can lift this cabinet up now?"

"Indeed."

"Well then, do your duty, my fine fellows." he continued casually, "Oh, and be careful not to cut yourself on the smashed vodka bottle in his pocket."

The cabinet was extremely heavy but Ingram and I managed to lift it off the corpse and ease it back under the window, matching the legs to the scuff markings on the floor where it had previously stood.

The dead man wasn't exactly dirty but he was dishevelled. He wore a creased, fur-lined coat over a smudged, side-fastened shirt. He had tight drawstring trousers on his legs and scuffed boots on his feet. Ingram searched the corpse's coat pockets and withdrew a broken bottle and some fragments of glass. We exchanged a look and shrug of the shoulders that was less about incredulity and more a sheer acceptance of Holmes's skills.

"If I didn't know better, Mr Holmes, I would say you witnessed this yourself or have an all-seeing eye trained over the world."

Holmes didn't reply. He was absorbed in scrutinising the velvet-lined cabinet shelves carefully, after which he turned his attention to the floor. Amongst the scattered objects was a gold brooch, an unopened packet of pastilles, a turtle-shell comb, a ruby ring, a pair of red leather gloves, opera glasses, a silver bracelet, a bauble necklace, and an illustrated children's picture book. I could not make out the connection between them.

"Hand me one of those candles will you, my good man?" said Holmes.

I handed him one of the votive candles and he withdrew a box of matches from his obviously deep pockets that probably also held four-and-twenty blackbirds, a cake that said "eat me" and more. But I am being ridiculous and I digress.

He lit the wick and peered into the cabinet for a few minutes, sweeping the candle side to side over the shelves so the flame illuminated something...I was not sure what. Then he reached for the scattered objects and began to install them again in a very precise order.

"How do you know which one goes where?" I asked.

"There is a slight indentation in the velvet which defines the shape of where each object rested. But more importantly, even though the cabinet faces away from the window and towards the *chaise longue*, the pervading sunlight will still cause fabric to lighten over time. Therefore, the velvet around each object has faded ever so slightly leaving a deeper shadow in the shape of each object."

"Brilliant." I could not help myself. I uttered the word spontaneously.

"Yes. I know."

"But look…this children's illustrated book is the first object she placed in this cabinet. Why? Nothing seemingly has a relationship yet this object is probably the most important."

Holmes opened up the book onto its front pages and read an inscription. He held it up and called out, "Brackenridge, what do you know of this?"

The young man peered around the side of the door and his features changed from worry to surprise.

"I can't swear it to be so but it looks like a book that belonged to me that disappeared when I was about ten or eleven. Whatever is it doing here?"

Holmes didn't respond but his eyes swept over all the items.

"There's something missing. Can you tell me what was standing right here?" he asked, pointing to an empty spot on the top shelf.

"I don't know," said Brackenridge from the doorway, "She never let me in here."

"It was oval shaped."

"I'm sorry, Mr Holmes, I really don't know."

"Have a look at the order in which these objects were arranged. The cheapest and oldest, to the most expensive and newest, yet this oval shape had pride of place."

Holmes's face suddenly brightened. He scribbled a few words onto a note pad with a pencil he withdrew from a pocket of his coat and then tore out a piece of paper, folded it and handed it to the policeman by his side.

"Ingram. Our work here is done. If you would be so kind as to despatch a telegram to Inspector Lestrade of Scotland Yard, I would be exceptionally grateful. This note will provide the contents of the telegram."

"Yes, of course. We'll clear the body first though."

"Well, I'm done," said Holmes, turning to go.

"Mr Brackenridge," said Ingram, "You're only permitted to travel between the hospital and these premises until we resolve this matter to my satisfaction."

"Yes, of course. Right now, my place is at my sister's side."

"Very well then. I'll be off. Mr Holmes, please escort your client downstairs and tell him he's under strict instructions not to enter this room again until we pronounce it habitable."

"I'm sure my client only wants to get to the bottom of this matter and will comply with your request."

Ingram moved out of the bedroom and down the hall towards the stairway and Holmes feigned to follow. However, as soon as the police sergeant was out of sight, Holmes doubled back, seized Brackenridge by the sleeve of his coat and demanded with a hiss, "Now tell us the whole truth. Where's the real dress Sophie was wearing when you found her?"

Toby's face fell. "How did you know?"

"You mentioned you had discovered your sister not much after eight. The hospital is five miles away so allowing for thirty minutes of search and discovery you should have got there no later than 8:45, travelling at forty-five miles an hour. Yet you got there at 9:30: that leaves forty-five minutes unaccounted for. Now, show me where you placed the items."

We returned to Sophie's bedroom and Toby reluctantly climbed into the cold fireplace, then put his arm up the chimney. He withdrew a slightly sooty pair of shoes with blood on their soles, and a ruffled blue lace dress with dried blood on its front. Holmes laid the dress on the bed and stretched it out.

"How did you know?" asked Brackenridge.

"You found her not on the floorboards near the door as you previously stated but fainted in the dead man's immediate vicinity. You dragged her away. Marks on the floorboards indicate that.

"The front and hem of her dress was saturated in blood from moving through the blood pool and then stumbling in hands first but it had not seeped through to her undergarments. You used the lemon water in the jug to wash her hands but you missed some of the blood which had collected in the crescents around her nail beds and which was visible, at least to me, when we were at the hospital. You poured the bloody water into a vase of flowers in the room but there is a slight residue of pink in the pitcher. You took her dress off but in the process transferred some faint blood drops from your own fingerprints onto the back of her corset, which I also saw at the hospital. You then grabbed another dress from that rack—a grand ball gown of all things, that she would never have worn for dinner with her brother no matter how conceited she was—and dressed her in it before driving to hospital."

"I have to protect my sister. I know she barely tolerates me but I swore an oath to my mother as she lay dying I would look after her."

"You're a fool. It appears for all intents and purposes from this cover-up that you've shifted the blame upon yourself and now you're a major suspect in this murder investigation."

Young Brackenridge maintained a bedside vigil by his unconscious sister for several days. My immediate thought was that it was because of his filial love for her but then I could not help but switch into a more suspicious part of my mind—Holmes had taken care of that when he planted the seed that Toby had whitewashed a most complex and heinous crime when he had tampered with the evidence. Perhaps Toby was being so attentive because he needed to get his sister to confirm his staged version of events before the police officially interviewed her. As a consequence, I began to adjust my behaviour so I was much less inclined towards compassion and much more inclined to cynicism when it came to conversing with the young man.

In the interim, Dr Lambert had performed an intimate exam on Miss Brackenridge. He was pleased to quietly inform us that the man who had been found in her boudoir had stolen nothing of womanly value.

Sophie woke up on the third day.

She did not remember a thing. Not a single scrap or morsel.

She did not remember her brother. She did not remember her house. She did not remember her grandfather had made his fortune in the Antipodes and had brought the family into wealth and repute. She did not remember when and under what circumstances her parents had died, let alone her parents at all. She did not remember the incident that had put her in hospital. And when Toby Brackenridge called out to her upon her waking, she did not turn towards him. She did not remember her name.

Dr Lambert examined her and said, "Miss Brackenridge exhibits all the signs of somebody with a memory deficit, yet there's no corresponding head injury."

There was a suggestion from the police she was feigning her condition but the doctor pronounced it not to be so.

"Whole or partial loss of memory," he told them, "comes about from disease, brain damage, mental or emotional trauma and the incorrect use of sedatives and mind-altering substances. In this instance, I'd diagnose her as having memory impairment brought along by her ongoing belladonna use, as she's still exhibiting signs of slurred speech, delirium, and blurred vision. We'll need to monitor her closely to establish whether her long term memories return, but this may take time."

I did not sense any chicanery about Sophie. Her energetic vibration was open and, although confused, felt unexpectedly peaceful. I got a sense she just wanted to bounce out of her bed with unabashed abandonment and that somehow we were constraining her.

The police still wanted to interview her once she recovered her memories, although there was no surety in that proposition.

Despite all that, Sophie Brackenridge, who was not privy to these mutterings, made an astounding recovery, which piqued my interest. One morning, her brother had taken his sister for a turn around the hospital garden. She had staggered around in sheer delight, smelling the flowers and stroking the bark on trees and sitting on the grass, which did my heart good to witness and made me question my suspicion. Despite a seeming lack of balance and coordination—no doubt a side effect from the atropine, the toxic alkaloid found in belladonna—I noted that the livid and pinched face I had seen when she was lying on her deathbed (so to speak) had been replaced by that of a seemingly robust and pink-cheeked teenager.

Holmes continued to pay acute attention to everything that was going on but said nothing. He was like an owl, watching from atop a tree, waiting for the scurrying mouse to expose its vulnerability so he could swoop.

It was Brackenridge who inadvertently provided some additional insight into his sister's condition. He now sat outside the hospital on a bench, looking perturbed.

I inquired as to his state of mind and after a while he replied, "I think I need to speak to Dr Lambert."

"There's nothing you can say to the physician that you can't say to us," said Holmes, striding up suddenly with his hands grasped behind his back. I was happy to be included in the collective "us". It meant that on some sort of trifling level I was proving to be useful to the great detective.

"Mr Holmes, I feel embarrassed to say this but your services are no longer required," said Brackenridge nervously, "The police have stopped probing. I'll settle your account by the end of the week."

"You hired me to discover the truth," said Holmes, unamused by this turn of events. "This case is far from closed but, very well, I'll abide by your wishes. I'm just waiting for confirmation from London on one of my theories and then I'll just turn all my notes over to the police."

"Perhaps I was…er…a little hasty…" replied Brackenridge, "I only want to get to the bottom of this so that Sophie is cleared of all innuendo and accusations and we can return to our normal lives."

"But why are you troubled?" I asked. "Your sister appears to be recovering nicely and the medical prognosis is looking optimistic."

"If you know more about this case than you've been saying…"

said Holmes.

"No, no, it's not that at all. It's just that Sophie's no longer her old self and I don't know what to make of it."

"Explain."

"Well, for one, prior to the incident she was always gritting her teeth whenever I was around, as if she barely tolerated me, and now her impatience is gone. She seems to be...dare I say it... happy now in my company."

"But surely that's reason to celebrate?" I asked.

"Are you sure it's not the consequence of no longer using those dreaded eye drops?" Holmes inquired.

"It's more than that. She never had the time or a connection to plants and animals like I did except to complain about them or to ride her old horse to hell and back. Dogs and cats would run away with horror in their eyes and hide whenever they saw her coming but the other day I saw her cooing to a dove and muttering sweet nothings to it.

"Moreover, she always used to loathe milk and now she drinks it readily...In fact, she only nibbled her food before—which was cause for great consternation in the house—but now...beg pardon the expression...she eats like a Suffolk sheep and they're known to be greediest food guzzlers of all the breeds. She is also quite content to keep her hair loosened on her shoulders— something she would never have deemed to do before. She was always preoccupied with outward appearance."

"Perhaps her flirtation with death gave her a new lease of life," I suggested. "It's been known to happen."

Brackenridge went silent.

"As a child she was adventurous and wild. She would scale the chestnut tree outside her bedroom and sit in the uppermost branches and look down on us all as if she was a haughty princess and we her subjects.

"In recent years she took to locking herself up in her wardrobe for days not eating or drinking. She rarely went outside except on rare occasions. On the day I brought my motor-car home, she deigned to grant me her company so I drove us to the Seven Sisters in Sussex for a picnic. She yawned all the way. We climbed to the edge of one of the cliffs and she looked down into the sea and this expression came over her and then she shuffled over to the edge and leaned over precariously. I wasn't paying attention but suddenly she was wrenched back from the edge as if by invisible hands. Do you believe in angels?"

"No," said Holmes

"Yes," said I.

"Because I tell you that she surely would have tumbled to her death without some divine intervention," continued Bracken-ridge.

"There was a time not long ago she decided to go for a walk. She didn't want any company and I didn't want her tramping around alone at dusk in the countryside so I asked Latch, the broom squire, to follow her discreetly from a safe distance. He told me quietly later he came across her at Gibbet Hill, kneeling at the foot of the Celtic Cross when she thought nobody was watching. She was begging for mercy. I don't know what sin weighed so heavily upon her conscience, as she has never been one to accept responsibility or to apologise or confess to anything. I asked Latch to keep this knowledge to himself but he did tell me when he left that there was a moment that struck him. Just as the sun went down, something came over her and perhaps it was his imagination or just a sunray streaming down at the right time but for a moment she seemed to glow. Then she got up and returned home."

Gibbet Hill: known as the hanging spot for highwaymen and other criminals. It was the second highest of the Surrey Hills, and sometimes I would go there myself to soak in the mystical emanation from the Celtic Cross that had been erected some time back to protect the locals from natural and supernatural misfortune. Perhaps she had connected with this force.

"She often said to me," Toby whispered, "That she was bored to death. But now she smiles…she smiles with her eyes as if she really means it.

"Dare I say it," he muttered quietly as if he was ashamed of what he was thinking, "But I believe I like my sister better now than before she had her accident."

I had been pondering these discussions and believed there to be more to this story than was outwardly observable. Holmes had invited me to accompany him to the Brackenridge estate again for a walk through the house with Miss Sophie but I had an agenda as well, albeit not an obvious one.

When the young woman was strong enough to travel we returned to her home. We did not tell the authorities. It was just Holmes, the siblings and I.

She wore a light blue travelling dress her brother had brought her from home and her hair was charmingly askew so that tendrils and curls escaped from around the hairline and at her neck. We showed her into the house but had to lead her to her bedroom because she did not remember the way.

She tentatively stepped into the wardrobe but seemed completely detached from it all. She walked around in silence, inspecting all its contents. Her face was contorted in a grimace as if she was trying hard to remember. She caressed the gowns with sensory pleasure. Then she turned around and asked, "Why in heaven's name are all these dresses blue?"

"Only you can answer that, Soph," answered her brother gently.

"But blue isn't even my favourite colour. I have a penchant for pink if you must know."

"You don't have to wear them if you don't want to."

"Very well then. Let's sell them and give the money to the hospital to thank the staff for caring so well for me," she said.

Young Brackenridge looked astounded at the request but acquiesced.

She continued towards the *chaise longue* on the platform and the now upright curiosity cabinet. The floorboards and blood-splattered areas had been cleaned so there was no visual sign that a crime had ever taken place but I still sensed the foreign energy-signature in the atmosphere. Sophie merely swept her gaze around silently, looking rather befuddled.

"I'm sorry but I can't help you with anything," she said after a while.

Young Brackenridge responded, "Well, how about we move you to the Rose Room so you can leave all your bad memories behind in this one?"

"I don't have bad memories of this one. I don't have any memories at all. But I suspect the Rose Room will be pink and more to my liking."

"Miss Brackenridge. There's one more question I have of you. There's a gap here," said Holmes, indicating to the empty space in the curiosity cabinet. "Can you tell me what has been moved?"

"I'm sorry. I have no idea," she said simply.

"Come," she suddenly pronounced, as if that was that and the subject was closed. "Mr Holmes, Dr Moriarty, do you have further need of us? I think I should like to stroll around the garden with my brother."

She hooked an arm into her sibling's, and then the two excused themselves and departed. It was a strange course of events to be sure.

I caught Holmes staring at the young woman as she walked down the corridor. He seemed to be...dare I say it...envious. Off guard for a moment he mumbled, "You know, dear fellow, it seems I understand this young woman more than you'll ever know. To be bored, so bored, that you long for an ending in totality..." he trailed off.

His energy retracted. I understood what he was suggesting and where he was going, and felt he had reached that precipice before. For a moment I connected with a deep loneliness of a soul who possessed a complete inability to just be still. I had seen his manner when he had seized the white powder from me a few days before. Its allure when he thought it was something else. The disappointment when he realised what it was. The addiction was a crack in his veneer but his true addiction was not to the drug. The true addiction was an almost fanatical need to keep his brain occupied, to being in a constant state of hyper-vigilance and intensity. Holmes had no real family, and in the end, mysteries were his children. They gave his life meaning. They were his calling. They were his challenge and they were his triumph. And when they were unavailable, he faced the reality of the empty nest and was without purpose but exposed to the miasma within himself.

"Mr Holmes," I said softly, breaking him out of his trance, "I have a request. Will you grant it?"

"What is it you would have me do?" he said turning abruptly around to face me. I could see that the revelatory moment had passed.

"I need to enter the wardrobe overnight to do my own form of investigation."

"You mean your psychic detective mumbo jumbo."

"Something like that."

"How much time will you need?"

"The equivalent of one of your three pipe problems."

He snorted with amusement.

"I suppose it will be a distraction. You do what you have to do and I'll smoke."

Although I knew better, I appealed to his rational self. "Must you? I didn't mean to suggest you actually regress. It defies logic that you would do so when you have come to Hindhead to heal."

"You're not my mother nor my physician nor my friend, Dr M. You're merely a foil, so I don't need to heed your advice," he replied. It was useless to argue.

"Very well. I'll need you to lock the door until such time I'm ready to emerge. Please ensure that nobody enters the wardrobe to disturb me. I'll knock when I'm finished."

He watched me step inside and then I waited for the click of the key in the door, which came in due course. Then I walked inside and sat down on the floor in the centre of the room.

I needed to enter a deeper state of meditation than normal, which demanded that I lay down. I propped a pillow under my head then closed my eyes and slowed my breathing and counted backward from ten to one. I felt a sinking sensation and a feeling of heaviness. I felt the floorboards beneath my body. I saw a swirl of dark cloudiness like ink in water. Before long I felt the cells in my body pulsating, quickening, vibrating as if each one of them had a heartbeat of its own and then a shudder as I felt myself exteriorise. I looked upon my material counterpart in repose below like a slipcover devoid of its book, and once I was content that my body lay tranquil and untroubled, I followed the trail of the faint and unfamiliar energy-signature that was present in the wardrobe to the astral plane. And it is here that I must halt my narration to protect the Right Path secrets to which I am bound. All I will say is that I needed to commune in a place where I could validate or discredit my hypothesis about what had occurred in that very wardrobe with Miss Sophie Brackenridge several nights ago. And just as I suspected, I found profound answers and brought the knowledge back with me, ensuring it would transfer from dream-state to waking, conscious thought.

What seemed like a short time later I returned from my astral wonderings and oriented myself to the here and now. I opened my eyes. I did not know how long I was gone but I could smell ash in a cold pipe and see how the light had changed to softened golden tones of sunrise. I must have been away all night. I sensed a presence in the room but it was not an out-of-world menace. It was merely Holmes standing in front of the window, gazing out at the chestnut tree and the gardens. He turned towards me. For the first time I was angry.

"Aaaah, you're back," he said.

"You really are very reckless, you know. You could have placed us both in danger."

"How so?"

"I've protected myself psychically but something could have easily slipped back to harm you."

"There's no more harm that can be done to me than I already do upon myself," he said with profound clarity. No words were truer said. A heavy pause hung in the air between us and then I started to compose myself again.

"Did you find the answers you were seeking?" he asked mockingly.

"Yes."

"As did I. While you've been floating about the netherworld I succeeded in solving this case.

"How?"

"It's said that eyes are the windows of the soul but what if windows were the eyes to the heart of this crime?" he said obliquely.

I had no idea what he was talking about but I did see from the gleam in his eye and his self-important and gratified manner he had come upon an answer. I caught the corresponding vibrational energetic shift—what I could only describe as *victory*.

"You piqued my curiosity," he said to me, "That rarely happens. I can usually discern a person's makeup and character in minutes; merely by observing the intricacies in their gait, their countenance, state of dress and demeanour. You, however, are a delightfully complex and intriguing archetype I have not observed in such close quarters before. I'll gladly add a new occupation and description to my catalogue—the Initiate. Bordering on the delusional, yet inexplicably promised to a path of healing.

"Come," he said suddenly clapping his hands, "We must assemble the players, although in this instance, I won't be inviting the constabulary until later. We should follow Miss Brackenridge's example from yesterday and take a stroll through the garden."

"I did not take you for a child of nature."

"I couldn't think of anything more detestable. In fact, I'll not lament when I return to the gas lamps and sewers of London. "

"I thought you had retired to Sussex."

"Under duress for a restorative stay."

For the first time we chortled together.

Holmes, the Brackenridges and I stood in the sunken garden at the back of the house, surrounded by azalea and rhododendron bushes and two red oak trees. Beyond that behind the break wall were other mature trees, trimmed shrubbery and an apple orchard. Sophie was garbed in a charming apricot dress and seemed in good spirits.

Holmes had need of a ladder and the gardener's was broken. He had determined that the nearest one was in the broom squire's cottage not far up the road and had sent me to fetch it. I had entered a yard full of well-cared caged animals—rats, weasels, ferrets and stoats. Latch, the scruffy but friendly broom squire whose job it was to collect heather and birch twigs to make brooms for a living, was cooing to a mink sitting on his lap. He gladly lent me his ladder with comment, "Glad to help out, Mr 'Olmes, for the favour he did me in bringing me precious Ellie back," he said, raising the mink up in the air as if he was toasting an occasion.

I had staggered back to the house with the ladder and, under Holmes's instructions, had propped it on the outside wall underneath the walk-in wardrobe. Sophie and her brother looked baffled.

"Miss Brackenridge, can you tell me what happened just before the incident in the wardrobe?"

She rubbed her neck and looked at us plaintively.

"No, Mr Holmes. I still have no memory of it. Everything in my mind is muddled and far away, as if I'm caught in fog and don't know what direction to take to get back home."

"I see. Well perhaps I can hasten your memory into recollection...but I fear you'll need to sit down for this."

We all sat down tentatively on the garden bench underneath the chestnut tree. The siblings looked fearful, clutching each other's hands. Holmes remained standing. He calmly lit his pipe. I smelled the revolting acrid fumes of a black shag blend, and took in a few gulps of clean air in an attempt to clear the scent from my nasal cavity.

The tree was gradually stripping itself bare and so I could see its branches from underneath extending upwards, and slivers of sky where the canopy was broken. A rake was leaning on the tree trunk, poised over a large pile of autumn leaves the gardener had not yet swept up.

After a few minutes, Holmes spoke up again.

"How do I put this delicately, Brackenridge…Your sister is a thief and a murderer!" he declared with great forcefulness.

"Now see here…" cried Brackenridge, jumping to his feet, "I hired you to find out the truth; not to invent it!"

"And I'm giving it to you."

"I don't understand," said Sophie forlornly, "How can that be? I promise you, Mr Holmes. I don't have murder in my heart."

"Everybody has the capacity to kill under the right circumstances," said Holmes impatiently, with a look of contempt on his face, "Even I."

"I'll gladly be held accountable if it be so it but I simply don't remember," she pleaded.

"Then let me recount the days leading up to the murder for that is what it was.

"Miss Brackenridge, you have been petulant and aggrieved for most of your life. You had a sense of self-entitlement and extended no care towards others. And then you started wearing blue eighteen months ago. That was a turning point."

Sophie sat quietly with a lost expression on her face. Brackenridge began protesting again but Holmes silenced him with a raised hand.

"You've done an admirable job of protecting her but you need to confront the truth."

The young man looked shaken.

"You said yourself that Sophie found her life tedious. Her days were spent in idleness, searching for stimulation, rather than searching for meaning. And then one day she found it. She was about thirteen and you must have been about eleven. She asked you if she could have your book and you did not give it to her so when you weren't watching, she stole it. That was when her crime spree began. She began to steal other things—a fan from a visitor, coins from the cook, a hair ribbon from the maid… Thievery excited her. It turned her towards even more sensation-seeking acts. Gave her a feeling of pleasure and power…albeit temporary. She needed to do it again. But pilfering from a brother or a servant was easy. If things went missing, one would just blame the help. What if she did it in the outside world? And so, once she was old enough to go on outings, she continued. At first it was a pack of pastilles from a corner shop. And then a handkerchief…Then gradually she became more brazen and the corresponding stakes and risks got higher.

"Once she grew up and sought some independence, I'm afraid that nearly every time she visited London she sought to steal something. She secreted the stolen items in her portmanteau. After all, nobody would suspect a lady of quality. And she was correct in this assertion. The blame would invariably fall on some innocent ragamuffin that happened to be in the vicinity.

"The curiosity cabinet became a resting place for her trophies. She would arrange the items in the order in which they were stolen, and every time she sat down and gazed at the objects from her *chaise longue*, she would relive the excitement of each deed.

"But there was one piece missing…this one had pride of place, and that is where the story begins anew.

"Eighteen months ago, Sophie Brackenridge performed the ultimate robbery. It was a crime of opportunity and one of great irony. She stole a package from an associate of the Sugarman Gang.

"The sugar in the letter…" I spluttered, making a connection.

"Yes, yes. We'll come to that in a moment."

"The Sugarman Gang is a burglary ring that fences jewellery, watches and other stolen goods. Scotland Yard has special interest in these blighters and has compiled a rogue's gallery of sketches and photographs of anyone in league with them, including one bald-headed Russian jewellery thief named Vasily Korotkin, the dead miscreant in your wardrobe. The reason I know this is because I remember seeing a sketch of a stolen bracelet in *The London Gazette* a few years ago…one of the many items in the cabinet upstairs. I commit the most mundane things to memory in order to exercise it properly and improve my recall. Inspector Lestrade confirmed several of the items as being stolen from various London shops. He also confirmed the identity of the dead man in the wardrobe."

"But what would I want with a gang of thieves?" asked Sophie, "And for that matter, I'm not interested in precious stones. I'd rather gaze at a polished pebble from a stream than gaze into the eye of a diamond."

Her brother turned towards her abruptly. He looked bewildered. And I knew why. The expensive contents in the jewellery case in her wardrobe spoke to the opposite of her claim.

"I'm coming to that…" continued Holmes,

"About two years ago you stole a precious object from Korotkin. I am surmising it would have been wrapped up in his pocket. He was passing a shop and saw he was about to be confronted by a gang of ruffians up ahead so he slipped inside and hid the package in a place from which he could easily retrieve it later. You happened to be there and witnessed him doing so. While he stepped outside for a moment, you took the opportunity to seize the item and stow it in your portmanteau. A few minutes later, with altercation avoided, Korotkin went to retrieve the object but it was gone. All he remembered was seeing a young woman to whom he had tipped his hat and smiled as he was going in and she was going out, and he knew you were the likely culprit.

"And correct me if I'm wrong…"

"I can't correct you. This is new information to me."

"When you returned home, you unwrapped the package and promptly became smitten with the object that lay inside, for it was the most breathtaking thing you had ever seen. It was blue."

"But what was it?" I insisted.

"In time," said Holmes, in such a way that I tapped my foot in impatience.

"It took all that time for Korotkin to track you down to Haslemere. He recognised you from a distance in London, and saw you were wearing a blue dress and carrying your familiar bag but he was too far away to pursue you. From then on, there were sightings in London of a woman in the blue dress that was always in the vicinity of a felony. The Sugarman Gang was apprised of this situation, kept an eye out for you and passed information on to him.

"And then a few weeks ago, he finally found you. He followed you to Haslemere by train. The broom squire told me he had hurried off a bald-headed itinerant a few days before the incident in the wardrobe, which leads me to conclude he had been watching and circumnavigating the house at night for an opportunity to get to you. The dilemma was that you rarely left your home.

"So several night ago Korotkin concocted a plan to get you to reveal where the object was hidden. He arranged for the letter to be delivered to you at precisely eight o'clock while you were at dinner. To intimidate you further, he put sugar in the envelope as a misdirect and a warning you were dealing with a highly dangerous criminal gang that had you in its sights. He knew you'd never give the object up willingly and, if he were found on the grounds, then he would invariably be arrested as a vagrant, a thief or even worse. He knew your first instinct would be to protect the treasure if you still had it in your possession. The reason the kitchen door was ajar at noon was because he slipped into the house and hid under your bed. He knew which room was yours by watching the gaslights being turned on and off at night and he must certainly have seen your silhouette in your upstairs third floor window.

"He had a small bottle of vodka with him to keep himself from falling asleep as he waited. Russians open their bottles by striking the bottom of it with the flat of their hand, which pops the cork. Contrary to popular belief that vodka is odourless; cheap vodka with its many impurities does have a rather unpleasant smell, similar to rubbing alcohol. Although it's difficult to detect on the breath, vodka often emits an unpleasant aroma from the pores. I found this out when I looked under the bed where he lay hidden for nigh on eight hours, waiting for you. I also found the cork."

He withdrew a cork from his pocket and held it up. We stared at it, voiceless and unmoving.

"Just after eight o'clock after you had received the letter, you rushed upstairs and unlocked the door to your walk-in wardrobe but forgot to lock it again behind you. You then climbed on top of the cabinet and pushed up the window, then crawled onto the branch of the chestnut and along the limb until you found your special hiding place. This was why your knees were scraped and why your stockings were torn and contained tiny splinters of bark. You also tore a fragment of lace from your dress when it snagged on a twig. I didn't see it the first time I visited because the view was misty from the rain. But while I was staring out of the window the second time, I saw it fluttering in the breeze. It's still up there if you care to look."

We all looked up. I didn't see a thing.

"Your little treasure was exactly where you left it. You must have been relieved. Then you crawled back and climbed onto the windowsill only to find Korotkin waiting to confront you."

"I can't remember, I can't remember," wailed Sophie with tears streaming down her face.

"You can't remember or you don't want to remember," said Holmes coldly.

He continued. "Korotkin advanced. It is here we must understand that despite being a heavy drinker and used to alcohol, he was inebriated after eight hours with no food to line his stomach. He was probably not in complete command of his faculties when you did the only thing you could think of. You sat down on the windowsill and, with all your might, you pushed the heavy cabinet on top of him with your legs. The glass shattered. Nobody heard the cabinet fall because they were at the other end of the house and several floors down. So he wouldn't survive, you then jumped on the back of the cabinet with all your weight. Indeed his sternum and several ribs were broken and a piece of glass was driven into his neck. He died in minutes from a combination of blood loss and crush asphyxia because the weight of the cabinet impeded his ability to breathe.

"You, Miss Sophie Brackenridge," Holmes cried, "Are guilty!"

The young woman wept. Her brother held her tightly, comforting her and muttering darkly, "I don't believe it. I don't believe it. You can't prove anything."

"A close examination on the back panel on the cabinet clearly showed several faint shoe impressions, which I matched to the pair Sophie was wearing and which you later hid in the chimney. Furthermore, when she jumped off the fallen cabinet and onto the floor, she picked up some blood trace on her shoes and left some faint bloody footprints as she attempted to move away."

"And now, Doctor, since you're an *amoureux de la nature* and I clearly am not, I suggest you climb that ladder and onto that tree branch to where I'm pointing."

I was speechless but did as he had commanded. Before long I was sitting on the sturdy limb that extended to the window of the walk-in wardrobe.

"What am I looking for?"

"The robin's nest."

"I won't disturb a nesting bird. It's sacrilege."

"It's time the robin flew south for the winter anyway. Isn't that what you said to me once, Mr Brackenridge? It's late in the season..."

I slid carefully down the branch towards the nest. The little red-breasted *brù-dhearg* flew away in fright. I pried the nest from the branch, clutched it to my chest, then clambered down the branch towards the ladder again and descended to the lawn.

Without a word, I handed the nest to Holmes. He moved some feathers and twigs aside, withdrew a blue egg and held it up to the light.

It was not a robin's egg. This one was about three inches in height and looked more like an exceptionally expensive Easter egg. It was enameled and reeded in royal blue and encrusted with gold, rose-cut diamonds and sapphires, as well as a diamond pushpiece. It was simply exquisite.

"Magnificent," I gasped.

The others looked stunned. I glanced over to Miss Brackenridge. She was mesmerised by the treasure in Holmes's hand.

"This is the Blue Serpent Clock Egg, handcrafted by Peter Carl Fabergé himself and intended for the Tsar, Alexander III of the Russian Imperial family."

"But there's no clock in it," I observed.

"That's because there's great confusion about this piece. There were actually two blue clock eggs. The second one in translucent blue was supposedly made and delivered to the Tsar in 1887. That one is currently held at the Anichkov Palace. It stands on a base of gold with an opalescent white finish and is about seven inches in height. It has three panels on its pedestal that feature motifs representing the arts and sciences. It has a diamond-encrusted snake coiling around the supporting stem and pointing its head and forked tongue upwards to the clock hour on a white, rotating ribbon of enamel that surrounds the egg. It also had gold handles.

"This one is the true 1887 Imperial Easter Egg, also known by the same name as the other. However, the more famous Blue Serpent Clock egg was crafted two years earlier by Mikhail Perkhin of Fabergé's shop."

"Then this is a fake." Brackenridge said with relief.

"No, this is the second lost egg."

"How do you know?"

"The 1887 egg had sapphires in it. This one has sapphires. The Tsar paid 2160 rubles for it instead of the expected 6000 rubles... why? Because it wasn't finished yet and the money paid was an installment. He would pay the balance when it was complete and then would take possession of it. He didn't get the opportunity to do so because it was stolen before Fabergé had a chance to add the pedestal and all its embellishments.

"Korotkin was the thief. He hid it for many years and then finally smuggled it across the continent eighteen months ago. He had made contact with the Sugarman Gang in London who were going to fence it for him, probably to a member of the English aristocracy who was prepared to pay a king's ransom to add the coveted item to a private collection. Your sister stole it first.

"You had every intention of killing yourself that night, Miss Brackenridge, which is why you put on your favourite blue lace dress, which is why you sprinkled rose petals around your chaise longue and surrounded it with candles. You've wanted to die for a long time but you wanted to do it on your own terms like a heroine from a romantic poem or drowned Ophelia from a Millais painting. You sought death but you wanted control over your death. At first you thought to make yourself look like death. It was not the fashion affectation I first suspected—it was a rehearsal, which is why you put the rice powder on your face and exacerbated the blue circles under your eyes and dilated your pupils. You wanted to look beautiful in death as you did in life. The problem was that Korotkin forced you to change your plans. You hid the egg in the robin's nest several weeks before your planned departure date, which is why the robin never left. She was still keeping that extraordinarily beautiful egg warm on instinct but it never hatched. Nobody would ever find it in a robin's nest until well after you were gone and, if and when they did, it would be a grand mystery as to how it got there.

"However, knowing you would be blamed for the murder, you staged everything to look as if Korotkin had attacked you and then you gulped down the remains of the belladonna solution. You collapsed from shock and lost consciousness in the middle of the room. If it weren't for the fact that your brother found you in time and got you medical help, and that perhaps the dosage was one berry short of being lethal then you would have surely died.

"And now, I'm afraid I'll need to take this information to the police and ensure the egg returns to its original owner," Holmes said, tucking it into his pocket.

Miss Brackenridge had collapsed onto the lawn, sobbing. "I can't remember. I can't remember."

"I believe her, Holmes," I said quietly.

"What you believe and what I believe are two different matters," he said sharply. "Miss Brackenridge is a fine actress, I can attest to that but the evidence speaks for itself. And justice must be served."

"Perhaps I can shed some additional light on this case that may not be obvious..." I said, "With your permission, of course."

He waved a hand at me with impatience.

"I believe there's a good explanation as to why Miss Brackenridge can't remember what occurred."

"And I believe I have covered it all. Sophie Brackenridge, memory loss or not, is the perpetrator of multiple felonies and a heinous murder."

"The thing is, Holmes, we're faced with a paradox. How can a murderer not be a murderer?"

He paused and looked at me. "You have my attention."

"Sophie doesn't respond to her name because she's no longer Sophie," I said, getting down on both knees beside her on the lawn and lowering my face towards her tear-stained one, "Your name is Tanith is it not?"

Sophie reacted immediately through her tears, turning towards her name like a dog turning towards its whistling master. "Oh, yes. That sits much more comfortably on me."

"Let me put it to you, Tanith, the reason you can't remember anything is because you've just been born into this body."

"What nonsense are you spouting now, Dr M?" exclaimed Holmes with derision.

"The only time the real Sophie was peaceful was when she was sleeping. That's why she retired to her wardrobe so often. The greatest trauma for her was waking up to face life's monotony and the slow, excruciating, ticking of a clock of a life that seemed pointless.

"Sophie was a tormented soul who knew herself to be hollow. She wanted to alleviate her ennui by leaving this earth permanently.

"Your soul, however, Tanith, was looking for an experience on earth and because bodies are scarce and Sophie had a viable one you came to an agreement on the other plane that would have her evacuate her body so you could inhabit it. You knew that Sophie was contemplating death. It was your spirit that saved her on the cliffs but it is at the Thin Place where you made your pact."

I looked up at Holmes to elaborate. He was a man of erudition but had no understanding about esoteric matters and the psychic realm. That was my domain.

"A Thin Place is like scrim between heaven and earth, between the two planes. It is said the distance between these two planes is three inches in such a spot.

"The area around the Celtic Cross on Gibbet Hill is a Thin Place, and that was why Sophie found peace there shortly before she chose to die because you both had an understanding it would happen on a particular night. Your soul approached Sophie's in a state of her prayer. Your soul needed a healthy vessel but it also needed the body to be temporarily weakened for the soul exchange to take place.

"This intersection point happens through accident, illness or meditation. It's as Mr Holmes said…on the night Sophie left this earth she was preparing for her death. But being proud and vain about her appearance she wanted to look radiant as she departed and so she prepared her death scene like one of her beloved romantic paintings. You, Tanith, needed her to loosen her connection to her body but not destroy it completely otherwise the entire exercise would have been fruitless. The belladonna solution was dosage enough to do that but not to kill her body outright. What neither of you anticipated—in either the earthly or spiritual plane—was that Sophie's crime would come back to haunt her on that same night."

I looked at Miss Brackenridge's face and tears ran down her cheeks.

"Is this at all possible, Dr Moriarty?" gasped Toby Brackenridge.

"Your true soul sister has turned to the Light. She is happy, but mark my word, she will atone for her sins threefold. She will not escape without making amends, whether it be now or in a future life. Your new soul sister who is without taint is in service to the Light. She doesn't recognise her life because she hasn't actually lived it. You are reminding her of memories lived by another.

"You see, Tanith is a *walk-in* whereas Sophie was a *walk-out*. A body can only have one soul in residence unless it is possessed by evil and this is not a possession.

"And here is the ultimate paradox…can Tanith be held accountable for the crimes of another who held court in the same body and who has now departed?"

I completed my summation and was met with silence. Toby slumped to the ground, holding his head in his hands. His sister stood perfectly still not twitching a muscle or blinking.

"So what's to be done here, Holmes?" I whispered.

He did not answer. Time passed slowly. I could hear Toby and Tanith holding their breath. I could feel Holmes trying to make rational sense of it all but not succeeding. And did I blame him? The explanation sounded preposterous. What sane adult or court of law could accept such a scenario?

As Holmes stood there under the chestnut tree, I noticed a solitary bee fly up from a wilting flower and land on the shoulder of his coat. His immediate reaction was to swat it and then he paused and offered it his hand instead. The bee crawled onto it without defensiveness.

"Fascinating insects," he said presently, examining it intently. "The only creatures on earth capable of creating a hexagon; 'the free yet enslaved'.

"I'm thinking of pursuing beekeeping when I return to Sussex," he mentioned casually, as he watched it crawl onto his upraised palm.

It was in that moment I understood something of great significance. The bee was a sacred symbol to King Solomon and, by extension over thousands of years, to my own kind and to me. Despite Holmes's blustering and his rabid insistence he was not aligned with any faith, the Grand Geometrician had chosen to align himself with him.

For Holmes was an advocate for righteousness. His mission was to redress imbalances in this world and whether he knew or didn't know that he had a higher purpose, was inconsequential. He just followed the directive of his own sacred blueprint.

Holmes suddenly walked into the sunlight and placed the bee onto a leaf.

Without warning, Miss Brackenridge slumped onto her brother. They hugged each other and she whispered her mantra again to him, "I'm sorry. I'm sorry. I didn't know. Please believe me."

Toby Brackenridge said, "I'll say I did it."

She replied, "No. Thank you for taking such good care of Sophie. Now let it be my turn to take care of you...Mr Holmes, I'm ready."

I was moved by their bond, and kept my gaze on them with a troubled heart.

After a few moments we turned around together to face Holmes.

We did not see him. He had silently departed. We did not know what that meant.

I stayed with the Brackenridges for the next few days to give them whatever comfort I could. We waited on edge for the constabulary to arrest one or other or even both of the siblings but nothing happened.

I decided to catch up with Ingram for the pint he had promised but my intent was surreptitious—I wanted to find out what I could about how the police were treating the case...anything... but he talked about other benign matters. I started to relax and in the middle of a guzzle I asked him, "So what happened with these suiciding hounds you once talked about? The idea has confounded me."

"Oh, it's quite simple really, Moriarty. There's a bridge nearby with a deep drop into a ravine. In recent months, several dogs walking with their masters over the bridge at night suddenly and inexplicably, as if driven by madness, jumped over the edge to their death."

"How horrible. I would not wish that on any animal or human for that matter."

"There were many theories for it...curses, spectres, you name it. Holmes didn't bat an eyelid when he was told about it. He merely informed us that dogs are dictated by exercise and live predominantly through their sense of smell. He said to look for an exotic...crep...crep...crepis..."

"Crepuscular?" I offered.

"Yes, that's it. An animal that is most active at dusk and dawn. It also had to have a strong scent.

"We set a trap in the ravine and sure enough after a few nights caught an animal that was rare for these parts..."

"A European mink no doubt," I answered, remembering something that had been mentioned to me a few days before. I knew they emitted a strong musty smell from their glands that no doubt would have been intoxicating to a dog that had never smelled it before.

"Why, yes. How did you know?"

"A mink by the name of Ellie."

"Yes, we returned it to Latch. He was delighted. Hasn't let go of her since. Loves that furry flea-ridden thing."

We clinked our beer glasses and toasted Holmes. Ingram did not bring up the case of the walk-in wardrobe and I did not ask him about it. The case appeared closed.

The next day I went to visit the great detective at Undershaw for that was the house where he had been staying and whose name I had forgotten. Its original owner—a man of letters and a knight of the realm—had vacated it shortly after his wife's death and a hasty remarriage. I knocked on the door and the windowpanes without response. The house was empty. I heard later that Holmes had moved back to Sussex. He did not return to the area again. I sent him a cosmic prayer to thank him for his mercy. I hoped somehow he would receive it consciously but knew in all likelihood he would not. I also left a short time later and returned to my family in Africa. It was to be nine years before I saw England again.

And now let me revisit the colour yellow.

Yellow is a feminine colour, a dainty colour that brings to mind freshly churned butter and ripe lemons and the stripes of bees. Yellow was Holmes's predominant colour. But yellow was also a contradiction to his nature because I sensed no female energy about him and indeed, he eschewed the company of women as if their very presence would taint his abilities. The yellow I speak of that dominated the ever-shifting spectrum of his aura was the yellow of intellect.

Holmes would not ever acknowledge that his intelligence could reflect in light and energy. He would happily claim his intellect with no thought to humility but a supercilious and at times gleeful celebration of his own prowess. But he would never believe in the yellow—the predominant colour that swirled around his head depending on his mood and inclination and his concentration—in muddy and even buttercup tones, unobserved by the masses and only discerned by the rare ones amongst us with subtle sight of which I am one.

Before you pounce upon me as a man of arrogance, please consider that I do not classify myself as special and if I had been born into another time I would have surely been burnt at the stake. I would rather categorise my gifts as an accident of birth that needed more tempering and training of the style I had learned from Holmes but now needed to redirect into the occult practises. For Holmes had the ability to focus on the minutiae of everyday life, to discern the extraordinary from the ordinary, to account for things that were out of place and therefore grounds for suspicion that would go about to right great wrongs. I, on the other hand, was only starting to scratch the surface.

And that is where the yellow came in. And that is how I will always remember him—swathed and bathed in a golden light around his noble head.

Curtain Call

J. SCHERPENHUIZEN

Sherlock Holmes was in a dour mood as the curtain fell on the latest performance of Christopher Marlowe's *Doctor Faustus*. The gleeful applause of Holmes's friend and chronicler, Doctor Hieronymus Mabuse, only seemed to deepen the detective's dark humour, and a saturnine sneer twisted his lips. Mabuse regarded his friend with no sign of concern and redoubled his clapping.

"Splendid," Mabuse said. "Splendid, quite the best production yet!"

"You should know," Holmes said. "You have seen the wretched piece to an extent which suggests an unhealthy obsession."

"Ah, a thing of beauty is a joy forever." Mabuse grinned, rising from his seat in their box.

"Familiarity breeds contempt," Holmes retorted.

"Surely not always?" Mabuse threw his arms wide as if he might embrace the world or possibly Holmes himself. "Look at all the years we have been the closest of associates and still we have not come to blows, despite the vow you made, the first week we shared lodgings, to knock my fillings loose if I persisted in my gambling. Here I stand, a frequent visitor to the Tankerville Club, teeth *in situ*, and my bank balance and reputation unblemished!"

"And you would be fully aware, I am certain, that you managed to curtail your dreadful whist skills with a combination of self-hypnosis and more careful selection of partners at the card table. In short, you took my advice, thus obviating the necessity of forcing you to see sense." Holmes hissed, but repressed a grin himself.

They were descending the stairs and there were few patrons in close proximity, yet the detective was ever mindful of his public image and was concerned that the personality of his at times boisterous companion, so different to that portrayed in his famous stories, would one day become an embarrassment to him.

"Ah," Mabuse smirked. "Forgive me. Despite the many years I have spent here, my values remain rather continental, and my manner more expressive than is the norm. I suppose I should be more mindful of local sensibilities. You British are so rigid, and codified—look at the way poor Oscar Wilde has been persecuted, for example."

"You admire Wilde?"

"Well, he's no Marlowe. Though I rather like *Dorian Gray*, there's nothing quite as magnificent as *Doctor Faustus* in his oeuvre."

"'Magnificent'?" Really, Mabuse, it is a tedious morality play, grounded in superstition, and your fondness for it remains a mystery to me. I only consented to accompany you because of your assertion that this new lead actor is a performer of genius— for you know my profession makes me curious in regard to the craft of the impersonator. Apart from that, what possible interest can Marlowe's dreary melodrama have to men of science like ourselves?"

"None whatsoever," Mabuse smiled, "unless, perhaps, there is a limit to what science might know, and a danger in the hubris of following knowledge whatever the cost."

"Pish! You love to test me." Holmes snorted. "Here we are with steam locomotives, gaslights and modern medicine. I suppose you think we would be happier being leeched by candlelight? And our eponymous protagonist, Dr Johann Faustus, is such a fool! He thinks he can make a pact with the devil and profit by it.

It is a silly tale about an imbecile!"

"Really?" Mabuse's cheer seemed a little diminished for the first time since Holmes had begun his tirade, and he kept his peace while they retrieved their hats and coats from the cloakroom, yet the detective was not yet finished.

"The entire piece is woefully predictable," Holmes continued. "Anyone can see the outcome from the very beginning."

"Perhaps," the doctor said, donning his hat as they stepped out of the theatre, "but not everyone has your powers of deduction, my friend. And let us be grateful for that. For if the world was not peopled by fools, they would not be so impressed by genius. They would not line up to read of your exploits as they do and we might have to get honest jobs. As it is, I am a wealthy teller of tales and you are allowed to amuse yourself with puzzles to your heart's content."

The detective made no response, but Mabuse was sure he was hiding a smile again.

Mabuse had agreed to join Holmes in enjoying a glass of sherry before repairing to his own digs. Arriving at Baker Street, the pair found Holmes's landlady, Mrs Hudson, at the door, a grave look upon her face.

"I must apologise, gentlemen, but a most insistent young lady is awaiting you. She is so agitated and distraught that I hadn't the heart to turn her away, unseemly as her persistence might be."

"Never mind," Holmes said. "I shall be happy to see the young lady. I am curious as to the nature of the dilemma that has inspired such behaviour."

As they entered the upstairs sitting room a young woman rose hurriedly to greet the gentlemen. In her mid-twenties, Elizabeth Durance was rather tall and bore herself with an unusual stateliness for someone of her age. Her eyes were large and spaced widely apart and her cheekbones were high. Her face was as strong as it was attractive, with a determined chin which thrust forward even as she offered her apologies for disturbing their evening. Assuring her he was more than happy to hear her case, Holmes bade her sit, and encouraged her to commence with her tale without further ado.

"My father worked exceedingly hard for many years in the goldfields of Victoria in Australia and amassed quite a fortune over a period of years. As his holdings grew he planned to return to England and envisioned a life for us here in which we might find a place in society commensurate with his wealth, and he had prepared for this by sending me to Switzerland where I would be groomed to become a lady. Sadly, toward the end of my stay in Geneva, my mother's health, which had been rather poor for some time, sharply declined. Thus, a journey here, where he would meet me was delayed until she should be fit enough to endure the journey. Unfortunately, contrary to our hopes, her condition declined further and she departed this realm."

"We're sorry to hear that," Mabuse murmured.

"Thank you," Elizabeth nodded in acknowledgement. The doctor studied her intently, with a look of intense compassion. She guessed him to be in his fifth decade but thought him unusually handsome, despite having reached such a venerable age. His long, slightly hooked nose divided a face of remarkable symmetry, and his eyes burned with a fire that she could not place.

"My father was a modest man despite his accomplishments. He was unlettered and everything he had achieved had been by dint of hard work, native wit and, as he was the first to admit, more than his fair share of luck."

"Hard working men with good wits frequently are lucky," Holmes said with a quick smile. "But I do not imagine it is his good fortune that brings you here."

"No," Elizabeth agreed, her head bowing with sadness. "My father was found dead, supposedly by his own hand, a few weeks ago."

"And, yet, you suspect foul play?" Holmes said gravely.

"It seems obvious to me that something unholy is involved in his demise," the young woman confirmed. "And I am sure that when you hear the circumstances, you too will be suspicious. While my father came here with a fortune and purchased a substantial estate, in the six months since he had been here, according to the police, he had gambled away his entire fortune and more, borrowing from the bank against the estate which will shortly be reclaimed to recover the debt. It is assumed that his suicide was prompted by his inability to cover his gambling debts."

"Did he not leave a note?" Mabuse asked diffidently.

"No. As I mentioned, he had no letters. All correspondence was dictated to his factotum, a man named Flanders. I do not see Father enlisting his aid in such a final communication."

"Ah, of course," Mabuse nodded. "I should have seen that."

"And the basis for your suspicions?" Holmes prompted.

"My father brought two other servants with him from Australia," Elizabeth said. "But they were given their notice by Flanders just some two weeks after the arrival. My father had taken ill, on the first day he set foot on English soil. I have since spoken to one of the servants who was dismissed, Elsie Jones. Elsie tells me my father was ill, acted peculiarly, and insisted on behaving the recluse after arriving here. In fact she only saw my father in his bed in dim light from the moment they settled in their new abode, however he did speak.

"Could an imposter have taken over your father's place?" asked Holmes.

"She believes it was him."

"And yet..."

"The pretext upon which she and the other servant were dismissed seemed concocted. And my father was a temperate man who never gambled. He was an individual with a strong character. Even if he had developed such a destructive habit, and even if he had lost his fortune, he would never end his life and leave me without means. He would have made another fortune."

"Gambling is a topic of considerable interest to the doctor and myself," said Holmes drily. "It is a vice which many apparently strong individuals have fallen a prey to, nonetheless I cannot ignore the fact that you have great faith in your father. And yet the police are unmoved, I gather?"

"They have mounted an investigation," Elizabeth said. "Armed with a photographic portrait and a description of my father they have discovered that a man very like him had been seen in many gambling dens about the city and also at the racing track, and his name was well known."

"Yet you do not believe it was him?"

Elizabeth wrung her hands in dismay. "It seems impossible to me that my father could change that much. I knew him, the police did not."

"Yet his body was found and positively identified?"

"Only by Flanders, who has since disappeared," Elizabeth said.

"Yet this is not enough for the police to consider the matter afresh?"

"No. The way they view it, my father was seen by dozens of people gambling his fortune away. He was attempting to move up in station which is not an easy thing to do in English society, and his wife was recently deceased. They consider it likely that he felt dejected and turned to gambling as a mere distraction, but it came to dominate his life and destroyed him. They consider me merely unwilling to accept the unpleasant truth."

For a brief moment silence reigned in the room.

"It is a reasonable surmise," Holmes conceded at last. "And yet this 'Flanders' disappearance is highly suspicious, as is the dismissal of the other servants. However, even if the police did agree that foul play was involved, proving it would be exceedingly difficult, and the authorities would rather not expend their energies upon unpromising puzzles that might defy them. That would look like a defeat. Better that they pretend there is no puzzle at all."

There was another moment of silence, then Holmes spoke decisively: "I will look into the matter myself."

"Thank you, oh, thank you so much," Elizabeth said, rising from her chair.

"I must go, too," Mabuse said. "Please allow me to see you to a carriage, miss."

"You're most kind," Elizabeth said with a small curtsey.

"You must both meet me here at six tomorrow evening," Holmes said. "I will have news for you then."

The following day had been grey and cloudy and rain chattered across the cobbled streets as the dusk fell and the gas lights were ignited. Mrs Hudson ushered Mabuse and Elizabeth into Holmes's study at precisely six p.m.

"Well, you are here, on the mark," Holmes remarked brightly.

"I am sure neither of us would be late for this particular appointment," Mabuse smiled. "I myself have been pondering our mystery much of the day, trying to imagine what you might discover that the police had neglected."

"I'm surprised you did not hypnotise yourself into focusing more on your work," Holmes said smugly.

"Hypnosis?" Elizabeth said. "Is that Mesmerism?"

"Yes, indeed," Holmes agreed. "Mesmerism shorn of its hocus pocus. While he is best known as my chronicler, our good Doctor Mabuse is also renowned, in certain circles, as a psychoanalyst and hypnotist."

"Ah, I did not know that," Elizabeth said. "I had assumed that the Doctor was a surgeon and a general practitioner."

"He is those things, too," Holmes said. "Our Dr Mabuse is a man of many parts. His knowledge is much broader than mine, I'm afraid. He knows of such matters as literature and art which psychoanalysts take an inordinate interest in. I'm afraid my attention is far too taken up with the criminal sciences to have attained his broad range of knowledge."

"Not to mention the newspapers and penny dreadfuls." Mabuse grinned.

"Both are an excellent source of information," Holmes said, smiling.

Mrs Hudson appeared at the door, carrying a tray with a tea service and biscuits, and the trio seated themselves and poured their beverages.

"Come, Holmes," Mabuse prompted as his comrade took a sip from his cup. "Don't keep us in suspense. What have you discovered?"

"Like the police, I showed the photograph around. A large number of cab drivers had a vivid recollection of dropping off someone of Mr Durance's description at the track, or in Chinatown. They also recalled his name. Apparently he paid generously. When they expressed their gratitude he was fond of making such pronouncements as, 'Don't let it be said, *Arthur Durance* hain't a genlman,' and '*Arthur Durance* hain't short a penny, my lad.' And, '*Arthur Durance* 'as nobless obleej'."

Holmes turned to Elizabeth. "Does that sound like your father?"

"Well, yes and no," she replied gravely. "The accent does, to some degree, and the vocabulary, too, I suppose, but my father was never in the habit of talking of himself in the third person."

"Few people are," Holmes mused, "unless they are acting in an expository role. What is immediately suspicious about this case is that this person was so easy to verify as being where Flanders had said he would be. It made it very straightforward for the police to confirm his movements. However, had they questioned more deeply, as I have done, they would have discovered how unusual the manner of this individual was, and how different from your father's. As it is, they were merely content to place him at the scene."

"What do we do next?" Mabuse asked. "It seems that we have established that Miss Durance's father was most likely being impersonated by some scoundrel. Nonetheless, Flanders, who is no doubt the mastermind, is missing and I imagine the imposter is, too."

"Perhaps," said Holmes. "But with my extensive network I have ways of finding missing persons. So I shall put together a drawing of Flanders and a description and circulate it among my associates. As to the imposter, there are two possibilities."

"What are they?" Elizabeth asked.

"Well, the first is that it was his body that was discovered in your father's house and identified by Flanders, in which case he has already paid for his crimes. Failing that, he is still at large."

"And how do we determine which is the case?" Mabuse prompted.

"Well," Holmes said tentatively. "Given the suspicions I have and my standing with the police, I imagine I could move to have the body exhumed. However, it is possible that the body is, indeed, that of Elizabeth's father.

"I would rather not say this, but it is possible, that while this charade was being played out, the poor fellow was kept sequestered and possibly drugged until the suicide scene was staged?"

Elizabeth drew a sharp breath and grew pale. She bit the back of her hand.

"Really, Holmes, could you not keep such speculations private?" Mabuse said, frowning.

"No, Doctor," Elizabeth breathed. "As horrible as such ideas are, I am already convinced that my father met with foul play. I would rather know the truth. If hypothesising along these lines is part of solving the mystery, then it is better that it not be stifled in deference to my delicacy." She turned to Holmes. "I suppose it would be up to me to identify the body?"

"You would be best able to do so," the detective agreed, "though the servant girl whom you have located could possibly do the task. And yet, perhaps it is not necessary to proceed with such a stratagem at this point. For if the victim is, indeed, Mr Durance, then nothing will be gained by the disinterment and the police will consider that their time has been wasted. The only point, in fact, in the exhumation, would be to prove that the body is not your father's and that some skulduggery is definitely involved. While foul play may still be a factor, the police will take this as evidence that it is not.

"Therefore, it seems to me, that it would be more advantageous to proceed as we would if the exhumation was not a possibility. Ergo, let us assume the imposter is still among us and make some small attempt to discover him, and approach the solution of the mystery via that avenue."

"And how shall we discover this individual?" Mabuse asked

doubtfully. "I do not believe there is a register of imposters."

"A register of imposters?" Holmes mused. "Well of course there is, or as good as."

"How do you mean?" Mabuse asked.

"Can you think of no profession which makes its living from imposition and disguise? You dragged me along to one such performance last evening…"

"Actors!" the doctor exclaimed. "Of course! Yet there are so many in London. Where on earth would we begin?"

"Yes, Mabuse, there is, indeed, a plague of vaudevillians, pantomime artists, thespians and diverse other mummers upon this city. Yet, for this charade to have been carried out successfully, the villain must have been able to have observed Elizabeth's father long and close enough to have mastered his speech and manner; at least sufficiently to fool the servants until Flanders dismissed them. Do not forget, the fact that the servant girl was convinced that it had been her master she had seen in his sick bed helped also to convince the police that Elizabeth's father had been master of the house, while I suspect that he had been replaced at the same time that Flanders became head of staff. The servants were kept on just long enough to be convinced that the imposter was Mr Durance."

"So it must be someone he knew in Australia?" Elizabeth suggested. "Perhaps," Holmes agreed, "Yet, I do not know how long this scheme was in the making. It is possible that the imposter knew your father much more recently, and it strikes me that the voyage out here would offer the perfect opportunity for close observation."

"Ah, I see," said Mabuse. "So you think that an examination of the passenger list of the ship that Mr Durance came out here on, may give us the identity of the one who took his place?"

"It seems a reasonable avenue of inquiry," Holmes smiled, pleased with this conclusion.

"Yes, I think so," Mabuse agreed. "So I suppose your next call is to the shipping office?"

"Indeed," Holmes nodded. "I sense we draw closer to unravelling this mystery."

"**M**iles Batersea," Holmes said. It was the following day and he had met with Doctor Mabuse once again at six o'clock in the evening.

"I beg your pardon?" Mabuse replied.

"Miles Batersea, was a passenger on Durance's ship."

"The chap who plays Faustus?" Mabuse said, apparently aghast. "No! The very man we just observed on stage!"

"You are surprised to discover that he has truly sold his soul to the devil?" Holmes grinned.

"By the Devil, this time you mean Flanders?"

"Perhaps," Holmes agreed, "if he is, indeed, the mastermind. Though I suspect some other devil."

"How do you know that Batersea isn't the mastermind, himself?" Mabuse enquired.

"He's an *actor*," Holmes said, raising his eyebrows haughtily.

"Extremely amusing, Holmes," Mabuse said, smiling. "Yet are you not, yourself, also an actor? Many is the time I have seen you transform yourself and play a role to the utmost. However, are you not also a mastermind yourself, if one who works on the side of the angels?"

Holmes smiled enigmatically.

"To think," Mabuse mused, "we saw him on the stage the night before we met Miss Durance." He pause an moment in thought, then asked, "So what are we going to do next, follow Batersea?"

"Hmmm, I don't see that just confronting him, at this stage, will do much. And certainly we have nothing particular to take to the police yet, by way of evidence, as being an actor is not yet a crime; not even if you are guilty of travelling on the same ship as a fellow who is recently deceased. So I imagine, yes, that we shall observe him for a while and see what we might learn in that way.

"Or rather *I* shall, for stealthy stalking is something I fear you are unsuited to, and while I am not averse to disguising myself as a coolie, a Mohammedan, or a lady of the night if need be, I cannot see you doing the same—at least not convincingly."

"I'm not so sure," Mabuse quipped. "I think I might make quite a fetching courtesan if the light were dim enough."

Holmes clapped his companion upon the shoulders. "Know thyself, my friend, and therefore your limitations; even in London there isn't a quarter dark enough for such a charade, not with *that* beard."

"So I must leave the front line to you, once again?" Mabuse said.

"You shall have word from me," Holmes assured him.

Doctor Mabuse was leaving his consulting rooms the following evening when he found himself approached by a bent Chinese man. At least he assumed it was an oriental, but the fellow was so bowed that nothing could be discerned of him save the top of his conical hat. The hat itself was so large as to obscure everything from view save the coarse garments that covered the fellow's lower limbs, the ragged slippers upon his feet, and the nether end of a crude cane. It was a wonder that he could navigate the streets at all, considering that he could not have seen more than a few feet ahead. It seemed that he was afflicted by some disorder, or extreme old age perhaps, for his passage was halting and disjointed.

Mabuse stepped to one side to allow this strange apparition to pass but the fellow changed direction and the doctor found his way still blocked. The Chinese muttered in annoyance and stood waiting, apparently, for Mabuse to make up his mind which way he was going. Yet when the gentleman moved so did the Chinese who grunted in frustration at the confusion.

"Go round, go round," he muttered. He waved the cane feebly, perhaps to indicate the possible directions the doctor might take, or perhaps as a vague and somewhat pathetic threat. Mabuse moved again only to have his movement mirrored.

A stream of curses in what might have been Cantonese cascaded from under the conical hat.

"My good fellow!" Mabuse began in remonstrance. Then he noted that the curses had turned to laughter which metamorphosed from the faltering wheeze of the old Chinese to the rich peal of amusement that could only belong to one man.

"Holmes, you scoundrel, you sport with me again!"

"Ah, forgive me, dear fellow." Stretching to his true height, Holmes smirked. "I could not resist."

Mabuse turned and continued toward his house, Holmes walking beside him.

"I take it you have trailed your quarry to the Chinese quarter then?" the doctor said.

"Indeed, once again the trail led me to the docks area."

"You say 'once again'. I know what the mention of that place conjures for you, Holmes, the image of an epicentre of crime you have often lectured me about. The realm of that criminal mastermind you have spent so much time trying to build case against. You suspect the involvement of Moriarty, *n'est pas?*"

"Well, yes," Holmes admitted. "You no doubt suspected that when Miss Durance mentioned gambling dens my mind was drawn to him. After all, as you are well aware, I have long proposed that Professor James Moriarty controls most of the illegal gambling operations among the underworld and the Chinese are inordinately fond of that particular vice. However, I did not want to mention it just yet. I know you think my interest in the professor is exaggerated. It is true much of it is based on rumour and possibly even myth. So many of the crimes that have defied solution seem to point toward his involvement; yet with so little that is concrete and nothing we can take action upon, I know you grow weary of my speculations."

"We all have our obsessions," Mabuse remarked with a smile as he slid the key into his front door.

"Yes," Holmes agreed. "You must forgive me for being so impatient with your excessive interest in Marlowe's play; it is hardly fair of me when you tolerate more than a few enthusiasms of my own that defy your sympathy."

"Well, I guess it is a fascination with devils we both share," Mabuse said. "It is only a matter of seeing whether yours, Moriarty, is more or less fabulous than mine. But tell me, what have you learned?" Mabuse asked, as he poured a brandy and Holmes sank into an armchair.

"Well, only that Batersea seems to like to spend his leisure time in the docks area frequented by a certain giant Afghan, Abdul Hakim, who is a known associate of the Professor."

"So we do not have anything truly incriminating?" Mabuse said.

"No," Holmes agreed. "It is but a start. They are a cunning bunch of villains. Though much is in doubt, I remain certain that Moriarty is behind it ultimately."

"Still," Mabuse observed, "at least we have Batersea, who is a villain if not the principal. If we bring him to justice would we not have achieved something?"

"We can hope for more than that," Holmes said. "If we can prove Batersea's guilt, then perhaps we can bring pressure to bear upon him to lead us to his master."

"Yet, it would be suicide for Batersea to do so," Mabuse said, "if Moriarty is indeed behind all this and he is the infallible and merciless tyrant you have always envisaged him to be. How could we ever convince him to risk such a perilous course?"

"I have an idea," said Holmes.

Batersea was due to play Doctor Faustus again that night and it was, therefore, with confidence that Holmes and Mabuse entered his premises. Due to his extensive knowledge of the techniques of burglary, it was a small matter for Holmes to gain access to the actor's lodgings from an upstairs window reached by way of a trellis. The lodgings, in a large, well-kept boarding house, were quite substantial. Moving quietly, Holmes and Mabuse made a thorough search of the premises. They had been there several minutes when Mabuse had cause to remark upon a set of goblets upon the mantelpiece.

"What do you make of these, Holmes?" he asked. "The material is quite strange."

Holmes took the goblet and turned it about in his hands, the handles, stems and bases were of finely wrought gold but the bowls were indeed of an unusual but rather beautiful material.

"Ah, Mabuse, your curiosity has borne fruit," Holmes said, smiling. "These goblets are uniquely Australian. The cups are of emu shell, if I am not mistaken." Holmes turned the piece upside down. "See here, on the underside of the base, the artisan's details are inscribed, 'Joseph Tucker, Melbourne.' Interesting. I was aware of Tucker's work in silver but have never heard of such items being made in gold. They must be incredibly valuable; somewhat beyond the means of an actor such as Batersea whose star is only just on the rise of recent times."

"You suspect he has purloined these from the Durance estate?"

"It seems most likely," Holmes agreed. "Perhaps while he was carrying out his charade there he became fond of the items and Moriarty agreed he might have them as a reward for his services, or he just helped himself to them, arrogantly believing that he would never be connected to this matter."

"Well, I hope the scoundrel feels sufficiently recompensed for the bad dreams he must suffer," Mabuse said ironically.

"Bad dreams?" said Holmes.

"I am sure you noticed the laudanum by his bedside," Mabuse said. "I assume his conscience plagues him and he needs assistance to find repose."

"I doubt conscience is something that has ever troubled our suspect overly," Holmes demurred. "But working for a ruthless fiend like Moriarty might well lead to a state of considerable trepidation."

Mabuse nodded thoughtfully. "True. Nor do I imagine that playing a role in which you are dragged off to Hell by a demon every night would do much to sooth the nerves, especially for one so clearly superstitious."

"Yes, he is a typical Papist at that," Holmes grunted. "Have you ever seen such a collection of icons?"

He pointed to the cheap plaster statue of the Virgin that stood on its niche in the corner and the daguerreotype of Holman Hunt's *The Light of the World* above the bed. A crucifix, bloody as anything in Grunewald's oeuvre, hung between the two and an engraving of St Peter was situated on the far side of the pre-Raphaelite masterpiece.

"Well, he's safe from vampires at least," Mabuse grunted. "Perhaps with his guilty conscience he would be happy to confess if pressured."

"Small hope of that," Holmes snorted. "Whatever nerves the villain may suffer from he has kept up the charade with apparent ease for a considerable time. If he lacks true confidence, he is a good enough actor to counterfeit sufficient courage to see him through."

"Doubtless you are right," Mabuse conceded. "Nothing short of a visit from Durance's shade would move him to confess. But I guess we cannot hope for that. Though if he overindulges the laudanum enough, he may conjure an apparition of his own."

Mabuse lapsed into silence and studied the books upon the sideboard dejectedly, noting the preponderance of ghost stories and books of a supernatural bent. Yet he was not long at this occupation before an exclamation from Holmes demanded his attention anew.

"Mabuse, you are a genius!" Holmes exclaimed.

"Thank you, Holmes," Mabuse said. "I wondered if you would ever recognise the fact. Now if you would just explain to me why?"

"That I will, indeed," Holmes agreed. "Now listen closely, my friend."

It was with a weary step that Batersea made the short journey from his cab to the door of his lodgings once he had finished the demanding role of Dr Faustus once more. He cast about nervously as he put the key in the slot, as if the demons he had escaped from in the theatre might attempt to reprise their role on the landing. Entering his bedroom he hung up his cloak and hat and stood briefly before the statue of the Virgin, head bowed, muttering a prayer.

He sat in apparent dejection upon the edge of his bed for some moments, as if pondering what he might do with himself, before turning to his laudanum and making the usual preparation. Throwing back the concoction he grimaced, as if the familiar brew was even more unpleasant than he was used to. Yet, having swallowed the tincture of opium which guaranteed sleep, his demeanour relaxed. Throwing his clothes upon a chair he donned his night gown and had hardly fallen back in the bed before a gentle snoring filled the room.

Batersea had not long to enjoy his repose before he felt himself shaken and awoke to find himself confronted by a tall striking figure with a bristling red beard and hair like straw that jutted from under his top hat. Though the figure's attire was of the finest quality, somehow it did not seem to sit upon him quite as it should.

"Batersea!" The figure moaned. "Batersea!"

"Who, who are you!" the actor shrieked, his eyes wide with terror.

"Do you not know me?" the apparition growled, coming closer to loom over the bed.

"It cannot be you, it cannot be!"

"So you do know me! Do you think the angels would leave me without justice?"

"No, you are some imposter!"

"Imposters! You know of that, eh?"

"Get out! Get out!" Batersea cried. "I will call the police! I have powerful friends!"

"And what will you tell them?" the figure cried. "That the spirit of the man you betrayed has come to haunt you! Will they arrest me? Will your powerful friends thwart heaven or hell for you?"

"What do you want?" Batersea cried.

"Confess!" the apparition cried. "Confess to your crimes if you would have peace! Or I will be here every night and you will see me during the day and when you close your eyes, too."

"I cannot," Batersea pleaded. "It is the gallows for me, if I do."

"But you already have," said Holmes, removing the wig from his head.

"Who are you?" Batersea demanded wearily. "Why this ridiculous imposture?"

"To establish your guilt beyond reasonable doubt," the detective said. "I am Sherlock Holmes, perhaps you have heard of me?"

"Yes, of course," Batersea said. "I have read many tales of you and your love of disguise. You are very good," he said grudgingly. "You almost had me believing."

"No doubt my colleague's meddling with your laudanum somewhat enhanced your credulity," Holmes conceded. "He is somewhat the expert when it comes to increasing the suggestibility of a subject."

Batersea smiled weakly. "Nonetheless, you have achieved nothing save taking some years off my life. You cannot prove a thing."

"Oh, I will have you convicted," Holmes said. "Have no fear of that. The passenger list shows you on the boat with Durance. You have his goblets on your mantle—his daughter has confirmed their provenance—and I have ample witnesses of your presence in the gambling houses where Durance lost his fortune."

"That last detail is of no importance," Batersea countered. "Many people visit the dens by the docks."

"Come," said Holmes. "I have you. And if I do not, I will get you. You know my reputation and my resources. Do you really want me as your enemy?"

"You speak as if I have a choice?"

"You are a villain," Holmes said. "Make no mistake, and you deserve punishment. But you are merely small fry. It is the one who orchestrated this evil whom I seek, Professor Moriarty."

"Professor who?" Batersea avoided Holmes's eye.

"I will not spar with you, Batersea," the detective said sternly. "I know you fear him as well you might. Yet, if you do not help me you are already dead. For I can make it known that I have uncovered your crime. Do you think he will let you live once he knows I am on your trail? You have been discovered and in his eyes that is already a failure. Moriarty does not tolerate incompetence. Once he knows you are even suspected he will have you eliminated rather than chancing that you would betray him or that somehow your blunder will lead us to him."

Batersea gasped.

"Ah!" Holmes exclaimed triumphantly, "realisation dawns, eh? You are lucky to still be alive as it is. Your cohort, Flanders, is dead I presume."

"I have not seen him for some time," Batersea admitted.

"He has ended his usefulness to Moriarty, just as you have," Holmes observed. "Yet he is gone while you are still with us. Have you any idea why?"

"I amuse him," Batersea speculated. "He enjoys my Faustus and admires my talent, though I know I am an amateur compared to him."

"He's an actor?" Mabuse ventured.

"Well, yes," Batersea said glumly, "even if he does not ply his trade upon the stage, but when it comes to disguise and deception, he has no equal. Not even you, Mr Holmes."

"Be that as it may," Holmes said. "The point is you have no choice but to help me. So long as Moriarty lives you are in peril. He and I have been playing out this game for years. I intend to win. If you help me, both of our problems disappear."

"What do you propose?" Batersea asked.

At four o'clock on the following day, Elizabeth Durance arrived at Sherlock Holmes's residence in Baker Street where she had been summonsed. Doctor Mabuse and the famous detective were awaiting her arrival and she was soon seated and equipped with a cup of strong tea, Holmes avoiding all questions until things were so arranged.

"You are no doubt anxious to hear of our progress," he said. "So I will leave you in no further suspense. I think it safe to say that we have discovered those responsible for your father's death and the disappearance of your inheritance."

"And may I ask who these villains are?" Elizabeth queried hesitantly.

"I am afraid you have fallen afoul of a man who is possibly the worst *villain* in the world," Holmes announced. "A man whose evil is so vast that it has given rise to legends that he is immortal, that he is assisted by demons or has supernatural powers—if he is not a demon himself."

"Goodness," Elizabeth gasped. "How is it possible for one man to have so much power?"

Holmes was sombre. "While a great number join this Napoleon of Crime's army willingly at first, no-one dares to desert should they become disillusioned at any time. His hold on the populace of fringe dwellers who inhabit his fiefdom is such that no one is willing to testify against him, lest their family be murdered. Yet it is not only through intimidation that his rule prospers, for his power and wealth are immense. Not only has he amassed vast fortunes through theft, but through graft and intimidation he has negotiated many lucrative labour contracts and trade arrangements. Therefore, there are also opportunities for advancement in allying oneself with such a one and being rewarded with a portion of these ill-gotten gains."

"But why would a man with such means and far-reaching power squander his efforts in fleecing my father?" Elizabeth wondered.

"Your father's fortune in itself is not significant to Moriarty, it is true," Holmes admitted. "But how much less so the few shillings a pickpocket must hand over from his earnings, yet do you think that the fiend, therefore, waves his tithe? No. For ten thousand times a few shillings is a tidy sum. And a hundred fortunes such as your father's is a vast amount.

"And Moriarty is also a patient, scheming monster. He is a genius, and whilst such men may struggle to find a challenge worthy of their abilities, he has found crime is able to provide a multitude of challenges to keep him stimulated, his interest fresh. Contemplating hundreds of these cases at a time, some taking years to mature, is the kind of mental juggling act that would engage his intellect fully."

"It seems you know this mastermind rather well," Elizabeth observed.

Mabuse made a short sharp laugh of admiration. "If you are

intimating that Mr Holmes knows him as a kind of kindred spirit, or rather the evil mirror of his own soul, you are correct. For just as Moriarty juggles a hundred opportunities at a time, Holmes keeps several hundred crimes, not yet solved, in his head, for one never knows when the solution or a new lead will suddenly present itself."

"Unsolved crimes?" Elizabeth said. "I hadn't thought of Mr Holmes encountering such things."

"They far outnumber the solved ones," Mabuse conceded. "We tend not to publicise the fact any more than the police do; it makes for rather a poor and unsatisfying story."

"And you cannot involve the police?" Elizabeth asked. "Surely, with all of this villainous activity, the scoundrel must have come under the suspicion of the authorities?"

"Not at all," Holmes demurred. "It is a small matter for such a one to conceal his true nature. As far as the public know, including the police, he is the very embodiment of respectability; an esteemed mathematician, author of the *Treatise Upon the Binomial Theorem* and *The Dynamics of an Asteroid.*"

"So how do you think it is that this brilliant individual has finally allowed an opportunity to trap him to arise?" Elizabeth asked. "You give the impression he is infallible."

"No human being is infallible," Holmes said. "Perhaps it is sentiment and the professor has an odd affection for Batersea as the actor hopes is the case. The fact that Batersea still lives suggests that he is a sort of pet. It would not be the first time such sentiment had been an individual's undoing. It is one of the reasons I avoid it."

"Yes," Mabuse noted, ironically. "I have observed, over the years, what an effort it has cost you to stifle the abundance of natural affection within yourself."

"You are amusing," Holmes said coolly. "*But sometimes, I wonder why, otherwise, I continue our association.*"

"Other than the fact that I have made your methods famous, and thus earned you the respect that allows you access to many of the continent's greatest mysteries, which your great talents alone might solve?"

"Ah, yes," said Holmes, "there is that."

Sherlock Holmes and Mabuse waited with Batersea in the sumpt-uous suite they had hired in a London hotel for their trap. Holmes's longtime collaborator, Inspector Lestrade of Scotland Yard, and a brace of five constables, were hidden behind the heavy damask drapes. Holmes had promised the inspector the breakthrough of a lifetime and that he would receive great credit for the part he was to play in the downfall of a villain whose capture would overshadow all else in his career. Holmes had confessed that the venture was somewhat risky and suggested that, if it proved a debacle, Lestrade should slip away with his reputation intact.

For the occasion Holmes had dressed himself as a tough and had groomed Mabuse in a similar manner. The doctor seemed rather to relish the role and strutted about loutishly practising threatening phrases in an execrable Cockney.

Holmes related to all present that Moriarty, on those occasions when he was seen in public, was generally accompanied by two bodyguards, and Holmes imagined that he would come no less equipped on this occasion. With Lestrade and the constables they were numerically superior, though all they hoped for was that Batersea would provoke the mastermind into an incriminating statement Lestrade could overhear, along with Holmes, Mabuse and the constables. That should provide sufficient grounds for Moriarty to be arrested and to arrange an investigation into his empire which, assisted by Batersea's inside knowledge, should prove most revealing.

The professor, a cadaverous man with a large skull and piercing, sunken eyes, arrived promptly at the arranged time. His bodyguards were imposing-looking characters. One was the huge, turbaned Abdul, sporting a vicious scar down the left side of his face that pulled his mouth into a permanent sneer. The other was a well-built man of military bearing, named Moran. Batersea arranged the seating so that he and his confederates were between the visitors and the door.

No sooner had the Professor been seated than Batersea leapt to his feet, pulling a gun! "Alright, Moriarty," he said. "I'm going to keep this simple. I have risked my life in your employ and helped you to attain a vast fortune. Yet you have fobbed me off with a very paltry sum!"

"What are you talking about?" Moriarty said, apparently startled. "Are you mad?"

The bodyguards reached toward their pockets. Behind the drapes, Holmes and Mabuse had their own weapons out already, anxiously monitoring the events. Holmes shook his head silently—Batersea was supposed to have been searched earlier—the constables had somehow missed the pistol!

Moriarty's surprise had given way to his former formidable calm. "I have always dealt well with you, Batersea," he said sternly. "What has unsettled you, out with it, now? Put down your gun and let us speak."

"Dealt well with me?" Batersea said. He was perspiring freely and nervously licked the sweat from his top lip. "Is that what you call giving me a few lousy pounds for helping you to murder Durance for his fortune?"

"This is madness," Moriarty cried, a hint of amusement in his tone. Holmes feared his intended victim suspected a trap, and was not about to fall for the ruse. "I am a scholar, not some brainless thug who must resort to crime to make his fortune. Are you unwell, you poor fellow? Tut, have you been over administering the laudanum?"

"Stop this charade!" Batersea screamed. "Oh, you're good! I thought you would threaten me; remind me who I'm dealing with, but you didn't get where you are by losing your control. You'll keep up this performance to the end. I'll never be free from you...unless!"

Holmes and the constables yelled and sprang from hiding, charging at the bodyguards, ready to stop the agitated actor, but too late. Batersea fired.

Moriarty was struck in the chest and screamed, his hands flying to his ribcage. Abdul and Moran were on their feet in a flash, pistols out and aiming toward their enemies, just as Holmes pulled the trigger of his own revolver.

Holmes's weapon misfired, even as a bullet from Moran's gun blew Batersea's head apart. Abdul swung his weapon toward Holmes, but Mabuse threw himself upon the detective screaming, "Down!" Holmes found himself smothered beneath Mabuse's somewhat greater bulk. Guns roared.

When the smoke cleared the detective saw that Lestrade had entered the fray. Smoke still plumed from the end of his gun. The bodyguards were both dead along with Moriarty and Batersea.

"My God," Holmes snarled. "I knew this was a perilous undertaking, but I never imagined it ending like this. How was it that Batersea had a gun! The men whose job it was to search him—by God, they should be horse-whipped!"

"Yes," Mabuse agreed, "this is something of a debacle, but at least it is the villains who are dead while we have all survived."

"Yet, without Moriarty's confession, what good is it?" Holmes demanded.

"You shan't need one," Mabuse said. "Lestrade?"

"No, indeed not, sir," Lestrade concurred. "and really, if there is no proof found of his guilt, it's simply a matter of this lunatic Batersea killing him for his own reasons, and no trail required there, either, gents."

"Come, Holmes," Mabuse said, noting that his companion's face remained downcast. "You have been convinced so far that Moriarty is the world's greatest villain. If so, he has been bested, even though it is through good luck more than good management. See what comes of a search of his residences and businesses. He will not have been able to hide all of the evidence."

"You're right, Mabuse," Holmes said, with a smile. "You must forgive me for my poor humour. It is churlish of me to sulk because the plan did not go according to my expectations."

"Well, life is somewhat less tidy than fiction," Mabuse said, "which is why I have dedicated myself to the latter. Rest assured that I shall bring the necessary improvement into my rendition of these events."

It was some months later that Holmes read of his latest exploits in *The Strand Magazine*, though the papers had been full of the sensational unveiling of the facts. Lestrade had claimed to have been working with Holmes for years to uncover Moriarty's empire of evil, much evidence of which had been found in the ensuing weeks since the gun battle. Holmes took no exception to the inspector's opportunism. Lestrade had risked a great deal in backing his gambit and if the fellow wished to garner more glory than was truly his due, Holmes would not begrudge him the bonus.

"What did you think of my rendition of events?" Mabuse asked, as he arrived for dinner.

"You have done an exemplary job," Holmes replied, "and mustered your most stirring prose in the service of inflating the tale into one redolent of heroism and genius, while deftly omitting anything which might cause any embarrassment. I am afraid you have been completely dishonest, in being rather too kind to me, again."

"How so?" Mabuse protested. "Did not events unfold exactly as I told them?"

"Now you know that isn't true," Holmes tutted. "It was my gun that misfired and you who leapt upon me, saving my life, not the other way around. And Moriarty did not confess nor begin the gunplay. Nor did Lestrade actually hit any of his targets, I believe, though you credit him with putting paid to a third bodyguard whose presence I do not recall."

"Well, Lestrade hasn't contradicted me," Mabuse grinned. "And in any event, you know how it is with eye-witness accounts—they seldom coincide. That is why I make sure I am the chronicler. I'm keen that my version of events stands. Now, what's this I hear about you planning retirement?"

"Ah," said Holmes. "Things are not quite the same since Moriarty is gone. Such mundane crimes as remain barely raise my interest."

"Well, you have earned your rest," said Mabuse. "I wish you the very best with your retirement."

"I'm sorry I will have no more tales for you to chronicle," Holmes said.

"Well, it is a great principle to leave your audience wanting more," Mabuse observed. "Perhaps there are already enough stories of Sherlock Holmes. I am thinking of attempting a historical fantasy set in the reign of Queen Elizabeth."

"I'm sure it will be a great success," said Holmes.

Many months later.
Sherlock Holmes was contemplating his options for the evening; cocaine or the violin? Or perhaps the cherrywood and a book? He decided upon the pipe but could not decide upon the publication and spent some moments poring over the titles in an overstuffed bookcase hoping for inspiration.

"May I suggest Dante?" a voice came from behind. "*The Divine Comedy* is always revealing, especially the *Inferno*."

Startled, Holmes spun about to find someone occupying his own chair by the fire, as if he were the room's rightful tenant. The newcomer was dressed in a fine set of Medieval robes that yet seemed oddly familiar. They shimmered in the gaslight, throwing up odd reflective shadows upon his saturnine face. That face, with its jet black, heavy eyebrows and moustaches, seemed the very epitome of evil.

From the first moment Holmes recognised the figure as familiar, yet its presence here so defied rationality that he could not credit it. It was the living image of Dr Faustus as played by Batersea upon the stage, but it could not be, for the actor was dead!

"Who are you?" Holmes gasped.

"Who do I appear to be?"

"Batersea? You can't be, Batersea is dead."

"You are correct, he is. But that is not who I mean. Did you ever see Batersea looking like this?"

"What do you mean?"

"Who do I look like?"

"You look like Batersea dressed as Dr Faustus."

"Are you sure?" The figure laughed. "What could you really detect from your seat in the theatre? How can you be sure it was Batersea you saw on the stage? That it wasn't me? All you can be sure of is it looked *like* me. But it could have been anyone with a talent for disguise. Like Moriarty."

"He's dead, too!" Holmes snapped.

"Yes, I must thank you for that," the figure smiled.

"Why? What is it to you?" Holmes demanded.

"Moriarty was a criminal genius," the intruder nodded, "almost everything you considered him to be. Yet he was not, in fact, particularly evil; no, he was actually an entrepreneur. Many of his victims were themselves exploiters of the poor, the working class, and Moriarty liberated monies they had little legal and no moral right to. So, a merchant, really, and as far as evil goes, an amateur.

"I have my own empire, you see. To villainy, true moral turpitude, true commitment to the perverse, I am what the British are to 'legitimate government'. There are few corners of the earth where my secret empire has not held sway. Moriarty was one of my few remaining rivals, it must be said. He brought order, and reward for effort, he was a clever, organised man. But thanks to you he is now dead and his empire has been added to mine. I can now ensure it runs *properly*."

"And you are saying I aided you? Ridiculous. Who are you and what do you want?" Holmes demanded. Thought his voice was resolute, there was, perhaps, a hint of fear in his eyes.

"I am Doctor Faustus. And I am immortal." Suddenly the interloper did not seem triumphant or to relish his words.

"And this is a burden to you?" Holmes observed.

"Time does hang heavily on my hands and I would gladly die," the stranger said, "if I only dared. Yet, I know I am destined for Hell."

"You fear a mythical doom," Holmes said, a hint of mockery in his voice.

"You would like to think so," the stranger said, "yet having met the Devil I can assure you that Hell is very much a reality."

"You have met the Devil?" Holmes attempted a laugh. "You are a madman. Oh, this is too much," Holmes gasped. "This is simply too much."

"And yet, here I sit before you. *Muss ich Deutsch sprechen, um Ihnen die Wahrheit zu verdeutlichen?*"

Holmes scoffed at the intruder's perfect German.

"*Ou français? Dans l'éternité, il y a beaucoup d'opportunités d'apprendre une multitude de langues...*"

"Enough!" Holmes snapped. "No matter how many languages you have mastered, it is no proof of your silly claims."

The strange figure nodded. "Yes, you are right. But that is not why I came here tonight. No, I am here to thank you and reward you with the truth."

"If you wished to express gratitude you might have done it by sparing me this nonsense," Holmes said.

"You are not curious?"

"As many parts curious as perturbed," Holmes almost sighed. "But yes, damn you, I must hear your tale, however disconcerting it might prove to be."

"Very well," Faustus said. "You want to know, regardless of the consequences. No one understands that better than me. Did I not sell my soul for knowledge? So this is my story. Not as Marlowe told it or Goethe, though there is much verity in both accounts. The main difference is that I was not dragged to Hell at the end, as the Elizabethan play portrays it."

"How so?" Holmes prompted.

"Satan's pleasure is in evil, it is that simple. What God hates brings him joy. I convinced him that I would be his agent on earth so long as I live; I outlined a plan to him that would make me the greatest villain of all time. And Lucifer knew I spoke true. If Jesus had been the avatar of God on earth, then I would be Satan's. And I have succeeded in as much as I promised and more.

"Yet, I was warned that the only way to avoid Hell was to be cursed to live forever. I readily agreed, not seeing that eternal existence could grow wearisome. Yet Satan knew. As much as he favoured me and as much as I did his work on earth, it is not in his nature to be grateful and show mercy.

"So one must find some way to relieve the tedium of endless years of existence."

Faustus fell silent and smiled at Holmes with a look of utter cruelty.

"So why do you come to me with this tale?" the detective said at last.

"Come, Holmes," Faustus replied. "Use your much vaunted powers of rationality and deduction. Tell me yourself."

Holmes's blood froze. These last words were spoken in the unmistakable voice of his companion of two decades, Doctor Hieronymus Mabuse.

"You are a genius of mimicry, but you cannot be Mabuse."

"Can I not?" Faustus grinned. He removed the moustaches and the cotton appliances that changed the shape of his eyes and nose. The face now laid bare was that which Holmes knew so well.

"Mabuse, why do you torment me like this? Why have you carried out this ugly pantomime?"

"I am not Mabuse," Faustus said evenly. "There never was a Mabuse, but the man you knew as him was always I, Johann Faustus."

"Rot!" Holmes roared, "What is the matter with you, man?"

"I told you, Holmes, I was bored. And you were an irresistible target. You reminded me so much of my youthful self when first we met. You were so full of arrogance, more interested in knowledge than anything else. More a calculating machine than a man. I had come to England to consolidate my empire here, intrigued by the idea of a joust with Moriarty, who was beginning to build his business. And it struck me, why not situate myself in the best possible position to learn about the Professor by becoming the confidante of his natural enemy; the Captain of the other side, if you like."

Holmes snatched up a pistol from the mantelpiece and aimed it at his tormentor.

"This is nonsense, Mabuse. I know we have had our tensions over the years but I never knew how much you hated me. Why do you antagonise me so with this fool game; do you hope to drive me mad? Is it intended to avenge some imagined slight? Did you take exception to the way I badgered you over your gambling and your vices?"

"My vices, yes! Dr Hieronymus Mabuse, the soak; Doctor Mabuse, the gambler, as long as I was guilty of that much you were convinced of your superiority over me."

Faustus rose now, and faced Holmes, who felt an eerie, unsettling feeling of unreality take hold of him, as if he had been transported into a performance of Faust, and yet the play was more real than what he had hitherto taken to be reality.

"All the world is a stage, eh?" said Faustus.

Holmes was startled by this apparent act of mind reading. Yet rallying what remained of his resolve he snarled at his former friend. "This is a stupid prank, Mabuse, vulgar and vile. Leave here and never cross my path again."

Faustus smirked. "You accuse me of having a low sense of humour? Well, yours is absurd, unless you really think that a pistol would give me pause. And if it could harm me, would you murder me for my prank? How would you explain that to Lestrade?

"But even if you did wish to slay me, I am who and what I say I am and no one can dispatch me but my Master, cursed with immortality as I am. I will leave here unmolested. But what will you do, now that you know the truth? For Doctor Mabuse will disappear. Will you write it down? Will you seek to set the record straight and reveal yourself to be a fool and the dupe of your chronicler? Will you tell how you only bested your greatest foe because I engineered it for my own purposes? No, no, I have a more attractive option: forget it all and bask in your undeserved glory for the years left to you."

Holmes's face twisted in rage, and his hand shook. Yet, before a shot could be fired, the gun was wrenched from his grip by invisible hands and returned to the shelf!

"Thank you, Azazel," Faustus said.

Holmes looked at the pistol on the shelf. "It's not possible," he gasped, falling into a chair afraid he might collapse. He looked at Faustus in despair. "How did you do this to me, Mabuse? Hypnosis?"

"What? Still searching for the rational explanation?" Faustus laughed. "Surely we have succeeded beyond our wildest dreams. Yes, of course, hypnosis it is the speciality of your old friend Dr Mabuse. Or am I Moriarty?"

Holmes looked at the fiend who had contaminated his life's work, his greatest achievement. He needed to calm himself, to think. He gripped his head, eyes closed, while he sought inside for answers. When he opened them but a moment later the intruder was gone. A shock ran through him, and for a time, the length of which he could not judge, it seemed he went into a sort of fugue. Yet, when his consciousness returned, he felt oddly calm, if somewhat grim.

"Moriarty!" he said. "It can only be you. I don't know how you did it, what drug you have managed to insinuate into my system, what hypnosis you have used to affect me so, but I will not be fooled. I will never give up my fight to put an end to you and your empire of evil, forever."

The words were rather grand but rang rather hollowly in the empty room. A sudden gust of wind outside rattled the windows and a chill ran up the detective's spine. He had told Mabuse he was thinking of retiring; perhaps it was best to revisit that plan. It would be wise to consult his trusted friend, as Holmes still thought of him, for it was impossible to believe that the uncanny individual who had visited him was indeed his trusted confidant of so many years.

Yet this course eventually turned out to be unavailable to the great detective, for, from that time forward, Doctor Hieronymus Mabuse was nevermore seen in this world.

The Investigation into The Dawning Od: A Sherlock Holmes and Dr Arthur Conan Doyle Mystery

ANDREW SALMON

My diary reveals that it was June of the year 1900, and I was stationed at Bloemfontein, South Africa with Dr Robert O'Callaghan's field hospital. The Boer conflict had turned in England's favour though we were ignorant of this at the time. Lord Frederick Roberts had taken Bloemfontein but had failed to seize the water supply at Sannah's Post some thirty kilometres away. The result limited us to rain water. Thankfully, we were in the rainy season. Still, this meant sporadic bathing and drinking water was restricted to half a bottle per man per day.

Dysentery ran rampant, and fever. The wounded were tended to by us doctors squelching through a layer of bloody, fetid filth at our feet. Flies swarmed in thick clouds about us. Thus you can imagine our reaction when Lord Roberts snatched the water supply from the Boers. However our instant elation cooled rapidly as the water did not flow immediately.

We soon learned that the insufferable Colonel Bartlett Stevens sought to earn the adoration of his thousands of troops bivouacked outside the walls by securing the flow of water for their exclusive use. As the wells used by the local herdsmen filled, the soldiers were given leave to drink their fill, clean themselves in makeshift tubs and fill every canteen they could get their hands on while our parched throats could not manage so much as a croak of protest. Had I known a spell to bring forth water I'd have used it. But, alas, my magic capabilities were limited to healing the sick and injured.

My writing had occupied my attention when the news of the water reached our hospital. I had spent that morning looking over my notes for the account of the Boer conflict I planned to finish upon returning to London and had lent the remainder of my creative energies to going over my latest *Secret Agent Holmes* adventure. These adventure tales had proved lucrative and an insatiable public had clamoured for more of them since I had first told the tall tales of this brilliant man of action whispered about in Whitehall in the months before we sailed for Africa.

A clerk had been placed at my disposal as a cricket ball to the leg had given me a pronounced limp. And so I sent the man to gather others of his rank with instructions to collect water outside the gates and carry it in, so that the wounded, as well as the staff, might wet their whistles. The wait was agonizing though of short duration. Being an invalid amongst the tumult around me was the epitome of frustration. The soldiers outside had been within minutes of marching to ships for home when news broke of the restored water. The camp and its personnel was to follow on their heels within the next week or so. The war, for us, was over and I shared the longing for home with my comrades.

The men returned, staggering under their burdens of clanking, glistening pots and bottles. We all but mobbed them. Of course, I could not push to the front of line due to my injury and instead watched the men drink deeply with one hand while holding bottles out to the patients with the other.

I called out to my clerk, Mark, asking if he might bring me some water after the wounded had been seen to.

"Sure thing, Dr Doyle," the tow-headed youth croaked. "'Ang on a minute."

He ducked free with two bottles filled to the brim with cloudy water which to me appeared as if it had been freshly drawn from an Arctic lake. My tongue ran like sandpaper across my parched lips as the boy returned to my bedside.

The thud of approaching hoofs outside reached me in my feverish state. A voice rang like a bell over the din, demanding the whereabouts of our commanding officer. Faint, muffled replies did not satisfy the speaker who flung back the netting at one door and strode boldly into the room.

"Leave that water alone, lads!" he roared.

Every head turned in his direction, for a moment. The urge to drink was simply too much for some in light of the dry weeks behind us and many continued to raise the bottles to their lips. Mark had been in the process of handing me a bottle prior to this interruption and my body's burning need for water overcame my reason. I reached eagerly for the container.

The tall, thin Major strode forward and slapped it out of Mark's hand. The bottle crashed against the bed frame, soaking the blanket over my feet. "Are you deaf as well as stupid?"

I looked the man up and down. Here was a tall, thin, cadaverous individual barely able to fill out the dusty uniform he wore, which was festooned with canteens. A gaunt, angular face with two small eyes set close together was thrust forward with intent.

"Major," said I as the man blinked heavily to aid his eyes in adjusting from the glare outside. "You can't come in here and tell thirsty men not to drink."

His eyebrows arched upwards and his eyes widened with revelation.

"You are that damnable Conan Doyle!" the man said as he regarded me angrily. "If we were not representatives of her Majesty's army, I'd thrash you!"

Furious at this attack, I sat up straighter in the bed and reached for my cane. "I'll not stand that, sir. Fellow Spiritualist or not. Who the devil are you to speak to me this way?"

"Major Sherlock Holmes," replied he with an insolent inclination of the head. "The man whose livelihood you have destroyed."

I was struck speechless for a moment at this revelation. The tall tales related to me of incredible exploits had led me to conclude that Sherlock Holmes was nothing more than a figment of the collective imaginations of staff officers with too much idle time back home, a rogue along the lines of Spring-Heeled Jack. To learn the man actually existed—it was extraordinary! Though I bristled at his ill manner towards me I now understood the cause. I settled back against the bed frame and returned my cane to its place.

"It appears we have much to discuss," I managed to croak. "Before we begin, I simply must trouble you for one of your canteens, if convenient."

Holmes flung one at me and it gurgled splendidly when it struck the blanket before me. He unburdened himself of the others, passing them to Mark with instructions that the contents be doled out amongst the wounded who, under no circumstances, must take the water flowing out of Sannah's Post and to spread the word about the non-potable water running into the town.

Mark dashed off with a nod from me and Holmes and I faced each other. Unfortunately fate was to postpone our discussion for the moment. A great ruckus outside heralded the arrival of Colonel Stevens who burst through the netting, flinging his gaze this way and that.

"Where is that rascal?" he bellowed. "I'll have his head!"

A junior officer approached the Colonel, saluted smartly, and made inquiries we could not hear from our spot across the room.

"I demand Holmes present himself immediately!" Stevens bellowed.

At this the Colonel caught sight of Holmes whose gangly form rose above the supine patients.

"Ah!" Stevens strode towards Holmes. Red-faced with rage, the mutton-chops he wore resembled vegetation from the surface of Mars. Stevens's stout form fairly trembled with the depths of his emotion as he glared at Holmes. "How dare you keep water from my men! I'll have your guts for garters for it, mark me! Place this man under arrest!"

With this last, he motioned angrily for the men at his heels to come forward and seize Holmes.

"Begging the Colonel's pardon," I dared to interject, "but shouldn't we hear the evidence upon which the Major based his rash action?"

"It's nonsense with no basis in fact." Stevens seemed to be enjoying having Holmes at his mercy and, like a cat playing with a mouse, desired to stretch out the moment. "Come now, Major! Let's hear it then. Why should we not drink this fine water? What is wrong with it?"

The piercing gaze of Holmes fixed on the watery eyes of Stevens. "Colonel, I have no idea."

On the verge of a stroke, Stevens staggered back a step in his apoplexy.

"I only know that my adversary was at Sannah's Post. With the tide of the war turning in our favour, the enemy must employ more clandestine tactics. Surely the flow of water into a British garrison suffering from months of deprivation is too compelling a target for the likes of him to overlook."

"Disrupting army routine on whims and fancy!" Stevens had regained his speech. "No, Holmes. This is the end for you and your grandstanding. Orderly!"

The man was at Stevens' side in an instant. In his fist was one of the bottles drawn from a well outside. The colonel accepted the bottle and thrust the container at me.

"Put an end to this, Doctor! Drink!"

I took the bottle and stared longingly at the contents as I brought the opening closer to my cracked lips. At the last moment my eyes turned to Holmes. With his thin lips a hard line, white against his tanned face, he shook his head. There was something about that earnest look that conveyed sincere assurance and emphatic warning. I hesitated.

"Doctor, I order you to drink that!"

I lowered the bottle.

"You refuse a direct order? We shall see about that!"

He snatched the bottle from my hands and raised it to his own lips. Holmes leapt forward and dashed the bottle from his fist. It shattered on the bed frame and the contents drenched Stevens from the waist down.

The stockade was a converted wine cellar and the cool, dark confines were excellent relief from the humid conditions outside. With nothing to do but while away the time while our fates were being decided, there was ample time to talk out our differences.

"Did you really defy the Colonel based on mere whim?" asked I.

Holmes propped himself up against an empty wine cask. In his pocket was a small flagon of water. He passed it to me and I drained it in two swallows.

"Facts. I had none," said he. "Only a conclusion based on experience. You must admit the resumption of water flow makes for an irresistible opportunity for our enemy."

"Granted." I handed the bottle back. "You suspected contamination. Of what kind?"

Holmes shook his head. "I cannot say. I know only that he was there. For me, that is enough."

"Who is this man?"

"He is the Merlin of Crime! A man whose influence pervades all the free cities of the world, yet so few have heard of him. I refer to Dr Otto Von Reichenbach. I hunted him from the shadows these last few years, kept my existence from he and his minions. When I tracked him to South Africa, I enlisted as an army spy so that I might get close to him before he divined the secret powers of the Od."

"What is the Od?"

"Black magic, forbidden knowledge and a gateway to another dimensional plane all rolled into one. Though I have dedicated years to learning its secrets, the full scope of the Od eludes me—as it does all who study it. It is believed Von Reichenbach uncovered some ancient secrets of the Od, studied them then destroyed them so none may follow in his footsteps. If he is not stopped, there is no telling the havoc he will wreak upon the earth."

My mind reeled at what Holmes related to me. "What would bring him here?"

"What, indeed?"

"You believe he applied magic to the water supply?"

"I know it. However I cannot prove it."

"Surely your own magic is of some use to you."

"I possess no magic."

"Nonsense," I retorted. "You discovered the taint to the water. You knew who I was, though we have never met. How do you account for that?"

"I observe and analyse. That is all. Magic is but an arrow in a man's quiver. However, it all too often becomes a crutch. For the mysteries the world holds; use the brain. To employ magic for such is a cheat."

"Is it not better to attack these mysteries with a full quiver at one's disposal? Why handicap oneself?"

"Magic has its uses, I'll grant," said Holmes reluctantly. "However it has been my experience that over-dependence on it dulls the intellect of those who practice. Recent events have done nothing to alter my conclusion."

"You use insults to cover what you refuse to face: you have the makings of a wizard."

"It is foolish to discuss this further, given our situation. Lives are at risk, I remind you."

"I have not forgotten it. If what you say is true then thousands are in harm's way. The men all but drowned themselves in the water flowing out of Sannah's Post."

"Now you finally begin to understand my earnestness. Those men are bound for Cape Town and then England as we speak, carrying whatever that devil slipped them. Consider that." Holmes threw up his hands in disgust. "It's no use. Whatever scheme Von Reichenbach hatched will succeed now. Your blasted stories have exposed me to the world and, most certainly, to Von Reichenbach. He will be ever more on his guard."

Here I explained my error in assuming the tales I heard were, by their very outlandishness, mere fabrication, and offered my apologies for any harm they may have caused. He was not in a mood to receive my heartfelt expression of regret.

"I hope the pieces of silver you earned from your stories bring you comfort," said he, "for a dark time will come upon the world and all the gold in England will not buy our way out of the dawning Od."

A n unscheduled rattle of the keys at our door stirred us from the reverie into which we had sunk over the last three days. Food and water was not due for an hour or more—though we touched neither—so we were at a loss to account for the clack of the bolt and the heavy door being flung open.

A stout figured stopped and entered. Once the man's face entered the faint penumbra of light from our small lantern, Holmes reacted instantly. He leapt to his feet and shook the man vigorously by the hand.

"General Watson!" exclaimed Holmes. "At last!"

I struggled to my feet and came to ragged attention.

"None of that now," said Holmes. "General Watson, I present to you Dr Arthur Conan Doyle."

"Doctor, is it?" said Watson with genuine warmth. "I tried my hand at that in Afghanistan but lacked the talent for it. Those damned spells, I dare say!"

Holmes clapped the man on the back. "Then it was the secret realm for you, eh? Doyle, the General here is my handler in the world of espionage."

"I see."

Watson turned to Holmes. "Conan Doyle? The very scoundrel who has been getting your name in every shop in London?"

"Yes, General," said Holmes. "However, grave matters are before us."

"Was it he?" asked General Watson. "Von Reichenbach?"

"It was."

"Damn and blast! And that fool Stevens locks you up! It's a three-day head start they have on you. I'll have his hide for it. Come along!"

The urgency that possessed General Watson was conveyed by the immediacy with which we found ourselves before Colonel Stevens in his office. We were given water from the General's canteens and some food from Watson's stores, but no opportunity to make ourselves presentable.

"General?" Stevens inquired in an ingratiating tone. "We had no idea you would be honouring us with your presence."

"My boots were cleaned before I set out and don't require licking," replied Watson. "Damn you, sir! By what right have you locked up my officer?"

"He struck me, sir." Stevens drew himself erect. "That is enough."

"I'll knock your fool head off in a minute! And the Doctor?"

"He refused to obey a direct order!"

"What was the order?"

"To drink the town's water supply."

"Did he give a reason for disobeying?"

"He sided with your Major who struck the bottle from my hand."

"In an attempt to prolong your miserable existence."

"General, I—

"Be silent!" Here Watson snatched up the water carafe on the Colonel's table and handed it to me. "Can you test this for magic?"

"I'll need a strip of paper."

One was obtained from a sheet on the desk. I infused the paper with a detector spell and inserted it into the bottle. The result was instantaneous. The entire contents turned black, bubbling and writhing as though the bottle were full of snakes. I almost dropped it in my sudden fright but managed to get a stopper into the neck.

"What is this trickery?" Stevens asked, his face blanched.

"Restrain the Colonel!" ordered Watson of the men closest to him. He whirled and faced the guards by the door. "No water for anyone in town! Effective immediately!"

The men were off in a flash.

"This confirms it, General," said Holmes. "I'm for England."

"You both are," confirmed Watson. "Doctor, do you know the nature of the enchantment?"

"A day or so of study and I'll have it."

General Watson shook his head. "You will accompany Holmes to London."

"I couldn't possibly, sir. The patients. My staff—"

"I left my mage in the Discovery Dream back at Sannah's Post. You have my word that once he awakens, I will have him brought here to put things right. To London, now; the both of you. I will prepare the necessary orders. Quickly, while there's still a prayer."

The ensuing hours proceeded pell-mell in a maelstrom of activity. Outfitted with horses and supplies, we were off through the town gates. The next two days and nights passed with a mad dash across the muddy wastes. Finally, Cape Town docks was before us with all its crisscrossing rail lines and Table Mountain at our backs. The *SS Briton* sat at anchor as stores were brought aboard. She was to depart in two days' time, which frustrated us no end. The *Londoner* assigned to carry the Colonel's men home had been in readiness and had set sail the moment the troops were aboard.

A change came over Holmes at this news as he succumbed to a singular brooding, with eyes half-lidded as if slipping into slumber. Yet his body remained rigid, motionless in his seat by the open window of his room at the Mount Nelson Hotel. He took only water during this period.

As Holmes was not forthcoming, I took it upon myself to be useful while we awaited our sailing. I contacted the neighbouring hotels to ascertain whether or not a man matching Von Reichenbach's description had passed through Cape Town. Tall, spidery, bearded, with hooded eyes and the black, lifeless stare of the cobra, our quarry cut a memorable figure and I soon had confirmation that not only had he reached Cape Town, he had sailed for England on the same ship as Stevens's men.

I brought this information to Holmes and received his embittered reply.

"Of course he was here," he snapped. "Any fool knows that."

This ended any future interaction between us on African soil. I took to my rooms and my work. The *Secret Agent Holmes* tale I had been working on at the field hospital was finished but I burned it in the wastebasket. The book chronicling my war adventures required my attention and there was my ending to *Drood* to while away the time with aboard ship. And yet my hand kept reaching for the books on magic I had brought with me. Having restricted myself to healing spells, the ominous warning Holmes had uttered had me thinking the time had come to expand my knowledge of the mystic arts and many an hour I passed in deep study.

The gloomy, drizzly day we departed was apropos and we left Africa behind to fade into the mist. London in June was not without its fog but the land would be in bloom, the sun would be shining and all about would be life sprung anew. A more welcome environment I could not imagine. With my work before me and home as journey's end, I forgot all about Sherlock Holmes and his missions of espionage.

My hope of summer rejuvenation was dashed when we caught sight of England. Dark clouds brooded over all and the London dock seemed half-submerged in rain when we stepped down once more on British soil. I supervised the off-loading of my bags as they contained some objects of a fragile nature. Holmes suddenly appeared at my side. He seemed rested, refreshed, his eyes blazing from his wet face.

"Returned to the land of the living, have you?" asked I, coldly.

"If we do not act swiftly and decisively, nothing will be alive for long. Come, Doyle!"

"Holmes, it is pouring with rain and I am tired from the trip. I should like to check in at home before I resume my duties."

"I'm afraid that is quite impossible," said Holmes. "I have been questioning the dock workers while you dawdled with the luggage. What I have learned is most disturbing and I have sent for the police in the hopes of learning more. It has begun, Doyle."

"What has begun?"

"The end."

I opened my mouth to demand elaboration but Holmes turned smartly and strode off. Rain streaming off my hat brim, feet squelching in my sodden shoes, I recalled my duty and, after a moment's wrestling with the irritation Holmes generated within me, I drove my hands into my overcoat and followed in his wake. A police wagon parted the teeming throng around the docked ships and Holmes made for it with haste. He had climbed aboard by the time I had pushed my way through the crowd. The bench was ample and I took my seat reluctantly beside Holmes. I knew better than to engage in conversation and we made our journey in silence.

Our destination was Whitehall and before us stood the skeleton of the new edifice being erected for Scotland Yard. Holmes sprang from the wagon before it had come to a halt and I lost sight of him as I climbed down.

"You'll be wanting to go that way, Doctor," the driver explained as he extended a long finger pointed over my shoulder to the left. "Inspector Lestrade is at the base of them poles. They've found another, they have."

Clueless as to the man's meanings, his directions were plain and I almost tumbled into the turbid Thames on the rain-slick boards leading down to the construction site.

"Ah, Doyle at last," said Holmes as I flailed against the slimy poles to maintain my balance. "Do stop messing about. There is work before us."

In defiance of Holmes, I took the time to dunk my hands at the river's edge to wash off the slime. With my handkerchief sodden in my partially dried hands, I stooped beneath the beams and joined the two men on the other side of the platform.

Holmes stood with a short, rat-faced man fairly swallowed up in his rain slicker. Watery eyes regarded me for a moment as I stood next to the man, then he and Holmes returned their gaze to the ghastly sight before us.

The torso of a woman lay at the water's edge. The remains were clad in a nightdress with more colour than the bloodless flesh. The figure's head and arms had been removed, leaving ragged flesh at the neck and one visible shoulder.

Lestrade turned to Holmes. "All right, you've seen it. What do you have to say?"

Instead of replying, Holmes turned to me. "Lestrade tells me these remains were found not twenty minutes ago. How about it?"

"Twenty minutes?" said I, considering. "The poor woman was not killed here—that much is plain. The blood loss from these wounds would have been enormous and even a downpour like this would not wash the boards clean. Also, the torso is clad in the remains of a nightdress. She must have been taken from her bed, murdered, and brought here."

"An excellent accounting of the obvious, Doyle," said Holmes. "Can you add anything pertinent?"

"See here, you vagabond," I began, furious.

Lestrade stopped me with a hand on my arm. "You'll get used to such treatment if you plan to continue your association with the likes of him."

"Believe me, officer, I have no intention of prolonging anything with Holmes."

"Stop that, you two," said Holmes.

"As to that, Holmes," said I. "Why don't you explain what I missed in my observation of the body?"

"There certainly isn't time to cover all that eluded you so I shall confine myself to the vital points."

I bristled but held my tongue.

"The woman was in her early twenties, married for the last two years. No children. She was no stranger to hard work but was not required to exhaust herself at it. Good nutrition means a husband who is not well off but does all right. Could be the wife of a civil servant, a policeman, soldier, mailman, iceman, milkman and the like. Blonde hair, five foot two or three."

"You are indeed a sorcerer, sir," said I with conviction. "Or a liar."

"I merely observe."

"It is impossible for you to deduce all that from mere observation. You made it up out of whole cloth or you have magic in you."

"Yes, magic," said Holmes. "I was hoping you would have the greater sensibility in that area and could shed some light on these matters. This is why I asked for your thoughts."

"Magic? I see no magic here."

"If you'll hazard a step forward to examine where the body was severed?"

"You might have suggested magic in the first place," I countered.

"Now that I am aware of your limited abilities, I shall do so in the future," said Holmes. "It is good to know the parameters of the brains assisting me."

"Shut up, will you?" I bent at the waist to see the torso better.

"I will not," said Holmes as I studied the remains. "I was called a liar and will explain my conclusions to you."

I was in no mood for that and replied "I would prefer you didn't."

Holmes ignored my reply and went on calmly. "The woman has blonde hair because two strands of it remain on the collar of the night dress. Her height is an estimate based on the length of the remains. Developed muscles in the visible deltoid indicate physical labour. The smoothness of the skin cries youth. The absence of scars show that said labour had not taken a prolonged toll. Overall musculature speaks of good nutrition. The hair of at least two cats, Scottish Fold and Bengal, is also present on the garment. The animals are house cats or else the hairs would not be on the nightdress. Money to feed and house the cats means a dwelling large enough to accommodate the ensemble. The narrow aspect of the lower back and visible abdomen indicates a childless union, which itself suggests relative newlyweds as income and living quarters show that money is sufficient though not ample—more likely suited to someone in the service professions I listed earlier. The nightdress is made of an Egyptian linen found in the finer linen shops this couple could not afford, which tells me it was obtained abroad. Our search may now be confined to sailors, soldiers or merchant seamen. Is this explanation enough? Or shall I go on?"

My brain whirled as I considered all that Holmes had related. So convinced was I that sorcery was at the heart of these abilities Holmes delighted in showing off that I was speechless in the face of the cold facts he had related. I could see the evidence now of many of his points and I did not doubt the veracity of the rest.

However they were put aside for the moment. For, upon examining the truncated remains, I observed that the torso was cauterized over the surface area of the cut. A foul-smelling, blackened mass could not hide the precision of the cut, which was straight and fine. Despite the burned aspect of the flesh and internal organs, neither the skin around the cut or the nightdress was burned. Holmes was right; only magic could be behind this. Black magic.

Holmes took Lestrade by the elbow. "With your permission, Lestrade, I should like to examine the other victims."

"Others?" asked I.

"A dozen, we reckon," replied Lestrade. "Pieces, really. Arms, legs, trunks and such. We don't hardly know if each comes from a separate victim."

"Dear Lord, what is happening?"

"What is occurring is secondary just now," said Holmes. "Stopping it is our priority. Accompany me to the Yard, Doyle."

After the grisly examination of decaying body parts, all bearing the same clean cut at the main severance point, we found ourselves back at the last crime scene. Holmes was on hands and knees in the mud, pawing at the ground where the torso had been discovered and since removed.

"Holmes, what are you looking for?"

"The locket, of course."

"What locket?"

"The one that had been around what remained of the victim's neck."

"I saw no such thing."

"That does not surprise me. There was a faint red mark, just discernible below the ragged flesh of the neck."

"Surely that occurred when the poor woman was beheaded. You are wasting your time."

"This poor murdered woman is but a link in a chain of evidence with which I hope to prevent a catastrophe," said Holmes, his eyes fixed on the water's edge. "If we cannot uncover something about her attacker in time, all may be lost."

"Then surely we should not tarry here, pawing through the mud in search of phantom jewellery."

"The straightness of that mark was incongruous with the other wounds," said Holmes. "She wore a locket and we must find it."

"If you are right I and do not concede that you are," I replied. "Would not the thing have been torn off in the couple's bedroom?"

"How did a woman and her attacker find themselves here at the water's edge?" asked Holmes, evading my question.

"I do not know."

"Neither do I," said Holmes. "But the locket must be here."

I could not fathom what Holmes meant by this and attempted to wrap my thoughts around all that had transpired since our return to London. The race against the homebound troops, the mystery of the cursed water, the human remains and now a locket—all of these swirled about in my mind until finally inspiration struck.

"You believe the murdered woman to be a soldier's wife!"

Holmes leaned back on his heels and presented me with the first smile of genuine emotion I'd seen him direct at me. "Bravo, Doyle! And here is our evidence."

He showed me a cheap, gold locket clutched in his fist. Holmes brushed away the sand and snapped it open to reveal a photo of a handsome army captain. Using his thumbnail, he slid the photo out and turned it over. In coarse script was the words *Captain Arthur Burke, 26 years of age.*

"We shall give this to the constable at the wagon." Holmes closed the locket. "And he will give it to Lestrade. The inspector will contact Home District and present the locket along with General Watson's report, which I have given him. There still may be time."

Holmes flagged down a hansom after we had sent the constable on his way. He gave an address on Montague Street in Bloomsbury.

"What the devil is all this about, Holmes?" I demanded.

In reply, he removed a large map of London and opened it up to the point where it served as a blanket over our legs. The map was dotted here and there with red Xs.

"Lestrade and I pinpointed the locations where the remains of other murdered women were found while you examined the collected remains," said he as he traced the red marks with one finger. "All along the Thames, do you see? Yet not exclusive to that waterway. See here, a foot found in the Serpentine at Hyde Park, an arm in Boating Lake, a torso near the Viaduct Pond of Hampstead Heath, two legs in the East Lake in Victoria Park, and so it goes. What is the common thread?"

"Water."

"What was Von Reichenbach's weapon of choice in Bloemfontein?"

"Water."

He indicated the downpour outside. "What do we seem to have more about us now than the air itself?"

"The same." I grasped at this thread. "You suggest there is a connection between him and this ceaseless rain?"

"I know it. It has rained every day since the ship carrying the returning troops docked."

"Amazing! And you credit Von Reichenbach with cunning and guile. Does not this overt move run contrary to that nature?"

"The Od is his ultimate goal, Doyle." Holmes nodded. "There is a larger game afoot. If we are able to stave off catastrophe tonight, there may be time to prevent Von Reichenbach from controlling this power."

"Surely there are mages in London who are better equipped to deal with magic of this sort?"

"There are," agreed Holmes. "And they are all engaged in defending the city from other threats. Their handlers require convincing before they may be diverted. I have sent Lestrade to them for that purpose. We shall see what is the outcome. Ah, my lodgings!" Holmes sprang from the cab, leaving me to pay the driver.

Inside the squalor of his rooms, Holmes set about donning dry clothing after tossing a bundle at me so that I might change out of my sodden attire. Under normal circumstances, I would have refused the offer but I was soaked to the skin and had no choice in the end.

Thirty minutes later Holmes received a telegram from Lestrade. That Home District had replied favourably was a wonder I believed had more to do with General Watson being behind Holmes rather than anything our flimsy evidence could relate. Be that as it may, the order had come down from the Commander-In-Chief of the Forces for soldiers and officers who had shipped aboard the *Londoner* to assemble at Regent's Park.

"Herding them together may limit the damage," said Holmes after I read the message to him. "But it brings us no closer to Von Reichenbach. How are you for wards?"

"Like any good physician, I possess a full retinue of ward spells. When the body is weakened by sickness, it is vulnerable to infection and must be protected during treatment. Wards are the best defence."

"Come, then!"

"We go in search of Captain Burke?"

"In a manner of speaking."

The rain had as much chance of washing the traffic from the roads as it would of washing one's sins away. Our cabman fought for every inch of road as we weaved our way back to the river. A stone's throw from our destination, the noise of a tremendous ruckus reached our ears. Holmes gripped my arm feverishly.

"Your wards!" he hissed. "Stand ready!"

It was our intention to proceed to Regent's Park in the hope of determining once and for all what threat we faced. Our journey had hardly begun before the first signs of commotion became apparent.

Nearby screams pierced the cacophonous clatter of the traffic. Holmes urged our driver to stop at once and we had just alighted before more cries echoed from a block over. These were followed by the clatter of boots on the cobblestones, then a gunshot.

"We are too late!" Holmes hissed. "Damn him!"

"What is it?"

"Summon your wards but have your pistol ready," replied he. "Noekken!"

I started at this. A water spirit! The mist surrounding our dilemma were whisked away. Holmes had already surmised the danger and the full implications of what Von Reichenbach had done at Bloemfontein descended upon me like a judgment. I broke into a run to keep pace with Holmes as he cut through a filthy alley towards the tumult.

"I see this has caught your attention," said Holmes. "Von Reichenbach is of Austrian birth but the magic of the world has been his playground over the decades. His powers encompass all folklores and legends."

Shouts rang out suddenly in front of us as we emerged from the alley. Figures dashed in every direction. Moments later, an upper flat was ablaze. Police whistles shrilled a street over and the noise of gunfire burst in rapid succession like fire crackers on Guy Fawkes Day. We cast our gaze about to see how we might be of use in this eruption of chaos.

A woman ran into the street not ten feet from where we stood. On her heels was the horrible figure from ancient lore. The Noekken was a terrible beast to behold. It stood over six feet and was possessed of large yellow eyes which glowed like hot coals. The body appeared shaggy as if covered, head to toe, in seaweed the texture of straw; dark, matted, slimy and emitting an odour most foul. More appeared in second story windows, exiting from the doorways lining the street, one on the rooftop across the way;

a dozen all told and Von Reichenbach's obscene crime in South Africa was realized.

He had enchanted the water flowing into Bloemfontein with a transformation spell. The soldiers had consumed the water and were cursed from that moment on. Gestating within them on the return journey, they had transformed here in London and would need to consume human flesh to complete the transformation. The presence of scattered human, female remains was instantly understood. Their wives had been savaged as the men awakened transformed and ravenous in their beds. I recalled Holmes's determination that the remains were located near bodies of water. Noekken were water spirits, the Thames their best hiding place. However, what I could not understand was how they got there without being detected.

"Doyle!" shouted Holmes. "A ward for that poor woman!"

This cry was followed by a shot from a pistol at the creature menacing the scrabbling woman. The bullet swayed the shuffling creature but did not slow it down.

I conjured a ward and sent it at the Noekken. A warding spell of this kind instills temporary paralysis as part of the healing treatment. The Noekken shuddered under the spell and froze on the spot, allowing the woman to disappear through a doorway. The paralysis was temporary and would gain us a minute or two before it resumed its rampage. Putting it to the torch would destroy the thing. However, before we could take steps along these lines, an intense flash of light shot from the eyes of the Noekken and it vanished.

"Can you explain that, Doctor?" asked Holmes.

I admitted I could not as I hurled a ward at a Noekken clumsily attempting to climb out a window.

The Noekken froze, losing its grip and started to fall to the pavement. Until a flash of light shot from its eyes and it, too, vanished.

Holmes paused in the process of reloading his revolver and struck his thigh with his fist. "I am a fool! The Od!"

He thrust his revolver into his pocket with one hand while extracting the map from the other. The rain soaked the paper instantly so he retreated under an awning two steps to the right. As the wards were stopping the creatures, I summoned all of my strength to conjure them one upon the other and let them loose at the Noekken. Flashes resembling fireworks ensued and they vanished one by one. I joined Holmes under the awning.

He had his fountain pen out and was tracing lines on the map.

"The power of the Od comes from another dimensional plane. One can be a conduit for its power," he was saying to himself. He noticed my presence. "The Noekken are mere diversion. Look! The marks for the remains found by the police." Here he used the pen to connect the locations. "You see how they intersect? Von Reichenbach must be using these beasts as batteries, drawing their strength. Each is consumed when their initial purpose is curtailed. He wants to open a portal to the Od and will attempt to do so at the intersection point. Here!"

He jabbed a long finger at the spot on the map. In the dim light, I had to lean in to see.

"Baker Street?"

Our journey was a desperate one. Chaos in the streets hampered us at every turn. The police were out in force, providing a barrier before the stalking Noekken and the populace. Soldiers in tight formations made their presence known as well; launching volleys into the dreadful figures while mages darted in with fire spells to finish the ghastly work. It appeared as if Lestrade had convinced them after all and I envied them their command of the mystic arts. Holmes pounded the roof in frustration at our slow progress while I exhausted myself sending wards at the monsters.

Baker Street was no different than the other avenues and we were forced to climb down and elbow our way through teeming throngs as we sought Von Reichenbach.

"He could be anywhere along here," I observed.

Holmes snatched up a straw broom a street sweeper had abandoned in the panic and thrust it at me. "Can you infuse this as you did the paper in Stevens's office?"

I caught his meaning and used my failing magic to do as he suggested.

Holding the broom high as one would hold a torch, we continued along Baker Street. The infusing spell would react when in close proximity to black magic as the strip of paper had done in the water bottle.

We were halfway up the street when the long bristles of the broom began to crackle and writhe. Holmes flung the broom about, trying to pinpoint the cause.

"He is here! Inside 221B!"

Holmes pulled his revolver. Mine was in my hand as well. The door to the flat leaned askew on the hinges and there was blood upon the steps leading to the upper chambers. A prone figure lay at the foot of the stairs. I pushed past Holmes and bent to examine the injured man. This took mere seconds as it was clear the elderly man was dead.

An unholy roar upstairs froze my blood. Holmes seized me by the arm and hauled me forward. We threw our shoulders against the door and it cracked inward.

Von Reichenbach stood with his back to us, arms outstretched over his head. His hands lay within globes of pulsating light. Before him was an undulating orifice. He was opening the Od portal!

Holmes aimed his revolver. The revolving interchange of the energy streams enveloping Von Reichenbach revealed the danger of what Holmes intended to do.

"Don't!" I cried.

I launched myself at Holmes the instant he pulled the trigger. Colliding with his slight frame, I succeeded in knocking him out of the return path of the bullet. I was not so fortunate. The bullet caught me on my right side. It passed through cleanly but in my already weakened state, it knocked the fight out of me and I lay sprawled.

Holmes was at my side in an instant, hands probing for injury. "Has he murdered you? The devil!"

He released me and rose to his feet, his body trembling with a rage that shocked me.

"Von Reichenbach!" shouted Holmes over the roar of air being sucked into the widening portal. "I'll have your life for this!"

Von Reichenbach pulled his gaze off the portal and regarded us over one shoulder. "Ah, Holmes! Bear witness to my triumph!"

"Bullets cannot stop him!" said I, but it was a whisper lost in the roar.

My energy was sapped from the battle with the Noekken but I had to try something. But what? It was no use, I was spent.

Suddenly an old woman appeared at my side. Her white hair loose and flowing about her head, she glared malevolently at Von Reichenbach.

"Let me have what remains, Doctor!"

I seized her hand and felt my power draining into her.

The woman had her hands primed to unleash a banishment.

Von Reichenbach turned to face us. A bloodless smile split his features. He raised his hands and the portal widened until it was as wide as the far wall.

"My army heeds me! They come!" he shouted in triumph. "Behold the dawning Od!"

At this the woman unleashed the banishment. It struck with terrible force and Von Reichenbach doubled at the waist; the grin, at least, was knocked from his ugly face. A howling multitude of voices from the Od reached us, growing louder. Von Reichenbach slowly straightened. The banishment had weakened him but had not finished him. We had lost. There would be no stopping his army now.

With a roar, Holmes launched himself at Von Reichenbach. He threw his long arms about the torso of the man in a vice-like grip and, driving with his legs, propelled Von Reichenbach towards the portal. The two tumbled into it and with a concussive blast that shattered the windows.

The portal was sealed.

In the weeks that followed, Mrs Hudson, for that was the name of the venerable sorceress, and I worked at setting the upper rooms of 221B to rights. It had been her warlock husband Holmes and I had found dead at the foot of the stairs, his heart having given out in his battle with Von Reichenbach. Mrs Hudson used reconstitution spells to great effect on the damaged furniture but I did not need to witness this to know that she was a witch of the first order. The upper rooms had been her late husband's laboratory, they were now vacant and I moved in as soon as the place was once again fit for human habitation.

From her I learned that the Od attempts to break through into this plane of existence every thirty days, though, without assistance from our side, these can be easily thwarted. That far wall of the flat is but one of the contact points. There were others spread across the world. It was for this very reason that the Hudsons had purchased the property, as they had been appointed to guard the portal.

I did not move in out of sentimentality for Holmes and his sacrifice. Mrs Hudson told me that the intersection phenomenon can, occasionally, allow something from the Od to pass through to this plane, if the breach is handled carefully. If Holmes was still alive, I owed it to him to wait and see.

As the days drew ever closer to this event, I was filled with anticipation. As irritating as Holmes was, he was still possessed of more courage than I'd found in most human beings and his intellect was capacious. If there was a chance he could be recovered, I owed it to myself and humanity to be there to help, if possible.

Until the next event, I had my Drood to labour over and Mrs Hudson's magic instruction to fill my time as I took my first steps into this new world.

Contributors

Philip Cornell is a writer, illustrator and caricaturist and has been a devotee of Sherlock Holmes since he read 'The Speckled Band' at the age of ten in a *Readers' Digest Young People's Annual*. Half a century later his enthusiasm for the Sherlock Holmes Canon is undiminished and he is a long-time member of The Sydney Passengers, the local Australian Sherlock Holmes Society, an organisation for which he has produced dozens of scholarly articles on the Holmes Canon for *The Passengers' Log* quarterly journal. He also wrote and drew a set of trading cards in comic-book form wherein Lee Falks's famous hero the Phantom encountered an evil British army colonel and his mathematics professor employer: *The Empty Cave*. A similarly Victorian-set story was Mr Cornell's collaboration with Christopher Sequeira and Dave Elsey on the *Sherlock Holmes: Dark Detective* series of graphic novels, and both his art and a short prose tale of his appeared in *Sherlock Holmes: The Australian Casebook*. However, his greatest claim to Holmesian fame may be the fact that the council responsible for the town square in Meiringen, Switzerland, commissioned him to produce all new colour art depicting events from 'The Final Problem' for permanent display on signs in the park!

Julie Ditrich is a writer, editor and comics creator, as well as the Founder and CEO of Comics Mastermind™, a professional development service for evolving comics creators. Julie has a BA in Professional Writing (University of Canberra), and has worked in mainstream publishing as a bookseller, publicist, marketing manager, editor and author. Julie contributed to the *Oblagon* comics anthology for Kaleidoscope, was co-writer on *ElfQuest: WaveDancers* for Warp Graphics, was cowriter on the *Dart* miniseries for Image Comics, a writer on the Supanova *Tides of Hope* anthology, and wrote the script for the epic fantasy *Elf~Fin: Hyfus & Tilaweed* comic book for Black Mermaid Productions, and she contributed a script to the *Australia* anthology for Comicoz.

Julie was the co-founder of the Australian Society of Authors (ASA) Comics / Graphic Novels Portfolio, and jointly hold the role between 2007 and 2012. In 2018 Julie joined the judging panel of the Ledger Awards, which acknowledge excellence in Australian comic art and publishing. Forthcoming work includes a new superhero character—Djiniri—published in *SuperAustralians* for Black House Comics, a story in *Cthulhu Deep Down Under 3* for IFWG Publishing, and Julie will also be the first Australian woman writer on *The Phantom* published by Frew Publications with the release of *The Adventure of the Dragon's Leg*.

Julie Ditrich—Acknowledgement: I am eternally grateful to Professor John Hilton, Consultant in Forensic Medicine, for helping me research the historical medical aspects of this story. John's openness and patience in answering my probing questions with such authority and with his own unique stamp of creativity were absolutely second to none.

Ron Fortier is a veteran comic book creator, best known for writing the *Green Hornet* and *Terminator: Burning Earth*, with Alex Ross, for Now Comics back in the 90s. Today, he keeps busy writing and editing new pulp anthologies and novels via his Airship 27 Productions (http://robmdavis.com/Airship27Hangar/airship27hangar.html). He won the Pulp Factory Award for Best Pulp Short Story of 2011 for "Vengeance Is Mine" which appeared in *The Avenger—Justice Inc.* from Moonstone Books and again in

2012 for "The Ghoul," which appeared in *Monster Aces.*

He continues to write his own graphic novels and series, such as *Mr Jigsaw Man of a Thousand Parts* via Redbud Studio. (http://www.robmdavis.com/RedbudStudio/index.html) and you can keep updated with his latest projects by visiting his personal website at: www.airship27.com

Nancy Holder is a versatile writer who has written over eighty novels and more than 200 short stories, essays, and articles; has been on *The New York Times, The Wall Street Journal, USA Today,* and *The Los Angeles Times* bestseller lists; has received five Bram Stoker Awards from the Horror Writers Association (HWA); and is well known for writing fiction and episode guidebooks for TV shows such as *Buffy the Vampire Slayer, Angel, Smallville, Sabrina the Teen Age Witch, Beauty and the Beast, Saving Grace, Wishbone,* and for novelizing movies including *Wonder Woman, Crimson Peak,* and the recent *Ghostbusters.* Her series, *The Wicked Saga,* co-written with Debbie Viguié, was optioned by DreamWorks. She is the writer on Kymera Press's comic book, *Mary Shelley Presents,* in which Mary Shelley and the Creature showcase works written by women writers from 1780 to 1920; and she's written and edited pulp collections and comic books for Moonstone Books, featuring the Domino Lady, The Avenger, The Phantom, Zorro, and other characters.

She also teaches seminars and workshops on writing comics and graphic novels for the Stonecoast MFA in Creative Writing offered through the University of Southern Maine, and she is an avid Holmesian, having written for the *Baker Street Journal,* as well as short stories for anthologies such as *The Further Crossovers of Sherlock Holmes, In the Company of Sherlock Holmes,* and *Gaslight Gothic: Strange Tales of Sherlock Holmes.* She has also written two games for the Storium™ storytelling gaming system: *The Unsolved Cases of Sherlock Holmes* and *Nancy Holder's World of Dracula.*

She is on the Board of Trustees for the HWA. Ms Holder lives in Washington State. Find her at www.nancyholder.com and @nancyholder.

Leslie S. Klinger is the *New York Times*-best-selling editor of the Edgar®-winning *New Annotated Sherlock Holmes* as well as numerous other annotated books, anthologies, and articles on Holmes, Dracula, Lovecraft, Frankenstein, mysteries, horror, and the Victorian age, including the Anthony®-winning anthology *In the Company of Sherlock Holmes,* co-edited with Laurie R. King. His latest books are *Classic American Crime Fiction of the 1920s,* also nominated for an Edgar®, and *For the Sake of the Game: Stories Inspired by the Sherlock Holmes Canon,* also co-edited by Laurie R. King. In 2019 he will publish *New Annotated H. P. Lovecraft: Beyond Arkham* and *Annotated American Gods* with Neil Gaiman. www.lesliesklinger.com

Rafe McGregor is the author of over two hundred short stories, novellas, magazine articles, and journal papers. His work includes crime fiction, weird tales, military history, and academic philosophy. As regular readers of *The Strand Magazine* will realise, his contribution to this anthology owes as much to L. T. Meade and Robert Eustace ('Followed', December 1900) as it does to Conan Doyle ('The Adventure of the Speckled Band', February 1892).

Brad Mengel works in Australia's criminal justice system. Before that he was trolley boy, a barman, an office manager and a teacher. A lifelong reader and pulp fan it was natural that he would turn to writing. His book *Serial Vigilantes of Paperback Fiction: An Encyclopedia from Able Team to Z-Comm* (McFarland, 2009) was the first book to examine vigilante fiction of the 70's and 80's. He has also contributed stories to *Tales of The Shadowmen#3 & #7, Pro Se Presents Nov 2012, Charles Boeckman Presents Johnny Nickle, Pulp Obscura: Senorita Scorpion, Blood & Tacos #4, Domino Lady Vol 2, Sherlock Holmes: Consulting Detective Vol 12* and *Poker Pulp.* His first novel *Australis Incognito* is coming soon from Pro Se Productions.

Will Murray has been writing about popular culture since 1973, principally on the subjects of comic books, pulp magazine heroes, and film. As a fiction writer, he's the author of over seventy novels featuring characters as diverse as Nick Fury and Remo Williams. With the late Steve Ditko, he created *Squirrel Girl* for Marvel Comics. Murray has written numerous short stories, many on Lovecraftian themes.

For this collection, he returns to two culturally significant characters he previously explored, H. P. Lovecraft's Dr. Herbert West ('Tombstone Tribunal' for the Herbert West Reanimated round robin tale) and Sherlock Holmes, whom Murray previously teamed up with Colonel Richard Henry Savage in 'The Adventure of the Imaginary Nihilist' for *Sherlock Holmes: The Crossover Casebook*.

Currently, he writes the *Wild Adventures of Doc Savage* for Altus Press. His acclaimed Doc Savage novel, *Skull Island*, pits the pioneer superhero against the legendary King Kong. This was followed by *King Kong vs. Tarzan. Tarzan, Conquer of Mars*, a crossover with *John Carter of Mars, is* forthcoming. www.adventuresinbronze.com is his website.

Dennis "Denny" O'Neil is a comic book writer and editor, principally for Marvel Comics and DC Comics in the 1970s. His best-known works include *Green Lantern/Green Arrow* and *Batman* with Neal Adams, *The Shadow* with Mike Kaluta and *The Question* with Denys Cowan, all of which were hailed for sophisticated (for the period, in the case of his 1970's work) stories that expanded the artistic potential of the mainstream portion of the medium. As an editor, he is principally known for editing the various *Batman* titles.

His 1970's run on *Batman* is perhaps his most well-known endeavour, getting back to the character's darker roots after a period dominated by the campiness of the late Golden-early Bronze Age. He particularly sought to emphasize Batman's detective skills. This grimier and more sophisticated *Dark Knight*, as well as new villains such as Ra's Al Ghul, brought Batman back from the verge of pop culture oblivion. His work would influence later incarnations of Batman, from the seminal comic **Batman: The Dark Knight Returns** by Frank Miller, to the movie Batman Begins in 2005.

Andrew Salmon has won several awards for his Sherlock Holmes stories and has been nominated for the Ellis, Pulp Ark, Pulp Factory and New Pulp Awards. He lives and writes in Vancouver, BC. His releases include: *Queensberry Justice: The Fight Card Sherlock Holmes Omnibus* containing the three *Fight Card Sherlock Holmes* books which introduced female Victorian bare-knuckle boxer, Eby Stokes. *Sherlock Holmes Investigates: A Quintet of Singular Mysteries, The Dark Land, The Light of Men,* and *Ghost Squad: Rise of the Black Legion* (with Ron Fortier) are also available. He has just released his first children's book, *Wandering Webber*. His work has appeared in dozens of anthologies.

He is currently at work on his series of Eby Stokes Victorian spy novels as well as a myriad of other projects. To learn more about his work check out: www.amazon.com/Andrew-Salmon/e/ B002NS5KR0

J. Scherpenhuizen is the author of numerous novels for children and adults, including *Twilight Age Vampires, Profile of Evil* and *Catvengers* (www.amazon.com).His short fiction has appeared in magazines and the anthologies *Sherlock Holmes: The Australian Casebook* and *Cthulhu Deep Down Under*. A mainstay of the Australian comics scene, his work includes both writing and illustrating the gritty horror graphic novel *The Twilight Age* (also published as *Time of the Wolves*); co-pencilling with Michal Dutkiewicz a number of American comic-books such as *Wolverine: Doombringer* and *Lost in Space*; and inking artist Chewie Chan's pencils on *Buckaroo Banzai 2*. He's also done a slew of work while teamed-up with Australian comics scribe Christopher Sequeira, with whom he has developed and created several properties including *Mister Blood, The Glowing Man* and *The Catamorph*.

His new superhero character, *Princess*, co-created with writer Jason Franks, will debut in a nationally bookstore distributed graphic novel in mid-2019. Scherpenhuizen is currently writing and drawing a 350 page hybrid literary novel-graphic novel-thesis as his doctoral project at Sydney University.

Christopher Sequeira is a writer and editor who specialises in short prose and comic-book scripts for the mystery, horror, science fiction and super-hero genres. He has also written scripts for flagship superhero comic-books, such as *Justice League Adventures* for DC Entertainment, and *Iron Man* and *X-Men* stories for Marvel Entertainment. His *Sherlock Holmes: Dark Detective* graphic novel with Dave Elsey and Philip Cornell is published by Caliber Entertainment, and an authorised revamp of Dr Fu Manchu with long-time friend and collaborator W. Chew Chan is in the works. He has edited (or co-edited with Bryce Stevens and Steve Proposch) the award-nominated anthologies *Cthulhu Deep Down Under* (three volumes) and *Cthulhu Land of the Long White Cloud* (both for IFWG Publishing); *Sherlock Holmes: The Australian Casebook* (Echo / Bonnier); and at time of writing the forthcoming *H.G. Wells's War of the Worlds: Battleground Australia* (Clan Destine Press), and the creator-jam-graphic novel *SuperAustralians* (for IFWG Publishing and Black House Comics).

I. A. Watson is the great-great grandnephew of Holmes's great friend and chronicler Dr John Watson. And if you believe that he also has a Thor Bridge to sell you. He's written about Holmes before—or discovered more of his famous ancestor's manuscripts, if you prefer—in Airship 27's *Sherlock Holmes Consulting Detective* volumes 1-12 and counting, and in the novel *Holmes and Houdini*. Several of those contributions were nominated for Best Pulp Story of their year and one got the trophy.

Pegged by editors as a go-to author for iconic or long-since-published characters, I. A. Watson has been seduced into penning the Robin Hood novels *King Of Sherwood, Arrow of Justice, Freedom's Outlaw and Forbidden Legend, St George and the Dragon* Volumes 1 and 2, *Labours Of Hercules, Women of Myth,* and half a dozen other books, plus contributions to around forty anthologies, and his first non-fiction essay volume 'Where Stories Dwell'. Occasionally he stops writing and eats. He is considering sleep. Full publication details with links to additional material and free stories are listed at http://www.chillwater.org.uk/writing/iawatsonhome.html

Luke Spooner, who created this volume's cover, is an artist and illustrator living in the South of England. He has a First Class degree in illustration from the University of Portsmouth and his current projects and commissions include illustrations and covers for books, magazines, graphic novels, books aimed at children, conceptual design and business branding.